NOT OK,
CUPID

Anna Kaling writes mostly British contemporary romances featuring lots of tea, rain, and passive-aggressive queuing. By day she writes about concrete erections for a construction firm, and by night she . . . well, never mind. She's working towards being an old cat lady and is a big fan of sharks, bad horror movies, and the Loch Ness Monster.

To find out more visit **annakaling.com,** or find her on Facebook **/annakalingauthor** or Twitter **@AnnaKaling**.

NOT OK, CUPID

CUPID

ANNA KALING

HEADLINE
ETERNAL

First published in 2020
by HEADLINE ETERNAL
An imprint of HEADLINE PUBLISHING GROUP

1

Cataloguing in Publication Data is available from the British Library

ISBN 978 1 4722 6637 8

Typeset in 11.55/16.25 pt Granjon LT Std by Jouve (UK), Milton Keynes

Printed and bound in Great Britain by Clays Ltd, Elcograf S.p.A.

Headline's policy is to use papers that are natural, renewable and recyclable
products and made from wood grown in well-managed forests and other
controlled sources. The logging and manufacturing processes are expected
to conform to the environmental regulations of the country of origin.

HEADLINE PUBLISHING GROUP
An Hachette UK Company
Carmelite House
50 Victoria Embankment
London EC4Y 0DZ

www.headlineeternal.com
www.headline.co.uk
www.hachette.co.uk

ACKNOWLEDGMENTS

Not OK, Cupid will always have a place in my heart for being my first published novel, but I wasn't expecting it to fill so many *other* places in my heart. Writing has made me so many new friends, and some old friends have been by my side the whole time, too.

Thank you to Amanda Jain, superagent, for saying, 'Yes,' to an unknown author. Thank you to Kate Byrne, editor extraordinaire at Headline Eternal, for saying, 'Yes,' to an unknown author's manuscript. Working with you has been a dream!

It took many people at Headline Eternal to bring this book to the shelves. By name I can thank Lucy Bennett for the beautiful cover, and Liz Hatherall for saving me from public embarrassment with her superhuman copy-editing skills. I know there are so many others who made this book possible but whose names I never saw – thank you.

Thanks to wonderful readers and wonderful friends AJ Watt, Cate Cameron, Jacqueline Rohrbach, Jill Corley, Jon Brierley, Kim Watt, Mandy Arnott, Martha Wilson, Natacha Billiet, Regina Partap, Sarah Stanton, Simon Reardon, Tani Hanes, and Thomas Roggenbuck.

CHAPTER ONE

~

$\mathcal{A}$lly Rivers narrowed her eyes at the woman's moustache. One remaining black hair moved up and down as she talked, waving like an antenna.

Ally readjusted the lamp to get it in focus. 'If you just keep still for a moment, Mrs McDonald, then we'll be done.'

Just as she wrapped the thread around the hair, it moved. Mrs McDonald cocked her head to peer up from the massage chair. 'You look tired. Are they working you too hard here?'

'Oh, no, Mandy's doing me a favour with the extra hours. I'm saving up for a holiday so I want as many shifts as I can get. If I just remove this last hair . . .'

As Mrs McDonald nodded, the hair glinted in the light. With her tongue poking out the corner of her mouth, Ally leaned in for the kill.

Mrs McDonald frowned and cocked her head the other way. 'It was Ibiza you went to last year, wasn't it? Where this year?'

Ally sat up, trying not to look at the clock. Mrs McDonald had described the office she worked in, where she was the only woman and all the men sat in silence. It sounded nothing like the salon, with its constant buzz of chat and people coming and going.

Making small talk with her was the least Ally could do while she ripped her facial hair out at the roots.

'If I win the lottery, the Caribbean,' Ally replied. 'But probably Ibiza again on a late deal. I'm not very good at saving.'

'I bet you're not.' Mrs McDonald grinned and the hair disappeared into a wrinkle. 'I was like you once, always out partying, always . . .'

Ally's mind drifted as she flexed her aching feet on the tiled floor. After fourteen days of extra shifts at the salon, the café and the bar, she'd seriously considered wearing her fluffy cow slippers to work.

This afternoon she was finishing early. Once the moustache was vanquished she could clean her station, collect her tips and top up her tan in the park for the rest of the day. That'd be kind of like a holiday – sun, sea (there was a lake), sand (in the children's play area), and . . . well, no sex, but there was an ice cream van. She could get one of those cider lollies that tasted like Barcelona. And maybe on her way to Mum's she'd buy some prawns so they could cook a paella together. With a glass of white wine and dinner on Mum's patio, it'd be like an evening in Spain. Sort of.

She blinked back into focus when she noticed Mrs McDonald's moustache had stopped moving.

'Sorry, what did you say?' she asked.

'I asked if we could speed it up a bit. I have a meeting at two thirty.'

Ally flexed her feet and showed her teeth. 'Sure. Just keep still for me and I'll finish up.'

'Ooh!' said Mrs McDonald, as Ally leaned over her. 'That's a lovely necklace. Where did you get it?'

* * *

Half an hour later, Ally stepped out of the salon into beautiful July sunshine. Her sore feet rejoiced in flip-flops – the cow slippers might've been a bit hot – and she could feel the vitamin D buzzing in her bare limbs. All she needed was a beach, but west London wasn't famed for its beaches.

At the end of the street she turned into the park and spotted the perfect patch of grass. It was soaked in sunshine, close enough to the stream to hear running water, but far enough away that she wouldn't get eaten by a swan. If only she had a set of watercolours with her to capture the scene. She needed to build a new portfolio of paintings to go with her new ad. Not that anybody would commission her to paint landscapes, but people liked looking at that sort of thing.

With a happy sigh she stretched out on her back, kicked off her shoes and spread her arms like a snow angel. Glorious. Who needed to be rich when you had grass and sunshine?

Her phone rang just as she got comfortable, and she pressed it to her ear without opening her eyes. 'Ally Rivers.'

'Hi, Ally Rivers. It's Samuel Kinsell.'

'Sam! Sorry, thought you might be a client. I put that ad up on a bunch of websites. How'd you like my professional phone voice?'

'Lovely. Beautiful, like you.'

Ally opened her eyes a crack. 'You want something.' Sam might have been the only man in her life she hadn't lost interest in within a few months – they'd been best friends for seventeen years – but he was also gay and never showed the slightest interest in her looks. In fact, he hadn't even noticed that time a bad dye job had turned her hair carrot-orange.

Best not to think about the orange hair incident.

'Of course I don't want anything,' Sam said. 'Hey, you remember when we were fifteen and I retyped your history coursework after you dropped it in the pond?'

'I couldn't help it. A swan looked at me.' She shot a look at the lake to see if they were listening.

'Yeah. But I still typed it up and you said I was the best friend in the world and you'd repay the favour one day.'

'You've been saving up that favour for thirteen years?'

'Yup. Will you come to a party with me?'

She kicked off her shoes. 'A party? Sure. You didn't need to guilt trip me into a party. Well, unless it's filled with my exes. When is it?'

'Um. Seven o'clock.'

'Today?' She dug her bare toes into the grass and felt them protest. 'Oh, Sam, I can't. I need a night off.'

'Ally, I need you,' Sam said in a wheedling voice. 'It's Gavin's engagement party. It's the first time Mum and Dad will be in the same room for ages, and I want them to remember how good things were so Dad can get over this mid-life crisis or whatever it is and move back in. But Gavin's bound to try to embarrass me in front of his friends and I'm already dying of heat exhaustion and I might end up battering someone with a champagne bottle. Look, there'll be cocktail sausages and Prosecco. And maybe I can find some rich aunts who'll hire you for portraits of my dick-head cousins.'

Ally closed her eyes and suppressed a sigh. Gavin. Sam had never been able to stand up to his bullying prick of an older brother, and things were awkward enough with their parents' divorce in progress.

'Well, if there's Prosecco, sure,' she said brightly.

'Thank you, best friend ever.' Sam's relief was evident. 'You didn't have plans, did you?'

Mum wouldn't mind cancelling dinner, and Ally could relax on her morning off next week. Well, it wasn't exactly a morning off, but her first shift wasn't until eleven so she could have a lie-in.

'Nah,' she said. 'When do you want to meet?'

'Three?'

That meant four, but he really wanted her to be on time.

'Three. I'll be there.'

After saying goodbye, she slipped her flip-flops back on and headed for the Tube station.

* * *

By three forty, Ally was ready in an azure cocktail dress with champagne nail polish. Twenty minutes to kill, and the sun was blazing through her living room window. She peered down at the front garden, fifteen feet below. It was in shadow thanks to the lime tree; nowhere to sunbathe.

Hitching the dress up her thighs, she hopped on to the window sill and swung her legs outside. Her anklet caught on the latch and almost unbalanced her, but she wriggled into a comfortable position without further mishap.

The sun spread over her skin like she'd stepped into a warm bath. She crossed her ankles against the brickwork and curled her toes in pleasure.

She leaned forward when she caught a glimpse of bare skin. On the opposite side of the road, a few doors down, a shirtless man dug in his flowerbeds with a spade. Ally positioned herself so he was in view, but he finished gardening and went inside. Spoilsport.

She retrieved her phone from her clutch and the OkCupid icon notified her of several new messages. She scrolled through the profiles. After discounting the ones who'd sent her unsolicited dick pics, she was left with two married men whose wives 'didn't understand them' and an estate agent. Not OK, Cupid.

'Ally, what the hell are you doing?' a voice called from the street.

Ally lowered the phone. Sam was crossing the road with his familiar stocky gait.

'Sam!' She swung her legs inside, hopped off the window ledge and ran downstairs.

Sam was waiting on the doorstep in a black suit and a blue tie that matched her dress and made his sandy hair look brighter.

'Hello, sexy.' She threw her arms around him, not minding that he was sweaty and radiating more heat than an atom bomb.

He kissed her cheek. 'What were you doing hanging out of the window?'

'Sunbathing.'

He pulled back and gave her a look. 'Out of the window?'

'I can't sunbathe inside, can I? Anyway, let's go. Your car has air con, right?'

Sam looked shifty. 'Can I come in for a minute? I need to talk to you.'

'Can't you talk to me where there's air con?'

'Um. You might not want to go after this.'

Ally stared. 'When have I ever not wanted to go to a party?'

'You've never been to a party like this. Trust me.'

Uh-oh. Maybe his parents were swingers, and they'd arrive to a house full of middle-aged people in lingerie and leather. She shook her head to dispel the image. There's no way Sam would want her in a room with his naked parents, let alone when they were . . . swinging, and Mrs Kinsell really, really didn't seem the type, unless all the time she spent at 'church' was a euphemism.

'I think you'd better come in,' she said.

In the living room she dropped on to the sofa next to him, fanned her face with a copy of *Vogue*, and braced herself. 'OK. Tell me.'

Sam cleared his throat. 'You're very generous, kind, helpful and, of course, beautiful.'

'What have you done, Sam?'

'Hey, I got you a present.' He proffered a carrier bag, and Ally drew out an adult colouring book – her latest hobby – filled with pictures of animals.

'Oh, great! Thank you.'

'There are no swans in it. I checked.'

Ally kissed his cheek again. 'You're the best.'

'No, you're the best. You're the best friend I could hope for and I know you'd do anything for me.'

'Hmm?' Ally flicked through the book to see if there were any cows.

'I was saying how generous you are to your best friend.'

She dragged her attention away from a drawing of a cute giraffe eating a branch. 'As much as I enjoy flattery, spit it out, Sam.'

'I have a confession to make.'

'Oh?'

'I told a lie.'

Ally waited.

Sam cleared his throat. 'You know my parents don't know I'm gay?'

'Uh-huh.'

'But I'm twenty-eight, so it'd look weird if I'd never had a girlfriend.'

Ally narrowed her eyes. 'Uh. Huh.'

'So, I told a little white lie.'

'Go on.'

'Hang on.' Sam dug deeper into his pocket and pulled out a lollipop. Coca-Cola flavoured. 'For you. Best friend ever.'

Ally snatched it. 'You said I'm your girlfriend?'

He grimaced and nodded. 'I mean, if I was going to have a girlfriend, it would have to be you. Since you're so beautiful, not to mention kind, and would do anything for your friends. Anything.'

Ally waved a hand to bat the flattery away. 'How long have I been your girlfriend?'

'Uh . . .'

'Sam?'

'Three years.'

'Three years?! Sam!' Unbelievable. Sam's outrageous lie was her longest lasting relationship. By almost three years.

'Don't be angry. I was forced into a corner.'

She folded her arms.

'I was!' he insisted. 'Look, I've been making up girlfriends since I was sixteen and Gavin brought a girl home to meet Mum and Dad. Every time they put pressure on me to introduce a girlfriend, she'd mysteriously break up with me. I tell you, it's lucky I'm gay because I have the worst luck with women.

'Then one year Gavin got really drunk at Christmas and started telling everybody I was making it all up, hinting that women weren't my type. Remember how he always called me a faggot when we were at school? So I blurted out that you and me had got together. I showed him a text where you said I was sexy and you loved me. I mean, he doesn't know that you always say that even though we'd rather wax our pubic hair with sandpaper than have sex with each other. It shut him up right away, because he always fancied you in school and knew he never had a chance.

'I was going to break up with you, I swear, but then Gavin started making digs about how far out of my league you are, and how you'd leave me for someone better-looking. So I made us more and more in love. Please don't be angry, you know I—'

Ally clamped a hand over his mouth. 'You know, I'm so damn impressed you've got away with this that I can't be angry. Man, how did you do it? Haven't they wanted to meet me before this?'

'Of course. But you've been working so hard at your career,

and you had a few placements at different hospitals around the country. It's amazing we lasted through all that long-distance stuff. We must really be in love. But Gavin keeps hinting so I agreed to bring you today . . .'

So that's why the big fat liar wanted her to go with him, not for moral support. Well, probably a bit of both. Gavin still terrified him, even though he was no longer a nervous schoolboy.

'Hang on.' Ally frowned. 'Did you say hospitals? And career? What career?'

'I told them you're a nurse.'

'Hey! What's wrong with my real job?'

Sam winced. 'Nothing. It's just that you're so caring and sweet. The perfect nurse. And, uh, Gavin's fiancée is a lawyer . . .'

'Oh, and being a starving artist isn't as impressive as being a lawyer?'

'I should've saved the lolly for this bit.'

'Does that mean you didn't bring any more gifts? No, don't answer that. You're not distracting me with lollies. You didn't think this through, did you? I can hardly keep my story straight when I'm telling the truth. And what if one of your relatives shows me a rash and asks me to diagnose it?'

Sam shuddered. 'I don't know. Just never, ever describe it to me.'

'Ugh. Are we going to have a fake wedding when they start hinting?'

'Uh, about that . . .' He rubbed his chin.

'Please tell me we're not married?'

'Not yet. But I proposed to you a few months ago.'

'Oh, Sam. You muppet.'

'Look, Mum and Dad have been talking more since Gavin and Kaitlyn's engagement. This party is the first time they'll have been in the same room in months. If they see us as well, all these happy couples, they'll remember why they got together in the first place and Dad might come to his senses, finally. Please, Ally. Mum needs him.'

Ally sighed. 'I am not having a fake wedding. Or a real one. When I become a world-famous artist, you're not getting half my paintings.' She shook her head at the window. Sam was usually so sensible, giving her a familiar, weary look when she confessed the latest foolish thing she'd done. But he wasn't sensible where his brother was concerned, forever seeking the prat's approval. If this was what it took to save him from Gavin's taunts, then fine.

She hopped up and looked down at her dress. Perhaps not ideal for meeting-the-parents; it just about reached mid-thigh, and the strapless sweetheart neckline just about covered her breasts. But screw it, she looked good and it was a shame to cover up on a beautiful summer's day. Or a day ending in Y. 'Come on, dear fiancé, or we'll be late.'

Sam followed her down the hall, looking delighted. 'You'll do it?'

Of course she would. She'd pretend to be a Teletubby if it would help Sam.

But she would make him squirm by laying it on thick about how in love they were.

She made a mental note to call their other best friend before he did. It would take some convincing for Rachel to believe Sam had come up with this hare-brained scheme, not Ally.

'Ally?'

She stopped, finding herself at the bottom of the stairs with Sam behind her, looking like a puppy who was trying so hard to be good and not snatch a treat.

'Oh, of course I'll do it,' she said. 'What are best friends for? But you owe me. Big time.'

He kissed her cheek, grinning. 'I do. I'll let you name all our fake babies.'

'Eurgh. No babies. Real or fake. Where is this party, anyway?'

'At Mum's. Essex.'

Ally forced her outraged feet into high heels – dark blue, strappy, and doing wonderful things to her calves – and followed him outside to his Honda.

'I get to control the radio today,' she informed him. 'For the rest of our lives, probably.'

She tuned it to Heart FM, and Michael Bublé crooned at them. Sam's eyes slid to the radio display, but he kept his mouth shut. Ally unwrapped her lolly and crossed her ankles on top of the glove compartment so the sun could catch them. She just had to remember to re-cross them every few minutes to get an even tan.

'Ally?'

'Mm?'

'Don't flirt with my cousins, will you? They're all arrogant pricks who'd only be interested in your body. Just your type.'

'Hey!'

Sam raised an eyebrow at her.

'Oh, all right,' she conceded. 'I won't. Spoilsport. Do you actually like any of your family?'

'Uh . . .' He tapped the wheel. 'My parents?'

'Well, that's a start. Do you really think they'd be upset if you come out?'

The tapping stopped. 'Mum would. She thinks it's unnatural. Perverted. When we were kids Gavin used to call me a fag when we argued, and she'd get so angry. Say it was disgusting even to suggest it.'

'Oh, Sam. But she loves you. She'd get over it.'

Ally had only met Mrs Kinsell once. She and Rachel had gone to Sam's place after school, back when the family lived in London. Mrs Kinsell, a petite woman with a strong limp who looked like a gust of wind might blow her away at any time, had hovered over them from the moment they arrived.

She'd given them orange squash and mini packets of Haribo, then told them fond stories about Sam while he sat red-faced and radiated silent apologies. For dinner she'd fed them chicken nuggets in the shape of dinosaurs with smiley potato faces on plastic neon plates, then insisted they go home for their bedtimes even though they were twelve and it was seven o'clock. They were out of the house before Sam's dad was home from work.

Even now he lived seventy miles away, Sam visited her weekly and called every other day. The strain of keeping up his lies must be awful.

Ally squeezed Sam's hand on the gearstick. 'She'd come round.'

'I don't want to upset her. She's really fragile. You'll see.'

And Sam blamed himself for her disability, even though it wasn't his fault she'd had pregnancy complications. That was yet another reason for Ally to use an IUD, condoms, *and* take a monthly pregnancy test just in case the universe hated her.

She was about to change the subject when 'Islands in the Stream' started playing, and she sang at the top of her lungs.

Sam suffered in silence and didn't even try to turn down the volume.

CHAPTER TWO

⁓

$\mathcal{S}$am and Ally arrived an hour before the party was due to start. The house was a run-of-the-mill semi-detached, clad in white stucco with picture windows. Well-kept but unremarkable, apart from the flowers – bright pansies and geraniums in window boxes, pink and yellow roses entwined around trellises, chrysanthemums and gladioli and flowers she didn't even know the name of in the borders around the driveway. It was surprising that Sam's mum could look after all these plants, but she did a great job.

'This'd make a great watercolour,' she said.

Sam wasn't listening. He stared with tight lips at a red BMW on the driveway.

'Gavin's?' she guessed.

Sam made a noise that might've been a confirmation. Ally took his hand, squeezed it, and dragged him to the front door. While he prodded the bell as if it were a ruptured cyst, she breathed in the scent of roses.

The door opened and Gavin smirked out at them. Ally was transported back fifteen years, watching him strut down the school corridor with a trio of giggling girls. Gavin would always pause to make them laugh by insulting his brother. Sam would stand and take it, frowning at the tiled floor like he could make himself disappear with the power of thought. It was Ally who told Gavin to piss off to the STI clinic where he belonged, or something equally mature. It was always her who fought with him until he gave up. Or sometimes Rachel, all five-foot-two of her blazing at the bully.

Even in appearance, Gavin hadn't changed. A tailored suit made his skinny legs look even feebler, and he seemed to have slicked back his hair with lard.

Ally tried her best to look besotted as she pressed herself against Sam.

'Well, hello,' Gavin said, looking Ally up and down. His gaze lingered for a moment on her cleavage. 'Barbie's finally come to meet the parents.'

She stopped herself rolling her eyes. The nickname hadn't been funny in school either, though Gavin found it ingenious. Instead, she beamed at him, full-on Stepford. 'Gary! How simply wonderful to see you again.'

The smirk slipped. 'Gavin.'

'Oh. Silly me. Of course. I'm always forgetting names. Hey, d'you remember Sara French from school? I saw her the other day in Waitrose, and I called her Sandra. Embarrassing. You know how you two dated for a while? Well, she came out as a lesbian soon after. Happily married to a woman called Jess now. Funny that, isn't it?'

'Uh-huh.' Gavin stepped aside to let them in. His expression had soured.

Sam leaned over to whisper in Ally's ear as they walked. 'I wish you'd bring mean Ally out more often. She's sexy.'

Ally tried to look offended. 'I'm always sexy.'

Gavin led them to the kitchen and introduced them to his fiancée, Kaitlyn. She was very pretty but spoiled her features by making a cat's-bum face when she appraised Ally's dress. Kaitlyn's was a similar blue, and probably cost six times more than Ally's, but it washed out her auburn hair and pale skin. She'd be a knockout in olive green.

'We were so sad not to see you at Julie's birthday party,' said Kaitlyn. Ally sat next to her at the breakfast bar and held Sam's clammy hand on her knee. 'It was absolutely gorgeous. Gavin got a cake specially made, in the shape of her church. He's so thoughtful.' Kaitlyn simpered at him.

'Ally was at work,' Sam blurted out.

Ally stroked his hand with her thumb. 'Yeah, you know nurses. Always short-staffed. It's hard to swap shifts. Being a lawyer must keep you busy.'

'It's not easy,' Kaitlyn agreed. 'Some days I don't leave the office until nine p.m., do I, darling?'

Gavin shook his head and winked at her as he lifted a cooler box on to the breakfast bar. 'Don't know when we're going to find time to make a little Kinsell. When are you two getting hitched?'

Sam was going to dehydrate if the rest of his body was sweating as much as his palm. Ally gripped it harder. 'We're in no hurry. We don't need to prove anything with a bit of paper.'

'Or a ring.' Kaitlyn lifted up Ally's free hand.

Gavin's eyes lit up. 'Sam, you didn't even get her a ring?'

Ally tugged at the gold chain around her neck, dragging her nana's antique sapphire ring from her cleavage. She put her best simpering smile on. 'I keep it next to my heart.'

Kaitlyn's smirk vanished as she examined her own ring finger. The stone was significantly smaller than the sapphire. 'How lovely.'

Gavin's eyes stayed on Ally's cleavage as she tucked the ring back into her dress. It nestled beside the crystal pendant Mum had given her, which was supposed to protect her from energy vampires and . . . materialistic zombies, or something. Mum had explained, but Ally had been too distracted by the way the crystal caught the light and cast rainbows on the wall.

They began unpacking food and drink from coolers. Ally stood between Sam and Gavin and kept up a flow of questions about the upcoming wedding. With Kaitlyn giving loud and detailed answers, there was no opportunity for Gavin to goad Sam.

She was running out of questions when her clutch vibrated half an hour later. An unknown number. Probably someone replying to the advert Sam had helped her create.

When she glanced at him, Sam pointed at a set of French doors. 'Garden's through there.'

Ally kissed him on the cheek and squeezed his shoulder on her way out. Gavin couldn't do much damage if she was quick.

'Ally Rivers,' she answered in her best phone voice.

The woman on the line had seen Ally's ad – result! – and wanted a portrait of her baby – sigh. Ally shut the kitchen doors behind her and followed a set of stepping stones to the sunny side of the house.

'Wow,' she mouthed. The sun beat down on a trimmed lawn, bordered by curved flowerbeds full of beautiful shrubbery. The only flowers were wild daisies, buttercups and dandelions. The rest was greenery in shades from chromium oxide to ultramarine.

She was too enraptured to notice the gardener until she'd taken in all the plants. He knelt at a flowerbed with his back to her, dark hair shining in the sun. Beneath a forest green T-shirt she noted a broad back and thick, tanned forearms.

Oh man, those arms. He ripped weeds out of the rich soil with a power that made her toes curl. Solid muscle flexed and relaxed in rhythm with his gloved hands. Judging by the rugged skin he was older than she usually went for, perhaps early forties, but he'd aged like a fine wine. Mature guys might be better in bed – less wham, bam, thank you, ma'am than the twenty-somethings. Trying an older guy would be a novel experience anyway, and she was running out of those.

'Excuse me? Are you listening?' snapped the woman on the phone.

Ally blinked, and strained to recall what she'd been saying. 'Yes, sorry. You want a picture of your . . . baby?'

The gardener looked round at the noise and smiled at Ally. Oh man. He was definitely her type, and definitely not too old. A younger man's smile wouldn't make his eyes crinkle at the corners in that rugged, George Clooney kind of way.

'Right,' said the customer. 'Can you do the seventh of August?'

'Let me check my calendar,' Ally replied. She didn't even own a calendar. Gardener Clooney watched her with an amused grin as she counted up to ten with her fingers. His strong jaw was dark with stubble and his eyes were a deep brown. Like a Jersey cow. Jerseys were the best.

'August the seventh will be gorgeous.' She frowned. Something hadn't come out right there. She forced her eyes away from Gardener Clooney's. 'I mean, August will have gorgeous weather, so if you're planning to do it outside we'll need some cover.'

'I'm aware of that,' snapped the woman on the phone. 'I have kept her alive for nearly a year and I don't need parenting advice. Are you sure you're a qualified artist?'

'Positive.' Well, she was, since being an artist didn't require any qualifications. 'I just wondered if you wanted me to bring a parasol.'

Mother-of-the-year was placated. Ally let her eyes drift back to Gardener Clooney as they finalised the details. He stared at her with crinkled eyes, his muscular arms propped on one knee.

Ally hung up and dropped the phone back in her clutch.

'You're an artist,' George observed in a voice like molten chocolate.

'You must be a detective.' Ally searched his left hand for a ring, but it was hidden in a gardening glove. A large gardening glove.

'Do you only paint babies?' he asked.

'Nope. I try to avoid it actually. Squirmy little beasts, and you never make them quite beautiful enough for the parents. Even when you don't paint the drool or flecks of vomit.'

His laugh was deep and sexy. This could last a few months – until they inevitably got bored of the sex and realised they had nothing in common – if those hands lived up to expectations.

And if there wasn't a ring on one of them.

'What about pets?' he asked.

'I love painting pets. They're much easier than kicky little babies. Clients just give me a couple of photos and tell me what they want the picture to look like.'

'You don't paint them live?'

'Nah. Hard to get them to sit still for that long. Hard for babies, too, but the parents always think they're angels.'

He stood and took a glove off to wipe his brow. The right glove, damn it, keeping his left ring-finger covered. 'Could you paint a dog who only moves if her life's in danger, or there's peanut butter on offer?'

'Any time! I love dogs.'

'Good. I've got a cocker spaniel on her last legs, and I've been thinking about getting a picture to remember her by.'

'Aw, I love cocker spaniels. You get a discount. I'll charge the baby lady extra to make up for it.'

He laughed. 'Why did you agree to it, if you hate painting babies so much?'

'I need the cash.'

He raised his eyebrows. 'Saving up for something?'

'Yup. Holiday. Sun, sea, sand and . . . sun.'

He showed more of those white teeth. Strong teeth. Was he a biter? 'You said sun twice.'

'I really, really like . . . sun.'

He blinked at her, then laughed. 'Well, nothing wrong with that. Will you paint Debbie?'

Ally reached into her bag and suppressed a smile. 'You'd better give me your number.' She unlocked her phone. 'I'll call and arrange a date.'

Damn. Date. She was here as Sam's date. No, his fiancée. She shouldn't be flirting with his mum's gardener. When she called she'd have to feel out how well he knew Mrs Kinsell and how likely he was to mention Ally. It'd be a shame not to try out those hands, but she wouldn't risk Sam's secret.

Once she'd programmed his number she straightened her dress. 'I'd better get back before they miss me.'

'You're here for the party?'

Damn. If he knew about the party, he was at least on chatting terms with Mrs Kinsell.

Ally nodded. 'Happy weeding.'

'Happy partying.'

She wondered if he was looking at her butt or her bare legs as she took the stepping stones back to the kitchen door. Just before she rounded the corner she glanced back, but he wasn't looking at her at all. He knelt on the grass, wrapping one gloved hand around a weed.

* * *

When Ally stepped into the kitchen, Sam's face was an unhealthy red as he stabbed cocktail sticks through sausages. Gavin, standing close beside him, looked very pleased with himself.

'Ooh, cocktail sausages!' Ally inserted herself between the brothers. 'Yum.'

Kaitlyn made a face and went back to chopping celery into batons.

'How's the colouring-in going?' Gavin the banker asked Sam the graphic designer.

Sam's fist closed around a cocktail stick.

'Great,' said Ally, as if the question had been directed at her. 'I still draw, and paint. You remember when you tried to buy my self-portrait in school?'

Kaitlyn looked up sharply from the celery.

'As a joke,' said Gavin. He cleared his throat and avoided his fiancée's eyes.

'Oh. Wasn't very funny. Then again, neither was that stand-up you tried to do at the talent show. Bet you still get embarrassed, thinking of that stony silence? Never mind . . . I'm sure you've got funnier in the last fifteen years.'

Gavin's jaw set as he ripped open a packet of profiteroles, then had to get on his knees to pick them up from the floor. Sam nudged Ally with his shoulder, the hint of a smile on his lips.

When the food was done, Ally helped carry the trays and ice buckets to the garden. Clooney was gone, but she heard a bang and spotted him dumping weeds in a compost bin at the side of the house. He took off his gloves, revealing a tanned – and ringless – hand.

Result.

He smiled at her and disappeared on to the driveway.

Please let him not be close to Mrs Kinsell. Besides anything else, she really wanted to paint the dog: she'd only sold two paintings since spring, though her ad was going to change that.

They set up trestle tables in the garden. Just as the sun went behind a cloud, the other guests started arriving. Sam shot Ally a pained look, took her hand, and introduced her to an endless line of aunts, family friends and people his mum went to church with. Ally squeezed his hand whenever someone asked her a tricky question, and Sam squeezed hers whenever her mind wandered.

Gavin stood with a group of men that laughed loudly every few minutes, spilled beer on the grass, and ogled any woman under thirty. When she met their eyes they smirked at her, brazen, and dropped their eyes to her cleavage. These must be the cousins Sam had warned her about.

Shame, because one of them was *hot*.

At seven on the dot, Gavin held up an empty wine glass and tapped it with a knife. The buzz of conversation stopped, and the thirty or so guests turned to look at him.

'Thank you everybody for coming,' he began, and launched into a very dull speech about the history of his relationship. Ally's mind wandered back to Gardener Clooney's hands, but she snapped back when she heard Sam's name.

'And today we finally meet Sam's fiancée,' Gavin said, gesturing at Ally with his glass. 'I hope he hasn't paid her to come along. Perhaps it was premature of me to say he was punching above his weight with pretty girls. Or girls with sight.'

Gavin's group snickered.

'Yeah,' Ally called out. 'From what the girls at school used to say, being premature has always been a problem for you.'

Subtlety had never been her forte, but Gavin's group seemed to appreciate directness. They laughed a lot louder than they had at his joke.

Gavin and Kaitlyn glared at her. Ally put on her sweetest Barbie smile and held up her glass of Prosecco to them.

Gavin seemed to lose his way after that, and abandoned his prompt cards unread. 'Anyway,' he shot another venomous look at Ally, 'today is a momentous occasion because our two families are meeting for the first time. Thanks to all of you, our beloved friends and relatives, for joining us. And my brother came along, too.' He winked as if it were a joke, and the crowd laughed. Ally made a mental note to grind her heel into his instep before she left. 'We want to give our special thanks to our parents, who've generously agreed to front the wedding costs. So please join me in a toast to my future parents-in-law –' he raised his glass to a couple standing near Kaitlyn – 'and to my parents.' He indicated Mrs Kinsell, leaning heavily on a black walking stick. Then Gavin turned and pointed the champagne glass at Gardener Clooney.

Mr Kinsell.

Gavin and Sam's father.

CHAPTER THREE

*S*am's dad. She'd been flirting with Sam's dad. Perving on him.

A bottle of brain bleach wouldn't be enough.

Sam's dad – his DAD – stood looking all handsome while his wife (oh shit, Sam's mum) made a speech to thank the guests for coming. He glanced around at the crowd and smiled when he saw Ally. Then his eyes travelled to her left.

To his son.

Holding her hand.

Ally pressed her cheek into Sam's shoulder, both to avoid his dad's eyes and to hide her blush.

Not only had she imagined screwing her best friend's dad, but she'd blown it as Sam's fake fiancée. Gardener Clooney – Mr Kinsell – Sam's *dad* – would tell Sam his fiancée was a cheating slut, or he'd work out their relationship was a sham. Either way, that prick Gavin would revel in his brother's humiliation and never let him forget it.

She had to fix this.

Everyone clapped at the end of Mrs Kinsell's speech. Ally hadn't heard a word of it, imagining the look on the woman's face if she knew her ex had been flirting with her future daughter-in-law. Although . . . Ally strained to remember the conversation, and her cheeks blazed. He hadn't flirted. Just smiled and stared. Shit, of course he'd stared. He'd wondered who this strange woman in his garden was, talking nonsense about parasols and how much she loved . . .

Great. Now he thought his son was dating a nymphomaniac cheating slut.

She'd even told him she was an artist, when she was supposed to be a nurse.

She really had to fix this.

The polite applause stopped, and everyone looked at Mr Kinsell.

'It's great to see you all here,' he said in that deep melty voice.

No, no, no. That was a rasping jarring voice. Not sexy. Yuck. He probably smoked sixty a day and that was why it was so deep, even though that made no sense, and he'd stink of cigarette smoke. And cough up black stuff in the morning. Ew. Who'd want to wake up next to that?

Everyone clapped again, though Ally was sure she'd only tuned out for a moment.

'Let's go and chat to Gavin.' Ally seized Sam's arm and marched him across the lawn.

'Why?' Sam hissed, dragging his heels. 'Are you a masochist?'

Ally ignored him. It was crucial she was with Sam and Gavin when their dad told them what she'd done. Damage limitation.

Sam had got away with this lie for three years, and she'd ruined it in three minutes thanks to her irrepressible libido. She was the worst fake fiancée ever, not to mention a terrible friend. Perving on his *dad*.

What the hell was he doing gardening, anyway? He didn't even live here any more. Unless Sam's scheming was working and he was getting back together with his wife . . .

Shit. If she'd thrown a spanner in those works, Sam would never forgive her.

Ally brought Sam to a halt beside Gavin and Kaitlyn just as a middle-aged woman descended on them.

'Gavin!' She took Gavin by the shoulders, kissed both his cheeks, then turned on Sam. 'Sam!'

'Aunt Jill,' said Gavin with an ingratiating smile. 'Have you met my fiancée, Kaitlyn?'

Once Aunt Jill had finished making a fuss of Kaitlyn's expensive dress, it was Ally's turn. 'Oh, now, look at you. What a beauty you've got yourself, Sam.'

Ally appreciated that, because it made Kaitlyn do the cat's-bum face again.

'What do you do, dear?' Aunt Jill asked.

'I'm a lawyer,' Kaitlyn answered immediately. 'Specialising in criminal law.'

Ally watched Mr Kinsell out of the corner of her eye. He stood by the buffet table, pouring wine and soft drinks for a stream of guests. Just before Mrs Kinsell reached the table, he moved to the other end and ducked down to unpack a crate of beers.

'And you, dear?' Jill asked.

'Hmm?' Ally dragged her gaze back to Jill. 'Oh. I'm an art—a nurse. An art . . . ery nurse. An artery nurse. I specialise in arteries.'

Jill's eyes lit up and she turned her back on Kaitlyn to face Ally.

'A nurse? That's very interesting.' She slipped a stockinged foot out of a pink, peep-toed shoe and pointed it at Ally. 'I've had this lump on the side of my toe for months—'

'Oh, Dad's free,' Sam interrupted. 'Excuse us, Auntie Jill. We haven't said hello yet.' Ally stared in horror at Mr Kinsell, who was arranging the beers on the tablecloth. Why couldn't they stay and examine Jill's bunions?

Sam steered her away. 'At least it wasn't a rash,' he whispered, with a shudder.

Ally's feet dragged of their own accord, and tried to stop altogether when Mr Kinsell caught sight of her.

She did the only thing she could think of. Lagging a few steps behind Sam so he wouldn't see her face, she locked eyes with his father and mouthed, 'Sorry. Explain later.'

He raised an eyebrow, but before he could say anything, a high voice said, 'Sammy!'

Mrs Kinsell was heading towards them, leaning on the arm of a woman who could only be her sister. It was like looking at before-and-after pictures for some revolutionary medical treatment, with the sister at least a stone heavier and a boulder robuster than Mrs Kinsell.

The sister eyed Ally as they approached, and Ally tried to smile. It felt maniacal.

'Hi, Mum. Aunt Virginia.' Sam kissed his mum on the cheek, and she drew him into a one-armed hug. He glanced from his mum to his dad, and shuffled closer to Ally. 'You remember Ally, Mum?'

'Of course.' Mrs Kinsell's smile faded when her eyes slid down Ally's tight blue dress. Mrs Kinsell wore a long skirt with tights covering her bare ankles and a long-sleeved blouse. Conservative. Smart. Not calculated to show the most flesh possible without actually breaking the law.

The sisters exchanged looks.

A thump vibrated through Ally's shoulder as Sam dropped his arm around her. 'Lots of romance around, isn't there? Me and Ally. Gavin and Kaitlyn. Must be something in the air. How are you, Dad?'

Ally fought down a wince, and adjusted her face to neutral. Something similar seemed to pass over Mr Kinsell's face.

Sam's mum looked up at him. 'Hello, Marcus.'

'Hello, Julie.'

'How's your new place?'

'Fine, thank you.'

'I'm sure it's cosy.'

'Yes.'

'You know this place gets chilly in the evenings.'

'Indeed,' said Aunt Virginia, looking straight at Marcus. 'It's not good for the joints. Especially ones that have already been through the wars.'

Silence fell.

'Great weather today, though,' Sam said. 'Suits the occasion. Love and happiness and all that. Bet Gavin can't wait to be married. We can't, can we?' He squeezed Ally's shoulder.

'Yeah. I mean, no. Can't wait.'

'A summer wedding would be nice.'

'Mm,' Ally said, then thought she ought to make more of an effort. 'We could have the reception outside. Like this.'

'Great idea!'

Ally risked a glance at Sam's father. He had an eyebrow raised again, and caught Ally's eye. She looked away.

'Sammy, your tie's crooked.' Mrs Kinsell leaned in and tugged at the knot around Sam's neck. Ally stepped to one side to give them space, and found Mr Kinsell square in front of her.

'So, Ally,' he said, in a low voice. She bet his chest would rumble if she put a hand on it.

'Hi,' she said, in a very high voice indeed.

Her pulse hammered in her veins as he looked down at her. Those brown eyes were dark and deep, contrasting with his blue shirt.

'Pleasure to meet you,' he said in his chocolatey voice. 'I should have come to say hello earlier, but I was on gardening duty. Forgive me.'

Forgive *him*? Was he playing with her?

'It's a beautiful garden,' was all she could think to say.

'I always think it'd make a good painting.' His eyes glinted. Penetrating. Penetrating . . .

Mrs Kinsell's voice carried into the silence. 'It does get lonely, yes.'

'About that painting,' said Mr Kinsell, his eyes still fixed on Ally. 'Come and meet Debbie, and you can give me a quote. My dogs are upstairs where they can't decimate the buffet.'

'I wouldn't charge,' Ally said hurriedly. 'Not for family. I'll give you a call when I have an opening.'

'Of course I'll pay. You have to eat, family or not. And you must meet Debbie. Don't want you turning up for our appointment and finding out you're allergic to her, do we?'

That was bullshit and he knew it; she could see the glint in his eyes. But if she refused to let him get her alone and quiz her about her behaviour? Then maybe he'd do it right here, a few feet away from Sam and his ex-wife.

'OK,' said Ally. One of her heels sank into the grass.

* * *

Ally followed Mr Kinsell inside, through the kitchen and up a flight of stairs in silence. Now they were alone it was her chance to explain, and she didn't have a clue what to say.

'I'm sorry,' she said, stopping on the landing. Well, there was no point putting it off. Mr Kinsell turned to her, looking bemused. 'I thought you were the gardener.'

He raised his eyebrows.

'Oh, crap, forget I said that, I mean—'

He grinned. 'It's OK. I am the gardener. Or, at least, I was. But Julie asked me to come early to help get the house ready, and I couldn't leave those weeds to choke the bluebells.'

A breeze fluttered in from the small window at the end of the hall and carried the scent of his aftershave to Ally's nose. Citrus, spice, and something deep and masculine, like leather. She hoped it was fake leather. No cow should have to die for cologne, even for a scent as bewitching as this.

She breathed in and tried to remember what he'd said. 'Uh . . . well, you know what I mean. I didn't think you were related to Sam or I wouldn't have been so . . . casual.'

'I like casual. Kaitlyn never says more than two words to me. Come and meet Debbie. She's in my room. Well, not my room any more, though I still have stuff to move out.'

Ally ground to a halt. Alone with him, in his bedroom? She'd self-combust.

Wait. *His* bedroom? Why not *our* bedroom? This had been the marital home, after all.

With a deep breath she followed him through a door and exhaled in relief. Not a bedroom, and it was clear why it was *his*. This was a man cave, all dark wood and charcoal furniture, with manganese-blue walls warm in the sunshine. It had the neglected look of a room in the middle of a house move: the shelves lining one wall were mostly empty, with isolated piles of CDs, DVDs and books among the dust. Another wall had a large discoloured rectangle on the paint, as if something had hung there and blocked the sunlight from the paint. The only furniture was a huge, squashy grey sofa, and a TV stand minus the TV.

Mr Kinsell picked up a cardboard box from behind the door, and began packing away books. 'What do you think?' He nodded at the window. Underneath it, a cocker spaniel was curled up in a massive dog bed like a single bean on a dinner plate. Squashed up beside it, a Newfoundland had one hind leg jammed into a cocker-spaniel-sized bed. He raised his head and thumped his tail at Ally.

'Oh my gosh, the cuteness.' Ally dropped to her knees and held out a fist to each dog. The cocker spaniel opened one eye, gave a cursory sniff, and went back to sleep. The Newfoundland ran his wet nose over Ally's knuckles like a vacuum cleaner, whined, and rolled over to expose his stomach.

'That means belly rub,' Mr Kinsell said.

There was a lot of belly to choose from. Standing up, the dog must have been as tall as her. He wriggled his butt as she rubbed the thick fur.

'Why is there a bear in your living room?' she asked.

'Julie wouldn't let me put him in the kitchen. He eats her friends.'

'He's not going to eat me, is he?'

'No. He had the postman this morning, so he's full.'

'That's a relief. I take it this is Debbie?' She jerked her head at the cocker spaniel, who snored.

'Yep. And that's Harry.'

'Debbie and Harry?'

He shrugged and gave her a sheepish smile. 'Never got over my Blondie obsession.'

Ally glanced at the bookshelves, but the row of CDs was too far away for her to make out the titles. 'Are you going to see them next month?'

'They're touring?'

'Uh-huh. I'm going to see them at the O2 on the twenty-fifth.'

'I didn't know. It's not really fair of me to leave the dogs in the evenings, anyway. A walker comes in while I'm at work, but they like company in the evenings. Especially that massive softie.'

'How much does he weigh?' she asked.

'Seventy-two kilos.'

Ally eyed the belly again. 'Man. He's heavier than me.'

'Get a treat inside him and he's heavier than *me*. It's my fault. We used to go running for an hour, morning and evening, but Debbie just wants to sleep these days. Harry won't leave her side, so the three of us crawl along like some kind of outing for disabled snails. Sometimes I can coax him to chase a Frisbee.'

'You could carry Debbie and run with him.'

Mr Kinsell snorted with laughter. 'I'm probably less fit than her. I haven't run since October, when the mornings got cold and I got lazy.'

'You look fit,' Ally said without thinking. She cringed. 'Er, I mean, you did all that gardening without breaking a sweat.'

'It's not exactly a triathlon. Anyway, enough about my laziness. If I start to feel guilty I won't be able to have a burger from the barbecue.' He put a final stack of books into the box and straightened up. 'I was hoping to talk to you about Sam.'

Oh, shit.

'Sam?' Ally said, her voice several octaves higher than usual.

'Yep. I would ask him, but it's such a sensitive subject for him. You two can't have any secrets from each other, being engaged and all, so I can ask you.'

Ally gaped at him. 'What subject?'

'A long time ago we talked about him having corrective surgery for . . . you know.' He gestured at his chest.

Ally stared at his chest, so horrified by this turn of events that she only wondered for a second whether it was hairy or smooth.

Mr Kinsell sat on the squashy sofa and gestured at the other side. Ally sat down with a bump.

'When he was younger,' he continued, 'I said I'd pay for it if he wanted it. But when I brought it up again he brushed me off and I could see he didn't want to talk about it. So you tell me, honestly, has he made his peace with it or does he want to go for the surgery?'

Ally's mouth was still open. She shut it with a snap and swallowed.

'Um,' she said. Think, think. What could be wrong with Sam's chest? 'Er,' she added, looking around the room as if the answer would be on a poster on the walls. As her gaze wandered back to Mr Kinsell, she caught a twitch of his lips.

She looked hard at him. 'Are you playing with me?'

His face rearranged itself into an innocent mask. 'I'm sorry?'

'You were laughing at me.'

'Me?' He cocked his head to the side. 'Why would I do that?'

'Because—' She shut her mouth again. She could hardly say *because you want to catch me out*.

'I'm just asking my son's fiancée a question.' He leaned forward, holding her gaze. 'You must know all about it.' He gestured at his chest again.

Ally's mind whirred. Did he know she'd never seen Sam naked? How could he know? She examined his face closely and could see no traces of a smile. His eyes were still glinting but maybe he just had glinty eyes.

'Well, so do you.' She crossed her arms and then, in a flash of inspiration, moved them below her breasts and pushed them up. A quick glance confirmed her cleavage was winning the fight with her dress. Trying to look casual, she bent her knees and drew her legs on to the sofa so the dress rode up her thighs.

It didn't have quite the distracting effect she hoped for. The git didn't seem to notice she'd moved, his stare fixed on her face. Her body was the only damn weapon she had and it wasn't working.

'You ask him,' she said, irritation making her voice more forceful. 'If he's not comfortable talking about it then neither am I. We protect each other's secrets.'

His dark eyes narrowed, and then his face broke into a wide smile. 'All right.' He nodded, as if conceding defeat. 'I'll ask him.'

'Well, good. You do that.'

He held her gaze. Ally refused to blink first, her eyes immediately watering. In an effort to distract him she pulled the crystal pendant out of her cleavage and rotated it to catch the light. A flash of white shone on the pale blue walls, but Mr Kinsell sat calmly and stared into her eyes.

Ally blinked first. It was difficult not to, because a blur of brown filled her vision a nanosecond before two paws the size of tree branches slammed into her shoulders. Harry pinned her to the sofa and nuzzled between her breasts, pushing the material aside to get at her pendant.

'Harry, no!' Mr Kinsell shouted.

Harry yelped as Mr Kinsell seized him around the middle and yanked him off Ally. She sat up just as Harry landed full-force on Mr Kinsell's chest, his massive paws waving in the air.

Mr Kinsell made an 'oof' sound, and Ally pushed Harry with all her strength. He slid off the sofa with a thump and stared at her with a hurt expression.

Mr Kinsell rubbed his stomach and winced.

'God, are you OK?' Ally bit her lip.

'I'll live. I've got a spare kidney if that one's broken.' He sat up gingerly. 'Excuse my dog. Harry!' The dog sat up straight and locked eyes with his master. 'You do not take off a lady's dress without asking. OK?'

Harry barked and shuffled his feet.

'Huh. Not many people call me a lady.' She tucked the pendant back in her dress and straightened the neckline. At least one male in this house appreciated her cleavage.

He smiled. 'So, when are you coming to paint Debbie?'

Ally thought fast for an excuse. 'It's too hard to paint animals from life. Give me some photos and I'll do it from home.'

'How can I get to know my future daughter-in-law if you're at home?'

She definitely wasn't imagining that mischievous look.

'Er . . . email?'

'All right. What's your email address?'

Trying not to show her relief, Ally typed it into his phone for him. Email was fine. She'd have time to form a convincing response, and he wouldn't be able to see her body language. She was transparent as a jellyfish when she tried to lie.

'One minute,' he said, taking the phone and tapping on it.

Ally's buzzed, and she took it out of her bag while he was still busy.

'Ugh,' she said. 'You're sneaky.'

He grinned.

Ally sighed at the email, from one Marcus Kinsell: *Nurse-slash-artist required to paint a cocker spaniel. Tuesday at six?*

'Fine,' she said. 'You win.'

'Great! I'll send you my address and we'll have a great time. I can ask you lots of questions about you and Sam. Won't that be fun?'

Oh, he was tricky. But Ally could be devious too. She adjusted her dress, tugging it down her bare thighs, and watched his face.

His eyes didn't stray from hers.

'Better get back,' he said with a smile. 'We can tell Sam. He'll be delighted that you'll be spending more one-on-one time with his family.'

'Mm. Delighted.' Ally narrowed her eyes at him and wished she could read thoughts.

He stood up and looked at his dog. 'Harry? There are absolutely no cocktail sausages in the garden, so don't bother coming to look. OK?'

Harry barked.

'Good boy.'

Ally tried to process the conversation as she followed him downstairs, but her brain wasn't designed for working out puzzles. She settled for watching the way his broad shoulders moved as he walked.

In the garden, Sam was hovering by his mum and her sister. His face relaxed in relief when he saw Ally, and he grasped her arm. 'Let's get a drink.'

Mr Kinsell's mouth twitched into a smile as he took in Sam's hand curled around Ally's forearm. It was the first time he'd looked anywhere below her neck.

Ally pressed herself against Sam's side as they went to the buffet table. She put a hand on his chest to feel his heart through the damp shirt.

Sam twisted away and flinched. 'Don't. I'm . . . I'm sweaty.'

'There's nothing wrong, is there?' Ally asked, squeezing his hand.

'No.'

'Your dad said something about your chest . . . I didn't know what to say. I kind of bluffed.'

His red cheeks clashed with his sun-bleached hair.

'Tell him it's none of his business,' he said, his voice uncharacteristically harsh. 'I shouldn't have brought you here. Why am I such an idiot?'

Sam's eyes flicked to the barbecue as they filled their glasses.

Gavin and his group stood there, drinking beer and smoking. Gavin caught Sam's eye, leaned closer to the cousins, and said something with a nasty grin. They all turned to Sam and laughed.

'Brace yourself,' Ally whispered into Sam's ear, then grabbed his face and kissed him like she wanted to count his molars.

She hoped he was a better kisser with men. He went limp, then grasped her shoulders with his arms sticking out like a crab and managed to move his lips.

Ally broke off, sighed, and stroked his cheek. 'Oh, Sam. You still make my knees weak after all these years.'

The gang stared at them, subdued. So did several shocked aunts, and Sam's parents. Mrs Kinsell and her sister looked horrified, but Mr Kinsell met Ally's eyes and gave a half-smile like they were sharing a joke.

Ally smiled around sweetly and poured herself another glass of Prosecco.

CHAPTER FOUR

～

*T*he café was quiet for Ally's Tuesday morning shift. She was nervous about seeing Sam's tricky, sexy dad that evening, but it was too nice a day to be in a bad mood. While she grilled a chicken breast for her lunch, she used the spatula to sing 'You're So Vain' with the radio.

'It's not "wife of a postman",' said a familiar voice.

Ally spun around and saw a grey-haired woman in a green sundress at the counter.

'Gran!' Ally skipped over to give her a kiss. 'What did you say?'

'The lyrics, dear. It's not "Wife of a postman".'

'Oh.' Ally sang it again in her head and it sounded right. Maybe Gran was going a little deaf. 'Want a cup of tea?'

'Irish coffee.'

'Gran, I've told you before. We can't serve alcohol.'

Gran sighed. 'Then what's the point of you? Fine. Tea. Two sugars, milk, and none of your skimmed nonsense, thank you very much.'

Ally rifled among the teabags for a Twinings English Breakfast and exhaled in relief when she found one. What was Gran going to berate her about today? Men, babies, or career?

She carried the tea to a Formica table, with a can of Lilt for herself. Gran inspected the mug for chips, pursed her lips, and glared at Ally. 'Now, Alicia, you know I'm dying.'

'Yes. Since the nineties.'

Gran waved a hand in the air. 'You don't get to my age by hurrying. The fact is, I'm dying. Your idiot father is going to get my money, and your grandpa's, God rest his soul. His idiot wife will spend it on impressing her friends. I'd write them out of my will but it'd upset your grandpa.' She blew on her tea and added, 'God rest his soul.'

Great; it was career today. Ally eyed Gran's viridian handbag, wondering when the cheque would appear, and gripped the Lilt can. 'You could leave it to charity?'

Gran gave her a look that suggested she'd spat in the tea. 'To feed a load of mangy donkeys that do nothing but eat and fart? Or buy a new bingo machine for a home full of feckless coffin dodgers?'

Ally glanced around to make sure her customers weren't listening. 'Well, spend it all then. Go on a round-the-world cruise.'

'Oh yes, I'd love to pay for some randy sailors to crash me into an iceberg.' She rolled her eyes. 'I'm dying but I'm not suicidal. Anyway, I didn't come here for ideas. If I needed someone with a list of a thousand ways to spend my money I'd go and see your father, and I'd rather have a smear test than visit him and Cruella de Vil without anyone holding a gun to my head.'

Ally choked on the Lilt and used her apron to wipe it up. 'Oh Gran, they're not so bad. Dad loves you, and Carly's just a bit . . . neurotic. She was born that way.'

Gran stared at her in disgust. 'When are you going to realise life's a bitch, Alicia, and people only care about themselves? Most of us make our peace with it when we're teenagers.'

'I like life. And people. You're one of my favourites.' Ally squeezed Gran's papery wrist.

'That's nice, dear. You're a fool. Now, listen. I'm leaving half to your mother, mostly because it'll annoy Cruella. But I don't want you to wait for her to shuffle off before you can have some.'

Ally's stomach tightened at the thought of Mum dying. She clutched the crystal pendant around her neck and wondered how to get Gran off this subject.

Too late.

'I want to give you some money to start your business again,' Gran continued. 'And this time I want you to do it properly, not a half-arsed job with a bunch of whining excuses.'

'Hey! I don't whine.'

Gran examined her. 'All right, you don't whine. You do make excuses though, all the time, and I'm sick of it. God gave you two gifts and you use one of them well enough,' Gran raked her eyes down Ally's body, making her shift guiltily, 'but not the one you actually have to work at. It's a waste and that's a sin and there's only one type of sin I encourage women to commit on a regular basis.' She leaned forward, hands clasped around her mug. 'How's sex these days? Has it changed since the noughties?'

'Oh, Gran, please don't tell me about Melvin again.' Ally got ready to stuff her fingers in her ears.

Gran grinned. 'Melvin with the wrinkly balls?'

Ally sighed. 'That's the one.'

'OK, I won't. All I'll say is "ancient basset hound" doesn't quite cover it and he's all set if he ever needs a skin transplant.'

Ally pushed her drink away and closed her eyes.

'Oi, listen to me.' Gran rapped Ally's knuckles until she squinted with one eye. 'Start your business again. I want my investment back in three years. Doubled. Then maybe I'll take Melvin on a cruise.'

Ally's heart sank. She hated letting Gran down, but that's exactly what she'd do if she took her money. Painting every now and then as a hobby was OK, but trying it as a full-time business had ended in tears. Literally. She just didn't have the attention span to do anything full time. There was a reason she had three part-time jobs with irregular hours: because she rebelled at any hint of routine and responsibility.

'I don't want your money, Gran. I can't even make sandwiches properly, let alone run a business. I was a disaster.'

'There you go with the excuses. Where would your mother be if she hadn't taken my money to set up her business?'

'That's different.' Ally eyed the café door and wished a customer would arrive. 'That was Mum. And people are willing to pay more for reiki and crystal healing than for a painting.'

'More fool them. Look, if she can do it with that hippie bollocks, you can do it with your talent. The two of you might as well be twins. Both of you bungalows, nothing—'

'—going on upstairs,' Ally finished. 'Thanks, Gran. But Mum's not a bungalow. She has stuff in the attic. It's just . . . a bit messy and disorganised. I have nothing.'

'Alicia, she's got a bomb site in the attic. Trust me, I saw enough of them during The Troubles. Now, no more backchat or I'll be angry, and you're not too old for a smack, young lady. Here.' She rummaged in her handbag, drew out a folded piece of paper, and shoved it down the front of Ally's T-shirt.

'Hey!' Ally fished it out and looked. A cheque for two thousand pounds. Ally knew she'd get all fired up, throw herself into the business with everything she had, then get bored in a fortnight and spend the rest on adopting cows in India. Again.

'Gran, I don't want this.'

'Tough shite. It's yours.' Gran sat back and sipped her tea. 'You should advertise in the Yellow Pages.'

'I don't think they print the Yellow Pages any more.'

'Then whatever flashy equivalent you kids have these days. Put an ad in Google, or that Face Magazine your Mum's always trying to put me in.'

The more Ally argued, the more stubborn Gran would get. Thank god nobody had told her about bank transfers; at least Ally could leave a cheque uncashed.

'OK, Gran.'

Gran scowled. 'Don't say "OK, Gran" in that "I'm just trying to shut you up" way. You do it.'

Was there *no* way to win this?

Only by satisfying Gran that she wasn't planning to work as a waitress-slash-barmaid-slash-beautician-slash-masseuse for the rest of her life.

'I did.' Ally sat up straighter. 'I put an ad on a bunch of websites and I got two calls. I'm painting a baby and . . . another baby, I think. Or maybe a kitten. I don't know, something small and noisy.'

'Good. When are you going to have a baby?'

'When I go insane or the world runs out of contraception.'

'You don't have to keep the man, you know. Milk him dry and disappear into the horizon with a chubby little baby.'

Man. She was going to get babies AND career nagging, all in

one conversation? Could she convince Gran she'd put an ad up for a baby, as well? Probably not. 'I want the man and not the baby.'

Gran made a face. 'Why? Did your father teach you nothing about men?'

'Not all men are like him. There must be one out there who I'll enjoy talking to as well as – you know.'

Gran tutted. 'Not for you. You choose the arseholes. Anyway, I don't have time to give you dating advice. I have salsa dancing class in six hours.'

Ally let her forehead hit the table top. 'You really cheer me up, Gran.'

Gran prodded Ally's shoulder blade with a sharp finger until she sat up. 'Look, forget about men. Get a vibrator and a career, and then you can play with a farting bag of testosterone if you want. When's your next painting?'

'This evening.'

Gran looked pleased.

'It's not a real commission though,' Ally admitted. 'I mean, it's for a friend. Well, a friend of a friend. Sam's dad.'

'Sam? I like Sam. Is he still gay?'

'Yes, Gran.'

'Shame. You know, Alicia, this is a very good cup of tea.'

'Thanks. I'll add your testimonial to my CV.'

Gran glared. 'You won't be making any more tea in crappy little cafés with skimmed milk. You're going to use that gift and be a world-famous artist.'

'Can't I just be a stripper?'

'No. You've only got a few years before everything starts going south.'

Ally squeezed her elbows against her chest and examined her breasts. 'They look all right.'

Gran snorted. 'Wait till you're my age. You can wear bras made of cloths and dust the floors while you walk.'

Ally slumped on to the table, and Gran patted her consolingly.

* * *

Gran left when the fire alarm went off.

Ally scraped the charred remains of her lunch off the grill, opened the back door to let the smoke out, and shouted apologies at the customers coughing their way out.

Brendan, the new cook, appeared through a haze of smoke. He'd taken the morning off for an appointment, and had seemed worried about leaving Ally to cope alone all morning.

'You've been cooking,' he observed, before dragging a stool to the middle of the kitchen. He stood on it and waved a tea towel at the fire alarm until it stopped beeping.

'I fancied a chicken salad, but I got distracted . . . anyway, I only got two orders wrong today.'

Brendan looked pleased for her. 'Hey, you're doing great! Still got your order pad?'

Ally grimaced. He'd bought her a phone case just the right size to tuck her pad into, with a springy cord that attached to her apron. For three days she hadn't been able to put the pad down and lose it.

'No,' she confessed. 'I forgot to unclip it before I washed my uniform, and after three hours of picking clumps of wet paper off all my black clothes, I gave up.'

'Aw. I thought we'd cracked it. Maybe we can get you a little dry-wipe board that won't dissolve in the washing machine?'

'You're so sweet.' Ally kissed his cheek. 'I wish Sam would stop being shy and come and meet you.'

'Me too. I know I'd like any friend of yours.'

'I'll get him here before you go back to uni. Somehow.'

Brendan smiled, then cocked his head at the radio. 'Hey, is that "I Wanna Dance With Somebody"?'

He grabbed her waist and led her in a solemn waltz around the kitchen, making her laugh. She was in much better spirits by the time the next customer arrived. When she cleared a table she paused at the bin, shredded Gran's cheque into tiny squares, and buried them in a pile of soggy beans.

* * *

After her shift she jogged home, showered, and deliberated over what to wear. Usually she didn't care what other people thought of her outfits, as long as she felt good, but this was different. This was for Sam.

She settled on a knee-length dress, rose-pink, that flowed out below the waist. Not tight, not too revealing, but cool enough for the weather. Sam's mum would approve – she definitely wanted someone for her son a lot more demure than Ally had looked in her barely-there cocktail dress. And Mr Kinsell . . . well, he probably just wanted a daughter-in-law who didn't chat him up in the garden.

Best not to think about that: when she looked in the mirror, her cheeks matched the dress. Ally pressed her face against the cold glass and wished she could stop going red every time she thought of Mr Kinsell. God knows, if she got embarrassed every time she screwed up she wouldn't have to buy blusher.

* * *

An hour later, Ally sat on the train with her art supplies in a battered satchel and a mounted canvas stowed in the luggage rack. She tried to concentrate on her book but there was hardly any breeze drifting through the windows, and she was distracted by visions of Tyson Beckford rubbing ice cubes all over her skin. When Tom Hardy joined in with a sprinkler, she gave up and put the book back in her bag.

The train didn't have Wi-Fi but her phone was stuffed to its limits with songs. She took it out and scrolled through her library, stopping at her Blondie playlist.

Debbie and Harry. She smiled.

Just as the train passed from London into Essex it got stuck at a signal. She messaged Sam's dad to say she'd be late, squirming in her seat at the memory of asking for his number. He replied to let him know when she was close to her station. With any luck he'd get Debbie ready before she arrived, so she could rush through the painting and get the hell out of there. The less time she spent talking to Sam's dad, the less likely she was to say something incriminating.

Finally, she got off the sweltering train, went through the ticket barriers, and opened her satnav app.

'Ally?'

Her heart sank and leapt at the same time.

Mr Kinsell stood by the taxi rank. He was in green again, a deep sage polo that went beautifully with his brown eyes and dark lashes, and charcoal shorts, showing off calves just as stocky and muscular as his forearms.

'Hi, Mr Kinsell.'

'Hi, Mrs Kinsell.'

'What? Where?' She looked around guiltily for his wife, but she was nowhere to be seen.

Mr Kinsell smirked at her when she turned back. 'You.'

'Me? Oh. Oh! Yeah. Right. Mrs Kinsell. That's me. Well, when me and Sam finally set a date.'

Smirking, he gestured for her to follow him to the car park.

Ally groaned in her head and trudged after him.

CHAPTER FIVE

✑

Ally couldn't help liking Mr Kinsell's car, even if the last thing she wanted was to be in a confined space with him.

Well, part of her wanted to be in extremely close quarters with him, but only if he was naked and not talking about Sam.

The Winsor-blue Subaru had a blanket in the back covered in fur, a dog-eared map in the door, and Heart FM on the radio.

'Good journey?' he asked, as she got settled.

That was a safe topic of conversation. Ally unclenched. 'Not bad. It was about three thousand degrees and I'm dangerously dehydrated because I packed a bottle of olive oil instead of water. But the view was nice, and I got a free newspaper.'

'Olive oil? You didn't notice the colour?'

'Nope. I'm not very observant. I'm surprised I didn't drink it.'

He glanced at her. 'What's the mortality rate like in your hospital?'

Crap. Technical questions about nursing. What was a realistic mortality rate?

'I think about . . . um . . .' She glanced around the car for inspiration and caught him grinning. 'Hey! Are you teasing me?'

'Me?' His eyes widened. 'Never. I'm sure you've never put olive oil in a patient's drip. Are you going to put your seat belt on?'

'Oh, right. Sure.'

He pulled out of the car park. A lazy breeze drifted in from the driver's side window and carried his aftershave to Ally. Different today. Cedar wood, jasmine and something fruity . . . blackcurrant, maybe. It was deep, rich, enticing. She wanted to bury her nose in his neck and take breath after breath until she'd caught all the notes.

'Ally?'

She blinked, and raised her eyes from his neck to his face. The car was stationary, at traffic lights, and he looked concerned.

'You were in another world.'

She wished. A world where he was free and single and not related to any of her friends. 'Yeah. You'll have to get used to that, I'm afraid. I have the attention span of a goldfish with ADHD.'

He laughed. The lights changed, and he drove off with his hand on the gearstick. Just a few inches, and he'd be brushing her thigh every time he changed up or down—

Sam's *dad*. Not a hot gardener. Man, this heat was making her randy. Well, to be fair, cold made her randy too.

She was lost in thought again, singing along to Heart, when she heard him laughing.

'What? Oh. My singing?' Madonna was on the radio. 'Sorry. Just pretend I'm drunk. It explains a lot of my behaviour.'

'Olive oil's pretty strong stuff.'

'Yep. Sam hates my singing too. He puts Classic on so the worst I can do is hum.'

'Tell him not to be so grumpy. You can sing as much as you like.'

'So you can laugh at me? I'll sit in dignified silence.'

'No.' His mouth twitched. 'OK, I was laughing. But not at your singing. It's just . . . it's not "touched for the thirty-first time".'

'Huh. Actually, that makes sense. Because she probably wouldn't be a virgin after being touched up by thirty other guys.'

'Probably. Unless she really enjoys foreplay.'

Ally watched his hand as he moved the car into fourth gear, and thought it best not to answer.

He pulled into a small car park at the front of a block of flats. They looked modern, each window identically framed and identically spaced, the front doors all the same colour with the same style of numbering and knockers. It would've been soulless, except for the borders of shrubs and flowers around the perimeter. Through an archway, there were glimpses of a lush green lawn with a curving path, and more bursts of colour at the edges.

'You do the gardening, don't you?'

He smiled, and though he was obviously trying to look modest, she could see he was pleased. 'I negotiated a lower rent for looking after the grounds. It doesn't take much work. Do you need help carrying your equipment in?'

'You can take the canvas. Thanks.'

Maybe this wasn't such a bad idea after all. Painting was always fun, the dogs were cute, and perhaps Mr Kinsell's identical twin brother would pop round and beg Ally to let him undress her and—

'Ally?'

A hand waved in front of her face, and she blinked. She was standing on a doorstep like a vacant milk bottle.

'Are you an only child?' she blurted out before she'd gathered herself.

'No,' he said, as if it were a reasonable question. 'I have a sister and a brother. But we all live at different ends of the country.'

She managed to stop herself asking if the brother was single.

The best course of action was definitely to get the dog, do the painting, and leave. Preferably in complete silence from beginning to end.

He lived in a ground-floor flat at the back of the block, overlooking a patch of rose bushes. The door opened on to Harry, whose face had been pressed up against it. He headbutted Mr Kinsell in the stomach, then bounded up to Ally and put his snout under her dress.

'Harry! In.' Mr Kinsell planted a leg either side of Harry, and shuffled him inside. 'We're working on guest etiquette.'

'I can see it's going well. Where's Debbie?'

Mr Kinsell ferried Harry through a door and shut it. Then he gestured at an open door, and Ally walked into a very clean kitchen.

'Drinks first, before you mummify,' he said. 'What do you want?'

'Whatever you're having. Well, unless it's alcohol. I'm drunk enough sober.'

'No alcohol. I've just bought a juicer, so I'm having whatever I dropped into it this morning when I was half-asleep. All I can tell you is it's green.'

'Sounds perfect.'

'You're brave.' He took a jug of green liquid from the fridge, added ice from the freezer and blended it into a slushie.

Ally took a sip and tasted lime, green apple, and something else fresh and zingy. 'Tasty. Are you on a health kick?'

'Something like that. Since I stopped running with the dogs I thought I'd better make up for it, so I stopped eating red meat and bought a juicer. I miss running though. And feeling fit. You're not helping.'

'Me? What did I do?'

'Sam tells us about all your running and yoga-ing and spinning, whatever that is. And you're disgustingly young.'

'Am not. I'm twenty-eight.'

'Exactly. I'm forty-seven.'

Older than she thought, but not *old*. He was practically a kid when he had Sam. Not that it mattered – it wasn't the age gap that was the problem. 'My gran's eighty-seven and she comes to yoga with me sometimes.'

'Get out of my house.'

Ally smiled and sipped her drink. 'I thought you were about forty when I met you.'

He paused from rinsing out the jug and cocked his head at her. 'Say more things like that.'

'Fragile male egos.' Ally shook her head and sighed.

He leaned on the breakfast bar and squeezed fresh lime halves into their drinks, his muscular forearms flexing and contracting. They were tanned on the upsides, the hairs bleached blond, probably from gardening in the sun. The undersides were pale with blue veins – visible but not bulging, just how she liked. If she ran the tip of her tongue down them even the most gorilla-like men moaned. No, not this one. He'd be a sigher.

Sam's dad Sam's dad Sam's dad.

She blinked at him like a drunk lemur. 'Sorry, Mr Kinsell, what did you say?'

His eyes crinkled in amusement. 'Marcus, please. I asked if you and Sam have plans this week.'

Oh god, questions about Sam. Ally gave it two minutes before she'd blurt out something about going to clubs to pick up men together.

Vague was best.

'Uh, not yet,' she said. 'We don't really plan in advance, because I forget what we agreed. He just calls or texts and asks if I'm free, then gives me a time an hour before he actually wants me to arrive. It means occasionally I'm on time.'

'Remind me never to get ill. Not if I end up in your hospital, anyway.'

Right, he thought she was a nurse. Time to change the subject again.

'Keep juicing,' she advised. 'So, I'd better get started while it's still bright. Where's my client?'

'In the bedroom. Why don't you go and get acquainted, and I'll set up. I thought you could paint her in the garden, if that works for you. If I put her cushion out there, she'll stay still until dinnertime.'

The bedroom was where Marcus had shut in Harry. He didn't seem to mind being evicted from the hall – he was lying on his back, limbs in the air, filling a diagonal patch of sunshine on the grey carpet. He thumped his tail when he saw Ally, and she rubbed circles on his stomach that made his hind legs twitch.

In a corner of the room, Debbie lay in a huge bed very like the one in Marcus's room back at Mrs Kinsell's house. She opened one eye as Ally gave her a hand to smell, then went back to sleep.

Ally manoeuvred herself between the dogs so she could stroke them both at the same time, and looked around the room. It wasn't the beige fest that usually came with new-build flats. The walls matched the carpet, with shades of grey cleverly chosen to make the average-sized room look bigger, and a steel-blue wardrobe and bedspread. It would've been cold and masculine but for the paintings – a seascape with the most beautiful blues and greens, and an impressionist oil painting of a field of poppies. With the windows open and the scent of roses drifting in on summer air, the picture came alive and the bright reds and greens made the grey walls pop.

Maybe he really did like art. Maybe she really was here just to paint Debbie.

'Ready when you are, Ally,' came his voice through the window. Ally tried to rouse Debbie, but the dog growled and refused to budge. Harry followed her into the garden, where Marcus had placed a fur-covered cushion in front of the roses. He'd arranged a blanket and a non-furry cushion for Ally, with her painting equipment sitting neatly beside them, and a little folding table. On it sat her drink, covered against the hopefully-circling insects, and an electric fan plugged into an extension cord.

The garden was obviously communal, spanning a courtyard leading to dozens of apartments, but it was deserted apart from Marcus, bent over a stack of 70-litre compost bags. He picked one up like it weighed nothing and carried it away from Ally's makeshift studio. The sack hit the ground with a thud, and Ally squeezed her thigh muscles as she busied herself with getting ready. Canvas first, then paints. Harry shoved his nose in her satchel as she took out her paints and, when she pushed him away, he shoved it in her cleavage instead.

'Harry!' Marcus strode over and dragged the dog away, but as soon as he was free he loped back to Ally and lay down with his head in her lap.

'He likes you,' Marcus observed, as she ruffled his head.

'I got that impression. I tried to bring Debbie out, but she went all Cujo.'

He grinned. 'I'll get her. Are you comfortable?'

'Very.'

He returned a minute later with Debbie in his arms, and set her down gently on her cushion. 'She's always loved the sun. She used to play in it, now she just sleeps. I think it soothes her arthritis. She seems stiffer in the winter, but there's only so much the vet can do for old age.'

His voice was normal, but it was obvious he didn't think she'd be with him much longer. Ally replayed the way he carried the dog like a precious china doll, and grasped her crystal.

Marcus glanced at her, and straightened up. 'What's wrong? Hurt your hand?'

'What? Oh, no. It's a crystal.'

'A crystal?'

Ally appraised him and decided he wouldn't laugh. 'My mum does crystal healing. And gemstone healing and reiki and acupuncture and stuff I can't pronounce. She's a bit of a hippie, and as distracted as me, if you can believe that. Anyway, I'm usually quite upbeat——'

He snorted with laughter, and she paused.

'Sorry,' he said. 'I mean . . . quite upbeat. In the way that water is quite wet.'

'Yeah, like that.' She cheered up. 'But when people are sad or angry, I get these horrible black clouds come over me. Mum says I'm an empath. Gran says I have the emotional maturity of a toddler. Anyway, this crystal is supposed to protect me from other people's energies. And it works because it reminds me of my mum and I can't be sad when I think of Mum. Plus, I look great in pink.'

The rose quartz was pale and pretty and went with nearly everything.

Marcus watched the clouds as if he was chewing it over. 'So, you're upset?'

'Not any more.' Ally chose a paintbrush. 'My moods change faster than my underwea—forget I said that.'

His deep laugh was so sexy. 'Do you mind if I stay or will I distract you? More than usual, I mean.'

'You can stay, but it's literally watching paint dry. It'll bore the pants off you.'

Ooh. Pants off. Boxers or briefs? Bad train of thought.

'Sorry, what?'

His smile was getting wider each time. 'I said it won't bore me. I'm usually out here alone in the evenings. Tell me if you get too hot or cold.' He arranged the fan so it blew gently on Ally then sat beside her. His enticing scent was faint in the breeze but very much there, and she tried to imagine it was BO and cigarette smoke.

Ally's mood soared as she set up the canvas. The garden was beautiful, the only sounds were bird tweets and insects buzzing, and a warm breeze rippled her dress around her knees.

'Ally?'

'Mm?'

'Why don't you wear an engagement ring?'

Ha. He wasn't going to catch her out with that one. She pulled her nana's ring out of her cleavage and showed him, trying not to look too smug. 'When I wear rings I play with them, and end up taking them off and leaving them somewhere. So I wear it round my neck where I can't lose it. That and my crystal. I always wear them.'

'It's unusual.'

'It's an antique. My nana left it to my mum when she died, and Mum gave it to Sam to give to me. It was all very romantic.'

'Huh. That's odd. At the party, I heard him say he bought you one. It was a size too small and you refused to marry him until he'd fixed it.'

Crap. She must've zoned out when Sam was telling that story.

'Uh, yeah, that's right,' she said, thinking fast. 'I really wanted to wear Nana's but he felt cheap not buying one so I have another one. He went back and got the right size. It's at home. In a drawer.'

That was a pretty quick-thinking lie. She tried not to smile in pride.

'Huh,' Marcus said, settling back on his elbows. 'That's even odder. I've just remembered it was Gavin who bought one too small, and Kaitlyn who made him return it.'

Ally whipped her head around. He was smirking. Eyes glinting. The whole shebang.

Ooh, he was devious.

'How funny,' she said through gritted teeth. 'Must be because they're brothers. That they both did exactly the same thing.'

He nodded. 'Funny indeed.'

Ally squeezed the tube of raw umber until her thumbs went white and imagined it was one of his tricky, gorgeous eyes.

She chose terre verte for the first wash, and wet a cloth with turpenoid to thin it down.

'What's that?' he asked.

She stared stonily at Debbie. 'Paint.'

'Not that.'

'Paintbrush.'

'Not that either.'

'I paint best in silence.'

He paused, nodded, then got up and walked away.

Ally regretted it immediately. She hated sitting in silence and she hated upsetting people even more. With a sigh, she started painting.

She jumped when something appeared in front of her face. A pink rose. Behind it, Marcus looked contrite.

'Sorry,' he said. 'Forgive me.'

Ally took the rose and slid it into her hair, trying not to look too happy that she had company again. Maybe he felt bad enough to stop prodding her about Sam. 'Forgive you for what?'

'Having a bad memory.' He widened his eyes.

Hmph. Or not. 'You're sneaky.'

Grinning, he sat down beside her and gestured at the turpenoid. 'Will you tell me what that is now?'

He seemed genuinely interested, and before long Ally was narrating everything she did. Marcus watched her face with those warm brown eyes and distracted Harry from pushing his nose in her cleavage. At one point, the dog stuffed his whole muzzle in, pushing the neckline of her dress down and exposing the top of her pink bra.

'You're a bloody sex pest,' Marcus scolded, keeping one hand on his collar. Harry looked up at him with puppy eyes. 'Well, you are. We're going to have a chat later.'

Ally wondered if Marcus had seen her bra. Probably not. He didn't seem to realise she wasn't a floating head.

'You're very knowledgeable,' he said, when Harry had calmed down.

'Ha. It's the first time anyone's ever called me that.'

'Nonsense. You're clearly made to do this. Why not do it full time?'

'You sound like my gran.'

'She has a deep voice.'

Ally burst into laughter. 'I mean she keeps poking me to start a painting business again. I had one for a few months, but it was a disaster. I was a disaster. Forgetting appointments, always late, not listening properly to what clients wanted. I need someone else to be in charge.'

'You seem very capable to me, and you sound far more enthusiastic talking about painting than nursing.'

'Really? How odd.'

Ally tried not to glow at his misplaced faith in her capabilities. He was just making up for being a devious arse and tricking her over the ring.

'What do you do?' she asked, before he got back on to the subject of nursing.

'Construction. Houses, mostly.'

Man, she always fell for the tradesmen. It was the muscly arms that did it. And the broad chests.

'You don't sound enthusiastic, either,' she said.

He shrugged. 'I wanted to be a graphic designer, like Sam is now. But Gavin came along while I was at university and an unqualified, inexperienced graphic designer wasn't going to make enough money to pay for a house. So I started labouring and worked my way up.'

'Does Sam know you wanted to do it?' she asked curiously. It seemed too much of a coincidence for Sam to have the same ambition as his father, but he'd never mentioned this as a reason for pursuing graphic design.

'I think so. We talked about it when he was choosing what to study. But I don't think he got into it because of me. He just inherited my eye for design. Anyway,' he said, standing up. 'For the next hour I'm a chef. You are staying for dinner, aren't you?'

Ally glanced at the fading light, startled to realise how late in the evening it was. He was easy to talk to. 'I'd love to. Let me pack up and I'll come and help.'

'No, no. You're a guest. I'll call you in when it's ready.'

Ally turned her mouth down. 'I like cooking. Let me help. I'll be sous chef.'

'Does that mean I'm head chef?'

'I guess.'

'And you'll call me Chef?'

'Sure. Chef.'

'Deal.' Marcus picked Debbie up in his arms and kissed her head before carrying her into the house. She licked his firm forearm and slapped her tail against his thick chest.

Man. Why did he have to be Sam's dad?

CHAPTER SIX

Ally left the painting drying in the warm evening air and joined Marcus in the kitchen. 'What are we having?'

'Grilled squid and salad.' He stopped slicing the squid and frowned. 'That's boring. I should've thought of something more interesting. I can make some chips to go with it?'

'Don't make them specially for me. I'll eat anything. Well, except liver. And fried tarantula.'

'Fried tarantula?'

She shuddered. 'Mum and I were on holiday and took the wrong boat, ended up on this island . . . I don't like to talk about it. Anyway, I'm easy to please.'

'We'll have chips,' he said. 'And maybe I can do something more exciting with our squid.'

'Seriously, don't worry about me. If you like it plain, we'll have it plain.'

'I don't. I lived on spicy food when I was at uni, but my ex-wife liked it plain, and I got used to cooking like that.' He looked down at the squid. 'Maybe . . . some sort of sauce? A . . . squid-type sauce . . . Hm. I'm out of practice.'

'I know one squid recipe. Salt and chilli calamari. Like from a Chinese takeaway.'

'I haven't had that in years. Not since I worked near China-town. What ingredients do we need?'

'Let me think . . . Cornflour, chilli, garlic, ginger, peppercorns.'

He opened a cupboard and pushed a bag of sugar out of the way. 'Uh. How much of that can be substituted with vanilla essence and balsamic vinegar?'

'You know what? I'm not that hungry.'

'Where's your spirit of adventure? All right, I'll go to the shop. There's a mini-mart down the road with a wall of spices. Enough chilli in there to fuel a small country.'

'How far is the shop?'

'Not sure. A mile or so?'

'I'll go. I need a run.' Her flat shoes weren't designed for run-ning but, like Gran said, her knees would be shot when she got old so she might as well use them now. Not that she thought Gran had been referring to running.

Marcus raised his eyebrow. 'You want to go for a run in this heat?'

'Well I overslept, so I need to get my hour in today somehow.'

'Ugh. Stop showing off and get out of my house.' He held her gaze as he pulled the guts out of a squid, and she gave him her sweetest smile.

Marcus glanced at Harry, who was pressed against Ally with his nose in the crook of her knee. 'Will you see if you can coax Harry out? He might leave Debbie for you. Just make sure your dress is on firmly. Turn left at the end of the road, then it's straight. You can't miss it.'

'I think you underestimate my powers of getting lost. If I'm not back in an hour . . .'

'Don't worry, your chips won't go to waste. I'll eat them.'

'Charming.' Ally put Harry's lead on and ran out of the door without waiting for him to notice Debbie wasn't coming. He loped along like a bear, gazed at her in adoration, and narrowly missed head-butting several lamp-posts. She managed not to get lost and was back with the ingredients in thirty minutes.

At the breakfast bar she chopped chilli while Harry sat pressed against her leg. When she turned to Marcus, he was wearing the exact same expression . . . whilst staring at the spices.

She was starting to get a complex about this. A gnarled ginger root was more attractive than her?

No, she was being ridiculous. Of course he was more enticed by the idea of playing with spices than playing with Ally, after years of plain food. Cooking it must be as dull as eating it.

She added 'likes spicy food' to her mental list of the ideal man, and stepped back from the chopping board.

'You know,' she said, 'I'll probably rub chilli in my eye. Will you take care of the calamari? I can do the salad.'

Marcus handled the spices like a child in a toy shop. Ally was content to be his sous chef and watch the grin on his face, but Harry was a health and safety hazard. He was determined never to be more than an inch away from Ally, even where there really wasn't room for two humans and a bear.

'He's in love,' Marcus commented.

'Me too. He's this close to getting my dress off voluntarily.'

'Could you leave the room first?'

'Spoilsport.'

Harry licked her knee.

'Well, somebody's got to stick up for your poor fiancé here,' said Marcus, shaking cornflour into a bowl. 'Speaking of Sam . . . I messaged him about the surgery and he didn't reply.'

Ally concentrated on chopping potatoes. 'Should've called him then, shouldn't you?'

'I didn't want to put him on the spot.'

Hmph.

'Come on,' he said. 'Just tell me if you think he wants the surgery. If he's got no interest in it, I'll leave it. I don't want to embarrass him.'

What bloody surgery? Obviously something optional, but what kind of chest surgery could be optional? She should've asked Sam about it. But he must have his reasons for keeping it quiet, and she wasn't going to force him to talk.

An idea hit her. 'Exactly!' She snapped her fingers, then grabbed a potato to stop herself doing it again. 'It embarrasses him, so I don't mention it. I don't know how he feels about it, but I love him just the way he is. So there.'

'Hm. All right.'

Ally congratulated herself on her lie.

'Go jogging together, do you?' said Marcus, as if it was a throwaway comment.

Ally sensed a trap, and thought quickly. Sam avoided exercise like the plague. He'd gone to the gym with her a few times and had been bright red, panting, and pouring with sweat within minutes. He claimed he was lazy and unfit. Ally thought it was because he'd turned up in a thick polo shirt. Rachel thought he was intimidated by the men with six-packs. But it must be because he had medical problems. Asthma? Was there surgery for asthma? Maybe experimental surgery that didn't always work?

'No,' she said, meeting Marcus's eyes to show him his trick hadn't worked. 'Jogging isn't a good idea with his chest problems, is it?'

'I see.' Marcus nodded and turned to the sink.

Ha. She'd outwitted him.

Pausing at the sink, he looked back at her. 'That's odd. He shouldn't have any chest problems.' He smiled. 'Is a wok OK for the calamari?'

* * *

Marcus didn't mention Sam's chest again, and Ally busied herself with cooking. He put the radio on Heart FM for her, and she danced around the kitchen until everything was done.

'Don't you ever get tired?' Marcus asked, leaning on the breakfast bar.

'Nope. Sam calls me Rampant Rabbit.'

'Does he now?'

'Just because I don't get tired. I mean, not when—Can we change the subject? Embarrass you for a change?'

'You can try, but I've never been compared to a sex toy.'

'It's not too late.'

He smiled. 'Will you bring the wine?'

She picked up the glasses and bottle and followed him, carrying their plates, into the living room. The colour scheme here was muted like the bedroom, but the walls were dominated by a framed oil painting of a Mediterranean harbour. A lone figure in a pink dress sat on a balcony, looking over the golden water as the sun set.

'That was in your room, in your old house,' Ally said.

'How did you know?'

'There was a dark square on the wall where it'd been hanging.'

'You're good. What's your expert opinion?'

'I'm not an expert.'

'I say you are, and it's my house, so I'm right.'

'Shouldn't you defer to guests?'

'Not when they're wrong.' He gestured to the table, and Ally sat and looked at the painting.

'I like it. The colours are beautiful, and she seems happy. Alone, but not lonely.'

'Agreed. That's why I bought it. Balsamic?'

'Uh, no.'

'Just wanted to offer something.' He poured her a glass of Riesling, and held up his own glass. 'Well, cheers to our new business relationship.'

'Cheers.' Ally tipped her glass against his, and their knuckles brushed.

* * *

Ally didn't realise how late it was until she had to squint to read the inscription on a book Marcus handed her. A copy of *Neither Here Nor There*, signed by Bill Bryson himself. She glanced at the window, and saw the sky turning burnt orange.

'It's on my bucket list to follow his route through Australia in *Down Under*.'

'I have no doubt you'll tick off everything from your bucket list, and some. Do you need to get home before Sam thinks I've abducted you?'

'Probably. Thanks for dinner, it was lovely. And you actually have a spice in your cupboard to keep the sugar company.'

'The sugar is delighted. Can I drive you home?'

'Oh, no, I like getting the train. Thanks though.'

'But it'll be pitch black by the time you get to Acton.'

'It's OK. I'm a vampire.'

'Nobody as lively as you could be dead. Or even undead. OK, but I'm driving you to the station. There are some dodgy people round here at night. Got all your things from the garden?' He took his car keys from a hook.

'You don't have to take me. I could do with a run.'

'I can't let you leave alone in the dark. What if something happened to you? Sam would be furious, and I'm pretty sure he could take me in a fight. I mean, I'm pretty sure *you* could, but I'd still rather drive you. Or maybe the dogs and I can walk with you.'

Ally needed to let off steam. Sitting still for long periods of time just wasn't her. 'I have a better idea. Let's race. You carry Debbie.'

'A race?'

'Yes.'

A slow smile spread across his face. 'I'm old. I can't race.'

'You're not old, and yes you can.'

'I can't run carrying a dog. Everyone will think I'm mad.'

She shrugged. 'Why do you care?'

'Because . . . oh, all right.'

Ally collected her supplies, attached Harry's lead to his collar, and stepped into the dark evening.

'Ready?' she asked Marcus, standing next to her with Debbie in his arms.

'No. This is a bad idea.'

'Set.'

'No. Ally, I'm an old man, I—'

'Go!'

'Ally!'

He groaned, but she heard him following.

Ally took it easy, but was still surprised by how soon he caught up with her. Long legs. He had to be about six foot, and in her flat shoes she was five seven.

When she finally outstripped him, it was close to her maximum comfort speed.

'You're sneaky. You're not out of shape.' She glanced back at him and came to a halt. He was sweaty and out of breath, making her simultaneously guilty and triumphant.

'Need to . . . start . . . smaller,' he panted, as he leaned on a lamp-post. Debbie snoozed in his arms. 'Going . . . to die.'

'Why didn't you stop?!'

'Wanted . . . to beat you.'

'Ugh. Male egos.' She swatted his arm with the back of her hand, pressing harder than was necessary so she could feel the outline of his muscle.

'Dying,' he insisted.

'If you'd been running every day since October, you'd be doing marathons by now. Come on, the station is just around the corner.'

'No it isn't.'

'Well, pretend it is. Ready?'

'No.'

'Set.'

'Ally.'

'Go!'

'Oh god.'

She took off again at a slower pace, then began sprinting when the station was in sight. When he caught up she beamed. 'I win.'

Marcus leaned on the wall and panted. 'Having . . . heart attack.'

'Drama queen.' She punched his shoulder.

'Debbie . . . slowed me . . . down.'

'Sore loser. We'll have a rematch without the dogs.'

He groaned. 'You'll kill me.'

'Not today. Thank you for dinner, and I had a great time doing the painting. I'll let you know when it's ready.'

He nodded slowly, catching his breath. 'Right. You don't need to come back again.'

'Nope. No more bullying you to run, don't worry. Look, I've got to go. My train leaves in a few minutes.'

Without thinking, she stood on tiptoe and kissed his cheek. It unsettled her because it was an unconscious decision, but on reflection it was OK. A perfectly normal thing for a daughter-in-law to do. Especially since they wouldn't see each other again.

She hurried for the platform.

'Ally?'

She turned around, heart fluttering, afraid she'd been too obvious and he was going to tell her not to kiss her fiancé's dad.

'Yes?' she said.

'You want to know something strange?'

'Sure. Especially if it's about UFOs or the Loch Ness Monster.'

He gazed at her for a few seconds. 'I always thought Sam was gay.'

The flutters turned into thumps. He knew. Of course he knew. This whole thing with the painting was a ruse to get her alone and trick her. All his attentiveness had been a way to relax her, lull her into a false sense of security, before catching her out with an innocent question.

Well, she wasn't going to confirm his suspicions. This was between him and Sam.

'Did you?' Her voice shook.

'Yes.'

'But I'm his fiancée. And I'm a woman.'

She refused to blink first this time, even when Harry drooled on her foot.

'Yes,' he said finally. 'You are.'

They stared at each other.

Ally heard a train speeding into the station, registered it a few seconds later, and ran for the platform.

CHAPTER SEVEN

*T*he following day, Ally and Rachel lay on a patch of grass in the park. Ally shielded her phone's screen from the sun and scrolled through OkCupid.

'Any luck?' Rachel asked, lying on her front and reading a book.

Ally put her phone down. 'Nope. If tonight doesn't go well, I'm screwed.'

'What's tonight?'

'Sam's finally agreed to meet Brendan, but he's nervous so I agreed to a double date. This guy that chatted me up at the bar while I poured him the wrong beer. He seemed a bit of a dick but hey, it's for Sam.'

'You like dicks. Uh . . .' Rachel frowned and looked up from her book. 'Let me rephrase. You like arrogant, selfish men.'

'Do not. They just like me. They're the only ones who like me.'

It wasn't her fault her libido was stronger than her brain and always won the argument.

At least she had good sex.

'Mm, maybe,' said Rachel. 'The nice quiet ones are too terrified to approach you. But one will stumble into your life when you least expect it. Mine did.'

'Show off,' Ally grumbled. 'Are you really still interested in him after all this time?'

'Yes. I want him more every day.'

Ally never ran out of things to talk about with Sam or Rachel or her mum or sisters, but after a few dates with a guy she was always scrabbling for topics of conversation. It was a mystery.

'Why do you never use his name?' Rachel asked.

It took Ally a moment to remember who they were referring to – Rachel's fiancé. She snorted in disgust. Use his *name* after he'd broken her best friend's heart. Rachel might have forgiven him, but Ally hadn't.

She thought of Marcus and felt her cheeks grow hot. That was different. Maybe she'd *thought* about things that would break Sam's heart, but she had no intention of *doing* them.

'It's been five years, Ally,' said Rachel. 'What does he have to do for you to forgive him?'

Ally dragged herself away from thoughts of Marcus. 'At least take a bullet for you. Or maybe fight off some crazed murderers or something.'

Rachel gently removed an ant from her arm and placed it on the grass. 'Mm. Anyway. Maybe you should reconsider the thirty thousand guys you rejected because of their profile pictures?'

'Nope. I'm shallow and I've accepted it.' It was only dicks that were attracted to her, so why not at least demand attractive dicks? She had to get *something* out of dating.

'You don't think maybe that's your problem?' Rachel asked.

'Nope.'

'That maybe you'll find someone you'll stay interested in if you judge them on their personality rather than abs?'

'Nope.'

Rachel nodded. 'I see.'

'Look, I've given up on looking for a relationship so I might as well have hot sex buddies, right? Except bloody Jason's got a bloody girlfriend.' Ally ripped a patch of grass out of the ground and threw it at a tree. It was a gnarled old tree that looked like a courtier in the middle of a bow, but Ally was too despondent to take a picture for painting later. 'Git. Sex buddies shouldn't be allowed to have girlfriends when I want sex.'

'So you want a committed relationship without any commitment?'

'Exactly! I mean, no. What I really want is a man who likes my defective mind as much as my body. Too much to ask?' Another patch of grass hit the tree.

She did want commitment. Being in love looked incredible. It'd changed Rachel almost beyond recognition, and Sam was always less anxious and more confident when he had somebody. But Sam and Rachel had attention spans wider than a tightrope. Ally had never found a man she enjoyed spending time with clothed and naked in equal measure.

'You won't find him at a bar or club or dating site,' Rachel said. 'Only the ones with supreme confidence are brave enough to talk to you. You need to meet someone in a non-dating context, get to know them, and see if it grows into something more.'

Ally considered it with scepticism. She had guy friends – either ex-friends-with-benefits like Jason, or men she wasn't attracted to. If she met someone and was attracted to him, why wait? 'That sounds long. Can't I just mail order one?'

Rachel sat up and inched into the shade. They'd been sitting in the sun for nearly her whole lunch hour. 'I don't like it when you're grumpy. It feels all wrong when you're not relentlessly cheerful.'

Ally beamed.

'That's better. Need a hug?'

'I need to get laid. But I'll take what I can get.' Ally put her head in Rachel's lap and closed her eyes. She listened to children playing football and the raucous call of a wood pigeon as Rachel read her book. When her phone rang, she answered without looking.

'Ally Rivers.'

'Hi. It's Marcus.'

She shot up, her heart racing. Mostly from fear, but a little bit from his melty voice. She was not going to talk about Sam. She had to remember not to say anything about Sam. Marcus was just a client who she'd done a painting for.

'The painting's not done,' she blurted out.

'I'm fine, thanks, and you?'

She rubbed her forehead, ignoring Rachel's mystified look. 'Fine. You?'

'No, we've done that one,' Marcus said. 'We've established we're both fine.'

'Oh. What do I say next?'

'You say "Yes, I'd love to come to Essex again."'

She stifled a groan and sank back into Rachel's lap. Hadn't he got the message from the four calls she'd ignored, and the email that she'd deleted unread? Sam's secrets were his to tell.

'I'm busy,' she said down the phone.

'I haven't said when I want to talk to you.'

'But I know I'll be busy at exactly that time.'

'You're sneaky.'

She couldn't help but laugh, even with her stomach full of dread. 'I'm not talking to you about Sam. You have questions, you ask him.'

'It's not about that.'

Ally unclenched. 'Oh. Phew. What is it about?'

'Harry.'

'What about him?'

'He's pining. You're his first love, and you just left him without a word. He carries the blanket you sat on everywhere. He looks miserable when he has to drop it to eat or breathe. He's lost two hundred grams. Wasting away.'

Ally snorted. 'Two hundred grams? What did he do, fart? Look, stick a dress on a blonde mannequin and let him hump it to his heart's desire.'

Rachel's mouth fell open.

'He's not that kind of dog,' said Marcus. 'He wants you for your mind, not your body.'

She snorted harder. 'That makes a change. Put him on and I'll talk to him.'

'I'm at work. Don't know if he's got his phone on him. Come and see him one evening.'

'I'm not dopey, you know. Well, I am, but not *that* dopey. You're going to get me alone and then demand to know things about Sam. Or, more likely, try and trick me into telling you things that are his business. I'm a loyal fiancée. Go away.'

'I'm hurt and offended at your unfounded accusations. So when are you coming?'

'Goodbye, Marcus.' She hung up.

'Marcus?' said Rachel.

Ally picked two daisies out of the grass and began making a chain. 'Sam's dad. I think he knows we're not really engaged.'

'That was Sam's *dad*? Why were you talking about humping?'

'Oh, long story.' Avoiding Rachel's eyes, she examined a daisy stem. 'I—' She sighed as her phone rang and answered, deadpan, 'Hello, Marcus.'

'Hi. Harry says he's going to have a medical emergency on Saturday and will need a nurse.'

She sighed again. He was persistent, she had to give him that. Perhaps if she met him one last time and showed him she wasn't going to spill Sam's secret, he'd lose interest in her. Then she could let the crush run its course and return to a pleasant, guilt-free existence.

Was this her mind's idea, or was her libido tricking them?

'Ally? I'm like a rash. I don't go away if you ignore me, I just get more annoying.'

A rash. She tried not to picture him spreading all over her body.

Yeah, it was definitely her body that wanted to see him.

'I'm busy for the next three years,' she said. 'Goodbye, Marcus.'

She hung up and put the phone on silent. Let him persist all he wanted.

Rachel cocked an eyebrow at her. 'Why are you flirting with Sam's dad?'

'I was not!' Was she that obvious?

'Were too. Does he look like Sam?'

'Not really.' If he did, she might have realised who he was in the garden. 'His hair's darker and thicker than Sam's. His eyes are darker too, like a good Scotch. They do have the same build, broad and solid and tall. But he's a bit Clooney and a bit that guy from *The Invaders*. You know, the hot one who—Don't look at me like that.'

'Well tone down the not-flirting a little, Ally.'

'Don't be disgusting,' Ally scolded. 'He's Sam's dad.'

Rachel gave her a knowing look.

* * *

On her date that evening, Ally couldn't decide what to pick from the restaurant menu. She liked all cuisines – though French wasn't her favourite; too much red meat and cheese – but preferred the clean, crisp flavours of the Mediterranean or the vibrant spices of India and Malaysia. But she'd found several things that made her mouth water.

The restaurant was nice, too; pricey, but she liked coming here when she could afford it. She liked the deep red walls, the dark wood chairs, crisp white tablecloths and oil paintings on the walls.

Her date was good-looking too. Oliver had dark hair, light blue eyes, a trace of stubble. He was a student, not her usual tradesman or labourer, but he made up for his lack of a manual job at the gym.

'I hope they know how to cook a steak properly,' he said, glancing over the menu. 'Last place I went to presented me with a lump of shoe leather and seemed surprised that I wouldn't pay for it.'

She had a feeling if he didn't fancy her, he would've demanded a refund when she'd messed up his order at the bar. 'It's lovely here. The lemon tart's like a warm hug.'

'Oh yeah? I'm not a big fan of lemon desserts. But warm hugs . . .' His eyes roved down her body. She couldn't blame him for liking her strappy pink dress that left none of her curves to the imagination, but she wished he'd at least pretend to be interested in her conversation.

She was so contrary. With Marcus, she'd been frustrated that he hadn't once looked anywhere but at her face. Now she was frustrated because Oliver was doing the opposite.

Maybe Rachel was right and Ally had it the wrong way around. The men she dated rarely needed encouragement to admire her body, but it was rare to find one she enjoyed speaking to. Someone who liked *her* could learn to love her body, but could anyone learn to love her fickle, distracted mind as much as her cleavage?

Unbidden, she imagined herself trying to seduce Marcus. Trying to make him realise she had something below the neck. Stripping for him, and watching a spark of attraction in those deep brown eyes.

The waiter appeared and asked if they'd chosen.

Ally snapped her mouth shut and hoped she hadn't been drooling. 'Oh, er.' She jabbed her finger at the menu. 'Moules marinière, please.'

'Oh, wow,' said Oliver. 'You can say the French words. I thought you were a waitress?'

Ally and the waiter both stared at him. 'Um, yes, I am. But I studied French at school for five years like everyone else.'

'You make French even sexier.' Oliver turned to the waiter. 'Is your chef good?'

The waiter blinked. '*Oui*, sir.'

'I mean, actually good? Does he know how to do a steak?'

'Er . . . *oui*. She is classically trained.'

'Oh, a woman chef? Good. They can usually take instructions.' He smiled at Ally. 'Chefs can be so arrogant. OK, waiter, I'll have steak. Rare please, and I do mean rare. If she overcooks it, start again. Don't try to fob me off.'

The waiter turned to Sam and Brendan. They were deep in conversation, staring into each other's eyes. She had to wave a napkin in Sam's face before he realised there was someone else in the room. She was happy they'd hit it off, but wished Oliver seemed more promising.

'You'd think they could hire real French waiters,' Oliver muttered to her.

'He wasn't real? Have I been hallucinating waiters again?'

'I mean he'd blatantly learned a couple of French words so they could claim they had French staff and put the prices up twenty per cent. He was probably born in Chiswick.'

'I doubt it. That seems like an awful lot of effort.'

Oliver laughed. 'You're so sweet. You don't know how ruthless these businessmen can be. For instance, I bet I know why the bar hired you.'

'Because I can make drinks and hand them to people?'

She thought of the several orders she'd got wrong that afternoon, and the several others she'd tried to give to the wrong customer.

He waved a hand. 'Anyone can do that.'

Charming. 'I wish you'd stop flattering me. It's embarrassing.'

'I am flattering you. They hired you because you're so hot,

and men will come in just to look at you. We all go to a place near campus because of the sexy barmaid, and she's not as sexy as you.'

It was half-true. Ally was pretty sure Barbara hadn't hired her for that reason, but it was probably why she hadn't been fired for all her mistakes. 'It's nice to know my skills are so valued.'

Oliver stroked her hand. She wrapped it tighter around her wine glass. 'I don't mean it like that. The world needs waitresses just as much as doctors, right? We can't all be academics.'

'Yes. Without us thick people, you doctors would have to pour your own beers. Heaven forbid.' Ally didn't know why she was getting so irritated. She was never going to be *Mastermind* champion and she didn't care. She'd rather be admired for her personality than her IQ. Why did she care that Oliver had pegged her as a dumb blonde?

Oliver walked his fingers up her forearm. 'Aw, come on. Don't take it the wrong way. I think you're really sweet.'

His arrogance wasn't turning her on like it usually did. She glared at him and poured herself more wine.

Surprise, surprise, Oliver didn't like the food. While he complained, talked about himself, and shot poorly disguised glances at her cleavage, Ally amused herself by giving her mussels names and backstories and then feeling too guilty to eat them. She thought of Marcus, asking her endless questions and listening intently to the answers. Older men could teach the younger generation something. Or perhaps it could only be learned through age.

'Uh, sorry?' she said, looking up from her napkin and the sketch of Molly Mussel she'd etched on it.

Oliver frowned. 'Do you have hearing difficulties?'

'Yep. I have hyper-waxability. I get a candle or two every week.'

He sat back. 'Gosh, I've never heard of that. Is there a treatment for it?'

'It was a joke.'

'Oh.' He smiled. 'Very good. Very clever.'

'Mm.' Ally sipped her wine.

'Have you ever tried modelling? I'm sure you could do it, and it must pay more than waitressing.'

'Standing around posing for photos is boring. I'd rather be taking them.'

'You like photography?'

A spark of hope for something in common. 'Yes, you?'

'Father gave me a Nikon for my birthday. Maybe you could come over and show me how to use it?'

The optimist in Ally tried to fight the assumption but she knew how it would go if she went to his place. Oliver would stare at her body, only pretending to listen to her. She'd sleep with him just to kill her boredom. If the sex was bad she'd turn him down when he asked to see her again, he'd get angry, and she'd watch *Bridget Jones's Diary* while eating ice cream. If it was good, she'd keep seeing him until she got too fed up of never having a proper conversation. It was becoming a routine, and she hated routine.

'Maybe,' she said.

He smiled. 'Are you having dessert?'

'No. I don't think so.' She hoped Sam and Brendan wouldn't either, so they could leave.

'Watching your figure?'

'I think you've watched it enough for both of us.' Ally was surprised at herself. She hardly ever snapped and couldn't blame him for staring at her in that dress. But she also couldn't bring herself to apologise.

He went red, and they sat in silence until it was time to leave.

'Well, I won't be going back there again,' said Oliver, as they stood up. He darted around the table to hold Ally's jacket while she slipped into it. As he smoothed it down her body, he smiled in what he apparently thought was an enticing way. It was about as sexy as watching a nurse approach for a smear test.

Sam and Brendan, clearly not ready to say goodnight, made plans to go on to a club. Ally debated going home, but she'd been strangely unsettled and bored in the evenings. She wished she had more portrait sittings to keep her occupied. Marcus's painting was taking for ever to dry.

In the club, she checked her bag and jacket and went straight to the dance floor. Oliver appeared in front of her and she let him take her hips. Perhaps he'd be sexier when he wasn't talking. Like her.

The thought upset her. Why couldn't she find someone who liked her infuriating quirks?

Definitely not Oliver. When he pressed his erection against her back, she snapped. Shaking him off, she slipped through the crowd to an Oliver-free part of the dance floor. She was happy dancing on her own, but when she opened her eyes someone was a few feet away, watching her. Not Oliver. She was about to brush him off when he smiled, and his brown eyes creased at the corners. His skin was sun-browned, too, and he had large hands.

'Hi,' he mouthed, and pointed to himself. 'Tim.'

'Ally.' The music snatched her voice away.

'Dance?'

She moved closer to him, and let the music sway her body. He smelled of good-quality cologne, and in the packed club it was mingled with just a hint of clean, musky sweat.

By the second song she was an inch from him, her nose brushing his jaw as she breathed in with her eyes closed. On her exhale she felt his sharp intake of breath, and fingers on her waist. When she didn't move away, he pressed his fingertips in and laid his palms on her hips.

His hands were as strong as she'd suspected, and her breath quickened as she thought of those fingers curling around tough weed stems and tugging them out of the dry soil with one flick of his wrist.

The song changed to a dance track with a deep, pulsing beat. A warm shiver swept up Ally's spine, and he responded by moving his hands down so his fingertips spread over her buttocks. The nerves sparked, and an ache throbbed between her legs that needed those fingers to work it out.

She closed the gap between them, laying her hands on the shirt over his flat stomach. Firm, muscled. His body heat mixed with the close atmosphere, and Ally took deep, long breaths. When her head started to feel light she turned around. His hands slid to the front of her hips, little fingers brushing the tops of her thighs, and her buttocks rested on a hard lump at his groin.

She closed her eyes as he pressed his lips on her neck, and it was easy to pretend they were the only two people in the room. Easy to imagine those large, strong hands sliding down her thighs and hitching up her dress. Dexterous fingers stroking the soft, sensitive skin on the insides of her legs, higher and higher until they pushed aside the flimsy material of her thong.

Warm breath hit the sweat on her neck. 'Want to get out of here?' he said into her ear, close enough that he didn't have to shout.

A voice somewhere reminded her he was off-limits, but it was drowned out by the buzzing in her nerves.

'Yes,' she meant to say, but as she drew back to look at him, it died on her lips.

The face was a shock. Deep brown eyes, sure, but everything else was wrong. The heat in her limbs turned to cold, and her treacherous eyes sought out Sam. He was nowhere to be seen.

'Fuck, I've got to go. Sorry.'

She pushed away from the guy, whatever his name was, and elbowed her way through the couples in heat on the dance floor.

Sam was in a dark corner, making out with Brendan. She tapped him on the shoulder and mouthed that she was going, busying herself with straightening her dress so she didn't have to look him in the eye. Judging by his hazy look, he wouldn't have noticed if she'd grown another head. Brendan smiled at her before gluing himself back to Sam's face, and she hoped she'd be seeing him around in the future. Sam deserved a break.

And he deserved better friends.

She waited impatiently at the cloakroom for her bag and coat, then hurried outside and sucked in cool air. That poor guy. Tom? Tim? She was no better than Oliver, using him as a humping surface. As some kind of prop in her screwed up fantasy.

She took out her phone and saw the envelope icon flashing. An email. From Marcus Kinsell.

Linseed oil is commonly used to thin oil paints. Yes/No?

She came to a halt in the street. What kind of question was that? She read it again with narrowed eyes, trying to work out the trick, but couldn't see it. Maybe he was at a pub quiz or something. The time stamp said it had been sent two hours ago, but she shrugged and replied: *Yes, told you that on Tues.*

Hmph. Not only had he failed to notice her body but he hadn't even been listening to her. There really was no hope of finding a man who did both.

She lost signal once she descended into the Tube station, and when she emerged in Acton there was a reply from Marcus.

Great! See you then.

She halted again, dumbfounded. See her when? What?

Scrolling down the email trail, she saw he'd changed his original question to: *You're getting the 11:52 train on Saturday to come and see Harry, aren't you?*

'Oh, for god's sake,' she muttered, shook her head at his deviousness, and called him.

'I did not agree to that,' she said, when he answered. 'You're sneaky.'

'I have it in writing.' His voice was gruffer than usual. Ally looked at the phone's time display and grimaced. Just past midnight.

'Did I wake you up?' she asked. The email had distracted her, but thinking of him in bed reminded her of Tim/Tom, and she grimaced.

'Yes, thank god,' he said. 'I was dreaming about health and safety inspections. Look, it's in writing. You're contractually obliged to be here on the 11:52 on Saturday.'

Ally sat on a bench outside the station. 'I watch *Judge Rinder*. That so wouldn't stand up in a court of law.'

'Judge Rinder runs a magistrate's court.'

'A what? What's the difference?'

'Oh dear.' Marcus sighed. 'You'll be taken to the cleaners by a proper judge. Don't make me do that to you.'

'I—'

'Hey,' he interrupted. 'You said you wanted to go to the Caribbean. Did you know they call Essex the Barbados of England?'

'Who does?'

'I don't know.' He yawned. 'People who've never been to Barbados? Look, I'll make it worth your time. I'll cook something Caribbean for lunch and we'll listen to reggae.'

'Do you even know how to cook Caribbean food?'

'No.'

'Do you own a reggae album?'

'No.'

Ally rolled her eyes. 'Then no.'

'Ally.' He said her name like a sigh, the syllables drawn out and his voice soft. Persuasive. Seductive. She closed her eyes and crossed her ankles tight. 'Please, Ally. Harry needs you. I can't bear seeing him so miserable, and he keeps making me play "All By Myself" on repeat while he eats ice cream.'

Ally burst into laughter. As exasperating as he was, she was content for the first time that evening listening to his voice. And she'd smiled more in two minutes talking to him than in four hours with Oliver.

'Fine,' she said, trying to sound reluctant. 'But I'm head chef and I'll bring the spices.'

'OK, Chef.' He sounded delighted. Ally hung up, and looked at the phone on her lap. She wished he was happy at the prospect of seeing her, not the idea of tricking Sam's secrets from her.

CHAPTER EIGHT

⌒

$\mathscr{H}$arry did have the blanket in his mouth when Ally arrived at the station. It trailed on the floor with white patches of dried saliva all over it. She tried to concentrate on Harry, not Marcus dressed in dark jeans and a white T-shirt that showed off his tanned skin and curved biceps.

Her cream skirt and orange strappy top didn't leave much to the imagination either. Not that he noticed. The git.

Harry dropped the blanket at Ally's feet, pushed his wet muzzle between her knees, and wagged his tail so hard his whole butt shook.

'Did you make him carry that?' she asked, looking hard at Marcus.

He handed her Harry's lead then tried to take the blanket. Harry sprang for it, growled, and shook his head until Marcus dropped it.

Marcus smirked, then handed her a carrier bag.

'What's this?' She extracted a can of Ting and a bag of plantain chips.

'It's just like being in the Caribbean,' Marcus said with a satisfied smile. 'You know what else they have in the Caribbean?

Trees and grass. There's a park down the road with trees and grass. But we're walking, not running. I'm sure I slipped a disc on Tuesday, thanks to you.'

He picked Debbie up in one fluid movement, the T-shirt rippling as his back curved and straightened smoothly.

'Liar,' she said, falling into step beside him with one hand on Harry's head. She waited for a breeze and took a deep sniff. Yes, different cologne again. Sandalwood. Saffron. Something sweet, subtle . . . vanilla. Even nicer than Tim/Tom's.

Best not to think about that.

'Ally?'

His voice was distant. She'd stopped walking, frozen at the entrance with Harry gazing at her in adoration. They must have looked like a weird art exhibition. She hurried to catch up. 'Uh, sorry. What?'

'I said maybe, *maybe* I don't have a slipped disc. But something in my back hurts.'

'Where?'

'The bit that's not the front.'

Ally sighed, but his smile was too infectious to be exasperated. 'Fine, I won't nurse you. And I'm not talking about Sam, before you start. I'm here for Harry and because you tricked me, but I'm not talking about Sam no matter how many types of courts you threaten me with.'

They turned through a green metal gate into the park. A concrete path wound through freshly cut grass, the scent strong and sweet among the sounds of birds chirping and shouts from the children's playground.

Ally opened the plantain chips and offered him one.

'Thanks. Look, Ally, I'm worried about Harry. The guilt of being in love with his brother's fiancée is killing him. Just look at that face.'

Ally looked. Harry's panting gave him a huge grin, and when she made eye contact he wagged his tail and shuffled his massive feet in joy.

'Oh yeah,' she said. 'He's a tortured soul.'

Marcus nodded, his expression solemn. 'If he knew you weren't really his sister-in-law, it would ease his conscience.'

'Even if I wasn't his sister-in-law, it wouldn't work out. Inter-species relationships are tricky.'

'He knows that. He's seen *King Kong*. He still feels guilty about maybe betraying Sam.'

Ally prodded Marcus's arm, mostly from frustration but also because it looked delicious in the white T-shirt. 'Why doesn't he just ask Sam? I mean,' she frowned, 'why don't you ask him?'

'Because if I'm wrong I'll look like a lunatic.'

'But you don't think you're wrong.'

'No.'

'Why are you so sure? Do you believe in damaging homophobic stereotypes?' She glared, and tried to sound offended. 'Because he wasn't out shagging loads of girls throughout his teens, he must be gay?'

'Because instead of going out shagging girls, he got an evening job so he could sit at the kitchen table every afternoon and watch the postman come up the path.'

Oh. The Italianate postman they'd nicknamed Luigi, because Sam was too shy to ever speak to him, even to ask his name.

'Well. OK. But why now? That was a decade ago.'

He was silent for a long moment, his eyes staring somewhere over her right shoulder, unfocused.

'Because I know what it's like to live a lie, and how it feels when you're finally honest with yourself. And I don't want Sam to wait as long as I did.'

Oh dear god, she'd been such a fool. It all made sense in a flash: Marcus was gay, too. It explained everything – the divorce, why he was so sympathetic about Sam's predicament, why he'd jumped to the conclusion that the engagement was fake.

It'd also make her feel a lot better about his complete lack of interest in her body.

'Oh, so you have a secret too, huh? Fine. You tell me yours and I'll tell you mine. And if you tell anyone what I tell you, I'll tell yours to anyone who'll listen.'

'Did you just invent a tongue twister?'

'I have a very dexterous tongue.'

He grinned, and Ally hoped to Cthulhu he wasn't gay. In her head, she was very much his type as she licked his skin, hot and hard, and felt those strong hands in her hair . . .

'Probably Hawaiian,' Marcus said.

Ally blinked. 'What?'

'We were just talking about favourite pizza toppings. I like pepperoni but I'd say Hawaiian's my ultimate favourite.'

'Oh.' Ally thought about it. 'I usually go for—Hang on! We were not talking about pizza.' She crossed her arms, heard a yelp, and loosened Harry's lead hurriedly. She scratched his ears in apology and he went back to sniffing lamp-posts. 'We were talking about your secret.'

She was even more confident now that he wouldn't trade.

'I don't have a secret,' Marcus said. 'The most interesting thing about me is how utterly boring I am.'

'Fine, then tell me your deepest regret. It's got to be something I can use against you. A security deposit.'

'Can't I just give you money?'

'No. Well, yes, if you want. But it won't get you anything in return.'

'I don't have any regrets. I don't get myself in awkward positions that could end in my humiliation and exposure as a liar.'

Ally threw a plantain chip at him. Harry ate it before she could pick it up. Then he whined and bounced on his paws, looking longingly into the trees. 'Don't you try and guilt me, Marcus Kinsell. You got me here under false pretences and you're trying to make me betray my best friend—'

She stopped abruptly. It was hardly fair to lay that accusation on him, with her filthy mind.

'I'm not budging,' she said. 'A trade is a trade. And I think we'd better walk Harry before he self-combusts.'

Marcus was silent as they walked along the path. Debbie snoozed in his arms and Harry sniffed at the grass, benches and lamp-posts, his tail wagging all the time. Marcus's face was serious, his eyes not focused on the concrete, and Ally let herself watch the way his arms flexed as he walked.

When he stopped abruptly, she nearly ran into him, and grabbed his arm to stop herself.

'It's not really a secret,' he said. 'Although I don't want Sam to know, so it counts as leverage, right?'

'Right, sure.' She needed to remove her hand, but his skin was warm and firm and he didn't seem to notice her touching him.

'My marriage has been over for years. Even when Sam was little, his mother and I only played at happy families. I lied to him, and Gavin, and everybody, including myself. I wasted the best years of my life, and now it's too late to have the things I really want. I don't want that for Sam. Not for anybody. Screw social pressure, social expectations. Everybody deserves to be happy. He deserves to find somebody he loves and who makes him happy and to enjoy that, openly, without worrying what other people will think of him.'

A flash of white over Marcus's shoulder sent a frisson of fear down Ally's spine. Filled with dread, she leaned a few inches to the left and let out a gasp. She'd been so captivated with Marcus that she hadn't realised where they were.

Beside the lake.

And they'd seen her.

A swan crept menacingly across the grass, evil black eyes fixed to Ally's right as if it hadn't even noticed her.

Ally knew better and backed away. She was dimly aware of Marcus falling silent, then asking her a question, but all she could think about was the advancing bird.

A high pitched *ee-ee* sounded behind her, the shrill warning of a whistling kettle about to boil over.

She whipped around to find another swan on the grass, closing in. They'd ganged up on her. It was like that movie Rachel had made them watch, the one with Samuel L. Jackson where sharks learned to hunt in packs.

Samuel L. Jackson got eaten. And that was *Samuel L. Jackson*, for goodness' sake.

Ally turned away from the pond and ran, but the other one

had circled around Marcus. She was trapped between the evil birds and the pond where the rest of the pack lay in wait.

'We don't have any bread,' Marcus said, waving at the swans. 'Shoo.'

A flood of adrenaline sent Ally's heart racing. 'Don't anger them!' she cried out. 'Just stay still!'

Trying to keep both swans in sight, she saw Marcus move from the corner of her eye.

'Are you scared of them?' he asked, his voice full of concern. 'They're only swans.'

Oh my god. He had no idea what danger they were in. 'You don't understand! You're going to get us killed if you don't stop moving.'

'Killed? Ally—'

Harry bounded over from the patch of reeds he'd been sniffing. He looked between Ally, Marcus and the swans, crouched low to the ground and growled at the birds.

Thank god. Bears were stronger than swans. Even swans who'd evolved into pack hunters. 'Harry, you little hero. Get them!'

'Ally, don't encourage him.' Marcus threw a stick towards the lake, sending Harry bounding away, then waved his arms at one of the swans. It fell back, hissing a warning, and stretched its wings. Showing him how big it was. Strong enough to break human bones.

Harry was gnawing at the stick with his back to Ally. She'd be dead by the time he heard her screams.

Her muscles cried out to run, but she couldn't leave Marcus to be eaten.

The swan hissed, regrouped, and came at Marcus with its chest thrust forward, wings spread wide. It was angry. Murderously angry.

Ally tried to move, tried to cry out a warning, but she was frozen to the spot.

Marcus shooed the swan again. Riling it up.

Movement to her left.

She'd let her guard slip. The other swan attacked in a blur of feathers, the *ee-ee* sound turning into the hiss of a viper. Its wingspan was so monstrously huge it filled her vision as it flew at her.

Ally screamed and stumbled back just as Marcus darted in between her and the swan.

The bird hissed as it slammed into this unexpected barrier, and Marcus yelled, 'Fuck!'

It'd got him. The swan had got him. They were going to die. Ally sobbed uncontrollably, her chest aching with every heave.

'Ally, calm down. It's OK, we—'

Debbie appeared suddenly, tearing across the grass like Usain Bolt being chased by a velociraptor. She lowered her head and crashed into the swan with the force of a small but very speedy car. The bird tumbled like a gymnast, flapped its wings furiously to right itself, and hissed.

There was no time to lose. Ally grabbed Marcus's hand and pulled him away from the lake as fast as she could run, calling for Debbie and Harry to follow. She looked back as they reached the tree line to see Debbie barking at the retreating swans. Ally vowed to buy her enough treats to fuel an army.

'Ally, slow down,' Marcus said, but the adrenaline wouldn't let her. He tried again several times as she raced down the path, Harry and Debbie now running alongside them.

When Debbie flopped on to the grass, Marcus stopped. Ally's hand was still in his and she jerked to a halt too, kneeling beside Super Debbie to make sure she was OK. The dog was panting but displayed her belly for a rub and seemed happy enough.

'You saved me,' Ally cried, kissing her head.

Marcus knelt beside her. 'Ally, it's OK. They're gone. They didn't even mean to get in our way, it's just that Harry scared them.'

She shook her head. 'No. They have it in for me. Swans. They . . . they hate me.'

'Why would swans hate you?'

Ally swallowed and tried to control her trembling. 'They sense my fear.'

'Why are you afraid?'

The lake was out of view. She was safe for now. 'I . . . I don't want to talk about it. You know the Queen is on their side, don't you? If you hurt a swan, she can behead you or something?'

Marcus's lips twitched.

'You're laughing! It's not funny.'

'I'm sorry.' He forced his face into a serious expression. 'I wasn't laughing. I was just picturing a world where people are beheaded for upsetting swans.'

'Well, that's not funny either. They're strong enough to break human bones. They can weigh up to thirteen kilograms. They're very dangerous. And the Queen's on their side!'

Marcus nodded quickly. 'You're right. I shouldn't have laughed. One of them did get me, you know, so I'm probably just delirious from pain. Forgive me?'

Her heart raced again. It'd got him. It could have broken a bone and he was just in shock and hadn't felt it yet and had internal bleeding and later on he would die and it would all be her fault for not paying attention and wandering over to the pond and antagonising the swans.

'Where?' she demanded. 'Where did it get you?'

'Don't worry, I was joking. It just bumped into my back, that's all.'

It might have got his spine or his kidneys or . . . other important stuff. Where was the spleen?

Ally pulled him on to the grass and tried to push him down. 'Sit.'

'It's fine,' he said, resisting. 'It only hurt because it got that muscle that always aches when cruel people force me to run.'

What if it didn't hurt now because it'd severed his spinal column and he had no feeling in his back at all?

'Sit, now. I'm a nurse, aren't I? You have to obey a nurse.'

Marcus sighed and sat on the grass. Ally scooted behind him and lifted his T-shirt, so worried her heart only skipped one beat as his bare skin came into view. It was smooth and tanned a healthy brown, with two columns of firm muscle either side of the spine. There would be some external signs of internal bleeding, wouldn't there?

'Where does it hurt?' she asked.

He prodded his lower back, just next to the spine. Ally pressed her fingertips on his warm skin and felt solid muscle. Not body-builder bulge but the lithe, toned power of manual labour.

The spot wasn't discoloured or swollen. He didn't react when she touched it gently, so she pressed deeper and felt an adhesion. A big one.

'I don't think anything's broken,' she admitted. 'But you have a huge knot.'

'Is that a compliment?'

She poked him in the ribs. 'That's why it's hurting. The muscle's tight.'

'How do I get rid of it?'

Oh, she shouldn't . . . but why not? It was harmless – in fact, it was helpful. He had a knot, and she was a masseuse. It was unprofessional for her not to do anything about it. Maybe even unethical.

'I'll work it out. Just relax.' She rubbed the knot to warm the muscle up, bracing her other hand on his shoulder as she increased the pressure. God, his body felt good.

As she worked at the knot, he made soft sighs of pleasure. Ally pressed her thighs together, trying to remember he was off-limits.

'You're wrong, you know,' she said. 'About it being too late. Plenty of people find love in their forties. It's hardly ancient.'

'Have you tried being my age and on a dating site? People seem to think anyone over thirty-five is dead from the waist down.'

'But you're not.'

He glanced at her over his shoulder, eyebrows raised. He said nothing, but looked amused.

Ally decided it was best to shut up and not pursue that line of conversation. She concentrated on the knot, and felt Marcus's breathing deepen.

'So,' he said finally. 'I told you, and now you tell me. You're not Sam's fiancée, are you?'

She had promised, dammit. And he already knew.

'No.'

'And he is gay?'

Ally stared fixedly at his back. 'I didn't say I'd tell you anything else.'

'Come on, Ally. You're not telling me, just confirming what I think I know.'

Ally thought of her reserved, quiet, sensitive Sam. She'd loved him from the moment she saw him on their first day of school, reading his book in his black square glasses and pristine shirt. How many playtimes had she glued herself to his side and talked at him until he started answering in more than monosyllables? He used to blush from head to foot when she hugged him or kissed his cheek, until he'd got used to her tactility.

His trust wasn't easy to earn.

'That's Sam's business,' she said.

Marcus turned to face her. Her fingers felt cold without his warm skin underneath them.

'OK,' he said. 'Then let's talk about a hypothetical scenario. Hypothetically, if I had a son who was gay, how would you advise me to get him to confide in me?'

She only knew two ways of loosening people's tongues, and one of them was illegal between a father and son.

'Alcohol,' she said.

Marcus made a face. 'I don't want him to tell me then regret it when he sobers up.'

'I didn't mean get him plastered. Just loosen him up a little so he's less anxious. Anyway, drunk people never do stuff they don't want to, do they? It's all the stuff we want to do sober but don't have the courage. So if he tells you under the influence, it's because he wants you to know. And if you're fine with it he'll be relieved, not embarrassed. As long as you make it very, very clear you won't tell anyone else. And maybe call him in the morning to reassure him.'

He seemed to chew it over. 'Well, I don't have a better plan. But we don't drink together. If I ask to see him he'll be nervous and on his guard.'

'Why?' Ally frowned. Sam hardly ever talked about his dad, but Marcus clearly loved him. What was keeping them apart?

'Because he'll know something's up,' Marcus replied.

'No, I mean why don't you two see each other?'

Marcus became very interested in Debbie's coat, picking a twig out of the curls.

Ally considered pressing, but decided against it. It was nothing to do with her. 'Where do you work?'

'At the moment, near Moorgate.'

'Hmm. There's a gay bar near Moorgate we go to sometimes. You could walk in and find Sam there.'

Marcus raised his eyebrows. 'Don't you think he'd want to know what his dad was doing at a gay bar?'

'Oh. You could say you popped in to use the toilet . . . no, OK, maybe not. Hmm. Oh! Bounce is nearby. It's so much fun there. They have ping-pong tables, and great music. And it's not a gay club. I mean, not gay only.'

'Why do I have to meet him in a club?'

'I can invite him out and get a few drinks in him, then you just happen to wander in. It'll be a happy coincidence and nothing to do with us plotting.'

She frowned. Was she really worrying about herself, about Sam discovering her part in this treachery? She should be worrying about him, and how he'd feel if he blurted out his secret. Would he regret it? If they reacted badly, yes. But Marcus was going to be supportive, so it'd be a relief for Sam, wouldn't it?

He nodded. 'OK. When?'

Argh. How had she got herself into this? Well, now she had, she had to do what was best for Sam. And, on balance, she thought telling his father would make him happy.

'Next Friday?' she suggested.

'Next Friday it is.' He arched his back and rolled his head from side to side. 'My back feels so much better, by the way.'

Harry flopped his head on to Ally's lap. She shifted his head a few inches, so he was drooling on the grass instead of her shin, and stroked him. 'You should go for regular massages. Not with me, because that would be weird, but I could give you some recommendations.'

'You're a masseuse as well as an artist and a nurse?'

'Uh . . . yeah.'

He narrowed his eyes. 'You have time to be a full-time nurse, a hobby artist, and a masseuse?'

'Yes.' She beamed.

'Ally.'

Ally sighed. There was no point pretending now the cat was out of the bag, but something in her wanted to carry on the lie. Wanted Marcus to keep thinking she was clever and resourceful and could hold down a responsible job.

'No. Fine. I'm not a nurse.'

'Why did you say you were?'

'I guess Sam wanted you to think he'd ended up with someone a bit more . . . respectable than me. I'm a part-time waitress, bar-maid and beautician, and a very part-time artist. Nice to meet you.' She held out her hand and he shook it.

'You've achieved a lot for your age.'

Ally lay back and slipped off her shoes so she didn't get tan lines. 'Very funny.'

'I'm not joking. You have three jobs and I know you're excellent at at least two of them.'

He seemed sincere, and he wasn't talking to her any differently now he knew she was a minimum-wage monkey. 'I—'

Marcus lay beside her and rested an arm behind his head. 'Look, modesty doesn't suit you. Accept the compliment.'

Ally shut her mouth, then beamed. 'You're right. I am pretty amazing.'

'Agreed.' Marcus turned on to his side so his face was inches away. His beautiful coral lips so close she could taste the mint on his breath. And his eyes . . . there was something in them as he looked at her. A hunger, an excitement that made her heart thud.

His lips parted and her breath caught as he spoke.

'What's for lunch?' he asked. 'Are there spices? I'm starving.'

CHAPTER NINE

The air at Bounce popped with the sound of bats and ping-pong balls colliding, and smelled of sweat and beer. Ally was on her third mojito, Sam his fourth cider, and he was loosening up. Music drowned out the conversations from surrounding tables; Sam and his father would be able to talk privately.

It was all going to plan until Sam had a phone call from his flat-mate. She'd forgotten her keys yet again, the cat hadn't been fed since morning, and Sam needed to go and rescue them both.

'Can't you wait half an hour?' she pleaded.

'Why? Tabitha's hungry.'

'Because . . .' She searched around for a lie and came up blank. 'I really want you to meet my friend.'

Sam narrowed his eyes at her. 'Are you trying to set me up again?'

'God, no! He's your—' Ally stopped herself just in time. 'Your . . . kshireish. Yorkshireish.'

She tried to look innocent as Sam stared.

'Yorkshireish?' he repeated.

'Yeah. You know. From Yorkshire.'

'Right,' said Sam slowly. 'As great as that sounds, I need to go.'

She had *one job* tonight – make sure Sam was there when Marcus arrived – and she was screwing it up. 'Oh, Sam, please. Just half an hour. For me.'

Sam drew his chair close and took her hands. 'Think of little Tabby. So hungry. Her little belly empty. Meowing pitifully.' He widened his eyes. 'Why haven't Sam and Sarah come to feed me? Why don't they love me any more? Why don—'

'Oh, go!' Ally put her hands over her ears. 'Don't make me cry. Go and rescue the kitty, Sam.'

Sam pecked her on the cheek and left.

She was relieved when Marcus's phone went to voicemail – at least she only had to confess her failure to the machine. Too disappointed to stay at the club on her own, she climbed the stairs towards the cloakroom and ran straight into Marcus.

He wore a blue shirt and dark jeans, had maybe two days' stubble on his chin, and carried the faint scent of orange, ginger and something spicy. Like a warming, satisfying, filling dessert that she'd have to eat all of even though it left her exhausted.

Seeing him unexpectedly was dangerous for her blood pressure. She inhaled a shaky breath and resisted the urge to pin him against the wall and see if he tasted as good as he smelled.

'Hi,' she managed.

Those warm brown eyes settled on her for about as long as it took to swat a fly. He didn't smile, and there was none of the usual mischief in his eyes. Ally, in her bright fuchsia dress that showed off legs *and* cleavage, felt like a potted plant.

'Where's Sam?' he asked, looking around.

Ally's heart sank further. 'He left. Sarah was locked out.'

'Sarah?'

'His flat-mate.'

'Oh.' Marcus deflated, but his eyes finally locked on to hers.

'I'm sorry,' she said. Somebody shoved past, forcing her closer to Marcus. She pressed his forearm in apology. 'I called but there was no reception.'

He nodded and moved out of the way as a line of women passed him to the toilets. 'Thank you for trying. Part of me's pleased. I'm not sure how he would have reacted.'

'Mm.' Ally's stomach knotted at the thought of Sam being angry with her. She was still uneasy about all this. Even if she did think it was better for Sam to have it in the open, she didn't have any right to force his hand.

'Hey.' Marcus nudged her fingers away from her crystal. 'Don't get upset.'

Ally swallowed and concentrated on not curling her fingers around his and pressing herself against him from head to foot.

Marcus shook his head, and for a second she was terrified she'd spoken her thoughts aloud.

'I've been unfair to you, Ally. All I was thinking about was getting Sam's secret out, not how you'd feel about giving it away.'

'You wanted to help Sam. You—'

'Don't make excuses for me. Should we get out of this corridor? I think we're a fire hazard.'

She didn't want him to leave.

'Want to play ping-pong?' she asked.

His smile broadened. 'Rematch for the race? You're on.'

There were no ping-pong slots available for twenty minutes, so Ally took Marcus to the table she and Sam had used. The music was loud, but she was afraid to sit next to him after three cocktails when he looked so delicious, so she sat opposite and strained to hear.

For once, he wasn't paying attention to her conversation, and it wasn't because he was enraptured by her figure-hugging dress. He glanced around the club nervously and averted his eyes if anybody looked at him.

'Sam's definitely not here,' she said. 'He left ages ago. You're off the hook from difficult conversations tonight.'

A petite woman in a black dress shouted an apology before diving under their table to retrieve a ball. She held it up, smiled at them both, then did a double take.

Marcus blushed, avoided her eyes, and seemed to be attempting to melt into the wall behind him. Ally felt a surge of jealousy. He noticed that woman in her little black dress but not Ally in hers? Maybe he liked petite brunettes, like his ex-wife.

Ugh. What was she doing? He wasn't hers to get jealous over, and she wasn't a jealous person anyway.

'I think I should go,' he said.

'What? Why?' Please say he couldn't see what she was thinking.

He looked around and cleared his throat. 'I don't belong here, do I?'

'What? Oh.' Ally caught sight of the brunette again. She would definitely have to show her ID to get served. 'You think you're too old.'

'I don't think. I know. Don't you see people looking at us? That woman was trying to work out if I'm a cradle snatcher or if I'm in a club on a Friday night drinking with my daughter like some sort of weirdo loser.'

'Silly. She probably fancied you. Or me, I'm hot. Anyway, look, that guy's older than you. And she's grey-haired. It's not stopping them having fun, is it?'

'Maybe they belong to a bingo club. Should I join?'

'I don't think you're in the blue rinse brigade yet. Anyway, don't forget you only look forty. Maybe thirty-five, since it's kinda dark in here.'

'All right, all right, don't go too far.' But it seemed to cheer him up. He smiled, and Ally had a strong urge to trace his lips with her finger. But she couldn't, because he was Sam's dad and, man, she wasn't touching that mess with a bargepole.

Though she kinda wanted him to touch her with his bar—No, bad train of thought.

But he *should* have someone, damn it. He was gorgeous and funny and caring and *funny* and if his confidence was this low, he probably hadn't had sex since Blondie was in the charts.

'You should think of it as an opportunity,' she said. A voice in the back of her mind told her it was the cocktails talking. A stronger and less coherent voice told it to shut up.

'An opportunity for what?'

'Meeting women. You're lonely, aren't you?'

His lips parted like he was surprised. She could fit her tongue in the gap. Just lean forward and poke her tongue between his lips and taste him, then maybe sit on his lap and nuzzle his neck.

So basically, she wanted to lick and sniff him? Maybe Harry was a better match for her than his human.

'Lonely?' He sounded shocked, like it hadn't occurred to him. 'I'm with people all day at work. And I do have a couple of friends. And the dogs.'

"S'not the same though, is it?' Ally poked his arm to emphasise her point. 'I mean –' she glanced around and dropped her voice – 'you could . . . you know. Find someone to *take home*.' She winked, then worried he'd missed it, so closed one eye.

He leaned in and matched her whisper. 'You know you once told me you're drunk enough sober?'

Ally nodded.

'You were right. When you drink, you just become more you.'

'Is that a good thing?'

'I think so. Definitely.'

'Hey, our table's ready.' Ally stood up. She was steady on her feet, and her speech was fine. He was right – drunk or sober, there was little difference.

Marcus was determined to win, dashing around and slamming the ball with powerful strikes that Ally could just about return. She became more and more out of breath until finally she lost three points in a row and conceded defeat.

Marcus was clearly delighted with himself, and she couldn't even pretend to be grumpy about losing. He was breathing hard but not panting like he'd done during their run.

'Have you been running?' she shouted over the music.

He looked even more pleased with himself. 'Yep. Every morning. I got up to a mile and a half yesterday.'

She beamed and gave him a thumbs up.

'Drink?' he offered.

Ally followed the path he carved through the crowd, noting from the way he walked that his back was still tight. When they dipped into a gap at the bar she felt for the big knot. Somewhere in the back of her mind an alarm told her the alcohol was making her too tactile, but she hit snooze.

'You haven't gone for a massage,' she said into his ear.

Marcus' stubble grazed her cheek as he turned his lips to her ear. 'For some reason, I feel strange about paying a stranger to rub me naked.'

Ally's fingers stopped circling the knot of their own accord and her pulse raced. Rubbing him naked . . . If he came into her salon asking for a full-body Swedish, she could hand him a little towel and tell him she'd be back in two minutes to rub him all over . . .

'I just saw the pope in a corner,' he whispered.

Ally pulled back. 'What?'

His lips parted into a smile, so close that all she had to do was tip her head back, and in less than half a step she'd be kissing him.

'Just checking,' he said. 'Thought you were spacing out again.'

'Me? Never.'

Marcus leaned over the bar and tried to catch the attention of one of the staff. Ally removed her hand from his back and fixed her eyes on the pale band of skin around his ring finger. Married or not, he was Sam's dad. Off limits.

'Hey.' Ally jumped as someone spoke close to her ear, the other side from Marcus. It was a tall blond guy with piercing blue eyes.

'Hi,' she said.

'Can I get you a drink?'

'No thanks.' She gestured at Marcus. 'We're together.'

Marcus looked around. Blond guy stared him up and down then smirked at Ally. 'Rich, is he?'

'Oh, piss off.' Ally turned her back on him, took Marcus's forearm, and waved at a barman.

Marcus was silent, his eyes fixed on the mirrors lining the back of the bar. Ally prodded him until he ordered – whisky – and tugged his arm to lead him back to their table. But the blond arsehole was on the next one, smirking at them, so she changed course and found a booth at the other side of the club.

It was quieter there, and she could speak without shouting.

'Ignore him,' she said. 'He's an arse.'

Marcus held his glass tightly and didn't respond.

'Don't get upset.' Ally squeezed his wrist, letting her hand linger. 'You were having fun. You beat me. You could probably beat me in a race now, too.'

He smiled, but it was forced. His eyes didn't crinkle. 'It was fun. I'm not upset.'

She tried to lift his mood, but for once it was him too lost in thought to listen. Ally babbled on anyway and hoped he'd forget about the blond arsehole.

When her fourth mojito was gone, she stood. 'Come and dance. I bet we have no trouble finding a woman who doesn't think you're too old.'

He blinked back to awareness. 'What? Oh, no. I haven't danced in years. I'd probably fall over and break a hip.'

'There isn't room on that dance floor to fall over. Come on, I'll show you how it's done.'

He shook his head. 'You go. I'll keep the table.'

'I don't care about the table. Come and listen to the music and forget that guy.'

'No,' he said firmly. 'I'll wait here.'

He met her eyes, and she knew he wouldn't budge. But she couldn't bear sitting there any longer, watching him feel bad about himself. Maybe he wanted her to go so he and his bruised ego could slip out, back home to his lonely life.

She made her way to the dance floor and lost herself in the thump of the music. After a few minutes she caught sight of a muscly guy with an afro in a T-shirt advertising that he was an 'Orgasm Donor' eyeing her appreciatively. He smiled as she met his gaze and asked her to dance. She agreed because he'd asked, and because his hands looked huge on her waist.

Orgasm Donor was a hip dancer. Ally debated asking for his number. His grip was firm, and there was power in that body.

When the next song started she turned her back to his chest. He spread his fingers over her hips, the little ones brushing where her panty-line would be if she were wearing underwear. Her fuchsia dress was too tight for anything but skin to fit inside.

Orgasm Donor bent his head to whisper in her ear, and as she twisted her neck to hear him better, she met Marcus's eyes. He stood stock-still in the middle of the dance floor and stared at her. Ally wrenched herself away from Orgasm Donor and stumbled towards him. He started, a blush creeping up his neck, and walked off.

'Wait!' Ally shouted, but the noise swallowed her voice. She darted through the crowd to Marcus's retreating back and grabbed his wrist. He turned in a flash and they were face to face, inches apart.

She realised she had nothing to say.

Marcus's expression was inscrutable, and Ally couldn't speak. She inhaled deeply and noticed for the first time how thick and dark his eyelashes were against those beautiful eyes, and a tiny scar in his left eyebrow where the black hairs didn't grow.

'Dance with . . . someone,' she said, changing it from *dance with me* at the last moment. If he touched her now, she'd be lost.

He carried on staring at her, then nodded. Ally led him back to the middle of the dance floor and turned her back to him before starting to dance. He'd be self-conscious if she watched him, and she had to get a grip on herself.

Orgasm Donor walked towards her with a grin. Ally shook her head and closed her eyes, letting the throb of the bass tell her feet when to move.

When the song ended she dared to look around, hoping Marcus hadn't gone back to the table, and widened her eyes. He was dancing with a woman. Platinum blonde like Ally, though out of a bottle by the looks of her roots. Her movements were out of time with the music, too. What was he doing dancing with her?

Marcus caught Ally's eye and gave a bemused half-shrug, as if he was asking the same question. But he was smiling, and Ally felt guilty for her mean thoughts. He was having a good time, and that's why she'd wanted him to dance.

But when she looked again and he'd swapped partners, she couldn't help frowning. This one was tall, olive-skinned, dark hair and eyes. Gorgeous, and she knew it. She swayed sensually, flicking her shiny hair around like she was in a L'Oréal advert. Marcus smiled kindly at her, blatantly unaware that she was trying to turn him on. She might as well be dry humping him on the floor.

He was too nice for a place like this, with women like that.

Oh for god's sake. Women like that? She glanced at her exposed cleavage in the skintight dress. Who the hell was she to judge?

She was just protective because this was Sam's dad, and he'd been out of the field for so long. He was her responsibility tonight.

Ally hovered near them. As soon as Sexual Dancer Woman got her grabby little hands off Marcus, Ally ducked in front of him.

His dancing slowed. 'Are you OK?'

Ally nodded. She forced herself to stop a foot away from him, and his movements ceased altogether. They stood still in the middle of a hive of gyrating bodies and stared at each other. Ally knew she had to step back. Leave the club. Stop pretending it wasn't wrong to be here with him. Hadn't been wrong to ask him to stay when their plans had fallen through.

OK, so Sarah locked herself out a lot, but what were the odds of it happening right before Marcus showed up? Maybe fate was telling her something.

Bullshit. She didn't believe in fate. It was her libido whispering sweet nothings into her ear.

Marcus held out a hand. His brown eyes were soft. When his fingers shook, Ally closed hers around them and, with her heart racing, put an arm around his neck. Marcus's fingers rested on her hip through the clingy dress. She was glad the music was loud enough to drown out her half-gasp, half-moan.

He bent his head to speak into her ear, and her head rested so naturally in the crook of his neck.

'She thought I was a mature student,' he said, pride and relief evident in his voice. He'd been accepted as one of the crowd.

Ally mentally apologised for her mean thoughts about Sexual Dancer Woman. 'So you're going to stop getting all oversensitive about not being twenty-one any more?'

'I wouldn't go that far. It's hard to forget when you have to

work twice as hard to stay in shape. And I have a grey hair. Look.'
He pointed. Ally couldn't resist the opportunity to touch his
hair with a valid excuse. It was thick and soft, and he kept his
head bowed while she took far too long pretending to look for a
grey hair.

'It's not there now. It must've realised that you're only in your
forties and fell out in a sulk. Anyway, running will keep you in
shape. And yoga is great, makes you feel strong and really in
touch with your body.'

'I tried it once. Everybody else in the class was female and shot
me dirty looks. I felt like a pervert.'

'Screw 'em. I mean, not literally.'

He laughed softly in her ear. 'I don't want to make anyone
uncomfortable. I found some tutorials on YouTube and started
doing those at home, but Harry and Debbie kept climbing on me.'

'We can do one together when I'm next there.'

But there wouldn't be a next time.

'Yes.' She knew from his voice that he'd realised, too. 'Next
time.'

He was lonely. Maybe he'd enjoyed her company while she
painted, even if he'd only invited her for Sam's sake. Maybe now
she'd helped him, he'd see her as more than a means to an end.
Maybe he'd realise she had a body below the neck.

'Do you want to come to Blondie with me?' she said in a rush.
She'd already invited Rachel, but Rach wouldn't mind. She didn't
like crowds anyway.

He didn't answer, just kept revolving on the spot with her.
Maybe he hadn't heard.

'I can't make it,' he said finally. 'Thank you, though.'

Right. He'd been thinking of a tactful reply. He was only dancing with her because Ally had forced Sexual Dancer Woman away. If she hadn't, would SDW have kept him company tonight?

Ally breathed in that deep, spicy scent one last time, then pulled back. 'I hate this song. Hungry?'

CHAPTER TEN

⌒

The August night was warm, and central London buzzed with life. Groups congregated outside every club and bar, smoking or drinking, and Ally watched Marcus's broad back as he carved a path for her. She wished she'd seen him with his shirt off, just once, to fuel the secret fantasies that Sam must never, ever find out about.

'Oh look, a dragon,' Marcus said.

Ally looked up. They were meandering beside the quiet grounds of St Paul's Cathedral.

'I'm back,' she said. A fantasy dragon scene in the cathedral grounds would make a good oil painting.

He grinned at her. 'What do you want to eat?'

There was only one answer when she was tipsy. 'Chips. Really greasy ones, with lots of ketchup.'

She loved the way he looked at her, like he was pleased with her answer.

They found a takeaway that screamed questionable hygiene, and bought two Styrofoam dishes of fat, shiny chips, with little wooden forks to spear them on.

Ally bit into one, felt it singe a hole in her tongue, and spat it out.

'Careful,' said the takeaway server in a monotone. 'They're hot.'

'Thanks,' she gasped.

Marcus ordered her a cold Coke from the fridge and she licked the bottle as they walked towards the Thames.

'Better?' he asked, as they sat on a bench next to the river.

She gingerly poked her tongue against her teeth. 'I'll survive. I regenerate, like Doctor Who.'

Marcus bit a chip. 'They're OK now. Do you always burn your tongue when you eat, or only with me?'

'Quite often. You know me. Act before I think, speak before I think. I'm amazed I made it to adulthood.'

A party boat blazing with lights sailed past. The raucous laughter of its guests carried in the breeze with the scent of vinegar and chip fat.

'You should definitely do yoga,' Ally murmured, watching the boat. 'It'll make you feel more flexible. More free.'

He watched the boat sail past. 'That'd be nice.'

'You could come to my yoga group. We're all women but I'll tell them you're my friend and you're not pervy. Just don't bring Harry because it could get really confusing with everyone shouting "downward dog".'

He laughed. Deep and sexy. If he did come to yoga, which she knew he wouldn't, would he notice her body when it was contorted into a pretzel shape? Or would he still be completely unaware that there was a body holding her head up?

It was silly to be annoyed by it. She didn't need validation from Marcus that she was sexy. She thought she was sexy, and that's what mattered. It was just annoying when she was so damn attracted to him and, even when she was dancing an inch away in her revealing dress, he acted like she really was his daughter-in-law. Had he lost all interest in women?

'How long has it been?' she asked.

He gaped. 'I . . . uh . . . that's a bit personal.'

Ally frowned, then realised. 'What? Oh, god, not that! I wouldn't ask that, even drunk. I mean how long is it since you were . . . living your lie.'

'Oh. Hard to pinpoint, really. We moved into separate rooms just before Sam was born.'

It was Ally's turn to gape. 'But he's almost thirty.'

'Yes,' he said. The smile was gone.

'Why did it take you so long?'

He put his chips down as if he'd lost his appetite. 'I couldn't leave her to raise two children alone, and I couldn't take them away from her. The only solution was to stay in the house. And by the time the boys left home, she couldn't look after herself.'

'But she could have had a carer.'

'She wouldn't accept care from a stranger.'

'She would have eventually, surely? I know it would've felt horrible to leave her with no choice, but . . .'

'No.' His voice grew heavy, and dull. 'Sam would have done it.'

Oh.

'She threatened it, when I said I wanted to leave. I had to get nasty. Said I would spend all the money, lose the house, before the divorce, so she got nothing. I'm paying for her sister to be official carer, though personally I'd rather have Hannibal Lecter as a nurse.'

He was right, of course. Sam wouldn't refuse his mum anything, especially if it was related to her disability. He would give up everything in a heartbeat.

'So you gave up half your life for Sam.'

'It's what parents do. No sympathy needed.'

She tried to look unsympathetic, and watched the water. Trying to imagine living with an ex for all those years.

'It's my fault she's ill,' he added.

'How is it your fault?'

'The doctors warned us,' he said. 'She had SPD with Gavin. It was bad. They said not to risk another pregnancy, because it'd be worse second time round. But she wanted another, and I didn't argue hard enough. I came to my senses after Sam, when I saw what it'd done to her, and had a vasectomy as soon as I could convince a doctor I wouldn't want more children in the future. She was furious – I think she would've put herself through it again for more kids. I don't wish I'd done it before Sam, because I'm very glad we had him. But I should've done it.'

Ally nudged his shoulder. 'I don't even know what SPD is but I'm sure it was nobody's fault. Sam blames himself too, you know, just for being born. You two are more alike than you think.'

'It's definitely not Sam's fault.' He frowned at her, like it was her suggestion. 'She'd go through any pain for him. He must know that.'

'Yes. But you're both being irrational and blaming yourselves.'

Marcus shook his head. 'Sam had no choice, but I did. I can't walk away from my responsibilities.'

'You were very young when you had them. That's a lot of responsibility, fast. I'm nearly thirty and I can't look after a potted plant, let alone a baby. Not that I want one. I mean, I'd quite like a potted plant, but no babies.'

'They weren't planned. At least . . . Doesn't matter. What's done is done, and all we can do is make the best of it. My boys are happy, and that's all I wanted.'

But not him. Ally imagined being alone in twenty years, and shivered.

'It's cold. Better get you home.' Marcus stood up, and offered her his arm.

As they walked to the Tube station, he kept shooting worried glances at her.

'I think your crystal needs cleaning,' he said. 'It doesn't seem to be working.'

Ally nodded, unable to smile.

'Hmm. Knock knock?'

She blinked at his expectant face. 'Who's there?'

'Impatient dog.'

'Impatien—'

'Woof.'

Ally sighed.

'Oh god.' He stopped in the street to stare at her. 'I broke you.'

'What?'

'You're sad. I've never seen you anything other than buoyantly chipper. Not for longer than a minute anyway.'

'Oh.' She smiled, making sure to show all her teeth. 'Better?'

'A bit Jack Nicholson, but better.' He tucked her arm in his and carried on to the station.

Most of the other passengers on the train were in high spirits, going to or from parties with their friends. Ally felt like an ink stain on a fresh white sheet, subdued and lifeless, while Marcus struggled to keep the mood light.

Ally roused herself just before her stop and said goodbye, but he insisted on walking her back.

'Look,' he said, when she argued. 'I'm from a different generation. Men made sure women got back home safely. I'm sure if we were attacked it'd be you defending me while I cried and begged for mercy, but let me keep up the pretence for my fragile male ego.'

Ally relented. When they stepped out of North Acton station, a cold gust of wind shocked her out of her miserable reverie.

She shivered, and Marcus held her arm again as they walked.

Outside her flat, she forced herself to disentangle her arm but wasn't ready to say goodbye. She hated the thought of him going back to a cold, empty bed. Both of them lying in cold, empty beds. 'Thanks. For walking me back. Do you want to come and see the painting? It needs a few more layers, but it's almost there.'

'I should get back.'

More crushed than she should have been, she tried to look as if she didn't care. It didn't work. His gaze was too shrewd.

'Changed my mind,' he said. 'I'd love to.'

He wouldn't love to. He wanted to go home. 'No, it's—'

'It's my painting. I want to see it.'

Too subdued to argue, Ally opened her front door and breathed in the comforting aroma of incense. She burned a stick every morning and every evening, like Mum always did.

Marcus sniffed. 'You're a secret hippie.'

'Am not.'

He pointed at a dreamcatcher on the back of the front door, and raised his eyebrows.

'Oh, all right. Blame Mum. I'm a flower-child's child. At least I don't dress like a hippie.' Ally's feet sighed in relief as she stepped out of her heels and led him upstairs.

The living room windows were open but the air was still warm from the day. Tiffany lamps cast a muted glow across the furniture, including the colouring book and pencils scattered across the coffee table, the stack of half-finished novels on the sofa, and the pile of to-be-ironed laundry on the armchair.

'I'm messy,' she observed.

Marcus didn't twitch at the sight of the clutter like Sam always did. 'This isn't mess. This is lived-in.'

Ally carried a lamp over to the dining room table so it illuminated the painting. She watched nervously as Marcus leaned his palms on the back of a chair and examined it.

'Well?' she said, unable to take the wait. She wasn't usually this nervous with a client, but usually the worst that could happen was they refused to pay. If Marcus was unhappy, he'd still insist on paying her, and she'd feel awful.

'It's beautiful.' He met her gaze. 'Beautiful.'

Ally swallowed. His eyes looked black in the dim light, and his cheekbones cast dark shadows on his jaw.

'You really like it?' Her voice came out as a whisper.

'Really. Don't change a thing.'

He hadn't taken those eyes off her. Her pulse was racing.

He was Sam's father.

But he was single.

He was nineteen years older than her.

But so sexy.

Ally touched the dark blue material of his shirt, just above the belt. Tentative. Just a brush with her fingertips. She could've just been getting rid of a bit of lint.

Marcus reached out and pushed a strand of hair behind her ear. Just moving it away from her face. It might have been annoying her.

Ally covered the distance between them in a rush, flung her arm around his neck and kissed him.

He tasted of good whisky. When his arm slid around her waist and his tongue pushed against hers, she felt it in her groin. A good kisser. Firm but not hard, lips soft and tongue controlled, the tip running across the inside of her lip and turning her stomach to molten honey.

She ran her hand from his stomach up to his chest, brushing her own hard nipple. He was solid, pliable, strong. The muscles not bulging but there. Not plastic but real, not perfect but human.

He wasn't exploring her body. He held her waist so tightly she could only draw short sharp breaths through her nose, catching burst after burst of his scent.

Ally pushed against him, crushing him nearer, but his hands flexed and then pushed her away. With a groan that she wasn't sure came from her or him, they separated.

'No,' Marcus said. He looked appalled. 'Stop. I'm sorry. I shouldn't have . . . Sam.'

Sam. Oh god, Sam. He'd never forgive her. Never.

'I'm sorry,' she gasped. 'I . . . don't tell him. Please.' She reached out to take his hand, but snatched it back.

'No,' he said, forcefully. 'No need for anyone to know. It was just the alcohol.'

'Right.' Ally nodded. He'd had one whisky. Her cocktails had worn off long ago.

'Not a word,' he repeated.

'No.'

They stared at each other, both breathing heavily.

'Ally, I wasn't coming on to you. Earlier. When we talked. I wasn't looking for your pity.'

Of course he wasn't. She was just a floating head to him. A way to get to Sam. So he'd reacted to the kiss – who wouldn't?

She'd got it so wrong.

'I'm sorry,' she whispered.

'Don't.' He reached out to sweep her hand from the crystal, but stopped mid-air. Ally dropped the quartz and stared at the carpet.

'Night, Ally. Take care of yourself.'

He left.

Ally stood frozen in her living room. She clutched Nana's engagement ring on the chain around her neck and prayed Sam would never find out what she'd done.

CHAPTER ELEVEN

*Ally was terrified of seeing Sam on their Monday movie night. She was convinced Marcus had confessed in a moment of guilt, and Sam would confront her. He'd be disgusted. Rachel would be disgusted. Ally would have to become a nun.

She preheated the oven for dinner and wondered how inconvenient a house fire would really be. It'd get her out of this movie night. But no – the firefighters might not arrive before the blaze reached her wardrobe.

When the doorbell rang, she forced her feet one step at a time to go and answer it.

Deep breaths.

She opened her front door to reveal Rachel, who held up a baking dish covered in tinfoil. 'Ta-da.'

'Oh, thank god.' She took the baking dish and drew Rachel into a tight one-armed hug.

'It's only aubergine moussaka,' said Rachel, patting Ally's back.

'You know how much I love your moussaka.'

'I do now.'

Rachel kicked off her shoes and followed Ally up the stairs.

'I'll put this on to cook,' Ally called, detouring to the kitchen.

The doorbell rang again just as she slid the dish inside the oven. Ally jumped so violently she grabbed the red-hot shelf with her bare hand, then snatched her fingers to her chest and hopped up and down in pain.

'I'll get it,' Rachel called out from the living room.

Ally whipped around in horror. Sam. Sam was here. He was going to run up the stairs and . . . would he hit her? He'd never been violent to anyone as far as she knew, but nobody had ever betrayed him so badly.

Ally found herself at the sink with the tap running. Why was the tap running? There was no washing up. To wash her hands? She squirted soap on her palm and yelped at the sting. Right. She was burnt. The cold water was soothing, but the moment she removed her hand it erupted into white-hot pain.

That was OK. She didn't want to leave the kitchen anyway.

But they would come looking for drinks soon. If she made them now, she could call Rachel to come and get them and buy herself more time before she had to face Sam.

Stretching so she could keep her left hand under the tap, she bent her back over the counter and took three glasses from a cupboard.

'Ally?' Sam's voice.

Ally spun around and dropped a glass.

Sam jumped away from the rain of shards, back into the hall-way. 'Crap, Ally, you OK?'

She stared at him in terror. Rachel appeared in the hall and leaned around Sam to see what the hold-up was.

'Ally?' Rachel waved at her. 'You're standing in a pile of glass.'

Ally looked down. There was a thin line of red blood on her bare foot, clashing with her hot-pink nail polish.

Sam stepped around the glass and took her arm. Ally looked at him in panic, but there was nothing except concern in his expression.

Of course Marcus hadn't told him. Of course. Marcus had even more to lose than Ally.

'Ally, are you ill?' Rachel stepped forward and felt her forehead, and she and Sam guided Ally to a chair like she was a child.

Well, she was. Sam had always been the sensible one, listening to her and Rachel complain about their lives and offering sound advice that annoyed them because they just wanted to rant. Now Rachel was the most sensible of them all, Sam was just as sensible, and Ally was still a screw-up.

'I'm fine,' she managed. 'Just thinking about something else.'

'As always.' Rachel put an arm around her shoulders while Sam got a dustpan and brush and cleared up the glass.

'Yes.' Ally sighed and leaned her head on Rachel's. 'Or not thinking at all.'

'You're burning up.' Rachel squeezed her burnt hand and stroked her hair like she was a child. 'Do you have a fever?'

'Maybe.' She could hardly say she'd worked herself into a froth of anxiety over seeing Sam.

'Sofa day for you,' Rachel insisted. 'No hostessing. We'll take care of everything.'

There was a bottle of aloe vera in the bathroom, instantly soothing and cooling on Ally's burn. Once that was taken care of, she wiped the blood away from her cut and examined it. It was one of those skin-deep ones that bled a lot, and stung like a bitch, but would heal up in a few days. She wrapped gauze around it, put a sock on, and joined her friends in the living room.

'I preheated the oven,' Ally said to them. 'Moussaka won't take long to warm through.'

'I'll take care of it,' Rachel replied. 'You just sit.'

Ally wished she could have the armchair, but Rachel was already in it. Ally and Sam always shared the sofa.

Ally perched on the edge and forced herself to look at Sam. He didn't look angry, but there was a strange expression on his face. Her heart thumped. 'Sam? Are you OK?'

He grimaced. 'Er. I need another favour and the shop was out of lollipops.'

Ally's heart sank. If only he knew how the last favour had ended. 'What?'

'Gavin and Kaitlyn are having a house-warming party on Friday, and he's invited you.'

'Who else is going?'

'Just us and my parents, though Gavin made it sound like it was a proper party when he invited them. We're trying to get them together as much as possible so they'll realise they miss each other.'

Ally pressed her burned palm between her knees. 'Sam, we can't keep this up for ever. They'll expect a wedding before long. Why don't you say we're breaking up?'

He rubbed the stubble on his chin. One of his father's mannerisms. Ally shut her eyes and shook her head.

'Gavin suspects,' Sam said. 'He keeps teasing me. Saying I looked like you were torturing me when we kissed.'

'You guys kissed?' Rachel grinned at them both.

'It was horrible,' Sam replied.

'Thanks,' said Ally. Her brain immediately compared the kisses of father and son, and she wished she could pull it out of her ear and soak it in bleach. 'He's probably just being a prick like he always is. Who'd suspect two people of pretending to be engaged? It's hardly the first conclusion you'd jump to, is it?'

'Why didn't you say I was your girlfriend?' Rachel asked. 'Is Ally a better pretend girlfriend than me?'

Sam shuffled and looked sheepish. 'Because Gavin fancies Ally, and I knew it would annoy him.'

Maybe she could snog him too, and make it a Kinsell hat-trick.

'Disgusting,' Ally blurted out.

'Aw. It'd be quite sweet,' said Rachel. 'Dating your best friend's brother. You'd be part of Sam's family.'

Ally wished the sofa would fold up and swallow her. She strained to telepathically shout Rachel a message to move right off that topic and never ever mention it again.

'I'd rather have Ally than Kaitlyn.' Sam sounded like a grouchy child. 'She's such a snob. I think she knows, as well. They're always smirking at me when I mention you.'

Ally thought desperately. 'Look, I'll call Gavin and make my excuses. I'll drop something in about how much I love you. OK?'

Sam's shoulders slumped. 'OK.'

It was the same look of defeat he'd worn in school every time Gavin insulted him for a cheap laugh. He'd never stand up for himself. That was Ally's job.

'Oh . . . fine.' Ally closed her eyes again. 'I'll do it.'

'Really? I'll love you for ever and ever.' Sam lunged across the sofa and hugged her. Ally squeezed him and rubbed his back. Softer than his father's. She couldn't feel any knots.

Oh man. She had to stop comparing. It was going to be hard enough seeing Marcus again without thinking about what it felt like to touch him, to kiss him.

Ally pressed her cheek against Sam's. 'You'd better love me for ever and ever, no matter what.'

'Course I will.'

She prayed that was true.

* * *

There was only one way to tackle the housewarming – act so in love with Sam that Gavin was left in zero doubt about the legitimacy of their engagement. Then he'd have to stop making jibes at Sam, and Ally wouldn't have to do this again.

She wore a short spring-green dress and put Nana's ring on a shorter chain so it was visible on her chest. Today, she couldn't forget even for a second that she was Sam's fiancée.

Marcus wouldn't give them away, would he?

No. He cared about Sam. Whatever he thought of Ally now, he wouldn't take it out on Sam.

Sam picked her up in the same suit he'd worn to the anniversary party. He was nervous, and Ally let him have Classic FM on in the car. How many hours of classical music would she have to listen to, to make up for kissing his father? There was probably a formula on the internet.

Gavin and Kaitlyn had moved into an apartment overlooking

Limehouse Marina. It was an ugly building, all cold glass and plastic, but she bet it had cost its weight in gold.

Ally pressed her side against Sam's and leaned her head on his shoulder as they waited for the door to open.

Gavin smirked out at them. 'Sammy and Barbie. How sweet.'

Ally flashed a smile. 'Hi, Gav.'

Sam made a noise that might have meant 'hello.'

All the blood rushed to Ally's ears as they followed Gavin into the living room. Her eyes found Mar—Sam's dad immediately. He sat on one end of the tiny sofa, body angled away from Julie, who was next to him with Kaitlyn on her other side. Ally plastered her Barbie smile on and moved her eyes around the room.

It was completely devoid of charm or comfort, with magnolia walls, pale laminate flooring, and stylish but uncomfortable furniture.

'Canapé?' Kaitlyn stood and proffered a tray of blinis. She wore a grey dress that matched Julie's trousers. Ally stuck out like an ill-judged centrepiece.

Ally took a blini before she registered that she was on the verge of vomiting from nervous panic. She was about to give it to Sam then, seeing that Gavin was watching them, fed it to him and kissed his cheek.

Now Gavin looked sick, too.

Ally sat on a chair in the corner to avoid the cramped sofa, where she'd be inches away from M—Sam's dad – or his ex-wife.

Too late, she realised he was in her line of sight. She angled the chair away from him and stuck her gaze on Sam's head, making sure she was smiling insipidly.

The room was small by anyone's standards, but with six people it was claustrophobic. Especially since Ally could only look at the left side of the room.

But she couldn't resist for long. While Kaitlyn was telling a long and dull story, full of '. . . oh, but I can't tell you about that, as it's confidential to my client . . .' Ally snuck a peek at Sam's dad. She took in the black trousers first, then risked the blue shirt, no tie, then her eyes slid up to his face of their own accord. He clearly wasn't listening to Kaitlyn either. He stared at the laminate wood floor in a world of his own.

'Ally?'

Ally jumped and found four expectant faces looking at her. Fear gripped her spine. She hoped she hadn't been staring at him for more than a few seconds. 'Uh, what?'

'Did you finish the painting?' Gavin said slowly, as if giving directions to a foreign tourist.

'Oh, um, almost. Oil takes ages to dry, you know. Just another layer or two.' Truthfully, she hadn't touched it since Sam's dad had been there. Too many bad – good – confusing memories.

'Not going to sit, Sammy?' Gavin raised an eyebrow at him. There were no seats left.

'I'm all right,' Sam muttered, avoiding his brother's eyes.

'You can't stand up all evening. Why don't you go over to Ally and she can sit on your lap? Or maybe you can sit on hers, if you're more comfortable.'

'Gavin,' said Marcus, in a warning tone.

Ally got up, grabbed Sam's hand, and pulled him down on the floor with her.

'That better?' she asked Gavin.

Kaitlyn looked horrified. 'You can't sit on the floor. Here, have the sofa. We'll stand, won't we, Gavin?'

As much as she didn't want to go near the sofa, this was too good an opportunity to pass up. Ally thanked Kaitlyn as sweetly as she could, nudged Sam to sit by his mum, and perched on the armrest with her hand still clutched in his.

Gavin, standing like an oversized ornament in his own living room, had a face like thunder. Kaitlyn and Julie were left to make stilted small talk until dinner was ready.

Ally didn't notice the food, but the wine was good. It seemed to disappear quickly, and she noted Marcus refilling his glass even more frequently than her. Gavin had almost polished off an eight-pack of beer by himself when dessert was served.

'So, booked a date for the wedding yet?' His words were slurred and Kaitlyn frowned at him.

'Er,' said Sam.

'Maybe next year.' Ally pressed her cheek against Sam's and adjusted her dress. Gavin's eyes travelled down to her cleavage and hovered there. 'We'd love an autumn wedding.'

Sam tried to smile. His eyes screamed panic.

'I must say, I'm surprised to see you here, Ally.' Gavin tore his gaze up to hers. 'All these years without a peek then we see you twice in one month?'

'She's been away a lot,' Sam blurted out. It sounded more like a question than a statement.

Ally nodded. 'It's been horrible being away from each other so much, hasn't it? But we're together now. And it's lovely getting to know you all.' She smiled around at all of them. All except one.

'I did wonder if he'd invented this relationship, for a while,' Gavin said, with a humourless laugh. ''Cause he couldn't get a girlfriend.'

Ally narrowed her eyes at him. 'Well, I'm very much real.'

'I bet you were his first, weren't you? He was hopeless in school and college. Thought he was a pansy for a while.'

Ally fired up. 'At least he wasn't a bullying prat.'

Gavin glared at her. 'Are you talking to me?'

'I'm looking at you, aren't I?'

'Oh, a prat? I was a prat, was I?' He stood up. 'I had loads of girlfriends, unlike that f . . .' he shot a look at his mum, 'that loser.'

'Gavin, shut up,' said Marcus. Nobody seemed to notice.

Ally kicked her chair away from the table and pointed a fork at Gavin. 'Oh yeah? Including Megan Fisher?'

'Yeah. Yeah. She was one. Of many.'

'Gavin!' Kaitlyn shouted.

'I bloody know she was,' said Ally. 'Because she wrote it on the wall in the girls' toilets, warning us that you tried to shove your hand up her bra on the first date, and your breath stank of cheesy Wotsits.'

Gavin's hands clenched into fists. 'And the boys got more than their hands up your bra, didn't they? Remember what we used to call you? Ally, the Bike of Brentford. Anyone for a ride, short journeys only, free of charge. Finger her on the first date, fuck her—'

'I said, shut up!' Marcus roared.

Everybody looked at him. Ally, caught unaware, stared right into his eyes. He was furious.

He stood up and threw his napkin on the table. 'Gavin, sit the fuck down and grow the hell up. How dare you talk like that to your brother, or his partner? Didn't we teach you any empathy, any manners? I'm fucking ashamed of you.'

Gavin sat down with a bump, his mouth hanging open.

'Marcus!' Julie gaped. She looked shocked.

'No, Julie.' Marcus faced her, his eyes ablaze. 'I'm not sitting back and watching him bully Sam one more time, let alone watch him insult his partner. Enough is enough.'

'It's true what I said!' Gavin shouted.

'I said shut the fuck up!' Marcus slammed his fist on to the table and an empty beer bottle smashed on the hard floor.

Sam clutched Ally's hand. He was trembling, his face pale. He was terrified of Gavin, even after all this time. Stricken, she sat down and rubbed his hand.

'I'm sorry,' she whispered. Sam shook his head and squeezed her fingers. Not her fault. But it was. She should have kept her mouth shut.

'Oh, I don't like this arguing.' Julie shot up, steadier on her feet than Ally would have guessed. 'I don't feel well. Call me a taxi, Gavin, dear.'

'Dad will drive you,' Gavin said, his white face blotched red. 'Won't you? Being such a gentleman, and all.'

Marcus's fist closed around his car keys. 'Let's go.'

Julie hugged Kaitlyn, Gavin and Sam before she left, but ignored Ally. Kaitlyn shot Ally a look of sour triumph, though Gavin still seemed too shocked to be nasty to her.

After Julie and Marcus had left, the four of them stood in the living room for a few moments.

'Well,' said Ally. 'Thanks for the invite. Hope you'll be very happy in your new home.' She grabbed Sam's hand and dragged him outside the flat. Julie would've had to take the lift, of course, and by the time they got the bottom of the stairs and left the building, there was no sign of Sam's parents.

CHAPTER TWELVE

⌢

*S*am wasn't angry with Ally. She wished he would be.

'It's my fault,' he said. He ground his teeth exactly the same way his father did. 'My bloody lies. Now Mum's ill because of me. Again.'

Somehow she knew Marcus was at home thinking the same thing about himself. These two needed their heads knocked together.

Sam let Ally fuss over him and bake his favourite coconut-and-lime cupcakes. He finally cheered up when his father called to say Julie was fine and he was to blame, not Sam. Ally wanted to grab the phone and insist it was *her* fault, but it would've been ridiculous for all three of them to fight over which one was more culpable.

He left looking happier. Ally ate too many cupcakes and wondered if they'd really called her the Bike of Brentford.

The following day when he came to see Ally at the café, he looked so happy that she asked if he was on drugs.

'Dad told Gavin off,' he said. 'He stood up for me.'

'He should've stuck up for you before now,' she said, trying to sound unimpressed. 'Gavin's always been a prick.'

'He hasn't come out with it like that for years. Calling me gay to my face, I mean. He just makes little comments that sound innocent to Mum and Dad.'

Ally deflated. If she could think badly of Marcus, maybe she'd stop thinking about him so much. But she couldn't. He was too damn caring, and it didn't help that he'd leapt to her defence as well as Sam's.

'How's your mum?' she asked.

Sam made a face. 'Upset. She's blaming Dad, even though it was Gavin's fault. He's such a turd. We got them together, sitting next to each other for a nice meal, and Gavin ruins everything because he can't stop being a dick.'

Ally sank down in the uncomfortable plastic chair.

'I don't think he's going to call me gay any time soon,' Sam said, with satisfaction. 'I won't have to come crawling to you for favours.'

'Pfft. Crawling. I'd do anything for you, silly.' Ally ruffled his lovely soft hair, and tried not to cry.

* * *

As August rolled on, Ally wanted the painting out of her flat. Every time she stepped into her living room it was a visceral reminder of her betrayal of Sam, and perhaps an even stronger reminder of the feel and scent and taste of Marcus. It was the only thing that made her stomach flutter at the moment, and she knew that mood. The only cure was to fuck him, and she couldn't do that.

Finally, she mustered up the courage to ask Sam to let his dad know the painting was done. Sam didn't seem to find it strange that he was delivering the message by proxy. That was much more normal than his best friend having direct contact with his dad.

Sam messaged Marcus right there and then, but there was no reply. He promised to let Ally know when Marcus replied, but as the days passed she realised he didn't want the painting. Of course not – it'd remind him of exactly the same thing as her. Next time she visited Mum, she'd take it and stow it in the loft. Maybe one day when this was all in the past, and she could look back on it and only cringe a little, she could sell it to a dog lover.

That Friday, as she exited the gym with a tote bag on one shoulder, she had a call. When she saw Marcus's name on the screen she stopped dead in the middle of the street. A woman walked into her back and cursed as Ally stared at the screen with her heart pounding in her ears.

'Hello?' she croaked.

'Hello.'

The silence dragged.

'Yes?' she managed.

'Sam said the painting's ready.'

'Yes,' she said. There was a silence as comfortable as a root canal. 'Do you want me to post it to you?'

'It's too big to post.'

He was right, but she couldn't invite him to come and get it. He might think she was going to jump his bones again, and he'd gently and excruciatingly explain that he wasn't interested.

Someone knocked into her shoulder as they passed, muttering about idiots standing in the middle of the pavement. Ally leaned against the wall of the gym. 'Well, I can bring it on the train, and you can collect it from the station.'

'You can't come all that way.' There it was – the consideration, the unwillingness to let anyone but him be inconvenienced. He hesitated. 'I can come and pick it up after work.'

Ally, surprised, didn't answer.

'No, forget I said that,' Marcus said quickly. 'Send it in a taxi. I'll pay for it when it gets here.'

That would be smart. They wouldn't have to see each other, and nothing could happen. But it'd be expensive. And, dammit, she wasn't going to jump his bones. She'd got the message.

'Oh, just come here and pick it up,' she said. 'I'll hand it to you and you can leave. No drama.'

A long pause. He must be searching for a tactful way to tell her no.

'OK,' she said. 'I'll send it in a taxi. When?'

'I can come today,' he said in a rush. 'After work.'

It was difficult to get enough breath in. There was something in his voice besides awkwardness, something that made her pulse race.

Maybe he was hungry again.

'What time?' she asked, before he changed his mind.

'Depends on traffic. Perhaps half six. Seven.' Yep, there was definitely something there. He was more animated than he'd been at the beginning of the conversation.

'OK,' she said, trying to sound neutral. 'See you then.'

At home, she sat on her bed and caught her breath. She was probably reading too much into his expressive voice. Picking up the painting from her flat was the most practical way to get it, and that was all. He'd given no signs of being attracted to her until she'd clamped herself on him like a sucker fish, and she couldn't blame him for getting caught up in it for a moment. She was a great sucker fish after all.

The likelihood was he'd knock, grab the painting, and run. But she had a date tomorrow and it was never too early to prepare, so it made sense to have a shower, shave, and wear her favourite underwear – the hot pink balcony bra with the matching low-rise French knickers. She wore sexy matching underwear every day, whether she had a date or not. Except for period days, of course, but this wasn't one of those. Thank god.

It was hot, so she put shorts and a pink tank top over her underwear then wrapped the painting. Then she unwrapped it, because he'd probably want to see it. Then she wrapped it again, because perhaps he wouldn't want to go beyond the doorstep.

She had a glass of wine while she waited, and then another, and then put the bottle in the fridge because she didn't want to be drunk.

Back on the sofa, her phone buzzed. Certain Sam had discovered what she was doing, she had a mini heart attack. But it was a message from Rachel – a picture of a wedding dress, with a question mark. Yes. Rachel would look beautiful in it and she'd get married with Sam and Ally as her best man and woman. The three of them had made a pact to be each other's best man and women when they were thirteen. Rachel didn't like the idea of a bridesmaid dress and a posy of flowers. Ally agreed that Best Woman was a much cooler title, as long as she could still wear a fancy dress.

What kind of best woman would sleep with her best friend's father? Would be sitting here in sexy underwear waiting for him and hoping? She was a terrible person and a worse friend. Her stomach knotted with guilt and disgust at herself, and then the doorbell rang.

Her stomach was so tight that it was difficult to uncurl and stand up.

Either her feet had gone numb or her mind was racing too fast to register anything happening as far down her body as that. She descended the stairs slowly, carefully. At the bottom, she laid her palm on the door handle and took a deep breath before opening it.

Marcus stood there in dark jeans and a forest green polo shirt. He must know how much dark green suited him and it was bloody unfair of him to use it against her.

Ally unstuck her tongue from the roof of her mouth. 'Hi.'

'Hello.'

'Come in?' She knew she should want him to refuse, but couldn't remember why now she was looking at him.

He didn't refuse, so she stepped aside and felt his eyes burn into her back as she led him to the living room.

'Here it is.' She pointed at the painting then saw she'd left it wrapped. Uncovering it gave her somewhere to look.

Marcus hovered nearby. Out of reach, but close enough to see the picture.

'There you go.' Ally fixed her eyes on Debbie's tail.

He took a step closer. 'It's excellent. You're very talented.'

'I'm sorry,' she blurted out, still looking at the tail. 'About Gavin's dinner party. I hope Julie's OK.'

'You didn't do anything wrong. I should be apologising for my son.'

She was about to protest then realised he meant Gavin, not Sam.

Ally stood up and dug her bare toes into the carpet. 'It was true, in case you're wondering. What Gavin said. I slept around a lot.'

'I wasn't wondering.'

No. He probably hadn't thought about her at all.

The nail polish on her little toe was smudged. A cotton bud would sort it out.

'I'll wrap the painting back up.' She worked in silence and Marcus didn't move. 'All done. It's touch dry, but if you put any force on it, the layers underneath will smudge. So just be gentle with it for a few months. You can get it varnished then, if you like.'

'Thanks.' He picked it up, and Ally stood aside, but then he put it back down. Her eyes were fixed on his feet, which turned to face her. 'Ally?'

Unwillingly, she raised her head. 'Yes?'

'It was my fault. Don't blame yourself.'

'It wasn't,' she said. 'I shouldn't have risen to the bait. I just hated seeing Sam like a twelve-year-old again, scared of the bully.'

'I'm not talking about Gavin. I meant here, after the club.'

He was obviously used to taking the blame. One more thing to feel guilty about would only weigh his shoulders down a touch more. One more secret would only give him another knot in a back taut and aching from them.

'Oh.' Her cheeks grew hot, and she dropped her eyes to his nose. 'That was me, too.'

'No,' he said sharply. 'It wasn't. I knew something was going to happen if I came in. I did it anyway.'

She cringed. Of course he'd known. She was as subtle as a Kardashian's make-up. He probably thought of her as a silly teenager with a crush on the teacher which, to be fair, just about summed her up.

'Please stop blaming yourself,' she said. 'I'm not worth losing any sleep over, really. I'm a bit of a disaster area when it comes to dating. I'll have forgotten all about this in a few weeks and moved on to some other man who's totally wrong for me.'

'Will you?' His voice was low. That smoky, sexy tone.

'I always do. I'm fickle. Goldfish brain.'

He picked up the painting with a crease between his eyes, then put it down again. 'You get this all the time? These feelings?'

Was he determined to humiliate her?

'Yes. I'm always lusting after somebody.'

'I'm not. This is new to me.' He spoke so quietly Ally wasn't sure she hadn't imagined it.

'What?' Her heart drummed. 'What's new?'

'Thinking about you. Picturing you. Imagining . . .'

Ally tried to catch her breath. 'Imagining what?' She wasn't sure if she was hoping or dreading he'd been imagining the same as her.

He stared at her for a long moment then stepped forward and cupped her face, pushing his fingers into her hair. His hands were firm, and warm, and electric. Then he was kissing her, running his free hand down her neck, her shoulder, into the small of her back, pushing her closer to him. She wrapped her arms around him and dragged him on to the sofa, on top of her, heavy and warm and solid.

Oh my god.

She wasn't a floating head.

His hand slid inside her top and caressed the bare skin of her side. His touch was gentle and slow, not like the way she wanted to dig her fingers into every part of him, but it still made her moan. She pressed against him to try and relieve the maddening ache in her hard nipples and clitoris and knew if he slid that hand inside her shorts he'd find her wet and hot for him.

But instead he took his gentle hands away, broke the kiss, and looked down at her with frustration and regret all over his face. 'I'm an idiot. I can't, Ally. Not Sam's friend.'

She couldn't either. Or shouldn't. But her body was crying out for an orgasm.

'Just once.' Her voice was no steadier than his. 'Get it out of our systems. Then we can pretend it never happened.'

He swallowed. 'It would never work out. The age difference, you being Sam's friend, everything.'

'I don't want to marry you. I want to fuck you.'

He ground his teeth. 'It's too risky. If Sam found out, he'd be crushed.'

Ally groaned in frustration. 'Don't. I know it already. You're killing me.'

'We can't.'

She thought of the guilty way Sam talked about his mother's illness, her helplessness, her fragility. Sam would be crushed if she were left alone.

'No,' she said, through gritted teeth. 'We can't.'

It wasn't the answer he wanted. His head dropped on to her shoulder, maddeningly close to her aching breasts, but the tension had gone out of him.

'Fuck.' Ally slumped back on the sofa and grasped her hair in her hands.

Marcus sat up, leaving her cold and wound tight. She was desperate for those hands on her skin, the taste of him, the smell of him. Goddammit she was horny.

He turned back to her. 'We almost lost him, when he was a baby.'

'What?'

'Sam. I knew you hadn't seen his scar. He had surgery, as a baby. Left him with a scar from here to here, and it didn't heal well. He always hated it. But he doesn't know how close he came to – to not making it.'

'Oh.'

That was why he wore collared tops to the gym, and wouldn't go swimming. That was why he'd never have casual sex, why it took him so long to trust a man enough to get naked with him.

Her Sam, so worried about a scar.

'I can't lose him, Ally. I almost lost him once, and I've had twenty-seven more years to love him since then. Even if I didn't show it very well. I can't risk losing him, no matter how much I want you.'

He was right. Sam would be devastated. Not just because this was his father, but because he was married to the mother he adored. The one he already beat himself up over. If he brought a cuckoo into her nest, he'd never forgive himself.

She was the worst best friend ever.

'You're right.' She got to her feet on uncertain legs.

Marcus picked up the painting.

'I'm sorry. I shouldn't have come. I shouldn't have done that.'

She didn't reply.

She waited until the front door opened then closed with a click, listened for the sound of a car starting and driving away, then lay on the sofa and let out a scream of frustration into the cushions. Lying on the sofa was nowhere near as satisfying as lying under him. It was cool, and soft, and didn't push back on her body.

Her nose caught the faintest remnant of his scent on the material, and she groaned. Not allowing herself to think, she popped open the button of her jeans and slid her hand inside.

She was so wet her finger slipped inside her, and it was almost painful when her palm brushed over her clitoris. It was engorged, sensitive, and she dipped back into the lubrication and circled it. Around it at first, and then closer, pressing into the hard nub.

His hand had been firm. A callous on one finger had scratched her skin like a teasing, tantalising fingernail. That touch was soft but his mouth was firm; his lips moving on hers, his tongue pushing into her mouth.

She bit the cushion, and drew her knees up to give her hand better access.

Those fingers caressing so gently, and then his mouth hard and insistent between her legs. Tasting her, licking her aching clit, lips enclosed around it until it was so intense it was almost painful, but . . .

She came with a cry, so worked up it'd taken barely a minute. The pulses were strong, her muscles clenching so hard she drew her thighs together to take the throb.

While her breathing slowed she lay with her face buried in the pillows, and tried not to think about how fucked up it all was.

CHAPTER THIRTEEN

Rachel called Ally on Monday morning. She was sure Sam wanted to break their pledge of no-partners-at-movie-nights but was too guilty to ask. They agreed to invite Brendan of their own accord, and Sam's smile when he arrived was worth it.

'You guys are the best friends ever,' he informed them.

Ally could barely force a smile.

Brendan, as the guest of honour, had chosen the movie. Ally's heart sank when she looked at it.

'*Something the Lord Made*,' she read, trying to sound enthusiastic. 'I used to love Sunday school. All those biscuits. Er, and the Bible, of course.'

'Oh, I don't think it's about God.' Brendan looked taken aback. 'Are you very religious?'

Ally beamed. 'Nope. Thank god for that. I thought we'd have to join hands and sing Hallelujah.'

'We should do karaoke soon,' Sam suggested. He held hands with Brendan on the sofa, like they didn't want to not be touching for a moment. 'It's been ages.'

'I love karaoke!' Brendan gazed at him in delight.

Ally sighed aloud and exchanged 'aw' faces with Rachel.

Romance definitely wasn't dead. She just had to find it, with someone she could actually have.

The movie turned out to be about two doctors who'd invented heart surgery. It wasn't their usual genre – Rachel always chose monster movies, Sam comedies, and Ally romcoms – but it was a refreshing change.

Brendan had to leave when the movie was over. Ally glanced at the front door as Sam said goodbye and saw him turn his head when Brendan leaned in for a kiss, pretending he hadn't seen. Brendan left looking hurt, and Ally watched Sam carefully. He was quiet, red-faced and not looking at either of them.

She plonked herself beside him on the sofa and bumped their hips together. 'What's up?'

'Nothing,' he muttered, going redder.

'Yes there is. You were fine before . . .' She trailed off as she remembered the movie. Heart surgery.

'He wants to have sex,' Sam blurted out.

Rachel caught Ally's eye. Ally tried to arrange her face into a look of confusion, but she finally understood why Sam got so anxious about first times. His scar. The movie had made it worse.

Rachel sat on Sam's other side. 'He wants to have sex with his boyfriend? The unreasonable fiend. This is a bad thing . . . why?'

Sam shrugged as if his palms were pinned to the sofa cushions. 'I really like him. What if he's put off?'

'Sam, he likes you. He's besotted. What's not to like about being naked with you?'

Sam's shoulders sagged.

'He told me about an ex,' Ally lied, crossing her fingers behind her back and hoping Sam would never ask him about this. 'This guy came in the café, all muscles of steel and hair in a ponytail and tattoos everywhere. He was totally eyeing Brendan up but when I nudged him he made a face and said this guy looked like his ex, and he never wanted to date someone like that again. He wanted someone who cared more about his mind than his body and spent more time with him than at the gym. His ex must have been hot if he looked like the guy in the café, but Brendan said his only redeeming feature was an appendix scar. You know how some people have a thing for scars? Anyway, I don't think you need to worry. He's not shallow. Like Rach said, he likes *you* so he'll like your body.'

Sam looked like a child waking up on Christmas Day.

'She's right,' Rachel said. 'Nothing to worry about.'

'Yeah,' Sam agreed. 'I'd better call him and apologise for being moody.'

Rachel gave Ally a thumbs-up as Sam left the room.

At least one good thing had come from her time with Marcus. Now Ally needed to give herself a dating pep talk.

* * *

Later that evening, Jason sucked Ally's neck while she counted the swirls on the ceiling.

'Uh, hello?' he said.

She blinked as his head appeared in front of her face. The sucking had stopped. 'Sorry?'

He propped himself up on his elbows. She usually couldn't resist squeezing his toned biceps when he did that, and running the tips of her fingers down the warm green veins, but today she admired him from a distance. Like a painter, not a sex buddy.

'I feel like I'm trying to seduce a sex doll,' he said.

'Oh. Right. What do you want me to do?'

'I don't know, move occasionally?'

'Move? I can do that.'

He moved in to kiss her, and she fought the urge to turn her head away. He put a hand inside her bra and squeezed one breast, then rubbed her nipple with his thumb, but it didn't even harden.

He raised his head again. 'OK, what's up with you?'

Ally sighed. 'I don't know. I'm just not into it.' He smelled wrong, and his lips were wrong, and his hands were wrong.

'Why didn't you say that?' He rolled off and lit a cigarette.

'I thought I might get into it. I need to get laid.' She turned on her side and pulled the sheets over her, because she couldn't be bothered to find her clothes.

'Yeah, well, I feel like a rapist and it ain't sexy. You can sort yourself out.'

'Oh, thanks.'

He peered down at her. 'I can give you a hand?'

She knew where her thoughts would wander, and it'd be all kinds of messed up to let Jason be part of that.

'Nah. I'm good.'

'So?' He raised his eyebrows at her.

'What?'

'What's up with you?'

She shrugged. 'I want this guy, and I can't have him, but I'm so set on him I don't want anyone else. I need to screw him so I can get it out of my system.'

'Why can't you have him?'

'You know the bro code? Like, you don't screw your friend's sister?'

'Right. Friend's brother?'

'Something like that.'

'Damn.' He offered her the cigarette, and she refused. 'Can't you just swear him to secrecy, screw him once, and get over it?'

'No. He won't do it.'

'Hmm.' Jason leaned his head back against the wall, then peered down at her. 'Want to shut your eyes and pretend I'm him? We can turn the lights off and do it from behind.'

'Uh, no. Thanks. But who said romance is dead?'

'Romance him then. You got the charms, so use them. Who could resist that?'

'You, apparently.'

'Yeah, but I have superpowers too.'

'Uh-huh.' She forced herself up and pulled her dress on. 'Maybe it'll go away with time. You know, like athlete's foot.'

'When you get an itch you gotta scratch it. Let me know if you change your mind about the doing it from behind thing.'

'Yeah. Don't hold your breath. See you.'

It was only a hundred metre walk back home. When Jason called to say he'd broken up with his girlfriend, and she once again had sex on tap just a minute's walk away, she thought the endless dates and browsing dating sites were over. At least until she got sick of him. Then Marcus had messed it all up with his irritating aftershaves and his irritating eyes and his even more irritating face.

Powerwalking home, she sent Marcus a text, reminding him that she still had a spare ticket to Blondie. If he said no, or got annoyed that she was contacting him, she could pretend she'd meant to send it to her Mum, next contact down in her address book.

The reply came almost instantly.

Don't think I should. Thank you though.

Ally didn't even bother pretending it'd been a mistake. She ran home, violently packed a tote pack, then went to the gym and pounded the treadmill like it was personally responsible for her dissatisfaction. Her mood declined further when she received a text, almost had an aneurysm, then discovered it was a deal for twenty per cent off a large pizza if claimed before Saturday.

Who did they think she was going to eat a large pizza with? Bastards.

In bed, after a mediocre orgasm, she was awakened by another message. She grabbed her phone, intending to put in a formal complaint to the pizza company about their disgusting timing, but it wasn't about pizza.

Can I change my mind?

She sank back into the pillows and sighed in relief.

CHAPTER FOURTEEN

Ally's mood didn't improve in the run-up to the Blondie concert. Everybody kept asking in surprise why she was so grouchy and moody, and she could hardly tell them the truth. Instead, she pleaded money problems. It gave her an excuse to stay home, eating so much junk food she had no choice but to go to the gym every evening.

Keeping busy. That was the trick.

It still seemed to take an inordinate number of days before the concert rolled around. Finally she was there, early for once, and in a good mood.

She sat in the foyer at the O2 and exchanged texts with Rachel about wedding dresses. It'd mostly been the two of them hanging out lately. Sam and Brendan had apparently cemented their relationship and now spent every moment of spare time together. Before long the honeymoon stage would pass and Sam would be back, sheepish and loved up, with Ally the third wheel.

Man, this self-pitying mood had to end. She didn't begrudge her friends happiness just because she was incapable of finding a man.

'Hi.'

She looked up into Marcus's beautiful eyes and her stomach dissolved into a quivering mass of lust. His short-sleeved T-shirt showed off his muscular arms, and he had the dark jeans on again. He could pass for late thirties, maybe. Not that she cared about his age. That was the least of their problems.

'Hi.'

He didn't seem to notice her outfit. Still? She was still a floating head?

OK, it was flattering, because finally somebody was more interested in her head than her more accomplished parts. But it was annoying because she worked hard on that body, dammit, and he was not showing proper appreciation. Especially since she'd worn her favourite seduction outfit: the poppy-red dress with the criss-crossed straps down the back. She'd been ahead of the trend but now BDSM was so hot, the tied-up-in-ropes look could snag any man.

Except this git. Marcus was focused entirely on her eyes.

'How've you been?' he asked.

'I've been fuc—' She clocked a group of middle-aged women staring at her raised voice, and swallowed an honest answer. 'Fine. I've been . . . fine. You?'

'Fine. But not an angry fine like yours.' He sat beside her. A different fragrance, again. Sandalwood, nutmeg. Maybe lemon. 'Are you sniffing me?'

She stopped abruptly and removed her nose from the vicinity of his neck. 'Well, you shouldn't wear such nice scents if you don't want to be sniffed. You're like a dessert today.'

He smiled, and she desperately wanted to kiss him. 'Speaking of dessert, I'm hungry. An early dinner before the show?'

Ally made him choose the restaurant, and they had burritos. She choked on a green chilli this time, and had to ask for a glass of milk to cool her burning tongue.

'Maybe I should stick to cold food,' she croaked.

'It might be safer. Want to order something else?'

'I'll be fine.' She dabbed her eyes. 'I learned my lesson.'

'We wouldn't be here if we'd learned our lesson.'

His frank stare made her horny. Hornier.

'Did the painting smudge?' she asked, to change the subject.

'No, it's perfect. I put it on my living room wall and rearranged the furniture so I can see it from the sofa.'

Well, at least he appreciated *one* of her talents. Gran would approve.

'How did the baby painting go?' he asked. 'August seventh.'

'You have a good memory. It was all right. The baby was cute, and she slept through most of it. I made her a little chubbier, and her eyes a little bluer, and Mummy was happy. I did charge her extra for giving me bottled water to mix paints with. Anyone who'd waste bottled water on that deserves to be overcharged.'

'Was I supposed to give you water?'

'Those were oil paints. Didn't I teach you anything?'

'Loads. I think I fell asleep for some of it, though.'

Ally crossed her arms. 'Hey, you asked, I answered. Not my fault if you were bored.'

'Not because I was bored.' He reached over, unfolded her arms, and put her fork back in her hand. 'Because your voice is so soothing. Why did you think I kept prompting you to talk?'

Placated, Ally speared a potato wedge. 'Most men want me to shut up.'

'Keep talking.'

She raised her glass to her lips so he wouldn't see her smiling.

* * *

Ally had bought standing tickets. They found a spot near to the stage, and new arrivals pressed them closer and closer to it.

She glanced around and panicked when she couldn't see Marcus, but a strong tanned hand appeared between the two men next to her and she grasped it. He pulled her through and held her hand firmly by his side.

A few minutes later, somebody crashed into Ally. She lurched into another man, spilling beer down his shirt. He glared at her, then shuffled off with a sour look. Marcus pulled Ally in front of him, folded his arms around her waist, and rested his chin on her shoulder. The crowd disappeared and it was only Marcus all around her, cocooning her in safety. She let herself curve her body around his and barely noticed when the band began to play.

The concert was a blur of music, singing, dancing and Marcus. His chest vibrated against her back as he sang and she was so happy he was letting loose. When 'Shayla' came on he held her hips and swayed with her, his nose buried in her hair. Ally was flushed with lust, straining on tiptoes and arching her back in the hope that his hands would go south. Even though she felt his erection pressing against her, and heard his breathing quicken in her ear, he stepped as far back as the crowd would let him.

Why the hell had he agreed to come?

Ally left the arena like a coiled spring. A grumpy one. Grumpy wasn't her, and she was even more grumpy thinking of how grumpy he made her. She tried to storm ahead of Marcus and lose him in the crowd but there was to be no storming in the packed exits.

Outside, he took her arm as someone knocked into her. 'Can I give you a lift home?'

She wanted to be churlish and refuse, but it was a long journey and she'd been doing a lot of dancing. So she shrugged, and sat in Marcus's car staring out of the window.

'Have I done something wrong?' he asked, after a while.

'No. You're doing the right thing, damn you.'

'You seem upset.'

'I'm horny.' There didn't seem any point lying. Gavin had already told him she was slutty, if he hadn't worked it out for himself. Not that she was going to apologise for that. Sex was good, when the man would bloody give it up.

'Does that normally make you upset?'

'Only when I can't do anything about it.'

He went quiet, and Ally didn't break the silence. She watched the lights of London whizz past the window and wondered why she kept putting herself through this. The smart thing to do was forget about him, however many guys it took to drive him out of her mind, and move on with her life.

Finally, they reached her flat.

'Night then,' said Ally, undoing her seat belt.

'Thanks for inviting me. I wish you'd let me pay for my ticket.'

She shook her head. 'I'm glad you enjoyed it.' She sat for a moment, waiting for him to make a move, but he didn't. He hadn't even turned off the engine.

'Night then,' she said again, waited another moment, then got out of the car and slammed the door as hard as she could. One of her neighbours glared from a window, and she glared right back.

She slammed her front door as well for good measure, then stomped up the stairs. Even after throwing her keys at the wall and kicking her shoes at the ceiling, she felt no better.

If Rachel was there, she'd force Ally to sit down and drink a cup of tea. It was worth a try.

In the kitchen, she had a strong urge to break a plate, but she only had three and that would leave her short on movie nights with her friends.

Two plates would be plenty if Sam found out what she'd done tonight. Or intended to do, dammit.

Her doorbell rang, and then there was a knock. Mrs Cooper from downstairs, come to complain about the banging. In this mood, Ally would probably end up in a slanging match like she had with Gavin. Better to wait until the morning and apologise.

But another ring and knock flipped a switch in her. Who the hell did both? Who did this woman think she was?

Ally flew down the stairs and wrenched the door open. 'Look, I never make any damn noise so—'

Marcus stepped inside and kissed her.

CHAPTER FIFTEEN

◡

*A*lly stumbled back. Marcus pinned her against the wall and ran his hands down to her hips in a way that made her legs weak. His mouth was hot and his body hard, firm muscle pushing against her breasts and her thighs.

His lips moved to her neck.

'Upstairs,' she gasped. 'Now.'

He cupped her buttocks and she hoisted herself up, legs around his waist and arms round his neck. As he carried her up the stairs she slid her hands up his T-shirt and pushed her fingertips into the hairs on his stomach.

At the top of the landing she pointed at her bedroom, unable to make words. They tumbled on to the bed still wrapped around each other and he sighed as she ran a finger down his happy trail.

She knew he'd be a sigher.

Ally took the hem of her dress, but he bent to kiss her before she could remove it and stretched his body out on top of hers.

If he didn't touch her skin soon, she was going to burst.

She pulled his T-shirt off and ran her hands all over his torso, itching to massage all the knots in his back but forcing her fingers up to the hard bumps of his shoulder blades. His skin was warm and caramel-coloured, and she expected to taste toffee when she kissed his neck. But all she could sense was his beautiful, subtle smell, pervading her nostrils like his mouth was enveloping hers and his hands were claiming her skin.

She raked her nails down his back until he sighed again, then tugged at his belt. He rolled off her to wriggle out of his jeans. Boxers. That was a nice surprise.

He flexed his fingers when she went to take them off, like he wanted to stop her, but didn't. And there was no reason for him to worry; his cock was a nice surprise too. Normal length but thick, already hard. His sigh turned into a moan when she explored it, but when she went to take her dress off he stopped her again.

'You want me to keep my clothes on?' she asked breathless, impatient.

'No.' He nudged her hand off him and kissed her mouth, then her jaw, then her neck. 'I want to undress you.'

She groaned as he trailed kisses down the sensitive veins in her throat. 'Quickly.'

'Slowly.'

She hadn't seen this coming. Not a teaser. She thought he'd be old-school vanilla – a kiss, a squeeze of each breast, then slamming into her until he came. She'd been hoping for it, wanting it to be bad so it'd cure her crush. Now he was here and naked – finally *naked* with her – she was bursting with anticipation.

'Don't tease me,' she begged. 'I need to come.'

He kissed her mouth and peeled her dress off. Slowly. It was more erotic than she'd expected, watching his face as he exposed her body. How the hell had he hidden this desire for so long?

When the dress was off she straddled his waist, breathing hard, and started to wriggle out of her knickers. But he took her arms, kissed each palm, and moved them out of the way. He ran his hands up her thighs and her back, drinking in the sight of her.

'I'm going to burst,' she said through gritted teeth.

Marcus sat up and kissed her, infuriatingly gentle. She wanted to crush their bodies together, she wanted him inside her, but she couldn't deny this teasing was making her hot as hell.

'I'm ready.' She squirmed on his waist. 'Just fuck me.'

Feather-light strokes on her back, then his hands working deep in her hair as he kissed her neck, then kneaded her buttocks when he moved his lips to her cleavage. She groaned in lust and frustration and curled her toes, right on the edge between pleasure and pain.

'Marcus,' she gasped. 'Please. I can't take it.'

He fumbled with her bra, and she remembered it'd been a long time for him. Years, maybe. She could be patient a few more minutes.

Especially since that meant it'd be over quickly.

When it was off he laid her on her back and ran a hand from her face to her hip. Her nipples were so hard they hurt.

'Please,' she begged again.

Marcus kissed her neck again, little kisses up and down, and pinched her nipple.

The sensation shot right down into her aching clitoris. She arched her back, trying to send his fingers south, but he moved to her other breast, and then her stomach, stroking and caressing every inch of skin.

'Marcus,' she groaned. 'Enough.'

He paused. 'You don't like it?'

He rubbed his thumb in the groove of her hip, his quick breaths hot on her neck.

'I like it,' she said through gritted teeth.

He kissed her mouth and she felt his smile. He stroked the inside of her leg with just the tips of his fingers and bolts of electricity slammed into her clitoris, inches away. Not long now. So close. But he slid his hands up to her stomach and she moaned, pressing her fingers into his sides and hoping it hurt.

'I want to feel you,' he murmured into her ear. 'Everywhere.'

It was so sexy and so maddening. He really meant everywhere, from her hair to her feet, every inch of skin caressed and stroked and tingling with pleasure. She lost track of time, in such a haze of sensuality that it felt like her body was singing. The nerves hummed even when he moved on, choosing a new place to worship.

She had no idea how long it was before he finished exploring, ending with her buttocks, and pulled her knickers off. She rolled a condom on to him, too eager to take her time and tease him like he had teased her. Ally gazed into his eyes as he looked down at her, then he kissed her mouth and in one fluid movement slid inside her.

Finally.

She exhaled a long, shaky breath and raised her knees to feel him deeper. Her skin still buzzed everywhere he had touched, singing, and now he was inside her too. Surrounding her. Filling her.

Even in her fantasies it hadn't been as good as this.

He rocked in and out of her and sighed her name.

'Mm. Harder,' she instructed, but she already knew he wouldn't, and in the back of her mind she knew why – because this would be the only time, and he wanted it to last.

'No.' She shook her head to drive the thought away.

'No?' He paused and gazed down at her.

'Yes. I mean yes.' She moved her knees higher and pressed her palms against his back. Her orgasm was building, each gentle thrust rocking her that little bit higher. Not long now. Not to be rushed.

She scratched her fingernails down his back, gently, not enough to leave a mark. Just wanting his skin to tingle like hers was.

'Mmm,' he sighed, right into her ear.

Her orgasm was so powerful she forgot her surroundings. All she could feel was his body on top of her and in her and hers contracting around him, not wanting to let him go.

His muscles tightened under her hands and he thrust into her harder, again and again, then froze and relaxed on top of her. He made barely any noise as he came, just soft sighs in her ear. She stroked his hair and felt him soften inside her but didn't want him to withdraw.

Eventually he moved, slipping out of her and rolling on to his back. Ally turned on to her side and stroked his face as he watched her.

'I have to go,' he said quietly.

'Why?'

'I left the dogs with my friend Paul, but I told him I'd be back tonight.'

'Paul knows where you are?'

He nodded. 'Don't worry, he doesn't know Sam. And he and Julie . . . don't get on, so there's no risk of her finding out and telling Sam.'

Oh man, she wished he hadn't mentioned Sam. She'd been doing well pretending Marcus was just a random guy she'd met.

She wondered what Marcus had said about her to this Paul. Had he really been thinking about her as much as she had about him?

'I like Paul,' she said. 'Paul's a nice guy. He'll look after the dogs until breakfast. Or maybe lunch. I don't have work until two tomorrow.'

He stroked circles on her hip and took a moment to reply. 'You know we can't do this again.'

Yes, she knew, but she didn't want to think about it. 'Tonight, we can. Just one night. Then we'll forget about it.'

'Forget about it.'

'Right.' She nodded. 'It never happened.'

He hesitated. 'One night. OK. One night.'

He called Paul, who was indeed a nice guy that sounded delighted his friend wanted to stay out all night. Then he pulled her to him and started driving her crazy all over again.

CHAPTER SIXTEEN

At Sam's house on Monday, Brendan occupied Ally's usual place beside him on the sofa. The two of them seemed unable to stop touching for a moment. Sam tried to eat popcorn with his left hand, holding Brendan's with his right, and spilled most of it on the floor.

'Come and sit with me.' Rachel patted the arm of her chair, but Ally took a cushion and sat on the floor. She took a grim satisfaction in the discomfort of the hardwood floor under the thin cushion.

In Sam's living room, drinking his wine and eating his food, she felt like a fraud. Anything less than her usual chirpiness would only confuse and upset him, but lying to him with every false smile was awful. He was so happy, gazing at Brendan with the kind of look Harry reserved for Ally, and all she could imagine was that happiness being ripped out of him if he knew what she'd done.

When she couldn't take it any more she slipped into the kitchen for some deep breaths.

'Ally?'

She spun around. Sam leaned against the doorway.

She forced a smile. 'I'm just getting some wine. Sorry, I should have asked.'

'Nah, it's fine.' He licked his lips. 'You do like Brendan, don't you?'

'Course. I wouldn't have introduced you otherwise, would I?'

'It's just you haven't looked at me once. Like you're avoiding me.'

She met his eyes and tried not to see his father's dark, thick eyelashes or the line of his nose. 'Haven't I? I didn't mean to. I'll make sure to distribute my vacant stares equally.'

Sam looked happier. 'OK. As long as we're good.'

Ally hugged him, and tried to transmit a silent apology with it. The first of several thousand. 'Of course. You're my favourite male best friend.'

'You're my favourite blonde best friend.'

'Damn right.' She kissed his cheek and carried the wine back to the table.

But as much as she tried she couldn't look Sam in the eye without wanting to cry. To break down and beg his forgiveness, even though she didn't deserve it. From the corner of her eye she saw him casting worried glances at her and before he could confront her again she claimed a headache and left early.

When he called the next day to see how she was, his concern made her so guilty she burst into tears. Sam was so worried she had to beg him not to come and see her, insisting she had a bad migraine making her sensitive and overtired. She carried on the lie beyond all plausibility, claiming she was ill until the weekend. Reluctantly admitting she was better, she made plans with Mum on Saturday and Sunday so she had an excuse not to see him.

The mounting lies made her feel as bad as seducing Sam's father had.

* * *

Ally knew she was pushing her luck when she claimed illness again on the following Monday. She told Rachel her usual awful period pains were in full force and she couldn't face socialising. But when she answered the doorbell to find Sam on her doorstep, she couldn't think of anything to say.

'What's wrong?' he said, the moment he came into view. 'You're avoiding us.'

Ally was so tired from broken sleep that she burst into tears again. Sam's hug made her feel better and worse. He coaxed her up the stairs and on to the sofa, where he put his arms around her again and patted her back.

'What is it, Ally?' His deep voice in her ear was familiar and reassuring.

'I did something terrible,' she said with a sniff.

'What?'

'I can't tell you.' That was the rub. Every night she tossed and turned in bed imagining telling him, imagining his reaction. Her thoughts went in circles and ended in the same conclusion: the only person it would benefit was herself. It'd cause unspeakable pain to Sam, not to mention Marcus.

Sam pulled back and squeezed her hands. 'Why do you have to avoid us because of it?'

'Because I feel guilty.'

'But it isn't terrible to us, silly.' His brown eyes were lighter than his father's and lacked the laughter lines. But they were just as beautiful to her, for different reasons.

'It is. If you knew, you'd hate me.'

Sam was shaking his head even before she'd finished speaking. 'I could never hate you.'

Ally sniffed. 'You would, Sam. I wish I could tell you because I hate having a secret from you. But I can't and it's eating me up. I never want to hurt you.'

'Have all the secrets you want, just don't avoid me.'

Ally couldn't stop her tears, and Sam drew her back into a hug.

'I love you, Sam. And I'm so sorry for what I've done.'

'I love you too. And whatever it is, I still love you.'

He patted her back like a dog until she stopped crying and pulled away to blow her nose.

'I don't deserve you, Sammy,' she said, wiping her eyes.

'Look, this is getting far too mushy. Stop whining, goldfish brain.'

Ally laughed. 'You can talk. You look like Grumpy Cat when the vet's rectal thermometer has just disappeared.'

'And that's why I love you.' Sam kissed her forehead, then went over to her DVD shelf. 'Me and you, movie night. *Anchorman* or *Life of Brian*?'

* * *

Clearing the air with Sam was the first step in moving on. The second would be to get back to dating other men.

OK, so their night together hadn't quite driven Marcus from her mind like she'd thought it would. OK, so actually she was thinking about him even more, and her vibrator had paid for itself several times over, but the night with him was history, and she had to move on. That was the one and only time she'd had sex since July. No, end of June. It was *September*. Had she ever gone that long without sex? She needed to get back in the game before her virginity grew back.

She had a shift at the salon from late morning to evening. It was a busy Friday, and although the distraction was nice, she was glad when it was time to shut up shop. She swept the floors while Micha dealt with the piles of towels and sheets that needed to be washed.

Jogging home, she wondered if she had the energy for going to bars or clubs. Well, she was going whether she did or not. She'd wear her lucky red dress, so she could wipe away the association with him. Perhaps even the hot pink underwear too. She'd bet tonight's man wouldn't wait so long to get them off her, or be as fascinated with her body.

She was so lost in thought, with her head bowed at the pavement, that she nearly walked into the figure outside her flat.

'Ally?'

She stepped back and gaped. 'Marcus.' Her mouth didn't want to work. 'What are you doing here?'

He looked pissed off. Jaw set, eyes hard. 'To see you.'

What had she done?

'You want to come in?'

He nodded. The brooding, dark look suited him. So did his burgundy shirt. Her nipples hardened and it hurt when her T-shirt brushed against them.

They were still standing in the street and staring at each other.

'Come in,' she repeated, and unlocked her door. 'Do you want a drink?'

'No.'

He stomped up the stairs while she closed the door behind her, and she bit her lip. Maybe he blamed her for seducing him, and now he was angry about his guilt.

In the living room, she perched on the edge of the sofa. Marcus stood by the table and glared at her.

'What have I done?' she asked in a small voice.

'I can't get you out of my head.'

Her heart leapt. Knowing he was suffering the same as her was a perverse comfort. Was she turning into some sort of sadist who enjoyed people's pain?

'Oh. I'm sorry.'

'I'm not blaming you.' He paced the living room. 'I don't know why I'm here. I promised myself I wouldn't come back. But nothing works.' He stopped and glared at her. 'I even joined a dating site. But it's not sex I want. It's you.'

Ally felt the weight of his anger and tried not to cry in case it irritated him more. 'I'm sorry.' Her voice came out high.

He shook his head, then grasped her arms and pulled her to him. 'I'm not blaming you.'

His touch sent waves of tingles all down her body.

'I wanted it to go away, too,' she said. 'I really thought one time would get it out of our systems.'

'Yes. I was hoping it'd be bad.'

'Mm. But it wasn't.'

'No,' he agreed.

He sat on the sofa and Ally sat next to him.

'Maybe if we did it again,' she offered, 'and tried to make it bad?'

He looked doubtful. 'How?'

'Um.' Ally thought. 'I don't like being hurt. Like hard bites, or hard slaps.'

Marcus looked pained. 'I . . . don't think I can do that.'

'No, OK.' She thought again. 'Or guys that have watched too much porn and think women really like to be degraded. Like, calling me a dirty whore.'

He seemed to shrink.

'No,' Ally agreed. 'Maybe not. Well, what don't you like?'

'I don't know.' He gave a small shrug. 'I haven't done much.'

What could she do? Lie there and stare at the ceiling in the way that'd turned Jason off so much? Well, she hadn't done a whole lot the first time with Marcus, and that'd still been amazing. Maybe she could give him a bad blow job, with too much teeth and choking noises.

But she didn't want to. She wanted to make him feel as incredible as he'd made her feel.

'Ally?' He touched her arm and then, like he couldn't help himself, ran his hand up to her neck and stroked her jaw.

The explosion of lust was instant and overpowering. The touch of his fingers brought everything back – every sensation, every satisfying orgasm of that night.

Without thinking, she straddled his lap and then remembered this was about getting rid of their attraction. 'I can make weird noises.'

'I like your noises.'

It was really difficult to think when he was thumbing the grooves of her hips. 'Um. I could wear granny pants. Well, I could buy some and then wear them.' She closed her eyes as he ran his hands up her back, inside her T-shirt. 'Mm. I have this really tight corset thing. You'll like that. Takes ages to get it off, so you can have your fun while I die of frustration.'

'That does sound fun.' He was tugging on strands of her hair. Way too gently to hurt, but enough to make her scalp tingle.

'Want me to get it?'

'Aren't we supposed to be making it bad?'

Guiltily, Ally stopped unbuttoning his shirt. 'Right.'

He gazed into her eyes and she couldn't help slipping her hands on to his chest. 'Oh, look, we've done it once, or a few times, so a few more won't hurt. Why don't we just carry on until we get bored? I think my record is about three months, but the average is more like three weeks. Then it'll be properly out of our systems and we'll be glad to see the back of each other.'

'What if Sam finds out?'

Ally gazed out of the window in frustration. That was the problem. But she couldn't feel guiltier than she already did, and the betrayal had already been committed. She doubted Sam would be any less gutted to know they'd done it just once.

'We just have to be careful,' she said, hating herself for every word. 'Cover our tracks.'

'How?'

'I don't know. I haven't had to sneak around before.'

'Nor have I.' He rested his forehead on her shoulder and she nuzzled his luscious hair. 'Although Julie does drop hints about dating into every conversation we have. I think she's dying to know if I'm looking.'

Oh, god. A jealous kind-of-ex-wife was the last thing she needed, and Marcus didn't need any more complication in his situation.

'Maybe this isn't such a good idea,' she said, closing her eyes and breathing him in. 'I don't want to hurt anyone but especially Sam.'

'I wish I was someone else.' The longing was evident in his voice and, when she drew back, his stare was so intense that she almost believed he could make it happen.

He wanted her as much as she wanted him and that made her horny as hell.

'Well, we can be other people,' she said. 'Call me Alicia. Or Lissy.'

He contemplated, then shook his head. 'You're an Ally. I was Marc, in uni. I'll be him.'

'Marc.' It tasted right. 'OK. You're Marc, a student, with no wife and no kids.'

He pulled away, still looking troubled, and tucked her hair behind her ear. 'And we'll get bored soon.' It sounded like a question.

'Definitely. Give me a few weeks.'

After a deep breath, he nodded.

Ally stroked his cheek. 'Actually, be Marcus again for a minute.' She slid off his lap and sat next to him. 'We still need to help Sam. All of this started because you wanted him to come out, and we failed miserably. If we can show him you won't disown him, well . . . at least we'll have done one thing right.'

He considered this. 'We need a new plan.'

'Right. I have an idea.'

It didn't take long to explain. It was simple, really, and they should have thought of it before the Bounce-alcohol-blurting-out plan.

And it eased her conscience, just a little.

When there was nothing else to discuss he kissed her, tentatively, and she tried to see a single man, unrelated to Sam. 'Then let's try it, Marc.'

'I have to go in an hour. Can't keep dumping the dogs on Paul.'

'Only an hour? Don't spend all of it undressing me, will you?'

'Spoilsport.'

CHAPTER SEVENTEEN

⌐

*P*ost-workout showers always left Ally feeling warm and relaxed. The hot water soothed the endorphin buzz into a pleasant, sleepy hum that made her limbs feel supple and heavy. She sat in the changing room in a towel and dried her hair with one hand while she checked her phone with another.

Four missed calls and a voicemail. A thrill fingered its way up her spine as she hit the icon with her thumb. Maybe Marc was free, and had tried to get hold of her in his lunch hour. He was much stricter than her about not using his phone at work.

But it wasn't Marc. All the calls were from Sam. Worried, she called voicemail and waited impatiently for the recorded voice to give its spiel. Then the new message played.

'Ally, call me back as soon as you get this,' Sam hissed. 'My dad came over, and—'

She dropped the phone and pressed a hand to her chest, unable to catch her breath.

Shit. Shit.

Why the hell hadn't Marc warned her he was going to confess?

Even if he didn't want to face her being upset, he could at least have sent a message and blocked her number. This was just cruel, selfish.

Cruel and selfish weren't two words she associated with him.

She gingerly picked up the phone and, with a knot in her stomach, played the message again.

'Ally, call me back as soon as you get this. My dad came over, and he's asking all these questions about you and me. I think he knows something's up. I thought if you came over . . . Fucking hell, Ally, I wish I'd never started this. I keep dragging you into it and . . . Look, I need to go. Sorry for whispering. I'm hiding in the bathroom. Just call me, please?'

With a huge sigh of relief, she called. It was several rings before Sam picked up.

'I'm hiding in the bathroom again,' he said.

'You're not on the toilet, are you?'

'It's the tap running.'

'Thank god. Sam, listen. Why don't you just tell your dad the truth?'

There was a long silence. 'It's been so long I don't know what to say. All the lies, all these years.'

'He'll understand. I don't know him that well –' she moved her weight from one foot to the other – 'but I got the impression he was pretty relaxed about stuff. And it's your mum's reaction you're worried about, not his, right?'

'Yeah. But what if he tells her?'

'Ask him not to. They aren't married any more so his loyalties aren't split.'

'But when they get back together? I can just imagine Gavin's wedding, with us pretending to be a couple and my dad knowing it's all fake.'

Ally dug her fingernails into her palm. 'Cross that bridge when –' *if* – 'you come to it.'

Silence.

'Won't it feel good?' she asked. 'To not have to lie to him any longer?'

'Yeah,' he said finally. 'Maybe. OK. No promises, but I'll try.'

'You can do it. Love you.'

'Love you, too.'

Half an hour later, he sent a text to say he'd done it. A month ago, Ally would never have tried to convince him to come out, but now she knew how Marc would react. At least one good thing had come out of this affair.

* * *

Marc turned up shortly after the text. Suspecting he would, Ally had left the door on the latch and heard him come up the stairs as she washed a carrot.

When he found her, he picked her up and kissed her with a broad grin. 'You convinced him. You're a genius.'

'He told you everything?'

Marc nodded. 'The fake engagement, his boyfriend, the lot. Brendan sounds great.'

'He is. So go on, how did you do it?' She stepped out of his arms and turned back to the carrot.

There was silence. She looked over her shoulder and found Marc staring at her with intense eyes.

'Hungry?'

'That dress.'

She looked down. It was a champagne bodycon dress and in it, according to him, she had looked naked as she walked towards his car from the train station last time she had visited. He'd driven way over the speed limit, and barely took time to shut his front door behind them before he pinned her against the wall in his hallway and took her right there.

'Oh, that dress,' she said. 'Such a shame it's too tight for underwear. It'd show through, you know.'

She turned back to the carrot and smiled to herself. A moment later, his arm snaked around her waist and he kissed her neck.

'You smell of raspberries,' he informed her, nudging her hair with his nose.

'What kind of weirdo notices how someone smells?'

She felt his lips curve on her neck.

'Anyway,' she said, 'this is very unprofessional behaviour for my sous chef. Make yourself useful and slice this pepper. We're having Thai red curry.'

He reached for the pepper and a knife with his arms either side of her, and nudged her carrot to one side of the chopping board.

'Right side is mine,' she said, shifting it back. 'You should know that.'

'How? We never sleep.'

He brushed her nipple with the back of his hand as he moved the pepper, and directed his exhales to the sweet spot in the crook of her neck. She fought a smile and ignored him. For once, she was going to ignore *his* hints and let him get worked up until *he* was begging her to touch him.

Instead, she grasped the carrot at the base and ran her fingers down it slowly, as if brushing off the water droplets. One remained on the tip. She collected it with the tip of one finger, turned her head so Marc could see, and placed it on her tongue.

His eyes flashed, but when he bent his head to kiss her, she turned away and tutted. 'Will you please concentrate on the cooking.'

'Fine.' He pushed one leg between hers. His cock was hardening, and the dress was very thin. The seam of his jeans rubbed against her inner thigh when he moved, which was more than necessary.

She fought an urge to turn around and kiss him. Focus on the vegetables.

Now she had to bite her lip. He hadn't quite cut the bell pepper in half, so the edges curved into lips. And not the mouth kind. He stroked the flesh inside to gather the seeds, then made a hook with two fingers and scooped them out slowly.

Last time they were together she'd been pressed up against the wall of his shower as he did that to her G-spot, until she came so hard he had to hold her up to stop her crashing into the tiles.

He must have heard her breathing grow faster, if he couldn't feel it with his arms around her ribs.

'What a perfect pepper.' He ran a finger down the groove in the centre, and Ally squeezed her thighs.

'Chef,' he said. 'Permission to wash my hands? You never know where a stray seed might end up.'

'Permission definitely granted.'

He shimmied them over a foot to the sink, and she watched his muscular hands as he soaped up and rinsed them off.

Now she had to distract him, because chopping the carrot into pieces might spoil the atmosphere somewhat. 'Hey, sous chef. Put some coconut oil in the wok to heat.'

'Yes, ma'am.'

He had to let go of her, and she took the opportunity to quickly slice the carrot – and to remind herself that she was denying him this time. No giving in until he begged.

'Dammit.' He sounded calm. 'The cap is broken. Oil everywhere.'

He put a leg between hers again and nudged her knees apart.

'See,' he whispered into her ear, and curled his hands around her bare thighs. His hands were indeed slick with warm oil – he'd remembered what she said in their massage lesson; that oil should be warmed in the hands before being applied to the skin – and the fragrance of coconut was delicious.

'You could've used a dish towel,' she said, voice unsteady as she gripped the edge of the counter. His hands rubbed circles to the inside of her thigh, and then glided slowly upwards.

He kissed her neck in reply.

'We need to finish cooking,' she said, closing her eyes and curling her toes on the linoleum.

He pushed her knees further apart, and brushed her lips with a slick knuckle.

Ally moaned, and pressed her buttocks into his erection so his fingers had more space to move.

'Aren't you hungry?' she tried in one last-ditch attempt at the whole Make Him Beg thing.

'Very.' He yanked the dress above her hips and knelt behind

her. Ally grabbed the counter and moaned as his tongue curled around her clit and his clever hands held her thighs.

He was good at this. So good. He took long, slow licks, tasting her, then circled her clit until she was panting.

She cried out when she was on the edge, when it was almost too intense to take, and in a flash he stood up, lifted her knee on to the counter and slid his cock into her. She drew up her other knee, trusting him to support her, and with her legs spread wide she felt deliciously exposed.

He kissed her neck, and even as he held her up his fingers stroked the inside of her thighs until her clitoris ached. She braced one hand on the window sill and moved the other under her dress, mimicking the circling of his tongue until she orgasmed.

Her forehead was still pressed against the cool window pane when he came with a groan, and it was only in the moments after that she realised her knees were aching from banging on the hard counter.

Gran was right about those. Wear them out while you can.

She turned around until she was sitting on the edge of the counter, her legs around his waist. 'Was it the dress or the pepper?'

'The Thai basil in your hair.' He plucked a sage-green leaf from her hair.

'I had that there the whole time?'

'Yep.'

She rubbed her oily thigh with a finger. 'I must smell like a Thai curry.'

'Mm.' He sniffed her neck, then pulled her into his arms. 'Now, about dinner.'

'Yeah, I think we have some disinfecting to do first.'

'Then screw dinner.' He lifted her up and carried her to the bedroom.

* * *

Later, Ally dozed with her head in the crook of his neck while he stroked her shoulder.

'Ally?'

'Mm?'

'Don't take this the wrong way, but why are you single?'

She walked her fingers up his stomach. 'I eat my fuck buddies after mating. You're OK because of the vasectomy.'

He winced. 'I wish you wouldn't call it that.'

Ally snorted. 'After all the things I've whispered to you, you get uppity about me saying fuck? Are you one of those men who thinks ladies shouldn't swear?'

Marc looked away.

'You're not, are you?'

'No. Seriously, why are you single? You have everything, but you talk like dating is trouble.'

'I'm pretty hard to live with.' She shimmied her head on to the pillow so they were face to face, his arm still around her shoulder. 'I know you find it funny when I'm not listening but most people get annoyed. Understandably. And I'm forgetful and messy and impatient and I always have to be doing some-thing. And even if a guy can put up with all that I get bored of him, like I told you. I'm a bit like a parrot – you need to keep buying me new toys to keep me occupied because I'm ditzy but also playful and easily distracted. One of my boyfriends got a parrot. He named it after me and taught it to say, "What did you say?"'

His laugh tickled her neck. 'You're not ditzy. You're really telling me there's never been anyone who held your interest? Nobody you wanted to spend your life with?'

'When I was younger and even ditzier, I used to get these insane crushes and think we were going to get married and live on a houseboat together. Always guys older than me . . .' She glanced at Marc and cleared her throat. 'I mean, like, I was a teenager and they were graduates. They just used me for a good time and left me when someone with wife material came along. I'm always attracted to cockwombles, but these days I don't get attached.'

Marc was silent, curling a strand of her hair around his finger.

Just as she was dozing off again, enjoying the gentle tugging at her scalp, he said, 'You know I'm not using you for a good time, don't you?'

Ally opened her eyes. 'Sure you are. So am I. Nothing wrong with that, as long as we both know it.'

CHAPTER EIGHTEEN

Marc cancelled his next visit because some cockwomble had delivered the wrong length of steel at work. Or something. Ally wasn't really listening, too busy biting back irritation. Not at him, exactly, just at the situation – which was that she was very horny and her favourite solution was no longer available.

OK, she had no claim on his time, but things were so new it was still exciting to see him and she'd been looking forward to it, dammit. Well, not really new . . . but it didn't feel like two months.

She made him promise to come on Tuesday, and she wore her nothing's-gonna-stop-me outfit: a red lacy balcony bra, with knickers that sat low on her hips, and her lucky dress – the scarlet one she'd worn to Blondie. With her clothes laid out on the freshly made bed, she went to the bathroom to get ready.

Ugh.

She stared in dismay at the toilet paper with its treacherous red stain, two days early. Even her ovaries didn't like routine, damn them.

With a sigh, she turned the shower off and ran the bath. Of course it hadn't been excitement making her stomach flutter. The cramps were coming, and for the next five days she'd be having as many hot baths as the water tank would allow. The rest of the time she'd lie on the sofa groaning.

Marc's phone went straight to voicemail. He was probably in the middle of laying tiles or something equally exciting, looking forward to laying her instead.

Damn human reproductive system. Evolution couldn't come up with something more convenient than this nonsense? How did fish do it? She'd never heard of a fish on its period, and wasn't it seahorses where the men had to give birth? Fish had the right idea.

She sent Marc a text telling him not to come, soaked in the bath until her fingers pruned then put her period knickers on, glaring at them as if it was their fault.

Stereotypes be damned: she grabbed a carton of Phish Food ice cream from the freezer and sat in front of the TV with a spoon, examining the chocolate-chip fish with a new-found respect. There was nothing good on, not even repeats of *Come Dine With Me*. Unheard of. The universe was obviously conspiring against her.

She called Rachel and invited her over, but Rachel was going on a date with her fiancé.

'Traitor,' Ally grumbled.

Rachel offered to cancel, but Ally refused. As much as she didn't like Rachel's fiancé, Rachel did, and they got hardly any time alone together.

As she hung up, an invisible boa constrictor tightened around her waist and flexed its muscles. She made herself a hot-water bottle and lay on top of it on the sofa, listening to a documentary about whales. There were lots of things she hadn't known about whales, and thought she would've got through life just fine without knowing them, but the remote was too far away to reach without getting off the hot-water bottle.

The documentary was almost finished when the doorbell rang. With a groan, she heaved herself off the sofa and held the hot-water bottle against her belly as she went downstairs.

Rachel was on the doorstep, and The Man waved at Ally from their car. Ally waved half-heartedly back and took the bag Rachel held out.

'Peanut Butter Cup,' Rachel informed her. 'I couldn't leave you without ice cream.'

'Love you. Even though you're a traitor.' Ally kissed her cheek and, as she pulled back, saw Marc's car pulling up behind Rachel's.

Oh shit. Talk about a traitor.

Ally lifted her hand up as if she were stretching and made a 'stop' sign, but it was no good. Marc was getting out of the car.

'OK, thanks for the ice cream, see you later!' Ally forced a smile at Rachel that, judging by her expression, gave off 'Here's Johnny' vibes.

'Ally? Are you OK?' Rachel asked.

Marc was at the gate now with a bag in hand. He glanced up, saw Rachel, and stopped dead.

Ally's brain went into full-blown panic mode, and instead of fight or flight, she froze.

As if in slow motion, Rachel turned around. 'Oh. Hello.'

Marc looked as terrified as Ally felt.

'Rach!' Ally found her feet and stumbled forward, almost knocking Rachel over. She steadied them, then whispered, 'He's shy. Love you, but go away.'

Rachel gave her a knowing smile then took a long look at Marc. A flicker of a frown crossed her face.

She'd seen the resemblance. Faint, but there.

'Come on, Steve!' Ally shouted, far too loudly. 'Rachel's leaving.'

Marc shrank into the hedge as Rachel passed him.

'Bye, Steve. Look after her.'

It seemed to take for ever for Rachel to get into the car, belt up and drive away. Her fiancé waved at Ally through the passenger window, and she was too distracted to make a face at him.

'We got away with it.' Ally leaned against the wall for support when the car was out of sight.

Marc looked worried.

'Don't worry. She'd never guess in a million years.'

'I hope so.'

This was Ally's fault. Why had she just texted him, and not called? 'I sent you a text. I guess you didn't see it.'

'I did.'

'Oh. So why are you here?'

He seemed confused. 'You said you weren't feeling well.'

'Yeah. Well, I have my period.'

Mrs Cooper's net curtains twitched, and a beady eye appeared. Ally waved at her, dragged Marc inside the hallway, and closed the door.

'I don't do period sex,' she said. 'My body goes all weird, and it hurts.'

'OK. Got it. No sex.'

She nodded and waited for him to leave. He raised his eyebrows.

'Do you want something?' She wanted to lie down.

'I don't understand. I have to go?'

'If you're expecting a blow job, I—'

'Of course I'm bloody not.'

Ally was taken aback at his angry tone. 'Well what are you here for, then?'

He recoiled like she'd slapped him. 'You don't even want to talk to me unless we're having sex? That's really the only thing you want from me?'

Were they talking different languages? Which one of them was missing the point?

She shrugged helplessly. 'What else?'

Marc's face was awful. He turned back to the door, then to Ally, then back again. 'OK. I'll go.'

'Wait, Marc!' She grabbed his sleeve, not wanting to let him go when he was upset. 'I don't understand. What do you want?'

He stared at her like she'd gone insane. 'To make you feel better? Cook you something? Watch a film?'

'Oh.' Silence while he stared sadly at her. She didn't want him to look like that, but she didn't understand. 'But . . . we're just doing this to get it out of our systems. Watching films isn't going to help.'

Those brown eyes hadn't looked away from her for a second. 'Are you getting me out of your system?'

'Not yet. But I will soon.'

'Oh, right. Good.' His voice was toneless.

'Then we won't have to feel guilty any more.'

'No. Right. That would be nice.'

'Yeah.' Ally ran her toe along a mark on the carpet. She'd have to buy some carpet shampoo, because the vacuum cleaner clearly wasn't getting it. It looked like a grass stain, maybe.

'What?' she said, registering Marc's voice.

He looked at her so fondly, and so sadly, that the butterflies fought with the boa constrictor for who could hurt her stomach the most.

'Am I allowed to stay?' he said. 'Even if I'm not performing a service?'

'If you like. I'm really not much fun though.'

'Ally, you're always fun.'

'Not when a boa constrictor is twisting my internal organs into one mega-organ.'

'You should be in bed.'

The snake clenched tighter and she doubled over, sinking almost to the ground. If the first day was this bad, the third and fourth were going to be hell.

'I'll just sit here,' she mumbled. 'It's nice here. Oh man, I wish I was a fish.'

Without a word he lifted her up, carried her to bed, and left. She couldn't blame him. Who wanted to sit around and listen to someone moan?

She almost jumped out of her skin when he returned. 'Jeez, don't creep up on me. I thought you'd gone.'

He tucked the freshly filled hot-water bottle behind her back and sat on the edge of the bed. 'Want me to get you some painkillers?'

She shook her head. 'I get headaches if I take too many, and a couple of paracetamol won't do the trick.'

'What else can I do to help?'

'I don't know. Knock me out and wake me up in five days?'

He shook his head. 'Who'd water your cactus? I'll have to do the best I can with you awake.' He lay down and drew her into his arms, sandwiching the hot-water bottle between them and rubbing slow circles on her stomach. 'Is it like this every month?'

He didn't seem at all uncomfortable about the subject, like some of her lovers had been. Living with a woman for thirty years must have made him used to it. Maybe Julie had bad cramps too, if he knew to refill the hot-water bottle without asking.

She banished the image of him soothing Julie like this. It made her stomach feel worse.

'It's always pretty bad. I'll warn you next time.'

His rubbing slowed. 'So I'll stay home? You really don't want me here?'

'I'm not very good company when I'm like this.' She snuggled back against him. His warmth was nice, and his gentle hand on her stomach.

'Are you going to tell me when you're getting bored of me?' he asked. 'Or just message me one day not to come any more?'

'Hey, I wouldn't do it over a message. I hate that. I'll at least call you. You might get bored first, anyway.'

He was silent for a moment. 'Did you say you want to be a fish?'

'Mm. I think they've got the evolution thing right. We made a wrong turn somewhere.'

More silence. Then, 'I think it was when we gave up fur. Look at all the disasters we've had trying to make up for it . . . dungarees, sandals with socks, shoulder pads . . .'

'Is this a roundabout way of telling me you have a furry fetish?'

'No. Just that if you're going to dress up, I'd rather Catwoman than a haddock.'

She smiled, glad that he'd come after all, and arched her back as he kneaded her belly with his knuckles.

'You don't have to go to work like this, do you?' he asked.

'Nope. That's the beauty of working shifts. I'll be watching DVDs and sea-life documentaries until the boredom becomes worse than the pain. Then I'll go back to work.'

'I can take the days off and keep you company.'

Oh man, that would be nice.

She shook her head.

'Ally, I can't leave you like this.' He squeezed her tighter, and the heat from the water bottle radiated through her aching back. Lying like this for five days wouldn't be so bad, except that she'd worry the whole time about Julie finding out or Sam turning up.

'I'll be fine. I've got my books and Rachel will probably come over tomorrow. What's in the bag?'

He'd left the carrier bag in the living room. 'Wine, and a bar of Lindt. Dark, with sea salt.'

'I love that!'

'I know. It's not a coincidence that I bought it.'

'Well, I'm not used to men listening to me. Gimme it.'

He kissed her shoulder before rolling off the bed, then came back with the chocolate. Ally broke off several squares for him, then nibbled the bar. 'Rachel bought me the sweetest ice cream in the world. I'm going to be at the gym for a solid week when this is over.'

'You do enjoy it, don't you? The gym. You don't feel like you have to go?'

'I love it. Well, you know how it feels after a good workout. Nearly as good as a good orgasm. Nearly. Maybe I should be a gym instructor, but I'm afraid I'd get sacked for hitting on the customers. It'd have to be more fun than making sandwiches.'

His lips curved into a smile on her shoulder. 'I thought you liked your job? Well, jobs.'

'I do, but . . .' But what? He was right. It suited her to work shifts, to keep busy, to be on her feet. What was she actually upset about? 'You're right. I'm being silly. All my friends are having babies and getting married and getting promoted and I'm just trying to remember what day it is and crying when I kill yet another potted plant because I forgot to water it. I know not everyone can be clever and there's plenty of things I'm good at, but I wish I could be clever enough just so that people . . . I don't know . . . thought more of me than my body or my face, I suppose. But then I like it when people admire my body so . . . I'm just impossible.'

'You think people don't like you for you?'

She winced and arched her back into the water bottle. 'Yes. Some people. But if they were asked that thing, you know, how to describe me in three words, what would most of them say? Distracted? Ditzy? Gullible? Hyperactive? Nobody would say I was reliable, or clever, or someone you'd want around in a crisis, or anything like that. I'd be the first person they'd eat on a desert island.'

Marc snorted with laughter. 'No, Ally. They'd say you're funny, and sweet, and kind, and definitely someone you'd want around in a crisis. Because you'd never let it get the better of you. If you were stranded on a desert island, you'd be enthusing about the sunbathing opportunities. Or how good coconuts are for your skin.'

'Yeah, see? I'm vain.'

He lifted his head to give her a look. 'Self-deprecation doesn't suit you. Cut it out. Anyway, you're not vain. You look beautiful without any effort. So beautiful that people think you must've made an effort.'

'Flatterer.' She bumped her butt against him.

'It's true. I've seen you first thing in the morning.'

He was so sweet.

'I don't just want to look nice, though. I want to achieve something using my brain, not my face or body.'

'Not many people can paint like you can.'

'Mm. But my brain lets me down when I try to do it as more than a hobby.'

'It's still a talent that doesn't come from your looks. What exactly happened when you tried it as a business?'

Ally sighed at the memory. 'I told you before – I was hopeless. I forgot to return calls and emails. When I did, I got distracted in the middle of the brief and painted the wrong thing. Or I made an appointment and then forgot it, or was so late they were too annoyed to let me in, or on time but on the wrong day. Even when I did manage to produce a painting, so many of them wouldn't pay the price they'd agreed and I can't play hardball. I just want to cry when people are being unfair. 'And even if everything had gone perfectly, I wouldn't have been able to make enough to support myself. There just aren't that many people wanting paintings these days, or willing to pay much for it.'

'Hmm. I think we can deal with the organisation problems. But maybe you'd need to offer something unique to get more customers and charge a premium?'

'Well, I had this idea. Because I get bored doing the same thing all the time, right? So I thought of this kind of package service for weddings. I'd do a spa day hen party with nails and hair and facials and all the stuff I do at the salon. And then hair and make-up on the wedding day, with photos and then a painting of the bride and groom. They could get the whole package or parts of it.

But I'd have to do a whole load of marketing and stuff to get anybody interested and . . . I don't know. It just seems like hard work.' She stopped and looked around at him. 'See? That's my problem. I want all the reward with none of the responsibility. It's no wonder people think of me as an amusing little child.'

Marc tucked flyaway strands of hair behind her ear. 'Ally, nobody could think of you as a child. Trust me. Anyway, being an adult doesn't mean getting a high-flying job and making yourself miserable. You're a different kind of adult. One determined to enjoy life. That doesn't make you a child.'

'Yeah well, you would say that, because you're fuc—' He winced, and Ally changed tack. 'Having sex with me.'

'I'd say it whether I was fuh-having sex with you or not.' His arms tightened around hers and she snuggled into him.

They watched movies – Marc tried to look enthusiastic about Ally's romcoms, but was obviously relieved when she put one of Sam's comedies on. Halfway through the movie she drifted off to sleep, and woke to find the start menu looping on the screen. Her insides felt like someone had knotted and unknotted them several times, but waking up cocooned in his warm arms with his fingers tracing circles on her stomach, she didn't care.

Until she looked at her clock.

'Marc,' she said heavily. 'You should go. You have work in the morning.'

His hands slowed. 'Will you be OK?'

'Yes.'

But when he stood up and his warmth disappeared, she was seized with panic. Alone for the next five days in her cold bed, eating crap and crying. She already felt on the edge of a big sob, worn down by the pain, and when Marc leaned over to kiss her cheek she bit her lip to stop herself crying.

'Ally?' He knelt on the floor beside the bed and cupped her face. 'Do you want me to stay?'

'No.' Ally smiled so he wouldn't feel bad about leaving her. 'If I need company I'll call my friends.'

'Your friends. Right.' His voice was dull. Maybe she'd reminded him of Sam, and he felt guilty? Before she could ask what was wrong, he tucked the covers around her and left.

Ally curled up into a foetal position and hugged the hot-water bottle. What was wrong with her? It was nonsensical to be afraid of being alone. She'd always have Mum, and her sisters, and Rachel, and Sam.

Unless they found out what she was doing.

That must be what she was afraid of. Not Sam's dad leaving her – that was silly, they weren't even friends – but Sam leaving her. Marc didn't resemble his son that much, but her brain was conflating them anyway, and her different feelings for both of them. Sam was her friend, Marc was her sex buddy. Temporary sex buddy.

Why did she keep confusing them?

Screw the headache. She took three painkillers.

* * *

Ally stayed in bed the next day, not getting up until her doorbell rang in the afternoon. A deliveryman carried a large cardboard box into the living room for her and when he was gone she opened it to find a whole collection of goodies. DVDs, novels, colouring books, heat pads for her back, and packets of healthy snack foods. Wasabi peanuts, seaweed crackers with a note saying 'For your fish fantasies', trail mixes. Plus a box of Lindt chocolates.

She called Marc, ready to demand he return it all and get his money back, but he was so nervous she'd be angry that she melted.

'You're so sweet,' she said, suddenly ready to cry again. 'But you don't have to look after me. I'm just a sex buddy and I'm not even delivering the goods.'

'Forget the damn deliveries. I just want you to feel better.'

She was unwilling to hang up, even when she could hear someone calling him about a problem with a crane.

'I can come tonight,' he said in a soft, tempting voice. 'All evening.'

In his warm arms, watching her new DVDs while he stroked her stomach. Like lovers. They couldn't be lovers, no matter how good it felt to be in his arms.

'I told you – I've got friends for that. I'll call you when it's over.'

There was a pause. 'Right. Your friends. I forgot. Hope you feel better soon.'

He hung up, and she wished she hadn't said it. She would've let Jason come over if he had any interest in listening to her moan in pain, so why was she pushing Marc away?

CHAPTER NINETEEN

Ally was unsettled and restless. Work was dull, the gym was dull, even reading was dull. All she looked forward to was going out and, especially, Marc's visits. The days between them stretched like elastic, the tension in her stomach growing tauter until he arrived.

This was bad. And it couldn't be because of Marc – he was very much off limits, their arrangement a temporary thing, and it was unthinkable that she would want more from him than sex. He was only exciting because he was something new, something different, and that was all. She needed something else to occupy her, something that wouldn't drive Sam away.

She went to the library and printed off the forms she needed to start a new business. As soon as she worked out the costs she got cold feet. To do a proper job of it, with advertising, she'd have to spend most of her holiday fund, and the business would probably be as short-lived as a holiday. Only with less sun and more shame. Well, maybe less shame – she'd done some pretty naughty things with a cocktail waiter last time she was in Spain.

She left them on the bedside table and went to get ready for Marc. It was OK to enjoy him, as long as it was just sex.

* * *

'There's a fire,' Marc said later, in bed. He stroked her back while she rested her head on his chest.

Ally came out of her reverie, registered what he'd said, and closed her eyes. 'OK. Wake me before it reaches the bed.'

'It'll be too late by then. Smoke inhalation will get us.'

'Oh well. At least it'll be painless.'

He pushed her chin up with one finger until she looked at him. 'What were you thinking about that time?'

'Some guy.'

'Oh?' Marc kissed her nose.

'Mm. He's big.'

Marc paused. 'You mean . . .'

'Oh, both. And gorgeous. Every time I see his face I just . . . melt.'

'He sounds great.' He moved his clever fingers down her back and around her hips.

Ally arched her back. 'He is. Just my type. Dark, strong, handsome. And he's an animal. The moment he sees me he wants my clothes off.'

Marc paused again. 'You're talking about Harry, aren't you?'

'Yep.'

'I'll show you who's an animal.' He rolled on top of her with a deep growl, and bit her shoulder. Two orgasms had left her body feeling relaxed and heavy, but when he cupped her buttocks so her clitoris pressed against his cock, the pleasant buzz turned into tingling.

He moved to her neck, taking the sensitive skin between his teeth. Each nip walked the line between pain and pleasure, leaving Ally hyper-aware of every sensation, her body on edge and crying out for more whilst afraid he would give it. She kept very still, fighting conflicting urges to arch her back, to push him away, to pull his mouth up to hers and kiss him hard. The pressure built until he ceased the little bites and sucked hard on her neck. She buried her fingers in his springy hair and clamped her legs around his back so his erection pushed harder against her hot skin.

'This isn't how the animals do it,' she said between breaths. 'I saw it on a documentary.'

He reared up on his knees, ran a hand down to her thigh, and turned her on to all fours. The strength in his hands made her toes curl against the sheets.

'Like this?' he said into her ear, pushing her knees apart until she almost unbalanced and then bracing her with his legs. If he moved, she would collapse. At his mercy.

'Something like that,' she said, but it ended in a moan as he cupped her breasts and pinched her hard nipples. Even with all that strength, he always walked the fine line between pleasure and pain. She trusted him and she didn't, and the fear heightened every sensation.

He pulled her nipples until it was on the tip of her tongue to tell him to stop, then released them and ran one finger along the sensitive curve under each breast where the skin was unused to being touched.

'I'm ready,' she panted, and pushed back against his cock between her buttocks.

'I know.' He traced the underside of her breasts until it stopped sending exquisite thrills straight to her clit and then stroked the inside of her arms, equally unaccustomed to attention.

All the time she tried to raise her hips so his cock would press where she wanted it, but she was trapped with his weight pushing her forward and her legs spread too wide.

She groaned in frustration and he ignored it, taking his sweet time. Then his hands travelled down her body and she took a mouthful of pillow in anticipation of that first electric touch between her legs.

But instead he found the crease between her lips and the top of her thighs.

Damn him. He knew every inch of her from those long, hazy moments when he touched her into delirium. And begging didn't work.

She tried anyway.

'Marc, please.'

He leaned forward and bit her neck again while his fingers stroked the inside of her thighs.

'Fuck me,' she said. 'Please. Hard.' She ground her butt against his cock, and heard his hiss of breath. She did it again, and felt a drop of precum on her skin.

'Feel how hot you made me. How wet I am for you.' She squeezed her buttocks around his cock.

He grasped her hips and his weight disappeared from her back and then he pushed inside her and she grabbed the pillow with a cry. It was hard and delicious. She braced against the wall and met his thrusts, then lost her rhythm when his fingers found her clitoris. It didn't matter. He was in control even if she wasn't, and she surrendered to his hands and his cock and came hard.

When she regained her senses she squeezed his cock inside her just the way he liked, and he held her hips as he came. He rested his head on her shoulder for a few moments, breathing hard. Then he pushed her legs together and let her down gently on to the sheets, which was nice because she felt too weak to do anything but collapse ungracefully in the wet patch.

Neither of them spoke for a while, until Marc reached for his drink on the bedside table.

'What's this?'

She opened her eyes, and saw him reading the forms she'd left there.

'New business registration. You're doing it?' He looked at her in delight.

Ally grimaced. 'I was thinking about it but . . .'

'But what? You've got to do it. Just think about it . . . Ally Rivers, CEO.'

She snorted. 'Ally Rivers, AWOL. She was meant to be with a client two hours ago but she got sidetracked watching a pigeon try to eat an entire Big Mac.'

He rolled his eyes. 'You've never been late for me. Haven't I told you before that self-deprecation doesn't suit you?'

'I tried before. I failed. I need to think of something else.'

'You didn't try this before. Anyway, you're older and wiser now.'

She snorted.

Marc narrowed his eyes. 'I'm not having sex with you again until you fill them out and send them off.'

'You're using sex as a weapon?'

'Yes.'

'But that's . . . evil.'

He leaned over her and pressed their noses together. 'I am evil. You haven't seen my dark side yet.'

Ally hooked her ankles round his waist and tried to pull him on to the bed. 'I want to see him.'

Marc resisted her efforts. 'You'll regret it. He's a bad, bad man. Do the damn forms.'

He dumped them on her lap and strode off to the bathroom. Ally sighed, picked up the forms, and snuggled her bare legs under the duvet. She was bored within five minutes when she'd already had to write her name and date of birth three times. Why couldn't there just be *one* form? Would Marc believe her if she said she'd posted them? Probably, but it'd be mean to lie to him.

Maybe she could—

Somebody knocked on her door.

Ally sat bolt upright in bed as adrenaline flooded her. Mum? Or Sam? Oh god, if it was Sam . . .

She grabbed a dress at random, pulled it over her naked body, and crept to the living room to look out of the window. She couldn't see whoever was on the doorstep, and they knocked again.

Trying not to make any noise, she unlatched the window and leaned her head out. A flash of dark red hair and a pale face. Rachel looked up at her. 'Ally?' She looked confused. 'Why are you hanging out of the window?'

'Uh . . .' The adrenaline made it impossible to think of a good lie. 'I've got company.'

'Oh.' A slow smile spread across Rachel's face. 'That explains the bed hair. Can I just come in for a minute? I need to borrow a dress.'

'Er, I'll bring you one down. What colour?'

'So I can get changed on the street?'

'Oh, right. I'll come down. Just let me get . . . dressed.'

She ran to the bathroom and found Marc stepping out of the shower.

'Stay in here,' she hissed. 'Rachel's here. Lock the door and don't come out until I tell you.'

Before he could reply, Ally ran downstairs and let Rachel in.

'I'll be gone in a flash,' Rachel said, with her hands in the air. 'But look.'

'Ooh.' Ally saw the blotchy red stain on Rachel's yellow dress.

'Doughnut. Jam doughnut.'

Mm. A doughnut would be good. 'Tasty?'

'Don't know. I didn't get any of the jam in my mouth. Help, please. I have a meeting with an investor.'

Ally led her to the wardrobe. Rachel smirked at the disarrayed bed and dropped her voice. 'Having fun?'

'Mm.'

Rachel took a dress at random and reached behind her to unzip the stained one.

'Not that one,' said Ally, fashion winning over the desire to get Rachel out of there ASAP. 'You can't wear dark blue with your skin and hair, and definitely not with that jacket. Have I taught you nothing?'

'You have, but I don't get it. I like blue.'

Ally sighed. 'We need another colour theory session. Or just let me buy all your clothes for ever.' She found a lime-green dress and swapped it for the blue one. 'There. That'll make your hair look more red and your skin glow. You're welcome.'

'You're the best.' Rachel slipped into the dress. 'So, do I get to say hello to your friend?'

Ally tried to stay calm. 'He's shy.'

'I thought you'd given up on the quiet ones?'

'Not all of them.'

'Good. Can I just wash my hands?'

Ally gaped like a fish. 'In the kitchen,' she said desperately. 'Not the bathroom.'

'How rude. The tradesman's entrance for your best friend.'

Ally followed her down the hall and skipped ahead to block the way to the bathroom.

Rachel looked around the kitchen with her eyebrows raised. 'This one's serious then?'

'What?'

Rachel nodded at the remains of their lunch. They'd taken the wine glasses to bed.

'And are those gifts?'

They were. A photography magazine, and a bar of Lindt with sea salt.

'He's just nice,' Ally whispered, hoping Marc wasn't listening from the bathroom. 'It's just sex. We don't go on dates or anything.'

'Gifts, a meal, and sex isn't a date? Things have moved on since I was single.'

A creeping shame twisted Ally's stomach. Rachel was right. Ally enjoyed clothed time with Marc so much that she'd strayed outside the boundaries of a sex-buddy relationship.

'Don't you need to go and get invested?' Ally said.

Rachel gave her a strange look. 'I didn't interrupt in the middle, did I? Why are you so tense?'

'Yes. You ruined my orgasm. Now get out, cockblocker.'

'Rude.' Rachel kissed her cheek. 'Have a nice orgasm.' She raised her voice. 'Bye, Ally's friend.'

Ally felt Marc's petrified silence.

'Aw, he really is shy,' said Rachel, as Ally prodded her down the stairs.

'Well he will be now, you embarrassing witch. Knock the investors dead.'

They kissed cheeks again, and Ally watched until Rachel closed the door behind her.

As she breathed a sigh of relief and sank against the wall, Marc appeared at the top of the stairs.

'All OK?' he asked nervously.

Ally nodded, and took the stairs two at a time. 'No way she can know who it was.'

She sat on her bed and watched him dress, enjoying the way his shoulders moved. 'Marc. You shouldn't buy me things.'

'Why not?'

'Fu—sex buddies don't do that.'

He frowned. 'I'm a guest in your house. I was brought up to bring a present for the host.'

'Sex is my present. Just don't, Marc. I feel guilty enough, without you spending money on me too.'

He sat beside her and took her hand from her crystal. Ally cursed herself for grabbing the damn thing all the time, so often she didn't even know she was doing it.

'It scared you?' he guessed. 'Your friend nearly walking in on us.'

'Mm.'

He wrapped his arms around her and even with his cologne washed off he smelled so good in her mint shower gel.

'Do you sniff everybody you meet?'

'No. I become an animal for you. Now get out.' She forced herself to look cheerful. 'But come back soon.'

He took a long look at her then stood up. 'Ally?'

'Yeah?'

'Do the forms, OK?'

CHAPTER TWENTY

⌐

Christmas with Ally's mum and sisters was the best kind of loving, manic chaos. On Christmas Eve they went to see Lucie in a matinée, where she danced the Harlequin Doll, and then Mum got to take her home instead of waving her off back to dance school. She held Lucie's hand all the way home, even though she was seventeen, as if afraid she would be torn away.

At home they decorated the tree, bought in a last-minute panic. When her sisters finally fell asleep, Mum leaned over with wide eyes and whispered to Ally, 'Help! I haven't wrapped their presents!'

Ally grinned. She'd already found the tape and scissors and stowed them in Mum's room.

'Do you think I got enough?' Mum asked, biting her lip as she examined the pile. 'It doesn't look like much. I was doing well with saving until the boiler broke . . .'

'Of course it's enough. They're not little girls any more, they want quality over quantity.'

'I got you least of all.' Mum curled a ribbon round and round her finger. 'I'll make it up to you on your birthday, I promise.'

'Mum, I don't need presents. Here, this is ready for a ribbon.'

She handed a wrapped Nintendo DS, Katie's main present, among the stocking fillers. Mum tied the ribbon then attached a label, hovering the pen over it for a long moment before she wrote. She added a label to Lucie's new shoes as well and put them both down with a sigh.

When they'd finished and were carrying the presents to the tree, Ally snuck a look at the labels. 'Lots of love, from Dad'. It was a good imitation of his handwriting.

'He didn't get them anything?' Ally asked.

Mum glanced up and reddened. 'No.'

'Cockwomble. And you're going to let him take credit for things you spent months saving up for?'

'It's not about him. It's about the girls. You stop caring so much about yourself when you have children.' Mum kissed the top of Ally's head, wished her goodnight, and went to bed.

As she changed into her PJs, Ally wondered how many of her Christmas and birthday presents from Dad had really been from Mum when she was growing up. Why was Dad able to forget about his daughters when other fathers would do anything for their kids?

Like Marc, giving up his life to care for a woman he didn't love, just to save Sam from the same fate. And now spending Christmas Day with them, when she was sure he'd be happier in his own flat and not having to play happy families, because Sam and Gavin had wanted to carry on their traditional family Christmas for another year.

Which of her parents did Ally take after? She used to think she was like Mum and would sacrifice anything for the people she loved. But now she was putting her selfish lust above Sam's feelings, and risking devastating him. Maybe she was more like her father after all.

* * *

Christmas Day passed in a haze of wrapping paper, food, mulled wine and games. Ally wore her pyjamas from breakfast to supper. She didn't think her jeans would've buttoned up.

In the evening she called Rachel to wish her a Merry Christmas and see if she liked her present, then Sam.

'I'm dying,' Sam groaned. 'Too much food.'

'Me too. Coming to the gym with me in the new year?'

'Don't even mention exercise. I'm not getting off this sofa until February. Can you believe my dad tried to get me to go for a run this morning?'

Butterflies exploded in Ally's stomach as she pictured Marc, full of energy on Christmas morning, going for a jog in the frosty air then coming home to cook dinner. No herbs in the gravy or stuffing, no cranberry sauce or bread sauce, no cinnamon and orange in the red cabbage. He'd eat the same as his wife and son, because Christmas was for family, and he put everyone else's wishes before his own. Would he wish he was with Ally, so they could run together then eat what they liked?

Of course he wouldn't. He probably hadn't thought of her at all and if he had, it'd be because looking at his son made him feel like an awful person.

'Ally? Ally? Hello?'

Ally roused herself. 'Sorry. Zoned out.'

'Say Merry Christmas to Ally for us, Sammy,' said a voice in the background. Julie. Of course, she still thought Ally was engaged to her son. How was Marc keeping all his lies straight?

She shouldn't have called.

'Mum and Dad say Merry Christmas,' Sam said.

Marc was probably staring at the carpet like he had last time the four of them were together, at Gavin's party.

'Merry Christmas to everyone. Mum and the girls said thanks for the gifts. Though I think you'll regret Katie's, because she wants to play the new game with you next time you're here. Speaking of which, I'd better go. She wants a rematch at Pictionary. Love you.'

'Love you too.'

It was even more difficult to concentrate than usual. The horrible fluttering in her stomach wouldn't go away. It was ridiculous to be this upset about Marc having a boring Christmas dinner, or spending most of the day in silence while Julie chatted to their sons, or being hurt that Sam didn't want to go for a run with him. Ally hadn't given a moment's thought to Jason, or any of the other lovers she was still in touch with, beyond sending a mass Merry Christmas text. She'd never looked forward to their visits so much, or been afraid instead of relieved that it was just a fling.

The unsettled feeling got worse.

'You're quiet,' Mum said.

'Stomach ache,' Ally replied. 'I have eaten about three tonnes of food today.'

'You've probably got an energy blockage.'

Ally had to lie on the sofa with her feet on Katie's lap while Mum waved a crystal around her stomach.

'Your chakra vortex is all out of alignment,' Mum announced.

Katie examined Ally's stomach and nodded. 'A big blockage in your heart chakra, too. Rose quartz, Mum?'

'You as well, Katie?' said Ally.

Katie beamed. 'I can see auras. Yours is pink.'

'Is it? Is it infected?'

Mum frowned at her. 'It means you're artistic. Or in love.'

'Oh. I wonder which one, after three hours of Pictionary.'

'Your dragon was rubbish,' Katie added. 'It looked more like a dinosaur.'

'You look like a dinosaur. All scaly.'

'Dinosaurs didn't have scales.' Katie looked uncertainly at Mum. 'Did they?'

'I don't think they worried much about their weight,' said Mum as she hovered her hands over Ally's chest. 'Your heart chakra is worse than your stomach. Have you been wearing your crystal?'

'Uh-huh. How long will it take to unblock? I want a bath.'

It took for ever. Baths always helped her period pains, but they did nothing for this ache. She sank into the water, her elbow propped on the side of the bath as she scrolled through her Facebook feed. It was quiet, with everybody offline for Christmas, and the few posts she saw were uninteresting. The one person she wanted to read about wasn't on Facebook.

She put his name into Google, expecting thousands of irrelevant results. But apparently it wasn't a common name, because most of the first page contained links to the same contractor's website. She clicked on the one with 'Moorgate' in the title, and gaped as it loaded.

The CGIs showed two massive skyscrapers set in immaculate landscaped gardens. One was to be a five-star hotel, the other a residential block where a one-bedroom flat would cost more than she'd earn in a lifetime. The development was going to cost twenty-four million, and Marc was listed among the six major people in charge of the project. In his headshot he wore a hard hat and gave a confident smile, looking calm and good-humoured and in control.

Ally stared at his face for a long time, wishing she could save it to her phone but afraid Sam might see it.

She'd assumed he was a builder, installing kitchens and bathrooms in nondescript terraced houses. Instead, he was leading multimillion-pound developments for companies so big even she'd heard of them?

She groaned, thinking of the times she'd whinged to him about her dull, minimum wage jobs, talking like he was in the same position and would understand. He'd been too kind to correct her and show her she was the only screw-up and he'd done very well for himself.

God, her self-pity must be unattractive.

The knot grew worse as she stroked his face with her thumb.

When she finally got out of the cooling water, Lucie had gone to bed to read and Katie was in her room, FaceTiming her friends. Ally cuddled up to Mum on the sofa and watched *Love Actually*.

'I made you some willow bark tea,' said Mum.

'Thanks.' Ally sipped it, but she knew it wouldn't help. This wasn't a muscle ache, or even the result of too much food. It was emotional.

Mum fell asleep on the sofa, and Ally roused her and sent her to her bedroom. Ally made up the sofa into a bed for herself and stroked her phone, wishing she could call Marc. Hearing his voice, and remembering that she shared her guilt, would be soothing.

This had gone too far. He wasn't just a sex buddy. He was a friend and a lover and a rock all rolled into one. She didn't just want to sleep with him, she wanted to be awake with him and use her mouth to talk to him and her hands to eat with him and what was that if not a relationship? And they couldn't have a relationship. Not a long one, anyway. Their days were numbered before they started, and if they didn't end it first it would end in catastrophe when they were found out.

From Christmas until New Year Ally argued with herself. As much as she wanted to keep seeing Marc, she couldn't make her desires stack up against all the reasons to stop. Her happiness couldn't be more important than Sam's, not to mention all the other people that would be hurt. She wouldn't be like her father, who didn't care how many hearts he broke when he left Mum.

When Marc finally called on New Year's Day, and she heard his voice, the arguments for following her heart suddenly seemed much more convincing.

'Hi,' she answered.

'Happy New Year. How was your Christmas?'

'Chaos, but lovely chaos. I've put on about fifty pounds, I'm a Monopoly master, and my chakras have been well and truly balanced.'

He laughed. That smoky, sexy laugh.

'I wish I could've spent some of it with you,' he said. 'Sounds much more fun than mine. I'm looking forward to going back to work.'

'When are you back?'

'Tuesday. Can I come and see you afterwards?'

She smiled. 'OK. I'll make you dinner. Something spicy. I'm guessing today's dinner wasn't very exciting.'

'Correct. Sure you won't get distracted and burn the house down?'

'Hey, I've only done that twice.'

He laughed. 'See you then. I—' He stopped abruptly and Ally gripped her phone hard. Had someone come into the room with him?

'What?'

'Nothing. See you soon.'

CHAPTER TWENTY-ONE

~

*B*y Tuesday, the butterflies were carrying out acrobatic training in Ally's stomach. What with Christmas shopping, seeing friends and family, and then the holiday itself, she and Marc hadn't seen each other in a fortnight.

If he even *tried* to tease her today she'd get her vibrator out and threaten to use it if he wouldn't give it up in a reasonable time frame.

The earliest he'd ever arrived was six-twenty, but by six she was pacing her living room and peering out the window every few seconds. When a car finally pulled up outside it wasn't a dark blue Subaru. It was a bright red Mini, parked crookedly.

'Oh for god's sake!' Ally mentally shook a fist at the bastard universe and its determination to prevent her getting laid.

Maybe it was someone else's Mini. There must be thousands of bright red Minis in London, right?

There was a knock at the door.

Ally groaned at the ceiling and traipsed down the stairs to open the door.

'Ally!' Mum burst in and grabbed both Ally's hands. 'I need

your help.' Her blue eyes were wide, her blonde hair in disarray, the three crystals on her chest rising and falling quickly.

'Oh, Mum. What have you done?'

'I forgot my taxes. Please help, Ally. You know I don't have your brain for maths.'

Ally let her head drop on to Mum's shoulder, then straightened up. 'Come in.'

Mum had a big black rucksack bursting at the seams. She heaved it on to the sofa between her and Ally and opened the zip. Scraps of paper with scribbled notes cascaded out.

Ally gaped at them as she dropped to her knees and helped Mum pick them up. 'You've had this many clients?'

'No.' Mum looked ready to cry. 'These are all notes from people who called or emailed. I don't know which ones I did or how much I charged. I'll have to cross-reference it with my diary and bank statements.'

'Oh, Mum.'

'Don't be annoyed with me.' Mum sniffed. 'I kept meaning to sort it all out but things kept getting in the way. Then it was Christmas and I forgot about the self-assessment deadline.'

'When is it?'

'The thirty-first.'

'Oh, that's OK. We have nearly four weeks.'

Mum drew back with an expression like a puppy being caught eating the toilet roll. 'I forgot to register. They said it takes . . . four weeks.'

Ally sighed.

* * *

Ally had only just created a spreadsheet on her laptop when Marc knocked. She'd completely forgotten about him in her efforts to calm Mum down.

He looked so sexy on her doorstep, with that joyful smile making his eyes crinkle and a wrapped box in his hands.

He cheated on the No Gifts Rule sometimes, even when it wasn't the first time they'd seen each other since Christmas.

'My mum's here,' Ally said. She could hear the frustration in her voice.

His face dropped. 'I have to go?'

Every fibre of her resisted it. 'You can stay, but we're doing her tax return. It'll probably take all night.'

'I could help. Then maybe it'll go faster.'

It was tempting. Mum would have no idea that Marc was Sam's dad, but the worry was that she'd mention him in front of Sam. Although Sam probably wouldn't make the connection between a man called Marc and his dad . . .

'Ally? Ally? Hey.' She didn't register the sounds until Marc cupped her face and made her look at him.

'Oh. Sorry. Look.' She dropped her voice to a whisper. 'We'll just have to be friends. No, that's a bit weird, with the age gap. Um, I'm teaching you how to paint, but we hang out sometimes before and after. OK?'

'OK. Take this and open it later.' He handed her a wrapped box, snatched a kiss that left her feeling giddy, and she led him upstairs.

Ally slipped the box into her room on the way. In the living room, Mum looked up from a scrap of paper and smiled at them.

'Mum, this is Marc. Marc, my mum, Rebecca.'

'Nice to meet you, Rebecca.'

'Likewise. A friend of yours, Ally?'

Mum seemed satisfied with the cover story.

'I'm sorry to ruin your lesson,' she said, as Marc took off his scarf and coat. 'I'm so scatty sometimes. When Ally was a teenager she had to wake me up and make me go to work instead of me badgering her to go to school.'

'I like scattiness,' Marc replied, without even a flicker of his eyes towards Ally. 'It can be very charming.'

He cleared a space on the coffee table to sit down, and Mum's eyes travelled from his handsome face to his beautifully sculpted forearms and the hint of soft chest hair on display in his blue polo shirt.

Ally nudged Mum's calf a little harder than she'd intended — more of a kick, really — and glared.

'What?' Mum mouthed.

Ally felt her cogs whirring. 'New divorce,' she mouthed back. 'Rebound.'

Mum shrugged. 'Still single.'

Ally shook her head vehemently at Mum, and stopped when Marc sat down and smiled at them.

Resisting an urge to sit on his lap and stake her territory, she plonked a pile of papers on it instead. 'We're sorting them into months. May starts there, April over here. If there's no date, they go here.'

Marc looked surprised at her arsey tone, but he didn't say anything.

'What do you do, Marc?' Mum asked.

'I'm a construction site manager. Dirt and diggers, not very exciting.'

'Oh, no, it's fascinating. That must be where all your muscle comes from.'

Ally made a face at her. Such blatant flirting. It would've been embarrassing even for someone who wasn't her mother.

Marc was very polite about it though. In fact, he looked quite proud. Ally kicked herself for not complimenting his body as often as she should have.

'I think Ally said once you're a healer. That must take a lot of emotional strength.'

'Oh, you're very kind. I don't think I look very strong at the moment though!' Mum reached up and smoothed her hair with a bashful smile, then adjusted her top. Was she trying to show more cleavage?!

'You look—'

'Can we concentrate on the taxes, please?' Ally snapped.

They both looked at her in surprise. Playing all innocent.

Ally dumped her laptop on the arm of the sofa so hard that it slid down and struck her elbow painfully, then shoved it on the floor and picked up a pile of papers.

After a few minutes of silence, Mum piped up again. 'How long have you been having lessons, Marc?'

'We met at the beginning of July.'

Six months. It really was six months since she'd had sex with someone else, not counting the entirely unsatisfactory attempt with Jason. Who had the last one been? A black-haired guy . . . the electrician. What was his name? She'd never be able to remember after all this time, if she'd even bothered to commit it to memory back then. Was that all she had to look forward to if she broke it off with Marc? Mediocre sex from mediocre men, where she was actually pleased about zoning out because it was more interesting than talking to them? Especially when they were so busy complimenting her body, and so determined to treat her like a trophy wife who needed managing, that she felt like a four-year-old who ate crayons.

She blinked back into awareness. Marc and Mum were both laughing at something, gazing into each other's eyes. Ally might as well be invisible, for fuck's sake.

She stood up, making sure to bang the coffee table with her leg so it jolted Marc. 'I'll go and make myself useful and get us all a drink, shall I?'

Their blinking expressions, like puppy dogs she'd just scolded for chewing a slipper, annoyed her. Ally stomped off to the kitchen and heard nothing but silence behind her. They were probably exchanging conspiratorial looks that said, 'Why's she being such a grumpy bitch,' if they weren't flexing their muscles or fiddling with their hair in an embarrassing peacock display. God, why didn't they leave Ally to sort the notes while they asked to borrow her bedroom?

Ally flung a kitchen cupboard open and took out three glasses.

A voice in her head told her she deserved this.

'Oh, shut up,' she muttered, knowing it was right. It'd be nothing but karma if Marc lost interest in her and went for her mum. What she was doing to Sam was worse, and she was such a selfish cow it hadn't stopped her. Why should Marc feel any loyalty to her? Mum wouldn't even think of flirting with him if she knew he was Ally's, but she didn't because Ally now lied to everyone – Sam, Rachel, Mum – even when there was no need.

What the hell had she turned into? This wasn't her. For all her faults, and her inability to think about lovers for longer than three seconds without getting bored, she'd always been a good friend. A loyal friend. Loving her friends and family to death. Now she was risking Sam feeling a hundred times worse than she was right now, with a new and more complicated knot in her stomach at the sight of Mum and Marc gazing at each other in amusement, all so she could get laid.

When she took three glasses of wine back to the living room, she was subdued. She had no right to be annoyed with either of them for flirting – she'd told Marc often enough they were just friends, even if she knew it was a lie. Mum wasn't doing anything wrong at all, just exchanging pleasantries with an attractive man.

Marc brushed her fingers with his as he took the glass. Ally met his soft brown eyes, and looked away in shame.

It didn't take long to sort the rucksack of papers into piles, but then came the tricky part. Mum had several paper diaries – one she kept at work and one by the phone at home, as well as an online one Ally had tried to get her to use. There were also numerous receipt books, as well as scribbled notes on days Mum had forgotten to bring one of them to the client's house, and they all had to be matched to online bank statements stretching back nearly two years.

Ally grumbled about it and, when she found yet another diary in the rucksack and made a noise of frustration, Mum became weepy again.

'I'm sorry, Ally,' she said with a sniff. 'I didn't mean to cause you all this trouble.'

Feeling even worse, Ally put an arm around her and pressed their cheeks together. 'I'm not upset with you. You did really well keeping all these records. We just need to sort them out.'

But Mum was so upset she kept matching up the wrong scraps of paper.

'Mum? It's gone eight. Why don't you make us something nice to eat while Marc and I carry on?'

Cooking would calm her, and remind her she was very good at some things.

'Are you sure you don't mind?' Mum looked to Marc.

'Not at all,' said Marc. 'I won't have anything, though. I need to go soon.'

Ally's heart sank. For a wild moment she wondered if she could sneak him into her bedroom while Mum was cooking and have a quickie before she returned. But it was far too risky, not to mention disrespectful to her mum.

The moment Mum left the room, Ally pushed the papers aside and sat on his lap, hugging him tightly. A spicy fragrance today. Cinnamon, and maybe lemon, with something she couldn't identify.

'I'm going crazy,' she whispered into his ear. His stubble scratched her cheek and she rubbed her face against it.

To her surprise, he pulled away and stared at her as if she had two heads. 'Ally, do you see yourself?'

She looked down at her body. Apart from the fact that her dress had ridden up to her hips, everything seemed where it should be. 'Yes?'

'Not that,' he said. 'This.' He gestured at the sofa with its piles of paper and Ally's laptop.

'My sofa?'

He shook his head. 'You. You're . . . you're *organising*. You're managing your mum's accounts. What's all this nonsense about you being too flaky to run a business?'

'Oh, don't be silly. I've got no choice because she has to get it done today. I'd be in the same mess if this was my business.'

'Does it matter, if you can pull it out of the bag when you need to?'

'Yes, becau—shit.' She jumped off his lap and sat on the sofa with a bump just as Mum came back.

'I'd better go.' Marc stood up. 'Lovely to meet you, Rebecca.'

'Oh, Becca, please.' Mum stood on tiptoe to kiss his cheek, and Ally saw her nostrils flare as her nose moved close to his neck.

Ally ground her teeth.

As they passed her bedroom, Ally ducked in and pushed Marc's wrapped presents into his hands – a drawing tablet for his laptop, a graphic design magazine subscription, and a Malaysian cookbook.

At the bottom of the stairs, she glanced up to make sure Mum was out of eyeshot, grabbed Marc and gave him a kiss he wouldn't forget in a hurry.

'What was that for?' His low, sexy voice right in her ear made her toes curl into the carpet.

'Nothing. Come back tomorrow.'

'Can't. Friday?'

Ally stifled a groan. 'OK. Friday.'

Three days felt like a very unreasonable timescale.

When they were finally done and Mum left, gone three a.m., Ally rubbed her sore eyes and sat on her bed with the box from Marc. The powder-blue paper was thick and embossed with white snowflakes, tied shut with a silver ribbon. Ally tried not to tear the paper as she opened it. The box inside matched it, white with silver and blue accents.

It was a lot more elegant than Ally's wrapping. She'd bought plain white paper and drawn cartoons on it to make him laugh.

Inside the box she found a beautiful lingerie set. Cliché, maybe, but she didn't care. It was a gorgeous Myla shell-pink corset and matching French knickers, with all the correct measurements. Maybe that was why he'd been so fascinated with her underwear lately; looking for the labels.

She took them out, stroking the silk and lace, and saw a lump underneath the pastel green tissue paper left in the box. This second layer was a pyjama set; cow-print bottoms and a long-sleeved top with two cartoon Friesians in a field. The soft cotton was warm, cosy and decidedly unsexy. Even more unsexy was the thick pair of black and white socks, complete with cow ears and marble eyes.

It was the kind of thing a woman wore for a winter night in on the sofa, watching movies and sipping hot chocolate, with a boyfriend she didn't need to dress up for because he found her sexy in a thong or in novelty slippers. A boyfriend who'd seen her flaunting her curves in lingerie, and seen her cleaning the bathroom in ten-year-old jogging bottoms and marigold gloves, and thought the world of her each time.

She put the cow socks on and made a puppet show with her feet.

CHAPTER TWENTY-TWO

~

$\mathscr{A}$lly's dad lived in a house much too big for him and Carly, and grumbled constantly that he wouldn't be able to retire until he was dead. The obvious solution of moving to a smaller house never seemed to occur to them.

Carly opened the door wearing a black skirt-suit and a blue silk blouse, even though Ally had tactfully told her several times she was *warm* toned and should wear warm colours. She'd even printed off a colour palette for her and offered to go shopping together.

It wasn't until Gran encouraged her to do it again that she realised Carly had taken offence. Ally had only wanted to play up her nicest features and make her look her best. What was mean about that?

'Ally!' Carly beamed and kissed both of Ally's cheeks.

'Hi, Carly. How are you?'

'Come in, come in. I'm fine. Phil's watching football.'

Instead of leading her to the living room, with its impractical white sofa and breakable things on impractically small tables, Carly led her to the master bedroom. Ally looked dubiously at the four-poster bed with gold gilt decoration. What if they'd, like . . . *stained* it?

Carly sat on the edge of the bed with a bounce and patted the space next to her, like she and Ally were teenagers embarking on a sleepover. Ally perched next to her and tried to relax.

'I wanted some girl talk,' Carly said, trying to sit cross-legged on the duvet. Her skirt didn't have a split down the side, so she abandoned this endeavour and settled for crossing her ankles and leaning back. It was a bit like a Playboy shoot gone wrong.

'Um,' said Ally.

'Phil and I want to renew our wedding vows,' Carly said, and giggled. 'We get another ceremony, another party, and maybe even more gifts.'

'Oh. That sounds . . . nice.'

Carly nodded, still beaming. 'Phil and I know how hard you've been working on your little business and . . . well . . . we'd like you to do it.'

Ally stared at her expectant face. 'Uh . . .'

'I know, I know.' Carly patted her hand. 'It's a lot of pressure. But we believe in you. And I'll be working with you every step of the way to make sure it's totally right.'

Ally hadn't been worried about her capability at all, but now she remembered Carly's wedding planning with horror. She'd badgered Ally to be a bridesmaid and didn't understand why she refused. Ally, trying to keep everyone happy, compromised by helping Carly make arrangements. Mum had been hurt and disappointed at her involvement. Dad had stayed out of it all, throwing money at Carly whenever she tried to get him to help.

After the wedding she'd been treated to an endless photo show from Carly. The napkins were folded into swans. The table centrepieces had been glass swans with lilies in them. The cake had been in the shape of a swan.

And Mum had cried the entire day.

'I'm sorry,' Ally said. 'I can't.'

Carly looked taken aback. 'Why not? We'll pay. I mean,' she nudged Ally's ribs and winked, 'with a family discount. It'll be so much fun! We can plan it all together. I can give you some ideas for the business.'

'Sorry. It's Mum. It wouldn't be fair on her.'

Carly frowned. 'Your mum? What do you mean?'

'Um. You know, she's still a bit upset about Dad cheating and then leaving her with three children to bring up?'

'Oh.' Carly looked confused. 'What does that have to do with you?'

'Uh, well, I'm her daughter. So it's a bit disloyal to do something that'd hurt her.'

Carly sat up and tapped an acrylic nail on her tooth. 'But we're offering to pay you.' She turned to Ally with a frown. 'You need money, don't you? You want to go on holiday?'

'Yes. But I won't do *anything* for money.'

'It's for your business though. We're doing you a favour! We could have gone with a professional after all.'

Charming. 'Thanks. But I really can't.' Ally stood up. 'I'll go and say hi to Dad.'

She left Carly looking bewildered and annoyed.

Dad was shouting at the TV when she descended the stairs.

'Hey, Dad.'

'What? Oh. Hi, Ally.'

'How's it going?'

'One all.' He glared at the TV. 'If we don't pull it back soon, we're out of the leagues.'

'I meant with you. Have you got Lucie a birthday present?'

Finally, he looked away from the TV. 'What? When is it?'

'Next Tuesday.'

'Dammit. What does she want? Send me an Amazon link, will you? Is it a big birthday?'

'She'll be eighteen. When's the last time you saw her, or Katie?'

'Oh, don't start that. I'm busy.'

Ally raised her eyebrows at the TV. 'Yeah. I see that. Did she text you about France?'

'France?'

'There's a school trip to France. She wants to go, but this time of year is slow for Mum. It's just over two hundred pounds, but she gets to go skiing in the Alps. You know how much she loves skiing.'

He shrugged. 'What's she done with her pocket money?'

'Spent it. She's a teenager.'

'Should've saved, shouldn't she? I'm not made of money.'

Ally suppressed a surge of anger. 'She's a teenager. All her friends are going, and Mum won't be able to afford a holiday this year. I'll give her some spending money if you just pay for the trip.'

'And a bloody birthday present, and new shoes last month? I won't let them take the piss out of me, Ally. They think money grows on trees. At least you never ask for anything.'

'Because I have a job,' she flared. 'Lucie hasn't finished training, and how's a thirteen-year-old supposed to support herself?'

'They have a mother,' he snapped back. 'What's she throwing it all away on? Coloured rocks and stinking oils.'

'That she needs for her *job*. Look, are you going to pay for the trip or not?'

'Not. She needs to learn the value of money. She's nearly an adult. Fuck's sake, I've missed half the game now.' He shifted irritably on the sofa and increased the TV volume.

'We've been talking less than five minutes,' Ally said coldly. 'About your daughter. Don't you think you have some responsibility for looking after her? You made her.'

'Your mother wanted to keep her. Don't blame me. You all could have come to live with us but you chose to stay with your mum. Make your bed, lie in it.'

Ally glared at him in disgust. Marc had spent thirty years with a woman he didn't love because he wanted to be a good father, and Dad treated his children like an irritation.

He didn't notice her leave. She ran all the way home to work off her anger.

* * *

Later, in her bedroom, Ally sat on the edge of her bed and looked between her new lingerie set and her new cow pyjamas. What to wear for Marc?

A woman like Carly wore silk and satin just for sitting around the house. Dad would probably make a jibe disguised as a joke about 'letting herself go' if she wore anything casual.

Dad tore up families and didn't care, because his happiness was the most important thing to him. He'd followed his desires and left four people sad and dumbfounded and two small girls wondering where Daddy had gone. People he should have loved and protected and who should have been able to trust him. Who should never have been betrayed.

Ally had sworn she wouldn't hurt anyone like that. That she wouldn't chase happiness at the expense of others. Especially not people she loved.

Marc deserved happiness though. He'd sacrificed a lot, made mistakes and tried to fix them, put everyone else first. It was his turn now, to do something he wanted. What he wanted was Ally, and she wanted him. Whatever she said to him, whatever she tried to tell herself, he was more than a sex buddy. He didn't just turn her on; he made her feel good, content, less ditzy. Or like her ditziness didn't matter, like she was fine how she was. Like he really wanted her and didn't just tolerate her.

Her, her, her. It was all about her. Like Dad's life was all about him.

She put on the lingerie. Marc could see her in it before she stopped pretending what she was doing was OK. She'd just give herself a few more weeks, so she could mentally adjust, and then she would end it.

Just a few more weeks.

CHAPTER TWENTY-THREE

*Next movie night, Ally watched *50 First Dates* with Sam and Rachel.

'Speaking of fifty dates,' said Rachel, turning to Ally. 'What's happening with you at the moment? Seems like for ever since you called to rave about a good date, or moan about a bad one.'

'Hey, I never moan. I offer constructive criticism. I haven't felt much like dating lately.'

'Are you ill?' Sam asked.

'Ha ha.' Ally poked her tongue out at him. 'No. I'm getting bored of flings. I want a proper relationship again.'

Sam stared.

'What's caused this?' Rachel paused the movie and leaned towards the sofa.

Ally tried not to think of Marc, or what she had to do. 'Oh, I don't know, I'm just getting old. Twenty-nine next month. I don't want wrinkles on my wedding day.'

'So you're going to start shopping for personality, not looks?' Rachel asked.

'I suppose. I just need to find a nice one who turns me on.'

Well, another nice one. It WAS possible. If Marc could do it, so could someone else. There was nothing special about Marc.

She squashed the troublemaking little voice that whispered all the special things about Marc in her ear.

After her friends left, Ally lay on the sofa and opened her dating apps. She hadn't checked either of them for ages and she had hundreds of messages to trawl through.

For a change, she didn't judge on the pictures. Unless they'd sent her dick pics, she read their profiles but still found herself discounting all of them. That one had never read a book. That one made jokes about fat women. That one had a non-ironic photo of himself kissing his bicep, which she thought counted as a personality issue rather than appearance. That one . . . um . . . was a Taurus and she was sure if she searched the net, she'd find a site somewhere saying they weren't compatible with Pisceans.

This guy . . . damn. Try as she might, she couldn't find a reason to discount him. He hadn't even listed a star sign. Usually she wouldn't have clicked his username because he had no pictures, but his profile actually made her laugh. He read the same kind of books as her, and also listed *Life of Pi* and *A Thousand Splendid Suns* under his favourites. What were the odds of that? Music, too – he liked eighties classics, including Blondie and Guns N' Roses.

But she didn't want to message him.

She had to. She had to stop seeing Marc as something permanent. He was one in a line – a long line – and she needed to keep it moving. She wouldn't grow old alone.

Like Marc.

Stopstopstop. Focus on the app.

Aha! She'd skipped over the most important info and now she had an easy out. He was forty-five. Way too old for her. Although . . . younger than Marc. What if it were life experience that made him so interesting, and good in bed? Maybe she was suited to older guys.

Undecided, she opened a message to him and saw he hadn't logged in for months.

Messaging him didn't seem such a bad idea now. She put a lot of thought into it, rather than relying on her pictures like she usually did. He was much cleverer than her judging by the way he'd written his profile, and she even put effort into making sure she spelled everything right. Instead of a bland greeting she talked about the books they'd both cited, then hit send.

He probably wouldn't get back to her, even if he did happen to log in. She couldn't decide if that'd be a relief or a disappointment.

* * *

Marc was due after work on Tuesday, and Ally's stomach hurt. Part of it was butterflies, some of it a crushing ache because their days were well and truly numbered now. When the doorbell went just before seven, the butterflies triumphed. She skipped down the stairs two at a time and threw her arms around him.

'Hello, handsome.'

He didn't reply, and he hadn't moved, leaving his arms hanging by his sides.

'Marc?' She drew back and her lips parted at his expression. Anger? No, something more. Pain? Maybe. Pain and anger, mixed.

For a moment, she was convinced something had happened to Sam. That he was about to tell her Sam had been in an accident, and was critically injured in hospital. Or worse.

'What happened?' she said. Her lips felt cold and numb.

He held out his phone. God, no. Had Julie or Sam texted him with an accusation? They'd been caught?

Ally took the phone with trembling fingers.

It was a message, but not a text, and not about Sam. It was the message she'd sent to Good Profile Guy on OkCupid.

'What?' She frowned at him. 'How did you get—oh. It's your profile?'

He nodded.

Ally cringed. 'I didn't know it was yours. You put the wrong age.'

Of course he had, considering his hang-up about age. She should've known when she'd seen Blondie, and hadn't they watched *Life of Pi* together?

Marc still hadn't moved. His eyes looked beautiful against his deep crimson shirt and he smelled deliciously of sandalwood and citrus.

'Is that why you wanted to see me?' he said finally. 'To end it?'

Mrs Cooper was peering out of her net curtains.

'Marc, come inside. It's freezing.'

'I don't want to come inside.' He followed her gaze and swatted at Mrs Cooper like she was a fly. 'Piss off, you nosy woman.'

Mrs Cooper gaped, and retreated into her living room.

'Marc! She's a nice lady.'

'You think everyone's nice. Every animal is cute. Every woman's pretty. Every man's good enough to fuck, for a few weeks at least.'

Ally flinched. 'You know what I'm like. I told you from the start. I'm not ashamed of sleeping with lots of men, and you're not going to make me ashamed.'

'I don't want you to be ashamed. I want you to want me.' He smashed his palm into the bricks beside her door, and Ally felt the pain in her own hand.

'Marc, don't.' She grasped his fingers and held them tight. 'Please come in. Not here.'

His hand trembled as she tugged him inside and she was afraid of the force of his emotions. He was usually so calm and good humoured.

'Ally.' He pushed her against the wall and cupped her face, staring at her with such intensity she felt breathless. 'What can I do to keep you? Just tell me. Tell me what you want.'

'Nothing,' she whispered, hating his strained voice. 'Marc, we can't do it for ever.'

'We can. I want you. Whatever you need, I'll give it. Just tell me.'

He moved closer. His warm, solid, comforting body next to hers. Ally laid a palm on his hammering heart and couldn't tear her gaze away from his eyes. 'Why are you so scared?'

'Because I love you.'

Ally blinked. She must have misheard. 'What?'

'I love you.'

Ally stared blankly at him. Computer wouldn't compute.

Marc pushed his hands into her hair. 'Ally. Talk to me.'

'What – I – what?'

He looked at her so fondly. Lovingly? 'I'm in love with you, Ally. You must know that. I don't want us to sneak around any more. I want to be with you, properly.'

It was too much to process. His words, his scent, the thud of his heart under her hands and the feel of his on her skin. She pushed him away and hopped on to the stairs, needing distance. Needing time.

'Ally.' He breathed heavy and hard, staring at her intently. 'Say something.'

'You – god, Marc, no. It's just sex.'

His body taughtened. 'It isn't. Not for me.'

Ally closed her eyes. OK, she knew it wasn't just sex, but how was she supposed to know it was this? This didn't happen to her. Men loved her body, and that was it. She loved their bodies, and that was it.

She thought of the unflattering, comfortable cow pyjamas. The way he'd held her when she was curled up in pain, sex the last thing on her mind, and would've carried on holding her for days if she'd let him. Christmas, when she'd missed him so much it ached.

'You don't feel the same?' Marc said, almost too quietly to hear. It echoed through her mind like a shout.

The crystal bit into her palm and she focused in on the pain so she didn't have to listen to her answer. Instead she forced herself to picture every detail of Sam's wretched face, Rachel's disgust, Mum's shock and pain and disappointment.

'No,' she said in a shaky voice. 'It's just sex.'

His eyes went in and out of focus. How many times had she looked into those eyes? Watched them watching her as they had sex – made love?

She loved Sam, and her Mum, and Rachel. And they would hate her if they found out what she'd been doing.

They locked gazes for a long moment, and Ally refused to blink first. Finally, he turned and left her.

Every muscle in her body screamed at her to let them run after him, to crush herself to him and feel him and breathe him in one last time, but she clung to the biting crystal until her palm turned hot and sticky, and watched the road long after he was out of sight.

Chapter Twenty-Four

$\mathcal{A}$ll Ally wanted to do was stay at home and eat things she'd regret. Instead, she forced herself to stay out of the house from morning to night and surround herself with people who expected her to be cheery and bright.

She almost gave herself Valentine's Day off, after working eleven days in a row. When she couldn't fill her days with shifts, she'd gone to the library to work on her new website and craft adverts for the business. It was working – she had one appointment to take pictures at a christening, and another to paint a pair of rabbits. Wedding business would be slow in trickling through, because people booked their photographers or make-up artists months or even years in advance. But that was good. Ally didn't want instant gratification. She wanted hard work with no return, like in the olden days when people had to do hard labour as penance. Maybe she could join a Catholic church? She'd heard Catholics were good at guilt.

Staying home alone on Valentine's Day would have been a mistake, but now she was here the café didn't seem like the best idea. All the happy couples weren't helping, acting like sucker fish or giggling as they ordered cheesecake to share. Usually a big fan of public displays of affection, Ally couldn't stomach it. She resisted the temptation to take an entire cheesecake into the back and eat until she was sick.

Every time she went behind the counter she checked her phone. If Marc loved her he'd be thinking of her. If he hadn't realised she was totally wrong for him; too immature, too flighty, too fickle.

If he lost interest, she should be happy. They couldn't be together, so it was better for him to forget her. But try as she might, as practised as she was, she couldn't find anything positive at all in him giving up on her.

She gave her first genuine smile of the day when Rachel came to visit in her lunch hour.

'Hello, gorgeous,' said Ally, and blew her a kiss.

Sam appeared in the doorway, and Ally's insides twisted at the sight of his so-familiar straight nose. She plastered her smile back on immediately, but Rachel gave her a strange look.

'Hey, sexy.' She kissed his cheek and inhaled deeply. Whatever aftershave he wore was nothing like his father's. If she looked at his fair hair and concentrated on the smell, she'd be fine. She wouldn't be reminded of anyone else.

'Are you sniffing me?'

Ally was transported back to the Blondie concert. Marc looked down at her with amusement while she pretended she hadn't been inhaling his seductive scent.

Yesterday, in a moment of weakness, she'd gone into The Perfume Shop when she was at the mall and tried all the men's fragrances until her head ached, her nose was incapable of smelling a thing, and the sales assistants were shooting her dirty looks. To make up for wasting their time, she bought one that was a bit like one of Marc's, if not as deep and bewitching. It sat on her bedside table so she could spritz his pillow with it.

No, not his pillow. Her pillow. He'd only ever been a temporary guest.

'Ally?'

She jerked back to reality when Sam prodded her. He was in a good mood, and his amused smile was just like Marc's whenever she returned from a zone-out. She looked away.

'Sorry, what?'

'Can we sit down?' he asked.

'Oh, right. Sure. What do you want?'

She got them both hot chocolates. Marshmallows for Sam, soya milk for Rachel. They sat on stools at the side of the counter so she could talk to them in between serving customers.

'Got a date tonight?' Sam asked her.

'Nah.'

Rachel paused mid-sip and both of them stared at her.

'What?' said Ally. 'I'm not buying into the Valentine's hype this year. I like being free and single.'

Rachel lowered her mug and narrowed her eyes. 'I thought you wanted a serious relationship?'

'I do. That's why I'm taking my time and not just dating anybody who asks me. Brendan said you're going to some fancy restaurant, Sam.'

'Yep.' Sam beamed. 'Next week I'm going to meet his parents.'

Rachel hadn't taken her eyes off Ally but now she turned to Sam. 'Wow! That's a big step.'

'I know,' said Sam in a rush. 'It's like we've known each other for years.'

If Sam was meeting Brendan's parents they'd want Brendan to meet Sam's before long. She pictured Marc and Brendan meeting and wondered how they'd get on. She wanted to talk to Marc but failing that she wanted to talk *about* him. It was an insane urge, one she needed to resist.

'What about him meeting yours?' she asked.

Sam gave a humourless laugh and stood up. 'Yeah, right. If I want my mother to disown me. I'd better get back to work. Coming on the Central Line, Rach?'

Rachel was still watching Ally. 'No. I'll stay a bit longer.'

As soon as Sam was gone, Ally spoke loudly to ward off any questions. 'So, what are you doing this evening?'

'What's going on?' Rachel said. 'You've been acting weird for months and don't think we haven't noticed.'

Ally stirred her hot chocolate and watched the liquid swirl. 'Nothing. I'm just a weird person.'

'Look, I'm going to ask you something. Don't freak out.'

'I think I left the fridge open. I'd better check.' Ally stood up, but Rachel grasped her wrist and tugged her back into her seat.

'That man I saw at your house once, when I dropped off the ice cream,' Rachel said. 'He looked a bit like Sam.'

Maybe if she ignored this, it'd go away. She examined her mug.

'Ally?'

Or not.

'Ally. Is something going on with you and . . . Sam's dad?'

She swallowed.

Rachel squeezed her wrist. 'You can talk to me. I don't think Sam suspects anything and I'm not going to tell him.'

Ally met her eyes and saw no hatred. 'We stopped. It's over.'

Rachel nodded slowly. 'When?'

'Last week.'

'And it'd been going on since . . .'

'Summer.'

'Jesus.' Rachel sat back and looked stunned. 'That's got to be a record for you. Why did you stop?'

Ally clutched her mug so hard her knuckles went white. 'Usual story. Nothing in common.'

'Then the sex must have been great for it to last, what? Seven months?'

'Yeah. It was.'

'Ally.' Rachel clasped her wrist. 'You look on the edge of a break-down. Talk to me.'

Ally's vision blurred. She wiped her eyes on her apron. 'I really screwed up. He said he was in love with me.'

'And that's a screw-up?'

'Of course it is. You know Sam thinks the divorce is some blip and they'll be back together before long. He would never forgive me for throwing a spanner in the works. And I won't lose Sam. I can't.'

Rachel patted her back. 'Oh dear. It is a bit messy.'

'I fancied him from the start.' Ally clutched her. 'I should've stayed away. I thought he wasn't interested but I should've been careful.'

Rachel stroked her hair. 'And you? How do you feel about him?'

Ignoring the knot in her stomach, she said, 'It was just sex. I screwed up.'

'Are you sure? You seem very unhappy for someone who only lost a sex buddy.'

Ally drew back and wiped her face on her apron. 'It's not that. I'm afraid of losing Sam too. I would lose him, wouldn't I?'

She looked beseechingly at Rachel, who shifted in her chair.

'Of course not,' she said unconvincingly. 'He loves you.'

Ally nodded and tried to hold herself together until Rachel had to go back to work.

* * *

When she got home that evening, Ally forced herself to change and go straight back out to the gym. It was almost deserted which was definitely a blessing and *not* a reminder that everyone else was out on dates.

She wasn't lonely. She had her friends and family and that was all she needed. Even if they were all on dates, including Mum.

Her phone rang while she was on the treadmill. She hopped off so fast she stumbled and wrenched her ankle.

It was Jason. Not Marc.

'Ow, hello,' she gasped, holding it to her ear.

'Hey. What are you up to tonight?'

Ally bit her lip. For once she just didn't feel like sex. Not with Jason, anyway. She pushed that thought out of her mind.

'Should be in bed soon,' she said, gingerly rotating her ankle, 'with my legs elevated.'

'Nice. You're still with that guy then?'

'What guy?'

'The one you've been seeing for months.'

Ally sat on a rowing machine. 'I haven't been seeing anyone. Tonight is just . . . casual.'

'Good. Want to go to Barbados with me?'

'Go to . . . Barbados?'

'Yep. My cousin and his girlfriend were supposed to go, but now she's pregnant and throwing up every half hour so they've given their tickets to me. I want to go with someone who looks hot in a bikini.'

Ally closed her eyes and imagined herself on a white sand beach with a cocktail in hand. 'I don't think I can afford it.'

'Flights and hotel are paid for, though you gotta share with me. All you need is spending money.'

Ally bit her lip again. She could do that, just about. Especially if she didn't drink too many cocktails. And even if she did have to share with Jason, he wouldn't expect sex if she didn't want it.

'I'm in. Thanks, Jas. You're the best.'

She hung up feeling happier than she had in weeks.

CHAPTER TWENTY-FIVE

~

lly sang 'Chiquitita' to herself as she packed. The hotel she and Mum had stayed at in Ibiza had played the song at least hourly, and she'd forever associate it with holidays.

Two hours until Jason would pick her up. By the morning she'd be in the Caribbean.

She hoped he'd packed lightly because her luggage was going to be way over her twenty-three kilograms allowance, even though most of the clothes took up very little space indeed. Some of her books and toiletries would have to go into his case.

Once everything was packed she had a long bath, painted her toenails, and lay on the sofa to watch snow falling past the window.

Fifteen minutes before Jason was due, she remembered she had to charge her phone and dug it out of her handbag.

Three missed calls. Marc.

Her heart thumped. She'd lost all hope of him calling.

Her finger hovered over the 'return call' button. This holiday was her chance to relax and unwind and forget about him. The last thing she needed to do was talk to him and start her ten days away on a sad note.

It still took a monumental effort to put the phone away and resist every urge to take it back out.

Ally slammed into Jason on the doorstep when he finally arrived.

'Uh, hi,' he said, as she shoved him outside and locked her door. 'Is something on fire in there?'

'Yup. Insurance scam. When I get back I'll get a whole new house.' Ally dragged her case to his car and hopped from foot to foot as she waited for him to open the boot.

'We've got two hours to get to the airport you know,' he said, lifting her bag in.

'Yeah, but I hate being late.'

He paused to stare at her.

'Oh, all right,' she grumbled. 'I'm antsy. I want my holiday. Thank you, by the way.' She threw her arms around him and kissed his cheek.

'Sure you haven't left the gas on or the water running or something?'

'As if I'd do a thing like that.' Ally beamed and hopped round the car to the passenger side.

She breathed a sigh of relief as Jason drove the car out of their road. They were on their way and nothing would stop them.

'How—' she began, and then her phone rang.

Marc.

Her heart thumped again.

This was different from a missed call. He was somewhere right now thinking of her. Wanting to talk to her. Right at that moment.

She ignored it and turned on the radio.

'Who's that?' Jason asked.

'Nobody.'

Ally pictured Marc's face with the expression he'd wore when he left her. She forced Jason to play the number plate game until they got to the airport, where they switched to I Spy.

'Ally, can we stop now?' Jason asked as they joined the back of the check-in queue. 'People are looking at us because we're nearly thirty and we're playing I Spy.'

'Why do you care what people think?'

'I'm a social creature.'

Marc wouldn't have cared. He didn't care whether she was stomping in puddles or running from swans. The only thing he'd ever worried about was that he was too old for her.

As if on cue, her phone rang again.

When she saw his name her fingers pressed the accept button before she'd thought about it.

'Ally?' His voice was wrong. Not as deep as usual. Not controlled.

'Marc? What's wrong?'

An announcement about unattended luggage blasted out from a speaker near Ally's head.

A pause. 'Ally? Can you hear me?'

She glared at the speaker. 'Wait, I'm going outside.'

Jason grabbed her arm. 'Ally? Where are you going?'

'Ally?' said Marc. 'I can't hear you.'

'Just wait! I'm coming.' Afraid he'd hang up, she shook Jason off and pushed through the crowd to the exit.

Outside, she stepped into the frigid air. Snowflakes hit her bare arms and shoulders and melted in an instant to icy droplets. She hadn't worn a coat, knowing she'd be in Jason's car and then in the warm airport. Her beach dress was thin and definitely not suitable for England. 'Marc, what's wrong?'

'Debbie.'

'Oh, no.' Her heart sank, and she closed her eyes. 'Is she OK?'

'She collapsed in the park.' His voice had risen a notch more. Still deep and rich, but edged with pain.

Ally squeezed her eyes tight. 'Where are you?'

'At the vets.'

She imagined him there alone. 'I'm coming. What's the address?'

Her voice, shakier than his, seemed to make his pain worse. She remembered the way he'd tell some terrible joke whenever he saw her holding her crystal.

'You don't have to come,' he said, his voice catching. 'I just . . . I don't know. I wanted to call you.'

Ally tried to pull herself together. If it made it worse for him when she was upset, she'd make it better by being strong. Or at least pretending to be. 'I want to come.' She held the phone away from her ear to check the Wi-Fi signal. 'Shit, my battery's low. Text me the address, quick, and I'll order a taxi.'

It'd have to go on her credit card. If she had enough left on her limit.

When the taxi app asked where she was, she remembered the holiday. Her heart sank at the sight of Jason, standing near the check-in desks with a pissed off expression.

'I can't come,' she said, cringing.

'What?' Jason's look of disbelief didn't help.

'My . . . friend needs me.'

'Your friend needs you,' he repeated, deadpan.

'Yes. His . . . well, his dog's not well.'

Jason peered at her like she was a Rubik's cube. 'You can't go for a holiday in the Caribbean because your friend's dog is ill?'

'Right.' Ally grimaced. 'Will you forgive me?'

Jason shrugged. 'I'll probably get over it. Is this the dude you've been googly-eyed over for months?'

'I have not been googly-eyed!'

Jason gave her a look.

'I haven't!'

'Right. Whatever you say.' Jason pushed the luggage trolley towards the exit, forcing Ally to skip after him.

'I haven't,' she insisted. 'It was just sex.'

'OK. Whatever you say.'

'It was.'

'Let's go to Barbados then. You can get sex there. Even sex with me, if you're lucky.'

Ally couldn't think of a comeback.

'Just sex, huh?' Jason smirked.

She forgave him because he waited with her until the cab arrived. He kissed her on the cheek, assured her he'd forgive her someday, and waved her away.

Ally begged the driver to be as quick as possible. The traffic near Gatwick on a Friday evening was outrageous. Ally was stir-crazy, desperate to get to Marc, and even considered telling the driver to wait for her at the end of the street so she could run around the block a few times.

The thought of Marc alone, knowing Debbie might die, sitting in some sterile waiting room . . .

'Is there another route we can take?' she asked.

The driver's eyes met hers in the rear-view mirror. 'Sorry. Everywhere's like this on a Friday.'

Ally slumped back in her seat and played the number plate game in an effort to distract herself. When she realised what she was doing, she burst into laughter and got a frown from the driver. Ally Rivers, trying and failing to distract herself? What had the world come to?

An hour later, with half her Barbados-flag-pattern nail varnish chewed off and a bitter taste in her mouth, the driver pulled up outside the surgery, a single-storey building surrounded by fields. There were two other cars in the small car park, and her stomach flipped when she saw the blue Subaru. Snow was building up on its windows, a powdery layer that would shift as soon as it moved.

Ally flung the door open before the taxi had fully stopped and jumped out. One heel sank an inch into the wet, muddy ground, and the other caught the side of a stone. She stumbled, grabbing the taxi door for support, and stepped towards the building.

'Hey!' The taxi driver got out of the car. 'Don't forget your bags.'

Bags? Who cared about bags? She grabbed her purse from the seat and pushed a five-pound note into the driver's hand. 'Will you unload them for me? Just leave them here. I need to go.'

Her heels sank into the ground again. With a noise of exasperation she tore them off and hopped across the gravel, ignoring the sharp pains.

'Hey!' the taxi driver called. 'The bags will get wet!'

Ally waved a hand behind her. Let them get wet. Her feet hit the smooth concrete path leading up to the door, and she ran.

Inside, there was a long, low-ceilinged waiting room. It was lit in garish fluorescent lighting, the room huge and stark with its single occupant. Marc, in a black overcoat and jeans, sat on a plastic chair with his head in his hands.

Harry, lying on the floor beside him, saw Ally first. He whined and thumped his tail, but didn't move from his spot.

Marc looked up, and wore the same expression as when he'd turned his back on her three weeks ago. Pain.

'Marc.' Ally ran forward as he stood up. In an instant she was in his arms, breathing in nutmeg and lemon and sandalwood with his warm body against hers.

'How is she?' she whispered.

He shook his head, and his stubble scratched her cheek. 'She's in surgery, but they didn't sound very hopeful. Kept saying how old she is.'

Ally squeezed him tighter. He rested his head on her shoulder and nested his nose into the crook of her neck.

They were still standing like that when someone cleared their throat near Ally's ear. Both of them raised their heads, and the woman in green scrubs looked apologetic.

'Sorry to interrupt.' Her eyes flickered to Ally's turquoise beach dress. Far too bright, too happy, for this place and for Marc, in his sensible winter clothes. 'Mr Kinsell, can we have a word with you?'

Marc grasped Ally's hand. She clung on, pressing her hip against his and craving his warmth.

'Come with me,' he said, his voice hoarse and his eyes beseeching.

Ally nodded. She didn't trust herself to speak.

The vet led them down a corridor into a room with an examination table, plastic cabinets and a computer. The heating was on, unlike in the freezing waiting room, but the tiled floor was still cold. Harry sat on her bare feet as if he knew, and her toes snatched his warmth.

The vet faced Marc across the table. 'I'm so sorry, Mr Kinsell, but the surgery was unsuccessful.'

He gripped Ally's hand so tightly it hurt. She gritted her teeth and stroked his forearm with her free hand.

'She's dead?' Marc whispered.

'No. Laura's just making her comfortable while the anaesthetic wears off. But her heart's giving up, Mr Kinsell. She might make it another day, or even a few days, with lots of medication and help to breathe. But she'd have to stay here, and it could be quite frightening and confusing for her. It may be kinder to help ease her away. It's your decision.'

Ally blinked furiously. He needed her to be strong.

'Can I see her?' Marc asked.

His legs didn't seem to want to work. Ally leaned into him and grasped his arm, half-dragging him down the hall. Debbie lay in a large cage on a mound of blankets, her eyes dulled. When she saw Marc she raised her head an inch and gave her tail one feeble thump.

'Hey, girl,' said Marc, stroking her head with his free hand. He was doing the same as Ally. Trying not to cry. Trying not to make it worse for his dog.

The vet pushed a box of tissues into Ally's hand and she pinched one against her eyes while Marc wasn't looking.

Debbie's breathing was awful. Laboured, heavy. She looked exhausted, miserable and confused. Harry nudged her with his nose and whined.

'Call us when you're ready,' the vet whispered to Ally. She nodded.

Marc stroked his dog. 'I'm sorry, Debbie. I didn't know you were so ill. I should have been paying attention.'

His voice broke and Ally buried her face in his shoulder for a second. Then she straightened up and squeezed his arm. 'She doesn't blame you, Marc. Look how much she loves you. Her eyes lit up when you came in.'

He sniffed. 'I don't think she's in pain. Do you?'

Ally stroked Debbie's curly ear and the dog's liquid brown eyes slid to her. Confused. Tired.

'No. I'm sure they gave her painkillers.'

'She's not happy though.'

Ally squeezed him again. 'It's a strange place. Confusing and probably scary.'

'And she'll have to stay here to die.'

Ally watched his face and hated that he had to choose. 'Maybe you can get painkillers, and take her home.'

There was a glimmer of hope in his eyes, and he sounded more animated. 'Yes. She can lie in her bed with me and Harry and . . .' He lowered his eyes to Debbie's. 'And lie there until her heart gives up. Until it's too much effort to breathe.' His voice was dull again. 'I can't do that to her.'

Debbie nuzzled his palm and gave a short whine before she had to take another laboured breath.

'I've got to let her go, haven't I?'

Ally swallowed. She wanted to plead ignorance and tell him he had to choose. But she could see the tug of war in his conscience, in the shake of his fingers on his beloved dog's head. If she made the decision for him, it would make it easier. Ease his guilt.

'Yes,' she said. 'You have to let her go.'

The only sound was Debbie's heavy breathing, and the shuffling of Harry's feet as he pressed against Ally.

'Will you stay with me?' Marc whispered, not looking at Ally, as if afraid she would say no.

'Of course I will.'

Silence again, apart from a clock ticking in the background. Steady and soothing, out of rhythm with Debbie's quick breaths.

'I love you, girl,' he said. Ally closed her eyes. How many times had he said that to a human? Did any of them return it? He and Julie had never really loved each other. His parents were dead. Neither Sam nor Gavin seemed the type to tell their father they loved him. How long since someone had told him?

He was still speaking softly to Debbie. Telling her how glad he was that he'd got her, and he'd never forget her. Ally's fingers were going numb, but she didn't complain or try to wriggle out of his grip.

Debbie seemed soothed by his voice. She laid her head down and closed her eyes.

Marc stroked her for a few more minutes, then turned and nodded at the door. It opened immediately, and the vet entered with another woman in scrubs.

'Have you decided what to do?' she asked gently.

Marc nodded, and Ally saw his throat move but no words come out.

'He wants to help her go to sleep,' Ally said, stroking his arm. 'So she doesn't feel any pain.'

Marc nodded and rubbed Ally's hand with his thumb.

'Do you need another minute?' the vet asked.

Marc smoothed Debbie's ears and she opened her weary eyes to look at him. Her breathing grew sharper. 'No.'

The vets spoke quietly, and one of them took Harry out of the room. He whined as he went and Ally debated following him, but Marc needed her more. She couldn't run away from this. Not when Marc had no choice. She held on to him while he kissed Debbie's head and whispered to her.

When the vet returned, she checked again that Marc was ready, then gently stretched out Debbie's paw and slid the needle in. Marc's fingers tightened on Ally's, which she didn't think was possible, and she bit her lip hard to stop from crying out.

Within seconds, Debbie's eyes fluttered closed again and her breathing slowed, then stopped. Marc bent to kiss her head, as his tears rolled into the curly fur on her ear.

CHAPTER TWENTY-SIX

*T*he vets slipped out of the room. Marc was still for a long time, then bent to kiss Debbie's head.

They walked back to the waiting room. The vets avoided Marc's eyes as they took his payment and arranged for Debbie to be cremated.

One of the vets held the door open for them.

'One minute,' Ally said. 'I need to get my shoes.'

Marc stared down at her bare feet, as if he'd only just noticed. He let go of her hand and she resisted groaning in relief as the pain ebbed.

No point putting her heels back on. It'd been snowing all the time they were inside, and the ground would be wetter than before.

The concrete path outside the clinic was icy cold. Ally tiptoed down it, exposing the minimum amount of skin to the white-flecked stone. When she went to step on to the gravel, Marc put an arm around her waist and pulled her back.

'You'll cut your foot.'

'I'm fine.' Ally's teeth chattered, making her voice shake. The snowflakes on her bare arms weren't melting on impact, but bouncing off her skin like sharp little pins.

Marc shrugged off his black overcoat, pulled it tight around her, then scooped her up in his arms much more easily than she'd imagined.

Ally buried her face in his neck and closed her eyes so his scent could envelop her. Man, she'd missed his fragrances. The nutmeg was so sweet and inviting.

It only took a few seconds to reach his car, and he let her go the moment she was in the passenger seat. She'd been clinging to him much tighter than he was holding on to her. Marc wasn't craving her closeness, wasn't desperate for her touch like she was for his. Maybe it hurt to see her and he regretted calling. Maybe even his cold, nagging ex-wife would have been more comfort than Ally.

While he retrieved her bags, she pulled the coat tight around her. His scent lingered on the collar and with the heavy, warm material it was almost like he was holding her. Almost.

Harry jumped into the back seat, pressed his forepaws against the rear window, and whined. Looking for Debbie. Ally shot Marc a worried look, but he was staring at the tree in front of the car, in a world of his own.

'Thank you,' he said. 'For coming.'

'I'm so sorry about Debbie.' Ally squeezed his arm. Marc reached up to grip the steering wheel, making her hand slip off him and on to the gearstick. Nope. He definitely didn't want to touch her.

'I'm sorry for what I said to you,' he said, not looking at her. 'I was unfair. You were honest. You're always honest. I'd just deluded myself, and it wasn't your fault at all.'

The temperature dropped another few degrees. Ally curled her legs underneath her and felt her icy feet through the dress.

'It's OK. I've heard worse.'

He looked like he wanted to say more, but swallowed and started the engine. Harry whined and barked as they drove off, looking back at the clinic as if he thought they'd forgotten his friend. Ally twisted in her seat and tried to distract him, even though Marc barely seemed to notice the noise.

They drove in silence, until he passed the train station.

'Marc? Where are we going?'

'Home.' He blinked, then he pulled over abruptly into a parking bay. Ally took in his white knuckles on the steering wheel and his pale face tinged yellow by a street lamp.

'I don't want you to go.' He met her eyes, finally, and his sadness punched her in the gut. Before she knew what she was doing she was kissing him, her arms around his broad shoulders and his soft lips hard against hers.

Marc gripped her waist, his fingers pressing into her hips. She wanted his hands everywhere, his mouth all over her body. Her knee hit the gearstick as she climbed on to his lap and crushed herself against him.

Marc broke the kiss but didn't loosen his grip. He leaned his forehead on her shoulder and Ally rubbed her cheek on his springy hair.

'I miss you,' he said.

Her toes curled. His breath was warm and tickly on her bare skin.

Ally couldn't say it back. It would give him false hope.

Harry's wet nose pushed into her knee as he sniffed. Probably wondering why she was climbing over his master.

Marc pulled back and looked into her eyes, his face expectant. Waiting.

'I . . .' Ally swallowed. They couldn't be together. Rekindling things would only prolong the agony. 'I'm sorry.'

He spread his fingers over her back and traced circles on her spine. Her skin was cold, and through the dress she felt every movement of his warm fingers.

'Were you with someone tonight? A man?'

Ally focused on his lips so she didn't have to meet his eyes. She couldn't tell him where she'd been going. If he knew what she'd given up he'd read into it just like Jason had. The silence dragged on and her heart beat faster, waiting for him to berate her again.

Instead, he pulled her close and kissed her cheek, then gently lifted her back on to her seat. She watched his blank face as he turned the car back. At the first roundabout he pulled out without looking, and an angry driver in a Mercedes hit the horn as he narrowly missed ploughing into them. Marc barely seemed to notice.

'Just take me to the station,' she said. 'You shouldn't be driving when you're upset.'

'I'll take you home.'

'No, Marc. It's not safe. Look, what about Harry? We have seat belts, but he doesn't. You need to get him home.'

Marc's fingers tightened on the steering wheel, his knuckles turning white. 'OK.'

At the station she shrugged off Marc's comforting, scented coat and left it on the passenger seat.

Marc saw it when he finished unloading her case, and handed it to her. 'Take it. You'll freeze.'

'It's yours.' If she took it, he'd have to see her again to get it. The best thing for him was to forget her before she forgot him. That way, he'd rejected her, and it wouldn't hurt him as much.

His precious face looked tired, those beautiful brown eyes sad. 'Ally—'

'I don't want it,' she snapped. 'It doesn't go with my dress. You know me. I'd rather freeze than look uncoordinated.'

'I do know you, and that's bullshit.' His voice was raised as well. 'You don't want it because it's mine. No need to lie to me.'

If she took it, she'd sleep with it. Every time she missed him, she'd sniff it. It would be pathetic and it would stop her moving on and when he came to get it they'd end up arguing again.

'Goodbye, Marc.' She moved forward to kiss his cheek but he turned away and held Harry's collar, even though Harry was sitting still beside him.

Ally wanted to hurry away, but her case was heavy and the smooth tarmac glistened with ice. Why had she worn heels? A rattle sounded, getting louder, and a train sped past her on the southbound side of the track. Shit. Another hour until the next one. She kicked her shoes off, bent to grab them, and dragged her case towards the platform as fast as she could.

At the sound of a car engine she spun around. Marc's headlights swept over her as he turned the car around and left her alone and exposed in the car park.

She'd refused the coat, and refused the lift, and if he was thinking straight he wouldn't have let her go barefoot, barely clothed, with a case she could hardly move. It was her fault he had left her, both times, but both times had struck her to the core.

She stared after the car until the train chugged, pulling out of the station, and groaned.

The air seemed to drop another few degrees when she thought of Barbados and trudged into the station. The ticket office was closed and locked this late at night, but the gate to the platform was open. When the ticket machine refused her card she tried again, then a third time, before admitting it wasn't a mechanical problem. She'd maxed it out.

After some experimentation, she was able to buy a ticket to zone five. At South Ruislip she could use her travel card to get a bus if they were still running or, if not, she could walk.

At least she hadn't completely run out of luck – the last train to South Ruislip was in thirty-five minutes, but that was better than there not being one at all.

After ten minutes on a freezing metal bench, she huddled down on her case in a corner, rested her forehead on her knees, and stopped fighting the images of Debbie closing her eyes, Harry nudging his friend in bewilderment, and Marc watching his beloved dog die. The movie reel froze on the last frame, and she sobbed into her cold skin, wishing she'd comforted him better. He loved her – or thought he did – and she'd let him down. Too concerned with managing his expectations so she didn't have to deal with the fallout. Not thinking of him, and that all he needed was a little kindness.

'Um, hey?'

Ally jerked her head up. A man in a dark suit frowned down at her. She scrambled to her feet and gripped one heel in her hand, ready to whack him round the head with it if he made a wrong move.

'Whoa.' He eyed the heel and grinned. 'Relax, honey. I don't wanna hurt you.'

She tightened her grip, even though he was clearly confident he could deal with her if she attacked. 'Glad to hear it.'

'You look like you need a hug. Come sit with me.'

Sour bile rose in her throat, but she didn't want him to see her swallow. Show no fear. That's what they always said in self-defence classes Rachel made her go to. 'I'm fine. I like it here. Alone.'

'Don't be like that. Come and hang with me.'

'I'm busy.'

He laughed. 'You're a challenge. I like that. Come.' He reached out, and Ally smacked his arm with the heel. Hard.

'Ow!' He clutched his forearm and stepped back. 'What the fuck? I was being friendly, you bitch.'

Ally's pulse pounded. Now he was angry, and she'd started the violence. She'd be no match for him if he was determined to get physical.

'I don't want any new friends,' she said, wishing her voice wasn't shaking. 'Leave me alone.'

'Everything OK here?'

Ally blinked over the man's shoulder. Another guy stood behind him in dark jeans and a jumper over a bodybuilder's physique. The arsehole looked him up and down, muttered 'everything's cool' and slunk off to the other end of the platform.

'You OK?' Bodybuilder took in her bare feet and shoulders. 'Want a jumper?'

Ally shook her head. 'Thanks. I'm good.'

'Your teeth are chattering.'

'It's my own fault.'

'You're punishing yourself for something?'

Ally realised how ridiculous she'd been over Marc's coat. She wasn't just cold, she was *cold*.

'Come on,' he coaxed. 'It'll give me a chance to show off my guns. Help my ego out here.'

Ally couldn't help but smile. His face was so friendly, and she felt no threat from him. Of course, that probably meant he was a serial killer, but at least she could die warm.

'I'd love a jumper.'

It was like stepping into a sauna, and she sighed aloud with contentment.

'I'd give you my shoes too, but I'm not that nice and my feet aren't that nice either.'

'I've got shoes.' Ally waved her heels and slipped them on.

They sat on the bench and waited for the train together. Her new friend, Simon, sat protectively between her and Arsehole, who paced up and down the end of the platform and shot them sour looks. He was honest, and funny, and his guns really were impressive. Dark hair, dark eyes, a hint of chest hair poking out of his white T-shirt.

All she could think about was Marc. Was he in his living room or his bedroom? Would Harry comfort him, or make it worse by nosing Debbie's bed and whining when he couldn't find her? Would Julie be sympathetic? Maybe he'd find comfort in her. Maybe they'd rekindle their relationship and he'd realise he should have been working on his marriage instead of chasing a hopeless airhead.

'Want me to cheer you up with some bad chat-up lines?' Simon offered.

Ally dragged herself back to the present. 'I bet I've heard them before.'

'Let's see.' He cleared his throat. 'Are you religious?'

'Nope.'

'Huh. 'Cause you're the answer to all my prayers.'

She burst into laughter. 'Please tell me that's never worked?'

He grinned. 'With this face? All the time.'

'Oh man. Got any more?'

'Something wrong with your left eye?'

'Nope.'

''Cause you're looking right, baby.'

Ally groaned.

She was feeling marginally better when a train pulled into the station eleven minutes before hers. Simon looked at it before glancing at Arsehole, who made no moves to board.

'This is your train?' she asked.

'No.'

'Liar.'

'Why would I lie? Tell me more about your business.'

He got her train, but she wheedled his destination out of him and made him get off at the right stop.

'You're sweet, but I'm fine now,' she said. 'I'll keep my phone in my hand in case I get into trouble.' She hadn't mentioned the dead battery. No need for him to worry about her.

Saying goodbye was a relief, even though she felt guilty because he was so kind. Giving up the jumper was more of a wrench, but she insisted. She sensed he was disappointed, and probably wanted an excuse to see her again. But the thought of dating him, sleeping with him, was all wrong. Like anybody she'd met since Marc.

Ally pressed her cheek against the train window and closed her eyes. It'd been seven months without so much as a tingle for another man. Longer than her longest relationship. Certainly the longest she'd been interested in a man since she was a teenager.

But that didn't mean it'd last for ever.

Just in time, she noticed that the train was still and she was staring right at a sign saying 'South Ruislip'. She slid out of the doors a second before they closed, and shivered on the platform.

She stepped into a nearly deserted street, and was covered in a frosty layer of snowflakes within moments. She dragged her case to the bus stop and wasn't surprised to find the last one had gone. There was nothing to do but start walking.

Seven months. It might be long for her, but it wasn't long for normal people. Maybe she was just growing up, and it didn't mean anything about Marc. It was just maturity – the way she finally enjoyed not-having-sex time as much as sex time. The way she wanted to share her dreams, and little moments of happiness, and her favourite meals, and comfort him when he needed it and seek comfort in him. The way she still ached for him, and had felt so empty and cold since he left. The way that, all throughout their affair, time without him was time wasted.

She wasn't in love.

The snow began falling in earnest.

* * *

Two hours later, Ally finally turned into her street. Her feet had gone mercifully numb some time ago, but every step took a supreme effort when the cold made her want to lie down and curl into a ball.

She'd taken to staring at the pavement and telling herself she only had to reach the end of the next slab. Twelve inches at a time. Now there weren't many twelve inches left.

She dragged her right foot on to the next crack and forced her left to follow it.

'Ally! Jesus, what are you doing?'

Blinking, she wondered if she was hallucinating from hypothermia. But when Marc clamped his arms around her and held her against him, he felt very solid and very real.

'What are you doing here?' she said. She wasn't prepared for this. Seeing him in the flesh when she'd spent the last two hours scaring herself with cyclical arguments about her feelings for him.

'I came to my senses and realised I'd left you in the cold and dark with a bloody great suitcase to carry. But when I got back to the station you were gone, and all I could imagine was you freezing to death somewhere. Jesus, you're cold. Thank god you're OK.' He exhaled into her hair and squeezed her tighter. He was so warm that she sank into him with a sigh of contentment, closed her eyes, and imagined him missing. If Sam called her, needing support because his father was missing. Not knowing if she'd see him again. Knowing she'd left it like this, with him thinking she didn't care about him at all.

Her chest tightened, and it was harder to breathe.

'What the bloody hell are you up to, anyway?' He pulled back, suddenly angry. 'Why are you barefoot?'

'My heel snapped outside the Chinese takeaway round the corner,' she mumbled. 'I really like their salt and pepper calamari.'

'And you don't have sensible shoes in your case? Or a coat?'

'I don't do sensible. And I was going to Barbados, not Antarctica. Can you shout at me inside, where it's warm?'

He picked her up, muttering darkly, and she clung on to his neck. He carried her and her case with apparent ease. When had he got so strong? She felt inside his coat and laid her palm on his chest until she could feel his heartbeat. Fast and unsteady. He was afraid. For her.

'I'm OK.' She rubbed her cheek on his chin and couldn't feel a thing.

'Your toes are probably going to fall off. And your nose.'

'Will you still l—will you still want me?'

He glared at her, but then hid a smile. 'Yes. You'd still have my favourite bit.'

Ally stared up at him. No trace of a smile. 'What bit's your favourite?'

'Your knees.'

'My knees?'

'Yes. They remind me you're not perfect.'

'You don't like my knees?'

'Right.'

Ally frowned and craned her neck to look at her legs. 'What's wrong with them?'

'Nothing. They're normal knees. But nobody has nice knees. Knees are ugly.'

'I don't think your knees are ugly.'

'You don't think anything's ugly. Keys?'

He stopped, and Ally twisted round to see her front door. She fished in her bag for the keys, and Marc carried her upstairs and into her bedroom.

Ally sat on her bed and examined her knees from different angles. They weren't knobbly, or wrinkly, or dry. Good, strong knees. What was his problem?

Marc rifled through her drawers, pulling out a bundle of clothing, then sat at the edge of the bed and picked up a foot.

'What are you doing?'

'Checking for frostbite.' He rubbed her foot with a towel, and she gasped as pins and needles erupted.

'Ow ow ow.'

Marc ignored her protests, rubbed her foot until the blood was circulating, then put a thick man-sock on it and turned his attention to the other one.

'Any of my toes fallen off?' she asked.

'Not yet.' He stood up and handed her jogging bottoms and a thick flannel shirt. 'Put these on.'

Ally stared at his back as he walked to the window. 'You can watch, you know. You've seen me naked loads of times.'

'I know.' He didn't turn around.

It was silly to feel hurt. But she was cold, and he was warm, so it made sense to want him to touch her, didn't it? She hobbled over to him, now that her feet were back to full feeling and full soreness, and put her hands around his waist. 'Come back. I'm cold.'

'That's why I want you to put dry clothes on.'

'The clothes are cold. You're warm.' She nuzzled his neck and inhaled his scent. The butterflies in her stomach went wild for it.

Marc turned his head towards her, and she thought he was going to kiss her. 'No more, Ally.'

'No more what?'

'Touching. Kissing. Sex. I've got to try and forget you.'

It felt like a punch in the gut, even though a few hours earlier she'd been hoping he'd forget her. Of course he didn't want to love her. She was a terrible lover.

'You don't want to see me again?'

He hesitated. 'Maybe we can try being friends. Just friends. No touching.'

Friends. Well, she'd done sex without feelings, so she could do the opposite. Maybe.

'Not even hugging?' she said, in a small voice.

He pulled her into his arms and her body moulded around his. Sex would be better, but if they could do this, she'd be OK.

'Last one,' he said. 'Because you're cold.'

'No! We can hug. Friends hug. I hug Sam and Rachel and Mum and my sisters all the time. It's a friend thing.'

'When I touch you in one place I want to touch you everywhere.' He ran his fingers down her spine and Ally arched her back, pressing her body closer to his.

'See?' He extricated himself from her arms, picked up the clothes from the bed and pushed them into her arms. 'Clothes. Now.'

He turned away before she peeled her dress off, and it would've been mean to trick him into looking at her.

'Are you staying?' she asked, when she was done.

Marc glanced around warily, then pulled the covers back until she crawled into bed. 'No. Harry was whining when I left, so he's probably keeping the whole street awake by now. He's not used to being alone. Without—' He clamped his mouth shut and swallowed.

Ally clasped his hand and tried to pull him into a hug, but he stood.

'New rules,' he said, staring down at her. 'It's OK to eat together, talk, spend time together out of bed. It's not OK to touch, or be naked with each other.'

'I don't like those rules. They're stupid.'

'Tough.'

'What's the game called?'

He pushed her gently until she lay down, then dragged the covers over her and met her gaze, inches from her face. 'It's called "Marc living in the real world, not fantasy." I'll call you tomorrow to see how many toes you lost in the night.'

'What if my fingers fall off?' she shouted, as he left the room. 'And I can't call an ambulance because my bloody stumps won't hit the right numbers? Marc? Marc?'

The front door closed with a click, and she sighed.

CHAPTER TWENTY-SEVEN

Ally logged into her banking app the next day to check the damage. It was bad. In an effort to forget Marc she'd been going out too much, drinking too many expensive cocktails, and ordering too many takeaways. The plan was to jet off to Barbados and ignore it, but now she had to face up to it.

Her first thought was to ask Gran for help. She'd get a profanity-laden lecture, a guilt trip that'd make her want to crawl into a hole, and a cheque.

Well, Gran couldn't make her feel any worse about herself than she already did and Ally would be able to say, truthfully, that she'd been working on her business.

But as she was dialling her fingers stopped. She'd put a *lot* of work into her business over the past few weeks but Gran wouldn't believe her. Why would she, when Ally was such a work-shy flake?

Flake? Yes. Work-shy? No. She didn't mind work, just hated routine and being tied down by people depending on her for things. It was like Marc had said: she was an adult, just an unusual kind of adult with commitment problems and minor brain dysfunctions. She could look after herself and she could get out of problems without crying to Gran. And there was still money on her travel card.

Half an hour later she was on her way to Central London with a sketching pad, pencils and a bright smile to lure flush tourists in for portraits.

* * *

Ally had taken eighty-nine pounds, including tips, before a jobsworth policeman told her to go home and get a street trader's licence. She went home to get a licence, discovered they were nearly four hundred pounds, and decided calling Gran for a cheque wasn't such a bad idea after all.

But she stopped herself again. On an average night out she spent maybe thirty quid, so if she stayed in she could buy the licence in two or three months.

Her nose wrinkled. No matter how sensible she forced herself to be she always wanted to work to live, not live to work. The whole point of working was to afford the things she loved – going out with her friends, the gym, holidays. All the things she spent money on.

Ally ran a bath and lay in it with only her knees and nose above water. Water in her ears always helped her think and most of her brainwaves came when she was swimming.

Hmm. There was an idea. A swim-only membership at the gym was almost half the price of her full membership. She'd miss the classes but she could still go running and use YouTube tutorials to do yoga. That'd save her forty a month, and if she went out but stuck to long drinks or even soft drinks instead of cocktails, she could afford the licence before too long. Once she had that, she could make enough money to branch into other things. Maybe buy a nice camera or a good set of make-up brushes.

Was it worth it? It was worth a try, at least.

Needing to discuss it with someone, she called Rachel. Rachel was just as excited as her and half an hour later she hung up convinced she'd be a billionaire by the end of the year.

Her optimism shrank when she went to put Rachel's advice into practice and called Sam. He'd make sure her promotional material was as good as it could be and he'd probably know the best ways and places to advertise for her longer-term wedding plans. But Ally thought it'd take another couple of decades before she had any right to ask Sam a favour, even if Rachel was right that she should act normally around Sam unless she wanted him to start asking questions. It was normal for her to shower him with love and hugs and he was tolerating her guilty affection with resigned stoicism.

In the end, she didn't have to ask for help. He offered it the moment she explained her plans and it would've looked strange to refuse. She added another couple of years to her penance calendar and used some of her earnings to buy ingredients for coconut-and-lime cupcakes. He was going to get all his favourites on movie nights for the next twenty-five years.

Still full of beans, she attempted to distract herself by tidying up her wardrobes and drawers. Five minutes in, with a mounting to-be-ironed pile, she gave up, added another year to her debt, and called Marc.

He brushed it off when she asked how he was, and changed the subject when she mentioned Debbie, so instead she babbled about her plans. He was as supportive and happy for her as she'd expected and she hung up satisfied that they really could be friends. As long as she brushed the no-sex part out of her mind, this seemed like a perfect solution. She wouldn't lose Sam, she wouldn't be responsible for making Marc leave his marital home, and she got to keep him. At least, some of him.

But the next time she called, she wasn't so sure. He was pleasant but quiet and made something that sounded suspiciously like an excuse, hanging up after a few minutes. Thinking he might be mourning and unable to talk about it, she drew a picture of Debbie frolicking in a field surrounded by trees, lampposts and treats with angels throwing balls and sticks, and sent it to Marc.

He seemed to genuinely like it when he called to thank her but he was still distant and hung up long before she was ready to say goodbye.

After several disappointing phone calls she challenged him. Marc pleaded ignorance and said he had to go and make dinner.

'Have you changed your mind?' she asked, hugging her knees and closing her eyes. It felt right to be held tight when hearing his voice. 'You don't want to be friends?'

He was silent for a moment. 'I don't know if I can. It's hard to talk to you.'

Ally pushed her eyes into her knee. 'Hey, I'm not that bad. I understand some big words.'

Marc laughed softly. 'You know what I mean. Look, I know you feel sorry for me, but you don't have to put yourself through this. I'll survive. You don't need to check up on me.'

'I'm not doing it out of duty,' she said, stung. 'Or because I feel sorry for you. I want to know how you're doing. I care about you.'

Marc paused. 'You do?'

'Of course I do. I miss you. You should come and see me. I mean, not for sex.' She straightened up. 'New rules, I know. Just for a catch-up.'

'I don't know if that's a good idea.'

'It's a great idea. Look, friends celebrate each other's birthdays so come and see me on mine. Sam's not coming over until eight.'

He was silent for a beat too long. 'Sure. I'll see you then.'

'Liar. You haven't even asked what day it is.'

Ally heard a faint bark down the phone and Marc raised his voice. 'Leave the squirrels alone, Harry. You think I don't know when your birthday is?'

'Why would you? We're not even Facebook friends. That's the only way I know anyone's birthday.'

'You told me when you were painting D—painting. I really have to go before Harry gets beaten up by a squirrel. Take care.'

At first she was stunned that he remembered her telling him all that time ago, sure *she* could never remember something like that. But when she cast her mind back she could see him as clearly as if he were in the room with her and saw his soft lips saying May twenty-fourth.

* * *

As much as Ally wanted Marc to forget his ridiculous rules she had to play fair. On her birthday she dressed in her normal friend-coming-for-dinner-in-winter outfit of jeans and a T-shirt. When she saw him on her doorstep with two days of stubble and the scent of cinnamon she wished she'd gone with stockings and a smile.

His Adam's apple moved as his eyes fixed on her face.

Ally made a noise like a hungry kitten and gestured for him to go upstairs first so she could watch his shoulders move. It didn't matter that he was wearing a thick winter coat – she knew every movement of his muscles well enough to imagine.

In the kitchen she collected herself, repeated 'friends' in her head and concentrated on not spilling the wine.

In the living room she smiled brightly, put the wine on the coffee table, and sat beside him on the sofa.

'Happy birthday.' He handed her a box wrapped in paper with cartoon cows.

Ally was afraid the gift would be expensive, but when she opened it she shoved it into his lap and withdrew her hands like it was a ball of fire.

'Oh, god, no. Return it! They cost hundreds. Thousands.'

He pushed the camera back to her. 'It's not for you. It's for your business.'

'Marc—'

He pressed a finger on her lips and the next thing she knew she was on his lap with his hands in her hair and his tongue in her mouth.

In an instant she was desperate for him. Not just to sit beside him but to be as close as she could get, wrapped in him. It wasn't lust but a ferocious need as strong as hunger.

He broke the kiss.

'No,' she groaned, before he could speak. 'Please, Marc. I want you.'

His fingers gripped her hips. 'You want me?'

She didn't have the strength to deny it when his lips were so close. 'Yes. I want you.'

He carried her to the bedroom and almost threw her on to the bed, tugging impatiently at her clothes. He didn't even notice her new underwear, pulling her knickers off without a second look at them. It was animalistic, urgent, and so hot she was squirming in her need for an orgasm.

There was none of his usual gentle teasing. He checked that she was wet and entered her, hard, without even taking her bra off. His sounds were different too. Not soft sighs but fierce grunts, matching his urgent thrusts. He hooked an arm around her knee and pushed it up. Ally moved her other leg as high as she could too, allowing him deeper, feeling his pelvis rub on her hard clitoris as he moved.

Her head slammed into the headboard and she didn't care, but he put his hand between her hair and the wood as a buffer. Not completely out of control then. Still the caring gentleman in there somewhere, under all this sudden passion.

Even though it was harder and faster than usual he took longer to come, and she had two orgasms just from penetration before he finally let out a groan then collapsed on top of her. Her hamstrings ached, her head ached, her neck ached, but a pleasant buzz from the intense orgasms washed over every muscle and she felt soothed, spent, satisfied.

In his arms, she breathed in his scent and rubbed her cheek on the soft hairs of his chest.

'We don't need to stop,' she murmured. 'We can be friends who sleep together.'

'That's a relationship, Ally.'

'No it isn't. It's friends with benefits.'

'I don't want benefits. I want love.'

How long had it been since he slept with someone who loved him?

'I miss you,' he said quietly.

'I miss you too,' she replied, without thinking.

As he stroked her hair, Ally traced circles on his stomach and tried to imagine how he felt lying there with her. What it meant to be in love. She was warm and contented and satisfied, the uncomfortable butterflies calm for once. Did he get the butterflies? That wasn't love, was it? Teenagers with crushes got butterflies.

'I told Julie about us.'

Ally blinked. 'I'm listening.'

'No, I'm not shocking you back to awareness. I mean it.'

The words sank in and she sat bolt upright. 'What? You're joking. She'll tell Sam!'

'I didn't tell her who you are. Jesus, she still thinks you're engaged to him. I just said I'd met someone.'

Ally tried not to imagine how Sam was going to feel. 'What did she say?'

'She was shocked. I'm pretty sure she thought we'd get back together. I really don't think she saw anything wrong with our marriage, even when we were sleeping in separate bedrooms, living separate lives. She wants a live-in handyman and cook, not a partner.'

Marc sat up and pulled her to him, noses touching, his scent in her nostrils and his warm body against hers. 'Try it, Ally. You and me, just like this, whenever we want.' He traced feathery kisses down her jaw and spoke low into her ear. 'No secrets, no lying. Imagine it.'

Ally imagined it. A relationship. Coming home to him in the evenings and sleeping with him every night. She wouldn't be alone in her new business venture. He'd be supportive and encouraging and help her stay organised. He'd celebrate her successes and stop her blaming herself when she failed. And he'd be there, every day.

But Sam wouldn't. Mum wouldn't. They'd both lose their families.

And she was so flaky. What's to say she wouldn't be bored of him in a few months and they'd both end up with nothing?

'No.' She extracted herself from his arms. 'I don't feel that way. I won't ever.'

'Then what is this?' he demanded. 'You miss me, you want to talk to me, you want to sleep with me. What's that if it isn't love?'

'It's not love,' she said loudly. Everyone else she loved would leave her if it was. 'It's friends with benefits.'

'So you feel the same about your other friends with benefits?' His eyes bored into hers. Intense. Alight. 'This Jason person. You miss him just the same? You like being with him just as much?'

Crap, Jason. She hadn't called since he'd got back from Barbados.

'I don't love you,' she shouted, to drown out an insistent voice in her brain.

'Then leave me the fuck alone!' She flinched at his roar. 'You enjoy messing with me like this? Calling me, reminding me of you, inviting me here, sleeping with me, and telling me it's nothing? Where do you get off on this mind fuck?'

Ally drew the covers around herself like a cocoon. 'I don't. I was trying to be friends.'

'This isn't fucking friendship!' He stomped over to his clothes and yanked them on. 'Maybe this is fun for you but it's not a game for me.'

It was a game and there was no way to win. Win Marc and lose Sam and maybe Rachel and Mum and god knows who else.

'I'm sorry,' she whispered.

He stopped, gazed at her for a second, then strode back to bed and crushed her into a hug. Ally clung to him. Heads or tails. Win and lose. Lose and win.

'Just tell me.' His voice had lost the anger. 'If you feel the same. And if you don't, let me go.'

Ally breathed in his scent, determined to remember. To find a bottle of it somewhere. Her hands traced the long curves of his back, still slick with sweat. His taste on her lips and his voice in her ears.

'I don't,' she said. 'I'll stop calling.'

* * *

There was only half an hour to pull herself together before Sam and Rachel arrived. Ally prodded Sam into talking about Brendan, hoping that would allow her to be silent without him noticing.

At the bar she busied herself with greeting her friends as they arrived and making sure everyone had drinks. Each time someone started a conversation deeper than pleasant small talk, she excused herself and went to a new group.

It was just good hostessing.

Sam and Rachel had clubbed together to buy Ally her licence. As overcome by gratitude (and guilt) as she was, part of her was disappointed. Earning it herself by sacrificing the things she loved had felt grown up, satisfying. And it would give her a reason to work hard.

Well, there were plenty of other things she needed to save for. Paid adverts, new make-up, better equipment.

Talking about her plans drove Marc out of her mind, so she let herself go and only stopped babbling when she saw Rachel suppressing a grin.

'I'm going on a bit, aren't I?' she said sheepishly.

Rachel shook her head. 'You're excited. So am I. I don't remember the last time you were this enthusiastic about work.'

'Oh, hey,' Sam said, shuffling down the sofa to join them. 'That reminds me. I've got a customer for you.'

'Ooh, really?' Ally's heart jumped. 'You're a legend, Sam, thank you. My next booking isn't for six months and man, it's hard to be patient. Who is it?'

'Mum.'

Rachel's face dropped into a mask of horror that Ally knew reflected her own.

'I can't,' Ally blurted out.

Sam blinked. 'Why not? You just said you were impatient for bookings.'

'Oh, er . . . I'm not working for friends and family. It's . . . not professional.'

He raised an eyebrow. 'I do loads of stuff for friends and family.'

Ally squirmed. 'I didn't mean unprofessional. I meant, you know, I can't afford to do mate's rates while I'm setting up and I can't charge friends full price.'

'Oh, don't worry about that. Mum saw one of those leaflets I made for you with the price on and she said she'd pay it. She's not expecting a discount. All she wants is her hair and make-up done for the wedding.'

Oh god, Gavin's wedding. Ally had been pretending it wasn't happening, even after she'd agreed to go as Sam's fiancée. She had no idea how she would keep up the pretence with Marc there.

'I didn't think your mum was into hair and make-up,' Ally said, lamely.

'She's not. But she was looking at the photos from her award ceremony thing and got upset about how old and ill she looked.'

'Award ceremony thing?' Rachel asked. 'You've got a way with words. What was she getting an award for?'

'Charity work.'

Ally was so surprised she forgot her horror. 'Charity work? Your mum does charity work?'

Apparently her tone had betrayed just how unbelievable she found it.

'Yes,' Sam replied testily. 'Why is that such a shock?'

'You didn't mention it before,' Rachel said, while Ally floundered.

'Yeah, well. She's afraid of spoiling Gavin's photos and says she'll look a mess again if she has to get herself ready. She's been feeling pretty weak lately.'

'Can't her sister help?' Ally said. 'The one who looks after her?'

Sam frowned. 'What are you talking about?'

'What's her name? Virgini . . .' Ally trailed off as Rachel made frantic motions behind Sam's head. Right, yes. Marc had told her about Virginia, not Sam.

'What charity does your mum work for?' Rachel said.

Ally exhaled as Sam turned to Rachel and said, 'She runs a fundraiser for her church. They build schools in India.' He looked back at Ally. 'You will do it, won't you?'

Ally scrambled for an excuse. 'I'm babysitting for Mum the morning of the wedding. I'll barely have enough time to get ready myself.'

Sam stared. 'No you're not. You said you were coming to mine first thing so I could make sure we were on time.'

'Oh, right. I've double booked. I'll have to tell Mum.' Ally cringed and tried to shrink herself.

'Why don't you want to do it? Don't you like my mum?'

Rachel grimaced behind Sam's back and shrugged. She couldn't help.

'Of course I do,' Ally said. 'I just feel bad charging her.'

'Yeah.' He turned away, clearly hurt.

'Oh, Sam, of course I'll do it.' Ally grabbed his arm and pulled him back. 'I'm being silly. I hate taking money from people I know. Tell her I'll do it.'

He seemed happier.

Behind his back, Rachel shot her a look of sympathy.

CHAPTER TWENTY-EIGHT

$\mathcal{P}$reparing for meeting Julie was like a MENSA logic problem. If Marc knows that Sam is gay but has to pretend he doesn't know to Julie, and Marc, Ally and Sam know that the engagement is a lie but Julie doesn't know, and only Marc and Ally know that they've slept together, is there actually *anything* Ally can say to anyone that won't incriminate at least one person?

Tonsillitis might be the safest course of action. She considered going to an ear, nose and throat hospital and kissing as many of the patients as she could until she was thrown out. If only she'd thought of it sooner . . .

She regretted being healthy even more deeply when she arrived at Julie's house. As Sam unlocked the door, she heard a familiar bark inside.

Harry was here. And if Harry was here, that meant Marc was here.

And if Marc was here . . . were he and Julie patching things up? She felt a lurch much more painful than the weeks of anxiety that'd led to this day.

The door opened. Harry barrelled into Ally, shoved his nose between her knees, and licked them.

'At least someone likes my knees,' she said, ruffling his fur.

'Who doesn't like your knees?' Sam patted Harry's back as he edged past him up the corridor.

'Just this guy.' Ally cleared her throat. 'Your dad's here?'

'Guess so. They must be spending time together again.' He gave her a broad smile and walked into a room to their left. Ally took a deep breath, followed, and showed all her teeth.

It took her a nanosecond to determine Marc wasn't there. Just Julie, perched on the edge of a sofa.

'Hi, Mrs Kinsell,' she said. At that pitch, Harry was probably the only one who could hear her.

'Ally.' Mrs Kinsell smiled, though it seemed strained. 'So nice to see you again.'

Ally fixed her eyes on the bridge of the woman's nose and tried not to think of Marc. Instead, she took in the bags under Julie's eyes and the pallor of her skin. Years of pain and immobility had taken their toll.

Sam blustered when his mum enquired about their own wedding date and Ally couldn't help him. Her plan was to say as little as possible.

Harry whined and pawed at the door.

'Sammy, will you take him out? Just take him around the block, anything.' Mrs Kinsell rubbed her forehead. 'He won't leave me alone and my allergy seems to be getting worse all the time.'

'You're allergic to dogs?' Ally blurted out.

The bridge of Mrs Kinsell's nose bobbed up and down as she nodded. 'Well, not dogs. Their fur. Or the saliva on their fur, to be precise. I'm all right as long as they don't get too close.'

Uneasily, Ally busied herself with rummaging in her bag. The image of Julie Kinsell she'd built up was very different to this woman who built schools for poor children and disliked dogs for medical reasons.

Sam left the room and called Harry to follow him. Before Mrs Kinsell could make more small talk, Ally launched into questions about make-up.

'Please, call me Julie. I don't know what I want, really. I've never been very fashionable. You pick whatever colours will make me look less old and tired.'

'You don't look old and tired,' Ally said automatically. 'What are you going to wear?'

'I was hoping you could help with that too.' Her thin lips smiled apologetically. 'Will you help me to my room? I'll show you what I've got, though I doubt you'll be impressed. You're such a glamorous little thing.'

It wasn't Julie's negligible weight that made Ally feel heavy, her feet dragging as they walked slowly to the bedroom.

The room was overheated and stuffy, but Julie pulled her cardigan tighter around herself and huddled on the edge of the bed. There was no fat on that body to cling on to heat. Nothing of substance between the bones and pale skin.

Ally glanced at her own tanned, toned legs and the solid knees that were the only part Marc could find fault with. She no longer felt like a cuckoo in Julie's nest. She felt like a vulture.

Julie shivered and pressed her knees together.

'Are you all right?' Ally asked with a waver in her voice. 'Can I get you anything?'

'I'm fine,' Julie said quickly. She straightened up with a wince. 'All my dresses are in there. Have a look and see what you think?'

Ally forced herself to concentrate. There was no choice but to look at Julie and assess what colours would be best for her. Mid-brown hair. Green veins, not blue like her ex-husband's. Don't think about that.

'This one,' said Ally, pulling out a coral dress. She lowered it when she saw Julie clutching her stomach. 'Are you sure you're OK?'

To her horror, Julie sobbed and buried her face in her hands.

'Oh god,' Ally blurted out. 'I'll call Sam.'

'No!' Julie shouted with such force that Ally stopped in her tracks. 'No, please. I don't want him to know—' She covered her mouth.

'Know?' Ally's heart thumped. Please god, not another secret from this family. Gavin would call her up next to tell her he was adopted and secretly in love with Sam and could she please not say anything . . .

Julie dropped her hands to her lap and twisted them. Her eyes were wide and her face had grown even paler. 'Nothing. Forget I said it. That one, you say?' She stood, reaching for the dress, then winced and sat back down.

Ally hesitated, then handed her the dress and avoided eye contact as she took out her make-up case. 'How about a neutral look? Mostly browns, maybe a peach blush to complement the dress. If you're not used to wearing make-up you'll feel self-conscious in bright colours.'

'Yes.' Julie sniffed and tried to smile. It looked garish beside her tear tracks. 'That sounds perfect.'

But when Ally forced herself to look into Julie's eyes, ready with eyeshadow, they were filled with tears. Julie did look old, and tired, and wretched.

'Do you . . . do you want to talk about it?' Ally said unwillingly as she put the brush down.

Selfishly, she wanted Julie to insist everything was fine.

'I'm sorry.' Julie drew a tissue from her sleeve and dabbed her eyes. 'You can't put make-up on when I keep crying, can you? I just feel so stupid trying to look nice with you here next to me so beautiful without anything on your face. You must think I'm a fool. What's that phrase – lipstick on a pig? That's me.'

'No, no—'

Julie didn't seem to hear. 'I just thought if I . . . if I try . . .' She melted into tears again.

Ally patted her arm awkwardly and Julie winced. She withdrew her hand quickly. 'Sorry.'

Julie took a deep breath. 'I thought if I try to look more fashionable, less pathetic, maybe my husband might come back.'

Cringing, Ally plunged her hand in her make-up bag and drew out the first item her fingers touched. It gave her somewhere to look.

She couldn't do this. She couldn't dress up Marc's ex to help her seduce him. It was sick.

'Maybe this isn't the way to do it,' she said, so desperate to get out of there she didn't care if she offended or not. 'I mean, you know what men are like. He probably wouldn't notice anyway.'

'He would.' Julie sniffed. 'I've seen some of the women he goes with. They're always in short skirts and bright lipstick.'

Ally shook her head as if there was water in her ears. 'What?'

Julie visibly paled. Her eyes were wide and scared with no hint of blame or calculation. 'Nothing. Forget I said it.'

Ally heard a muffled crack as the bronzer slipped out of her hand and hit the carpet. 'He . . . has a lot of women?'

Julie nodded and bit her trembling lip. 'All through our marriage. I tried, but I wasn't much of a wife, I suppose. My health has been poor for a long time, and even before that I wasn't the blonde bimbo type he goes for. Then one night he brought one of them back here, walked right past me in the hall and up to his bedroom with her. It was the last straw, and I asked him to leave. But now . . .'

Ally stood up and sat down again. She wanted to run. She didn't want to hear this.

'He's got a terrible temper,' Julie whispered. 'He wants everything in the divorce. Everything. He says he'll spend every penny rather than let me have any of it, and what will I do? I can't work. He took all the savings when he left. I'll be homeless.'

It had to be lies, didn't it? A double bluff from Julie, who'd somehow found out about Marc and Ally. That was why she wanted Ally to come here today.

Julie gripped her arm. 'I shouldn't have said anything. Oh, don't tell Sam. Please.'

That was fear in Julie's eyes; genuine fear. Was it? Could that be faked? Ally was a crap actress, transparent as cling film, but not everybody was.

'Please, Ally.'

The shake in her voice, the dilated pupils, the plaintive expression. It seemed very real.

Ally shook her head. It was a nightmare. It had to be. 'Why are you telling me?'

'I'm sorry,' Julie hunched and stared at the carpet. 'I shouldn't. I know. I just . . . I don't have anybody. He didn't like me going out, making friends, talking to people. Even when my sister visited he hung around, checked up on us. And everyone thinks he's so calm and gentle.'

He was. Calm, and gentle, and sweet.

Except when he'd confronted her about the message on the dating site. She'd been scared of him just for a moment. And that time he'd been waiting outside her flat, after they'd slept together for the first time. She'd been afraid for a moment then, too. But he hadn't done anything either time. He'd never been violent.

But he had told her, from his own lips, that he'd threatened Julie he would take all the money. She wasn't lying about that.

'I think the latest one's left him,' Julie whispered, still holding Ally's wrist. 'He's been so moody. His temper is always bad but it's worse when he's frustrated. He lashes out.'

'You argue?' Ally asked, a pleading note in her voice. That's what she had to mean by his temper.

But it was Julie's turn to shake her head. 'I stopped arguing years ago. I try to placate him but it . . . it doesn't always work.'

'He hits you?' she asked in a whisper, and regretted it immediately. She eyed the cotton balls in her make-up bag. How quickly could she shove them in her ears and leg it to the station?

'Sometimes.'

'No.' Ally stood up without meaning to. Even if Marc hadn't told his wife, she must have guessed. Of course she'd guessed. Nobody decides to leave after thirty years unless something – or someone – has changed everything. 'He wouldn't do that. He wouldn't hurt anyone. I mean you have no bruises, no—'

Julie shrugged one shoulder so her cardigan dropped. She wore a sleeveless nightgown and, vivid and glaring on her white skin, an oval bruise sat on her wasted bicep. Purple and red, the colours of ravaged blood vessels.

She lifted her arm away from her body to reveal four more ovals on her inner arm. Four fingers, with the thumb gripping the other side all alone. Not a bruise from a knock, cynically blamed on a fist. A handprint. Fingerprints. Evidence that couldn't be faked.

Ally's hands clamped over her mouth but she retched anyway, her body convulsing as if it could force Julie's words out of her brain by force. Saliva caught in her throat and she coughed, heaving in a wheezy breath and sitting heavily on the bed before she fell.

Julie clapped her on the back and shook her wrist. 'Ally? Are you OK? Oh, no, I've upset you.'

'Upset . . . me,' Ally gasped. She shut her eyes and drew a shaking hand across her mouth. Then she fixed her eyes on Julie's, desperate to find a trace of a lie in her expression. Anything she could cling on to.

A door slammed somewhere far away. Another one swung open.

'Don't say anything,' a voice pleaded. 'Please. You promised.'

A blur of dark blue filled the doorway. Ally wiped her eyes and blinked furiously but the blur didn't sharpen. She knew it was Marc, his stance and his aura and the feel of him so different from Sam's that she would've known blindfolded. This was the body she knew intimately, the hands that had made every inch of her skin hum.

The same hands that had made those bruises?

Somebody else could have given her those bruises. Maybe Julie was having an affair.

An affair with a man who beat her? Unlikely.

'You're back quickly,' Julie said brightly. Marc held several shopping bags. 'Don't worry about putting everything away. Sam will sort it out when he's back from walking Harry. Ally and I were just talking about make-up.' She pressed a hand into Ally's back, and Ally tried to compose herself. She slid her eyes away from Marc, stretched her mouth into a smile and unclenched her fists.

'What's going on?' asked Marcus.

Shit. He wasn't playing along with the charade. Bile threatened to splatter Julie's carpet and that would be so damn rude when Ally was a guest. She turned away, fumbled blindly for the box of tissues on the bedside table, and pressed them so hard into her eyes she saw spots. Spots were good. Spots were much better to look at than this nightmare playing out in front of her.

Hell, *The Human Centipede* was better viewing than this, and Rachel was still apologising fourteen months after choosing that for a movie night.

'Ally's making me look nice for the wedding.' Julie *was* a good actress. Ally, finally able to see, glanced at her face: calm and pleasant. No traces of fear or panic. But which one was acted? The fear, or the calm?

'Ally, what's wrong?' Marc asked gently. Gently. He was gentle.

Except when they argued and his temper rose, or on her birthday when he'd thrust into her like he wanted to release more than an orgasm. But lots of people had hot tempers and weren't violent. Lots of people had rough sex without being rapists. She hadn't been scared, had she? If she'd asked him to stop, he would have, but she was enjoying it. He knew she'd enjoy it. He wouldn't hurt her. Would he?

'It's the pollen,' Julie said. She gestured at the vase of gladioli next to her bed. 'It's been making her eyes water since she got here.'

Julie was such a good liar. It was so convincing.

Because she had to act to avoid violence from her husband? Or was the violence another lie?

The bruises. They weren't faked.

Marc crossed the room in a few strides and carried the vase into the en-suite bathroom.

'You promised,' Julie hissed, while he was out of the room. 'Act normal!' Her mask had slipped. Now she looked angry and disdainful – the way she'd looked at Ally in her tight blue dress at the anniversary party.

Once, when they were all watching a Bond movie, Rachel's man had launched into a detailed explanation of body language and signs that someone was lying, scared, or getting ready to make a move. Ally had been determined not to hear him and tuned him out to watch the film. Now she would've given anything to rewind her memory and remember his tips.

He'd probably been talking bollocks anyway. What did a gym instructor know about how people acted under torture? He was so full of shit.

Somebody shook Ally's arm, fingers digging hard into the sensitive veins of her elbow. She winced and blinked down at Julie's glare.

'Julie, you're hurting her!' Marc was back, a blur of blue again as he pulled his wife's hand away from Ally. As he made a half-turn towards Ally, Julie grimaced. Her hand flew to the bruises and rubbed; an automatic gesture, like any touch from her husband was a reminder of her sore flesh.

'Don't touch her!' Ally blurted out. She darted next to Julie, guarding her and staring Marc in the face. 'Leave her alone.'

His mouth fell open, then his gaze whipped to Julie. 'What the hell have you been saying to her?'

He wasn't confused or stunned, which would surely be natural for an innocent man. An innocent man wouldn't jump to the conclusion that his ex had blabbed.

'Nothing,' said Julie. 'You did push me rather hard, Marcus, can you blame her for overreacting? Look, why don't you leave us so I can get dressed?' The familiar shrewish tone was back in her voice. No traces of fear at goading her husband.

A headache was starting behind Ally's eyes. A combination of hot pressure trying to force tears out and utter bewilderment at who had lied to her.

She trusted Marc and she knew what Julie was like. But she knew what Julie was like because he'd told her. Maybe she was shrewish because it was the only way she knew how to cover up her unhappiness and fear in front of others.

And the bruises. It all came back to the bruises. Not even an Oscar winner could act those.

The sight of those ugly, deep bruises reared up, and made Ally feel nauseous again. She'd sit through the whole Human Centipede trilogy, in HD, if she could only forget the image of Julie's ravaged skin.

'Ally, for god's sake, what's wrong?'

Another hand on her elbow but this one gentle and comforting.

'Don't.' Ally moved out of his reach, the knob of the bedside table's drawer pressing into the small of her back.

'Look at her,' Marc demanded. Ally knew he was talking to

Julie even if her eyes had gone blurry and hot again. 'What have you said?'

'Nothing!'

'Bullshit! She's crying. She looks like she did when Debbie—' Marc caught his breath as if the name had snatched it.

'When Debbie what?' Julie snapped. 'You've only met Ally twice. Why are you shouting at me for upsetting her?'

'Oh, give it up,' Marc snapped back. 'I thought you knew and now I know you do.'

God, no. Was he referring to their affair? He must be. But if she knew—

'Dad?' said a voice from the doorway.

Ally crammed a tissue into her eyes and straightened up. Oh god, Sam. Sam was back and a furry wet face pressed into Ally's hand. She closed her fingers on Harry's head and pressed her leg against his solid bulk. At least Harry couldn't lie to her.

'What's going on?' Sam stared at the three of them with a deer-in-the-headlights look. 'What does Mum know?'

No, no, no. This couldn't be happening.

'Sammy.' Julie beamed at him. 'Dad got me some shopping. Will you help put it away?'

Ally was going to need an encyclopaedia to keep up with the lies. Was Julie double – triple? – bluffing, or was her story straight and Marc was referring to her knowing something else?

Ally needed a shitload of alcohol.

'Why's Ally crying?' Sam asked.

Goddammit, why hadn't she got control of herself yet? She needed tips from Julie. Or Marc. Or . . . dammit, whichever one of them was lying.

'I think your Mum's been telling lies,' Marc replied with a hard edge in his voice. 'She's had a lot of practice.'

'How dare you!' Julie shot to her feet, no signs of pain or difficulty on her enraged face. 'You're the liar!'

'Shut up,' Marc hissed. He gripped her arm and pointed at Sam.

'Ow,' Julie whimpered.

Marc's eyes were blazing. He was angrier than Ally had seen him, towering over his petite wife like an executioner, and her fear looked genuine.

'Please don't hurt her.' Ally pushed herself between them, unable to bear it. 'She didn't say anything. It was the flowers. Don't be angry with her.'

'She said I hurt her?' Marc spoke softly but he was so close Ally heard every word almost as clearly as she smelled his bewitching spicy scent. 'You know I wouldn't do that.'

Again, no traces of shock or confusion. He knew what Julie would say. How would he know that, why would he jump to that conclusion, unless it was true? Maybe if he'd heard it before . . . but he said he kept his girlfriends away from Julie.

Were both of them lying?

'What is this?' Sam spluttered. There was enough shock and confusion on his face for the whole family. 'Why are you talking to Ally like you know each other? What does Mum know?'

Marc ignored him, his gaze fixed on Ally. 'You know, don't you? That I wouldn't hurt her. Or anyone. You believe me?'

Her thoughts spun in circles. Like that Dusty Springfield song. Circles in spirals, wheels within wheels, windmills in the willows. Or something like that. Round and round with no answer. Julie was a good liar but maybe she'd got her practice pretending her marriage was fine and her husband not violent. Marc couldn't hurt anyone but how did he know what Julie had said and how had she got those bruises? Abusers always started out charming. It'd been months before Ally had seen his temper, and the longer the affair went on the moodier he became. One day, would he have switched on her?

'Someone bloody speak!' Sam shouted. Ally tore her eyes away from Marc to look at her friend, red-faced and pale at the same time, beautiful and sweet and shy and loving Sam, her Sam, one of the two friends she would've died for. That she'd betrayed.

'Let's go,' she said. 'Sam, let's go home.'

Sam gaped like she had two heads then turned to his father. 'What the hell is going on? Did you hurt Mum?'

'No,' Marc replied instantly. 'I've never laid a finger on her.'

'This is all just a big misunderstanding,' Julie said. 'Ally saw a bruise and jumped to the wrong conclusion, didn't you?'

It was Ally's turn to gape like a startled cod. A quadruple bluff? It had to stop here because she didn't even know what came after quadruple. Fiveruple didn't sound right.

They were all staring at her expectantly. Even Marc.

She couldn't think of anything to say but the truth. Well, some-one had to. 'It's a handprint. Who could have done that to her?'

It wasn't a rhetorical question. She wanted an answer from Marc.

'A handprint?' Finally, he did look surprised. 'Where?'

Julie clutched her cardigan around her. 'It's not. I knocked it on the door.'

'It's a handprint,' Ally repeated. She had no idea whose side she was on any more. If telling Marc would put Julie in danger, or expose her lies. 'There, on her arm. And . . .' She couldn't say it in front of Sam.

'*What*?' Sam exploded.

'I haven't laid a finger on her,' Marc said, eyes locked on Ally's again. 'I don't know where she got it, but it wasn't me. You know why she's doing this. Because I've moved on and she knows it. I don't know how, but she knows.'

'Knows *what*?' Sam yelled at the top of his voice. 'I'm going to go insane if you lot don't start talking sense. I mean actually, legitimate Bates Motel insane. And if you fucking hurt her I will hurt you.' Ally had never seen him threaten anyone before, but he looked ready to kill his father.

'Of course I didn't hurt her.' Marc faced his son head-on. 'She knows I met somebody else. That's why she's made up this bullshit.'

'You met someone?' Sam's face was ashen.

'Yes!' Julie shouted. 'And you want to know who, Sam? Your precious Ally. I told you what type of woman she was.'

Ally groaned in despair, though she wasn't sure any sound came out. This was a waking nightmare. In fact, she'd had nightmares pretty close to this once or twice over the past year.

'What?' Sam said again. His voice was blank, like it was too much to process. Slowly, he looked from his mum to his dad and then to Ally. His face changed and she knew she'd given it away, like she always did with her treacherous, transparent face.

'I've never hurt your mother,' Marc said flatly. 'Never.'

'Liar!' Julie scrambled at her cardigan and exposed the garish bruises again. 'There you go. Happy now I've had to show him?

Happy to humiliate me more? You knew I didn't want him to know, you piece of shit. What kind of man sleeps with his daughter-in-law? You're disgusting. You don't deserve to be called his father.'

Marc reddened at the sight of the bruises. Guilt or anger?

'I didn't give you those and you know it.' He turned his back to her. 'Sam, I didn't. Ally. You know I wouldn't.'

Hopelessly, she watched his expectant expression turn to shock, disappointment and pain when she didn't answer.

'You bastard,' Sam whispered. In a flash he barrelled forward and punched his father in the face. There was no sound like in the movies, but Ally felt the impact anyway as if it had smashed into her own cheekbone.

It only took her a few seconds to recover from the shock but by then they were on the floor, a flailing mass of kicking legs and swung fists, limbs jerking out of each other's grasps. Marc was trying to pin Sam's arms to his sides to stop him punching but Sam was like a man possessed. Harry stood a few feet away, moving closer then back, closer then back, barking.

'Stop it!' she and Julie screamed in unison, then shared a horrible look of mutual understanding.

Anything was better than that mutual understanding, including being in the middle of a fight. Ally launched herself at the pile of limbs and grasped Sam's upper arms. Marc made a grab for them at the same moment and his fist caught her on the jaw, snapping her head back and wrenching her neck.

Ally fell back against the bed, clutching her jaw. The pain was so exquisite her eyes watered and nausea hit her again.

'Ally!' Marc sprang up and she realised Sam had stopped his

attack. Marc knelt beside her, pulled her hand away from her face, and tipped her chin with the tip of one finger so he could see her jaw. 'Christ, I'm sorry. I didn't see you in time. Can you move it? Can you talk?'

Ally experimented gingerly. 'I think it's OK.' The pain didn't seem important with him so close, an angry red patch on his face where Sam had thumped him, their secret out in the open and lies clouding the air. Even now she wasn't afraid of him, couldn't imagine him hitting her on purpose.

Marc brushed her hair behind her ear and stroked her sore jaw. 'I swear, Ally. You're the first woman I've hit.'

Ally almost laughed until she caught sight of Sam. His face was sweaty and flushed, his whole body shaking. He was devastated and she'd done it to him. Even if she wasn't the cause of Julie's bruises – even if Marc wasn't – she was the cause of Sam's pain. And the shiner Marc was going to have in the morning.

'Ally,' Marcus urged. 'You don't believe her, do you?'

She'd never seen contempt on Sam's face before. Definitely not when he was looking at her. Would he ever forgive her? Maybe, if she stopped now. If she showed she was sorry, that it was a mistake.

Marc wasn't a mistake. The thought came to her, illogical and unbidden. Of course he was a mistake. A married man, her best friend's father, twenty years older. A ridiculous mistake.

It was Sam she loved, not his father. Romantic love didn't last – not with her. Sam had been by her side for seventeen years but Marc had never been hers, and never would.

'Ally?' He spoke so softly it was like they were the only two in the room.

She thought of all the lies Julie had told today, her acting, her abrupt switches from fear to calm to anger. She thought of Marc's gentle kisses, the way he stared into her eyes, the way he'd slammed his fist into the brick wall outside her house. She thought of Sam's shock and Rachel's unease and her mum sobbing into a cushion for days and days after Dad had left.

With a deep breath, she pulled herself together and met his eyes. 'It doesn't matter who I believe. It was all a mistake, and we're finished.'

She looked away before she could register his expression. Sam. She had to focus on Sam. Losing him was unthinkable.

'Sam, I'm sorry. It was a mistake.'

Sam's expression hardened. He wouldn't look at her, but clenched his fists and addressed his father. 'You're leaving Mum for her?'

Her. With that one word Ally understood her new place. An outsider, a stranger in Sam's life. Unimportant. The cuckoo in the nest that'd broken up the people who mattered.

She almost used Marc's shoulder to get to her feet but clutched the bed's footboard instead.

'I'm sorry,' she mumbled again, as she grabbed her bag, left the room, tore open the front door, and broke into a run.

CHAPTER TWENTY-NINE

Ally wanted her mum. But when the train pulled into North Acton she stayed in her seat, holding tightly to her dress in its dry-cleaning bag. Mum would want to know what had happened and Ally couldn't confess. Sam's disgust was bad enough without adding Mum's to it.

She wanted Rachel, but when she called it went straight to voicemail. It could have been off, or it could have been anyone on the line, but she knew it was Sam and she could imagine what he'd be saying.

Jason was a last resort. She knocked at his door with a bottle of vodka, a bottle of rum and a lemon, the crumpled dress bag under her arm.

'Uh-oh,' he said, appraising her from the doorway.

She woke on Tuesday afternoon, lying diagonally across his bed. At least she was fully clothed – not that he would have taken advantage of her anyway, drunk or not.

She curled into a foetal position and buried her head in the soft pillows. She trusted Jason, a casual friend, but she hadn't given Marc any benefit of the doubt. Marc, who loved her. Who said he loved her.

'You look a mess,' said a cheerful voice.

Ally didn't look up, the pillow muffling her voice. 'I feel a mess.' Her jaw hurt when she spoke, and she remembered Jason raging that he was going to beat the shit out of whoever had hit her.

Something hard bounced off her back. 'Your phone kept ringing and you wouldn't stop snoring so I turned it off.'

Ally fumbled for it and blinked the screen into focus. No missed calls from Sam – not that she'd really expected any. Several from Rachel. One unknown, probably a client. And two from Marc.

She badly wanted to talk to him. If she did, Sam's name would never be in that list again. It was Sam's name she wanted there, not Marc's.

No. Both.

She couldn't have both.

Relationships and Ally weren't compatible. Experience had proved that, time and time again, even if she'd never felt quite like this. But Sam had been there through every break-up, every time she got fed up of being single, every time she needed a wingman for prowling in clubs. Sam and Rachel.

She sat up and yelped in pain. Her neck felt like she'd got carried away at an Iron Maiden concert, screaming in protest when she tried to bend it. Marc had got her good. Probably damaged her tendons or ligaments or whatever they were.

She relished the pain. She deserved it.

She called Rachel.

'Are you OK?' Rachel said, by way of a greeting.

'No.'

Rachel let out a long sigh. 'It's a bit awkward, isn't it?'

Ally had to agree. 'Will you come and eat junk food with me?'

Rachel hesitated.

'Don't worry,' Ally said quickly. 'You're busy. It's a work day. I shouldn't have asked.'

'No, it's just . . . I said I'd go and see Sam.'

'Oh.' It'd started already. Rachel – sensible, maternal Rachel – was caught in the middle, wanting to comfort both of them. She'd have to choose Sam because he was the innocent one. Rachel would feel awkward and stuck and Ally would have to stop calling so she didn't have to choose and *fuck* she was going to look terrible in a wimple because black *so* wasn't her colour.

'I can come over later,' Rachel offered.

'No, no. I'll be fine. I'll go and see Mum . . . or Gran. Maybe Gran.'

'I'm sure she'll be a great comfort,' Rachel said, in a tone that suggested she thought the complete opposite.

Rachel had met Gran, twice.

'Yeah.'

'Sam believes his mum,' Rachel said neutrally.

Of course he did. He adored her. Ally had believed her too and still couldn't shake her doubt because of those damn bruises. Rachel was smart – Rachel would come up with another explanation, if there was one.

'I saw her bruises,' Ally said. 'They were hand marks. Who else could have done it?'

'I don't know. Could she have done them herself?'

Ally's heart leapt. 'I don't know, could she? Hang on.'

Ally pinned the phone between her ear and shoulder and grasped her upper arms, squeezing as hard as she could. 'Man, I don't know. I don't think I can do it hard enough to bruise. My brain's like . . . dude, you don't want to do that.'

'Maybe if you were desperate?'

'I *am* desperate.'

'True,' Rachel said. 'Look, you're never going to know for sure, are you? You can't exactly dust her arms for fingerprints and get proof. Either you trust him or you don't.'

'I think I loved him, Rach,' Ally said before she could think.

From Rachel's sad sigh, Ally knew she'd known all along.

'I don't know what to do,' Ally said miserably.

'Give yourself some time. When your head's clear you can see him, if you want, and hear his side.'

'It doesn't matter. I mean, it matters for him, and his wife. But I can't have him even if he's telling the truth. Sam –' she tried not to cry – 'Sam might come round if I don't see Marc again. What . . . what did he say when you spoke to him?'

Rachel paused and Ally's heart sank.

'He's a bit upset,' Rachel said. 'I'd give him some time too.'

'How long?'

Rachel paused again. 'What's the average life expectancy these days?'

Ally closed her eyes.

* * *

Gran wasn't a great comfort.

'Holy Mary, mother of God,' she said, when Ally had finished explaining. 'What a fecking disaster. I blame your father.'

'What did Dad do?'

'Gave you abandonment issues. Now you're chasing after men like him.'

'Marc is nothing like him!' Ally sat up, stung. 'He stayed with his wife for their children, even though he was miserable. He didn't abandon them, like Dad. Dad's selfish, always thinking of himself, but Marc puts everyone else first. He always tried to do what he wanted and he was so caring when I was in pain and he was always there when I needed him and—'

'Huh,' said Gran. 'Doesn't sound much like an abusive rapist, does he?'

Ally gaped at her and couldn't think of anything to say.

She swore Gran to secrecy but knew she'd tell Mum the next time they had a whisky and bridge night. The sensible thing to do was confess before then so at least Mum heard the unembellished and unintoxicated version.

Instead, Ally decided not to mess with a winning formula and threw herself into work again. It felt wrong to use the ads Sam had designed for her, so she called an art student she'd had a date with the year before and charmed him into sneaking her on to his campus and logging her on to a computer. She'd never used image software more advanced than MS Paint. It was an excellent distraction spending four and a half days mastering InDesign and producing half-decent posters and ads before the librarian caught on and threw her out.

'I paid for the printing!' Ally yelled, as the door slammed behind her. 'I'm not a criminal.'

She muttered to herself as she walked to the Tube station.

Instead of going back to Acton she got off in Oxford Circus and browsed the clothes shops to cheer herself up. One sunset-orange dress screamed out at her to buy it, but all she could think of was the look on Marc's face whenever he saw her in a new dress. No – the look on his face whenever he saw her, new dress or not.

And it was finished. He'd never look at her like that again and that was good because it meant Sam might forgive her. It was good. It was.

She left the dress in the shop and walked to Regent's Park, trying to think only of the clear spring day and avoiding the lake. There were swans. On the whole she did well, except that every flower bed made her picture Marc kneeling in the soil tending his wild flowers.

Ally made herself focus on the buildings instead. The bricks, the ivy, the sign advertising it as a wedding venue.

Would she still be able to go to Rachel's wedding? Sam would probably refuse to go if Ally was there, and he shouldn't miss the wedding because of her. Rachel could still have her best man, but not her best woman. Ally had ruined that pact.

Hang on . . . weddings . . .

Ally smoothed her skirt, practised smiling until it felt natural, and breezed into the ivy-covered building.

When she first saw the stony-faced manager she thought it was a lost cause, but the moment the woman looked at Ally's leaflet her eyes lit up.

'Oh, look at him!' she cried, putting a hand on her chest. 'He's adorable. The three-legged cat! My Lily has three legs too. Isn't it amazing how quickly they learn to walk again?'

Ally's heart leapt. 'He's my friend Rachel's cat. It was his tenth birthday a few weeks ago. We stuck a candle in a tin of tuna and sang happy birthday to him . . . he seemed to enjoy it. The tuna more than the singing, I think.'

'Oh my goodness, I'm going to do that for Lily's fourth in September!'

From then, it was smooth sailing. Ally's leaflets would be in reception and, if she brought her portfolio sometime and filled out some paperwork, she could be on their list of recommended suppliers for make-up and photography.

As she exited the park, buoyant and not paying attention to where she was, she found herself in front of a large church. Churches meant weddings and vicars were nice, so she went in and tried her luck again.

The vicar *was* nice, and let her stick up a poster on her notice-board. A bright love heart on another ad caught her eye. Speed dating, in a church? Was that normal? Come to think of it, Gran would probably love it – Jesus and single men all in one place.

Dating would be good for Ally. It'd been too long since she'd seriously looked at a man besides Marc and maybe if Sam heard she was dating, he'd know she was really finished with his dad. Maybe he'd forgive her. Maybe.

Ally sent a text to the organiser asking for details of the next event, then walked around central London visiting as many wedding venues as she could until everywhere was closed.

CHAPTER THIRTY

'Big smiles,' Ally instructed. 'You all look gorgeous.'

The wedding party beamed and Ally took several photos in quick succession.

This was fun. Ally wished she could've done their make-up too, because some of the bridesmaids' lipsticks were totally the wrong shade for them, but she'd only got the photography gig because they'd been let down at the last minute. The three-legged-cat lover had recommended Ally. Well, she'd probably recommended others but newbie Ally was the only one available the next day.

Although it was the beginning of summer and prime wedding season, Ally had none booked until Christmas. Her diary was filling up for next year, but people just didn't book hen parties, make-up, or photographers late in the day. She was in this for the long-haul and, so far, wasn't getting bored of waiting. Impatient, yes, but not bored.

At least she'd had several non-wedding bookings to keep her motivated. She'd advertised a makeover and photoshoot service and that'd been going well – mostly parents arranging it for teen-aged daughters, or men for their wives or girlfriends. She loved seeing their faces at the big reveal in the mirror, making them feel good about themselves.

She was getting much better at concentrating, too – during all her lonely evenings she'd been playing brain-training games to teach her mind to stay focused. It seemed to be working.

When she'd taken all the shots the bride and groom had asked for, and a few extras they might like, she followed them to the reception hall and snapped the speeches, the cutting of the cake, and the dancing. It was a long evening but she got a free three-course meal and even a bit of the cake.

Life was good, except for the gaping hole where Sam and Marc had been. Sam still wouldn't answer her calls, and Marc had given up calling her. Rachel was still trying to balance keeping Ally and Sam in her life but the strain was showing. It was clearly upsetting Rachel that her friendships had fractured, and it added to Ally's guilt every day. She couldn't keep doing it to her one remaining best friend. Before long, she'd have to let Rachel go. Let her become one of those friends she saw occasionally.

Mum was trying hard not to show her disapproval, not to show her hurt that Ally had broken up a family the way Dad had. But Mum was about as accomplished at acting as Ally, and even the girls had noticed something was wrong. Ally still went to babysit, but she didn't stay so long when Mum got home, and she'd stopped calling so often.

As she was walking to the station, her phone sang the arrival of an email. Ally opened it, stopped dead in the street and laughed aloud. It was an invitation to a speed-dating event in Camden – probably the one she'd taken the details for months ago. The one she'd been ignoring invitations to ever since. Mum would call it a sign that a new invite had arrived when Ally was thinking about how lonely she was. Gran would say fate was a load of bollocks but Ally didn't need a sign to know she had to get laid while everything was still pointing up.

The only problem was the thought of any man except Marc did nothing for her.

But it was too late for that. She'd spent all their time together trying not to feel anything for him, worrying about Sam, and now she'd lost both of them. Marc would feel just as betrayed as Sam, after what Ally had said in front of his family.

She messaged the speed-dating organiser and booked herself a place.

* * *

On speed-date night, Ally chose a pink polka-dot dress with something of the fifties about it, and sensible heels. As much as she still believed in dressing to feel good, not for other people, she had to admit first impressions counted. She wasn't just a young, fickle, irresponsible waitress now. Still young, but ditziness wouldn't be as charming in a thirty year old as a twenty-something, and she didn't have long to go. Still fickle and distracted, but with a lot of effort she was getting better at not zoning out in front of clients. Still a waitress, but maybe not for ever.

It was a warm May, and the Tube was filled with a fug of hot, rebreathed air that made her feel suffocated. To keep her mind off it she studied the map on the curved ceiling and tried to remember all the stations. Moorgate stuck out as if it were in neon rather than black, one stop away from her destination.

Was he still working there? Must be. Buildings like that took years to complete. Had his life changed since the truth had come out? Did their mutual friends, families, know about Julie's accusations? Was he even lonelier? Who would he be spending his birthday with? Rachel had told her snippets gleaned from Sam at first – that Gavin had also cut off his father, that one of Kaitlyn's hot young lawyer friends had stepped in to take over divorce negotiations – but she was clearly uncomfortable, and eventually confessed that Sam had sworn her to secrecy. He didn't want Ally knowing what was going on with his parents. From that moment Ally stopped asking, and lost her only source of information. Now all she could do was imagine, which she often found herself doing when she wasn't working and wasn't brain training—

Brain training. That's what she should be doing now. These were Bad Thoughts. No Marc. What station came after Moorgate? Hers. It was too late for him to still be at work, but she felt close to him anyway.

The train seemed as sluggish as the commuters in the hot, heavy air, but finally Ally was breathing in fresh oxygen outside Tottenham Court Road station. Well, some kind of mixture of oxygen and pollution and cigarette smoke and McDonald's fumes but hey, at least it was cooler outside. Refreshed and full of energy, she made herself think positive thoughts about the evening.

Speed dating had been fun the couple of times she'd tried it before. It was all a big gimmick, of course, but in those days she didn't care – all she'd wanted was a fling, and three minutes was enough to decide if a man was sexy enough for sex and bearable enough for the polite small talk that had to be made first.

But tonight was different. She was going to find someone she wanted to go on a date with, and then another, and then another, and then she might sleep with him on the fourth date but only if they hadn't run out of conversation. It seemed a good rule of thumb to start with.

She recited the stations of the Northern Line in her head and almost walked past the restaurant. The maître d' showed her into a private room where ten tables-for-two were lined up in two rows, and five people shuffled about the chips'n'dip trays looking sheepish.

'Hello!' said a woman in a smart black dress, far too loudly, as she rushed over to Ally. 'I'm Fran. Lovely to meet you.'

Ally forced herself not to step back as Fran descended on her with an awkward kiss on the cheek. 'Oh, hi. I'm Ally. Er, Alicia Rivers.'

'Such a gorgeous name!' Fran trilled. Her hand shook as she crossed Ally's name off the list.

'This is the first event, isn't it?' Ally asked.

Fran's head snapped up and the pen jerked, crossing out several names. She looked around wildly at the assembled guests. 'Don't worry,' she said, still speaking as though they were all nearly deaf. 'I assure you I'm qualified and we're going to have an amazing night! In fact, I sense a marriage coming out of this one, ha ha!'

Ally resisted an urge to pat her on the back and buy her a

double vodka. 'Sorry,' she said in a low voice, as if it'd balance out Fran's shouting. 'I didn't mean I was worried. The room looks so beautiful I was sure I must have misheard when the email said it was the first one.'

'Oh, thank you.' Fran looked so thrilled that Ally wondered how excited she got during orgasm. 'I . . .' She dropped her voice to a near-whisper. 'I suppose you could say I'm a little nervous.'

'You'll be fine,' Ally whispered back, smiling encouragingly. 'Anything I can do to help?'

Fran shook her head. 'Here's your name badge. I'd say to mingle but . . . you're only meant to get three minutes with each other, so I suppose just help yourself to a drink and, er, don't talk to anyone.'

Ah. That explained the deadpan atmosphere and the four men pretending to look at cheap prints on the walls. She debated telling Fran that the other events she'd attended weren't quite so regimented, but decided against it. It might induce a panic attack.

It was going to be a long ten minutes waiting for the event to start. It was unusual for Ally to be early, or even on time, but she was trying to discipline herself so she wasn't late for clients. Being a businesswoman was very demanding, but she was determined to be a good one and not to feel embarrassed about giving herself the title. No imposter syndrome for her when she inevitably became a millionaire.

OK, maybe a little overconfidence, but that'd never hurt anyone.

Ally chose a glass of Prosecco and a nice piece of wood flooring and planted herself there to admire a cheap print on the wall. The still-life bowl of fruit got boring pretty quickly, but she amused herself by counting how many times Fran looked at her watch compared to how many sips of champagne the poor woman drank. It only let up when other daters arrived, and both counts were evening out at almost fifty when Fran glanced at her watch, jumped, and shouted, 'It's time!'

Everyone started, apparently alarmed at her volume.

'Oh gosh, there's only eighteen of you,' she said, clearly panicked. 'Er . . . oh, it's OK.' She exhaled a shuddering breath and pressed a hand on her chest. 'We're missing a man and a woman so we can still go ahead.'

Fran's blood pressure must be frightening.

'Is everyone familiar with speed dating?' Fran asked, fumbling with her papers.

About half the crowd had tried it before, the other half newbies, so Fran stammered her way through an explanation. A few minutes later the door opened, and two figures hurried in and stood at the back.

Ally was pleased for Fran. A full house would boost her confidence.

Apparently calmer now, Fran finished her speech then asked all the women to sit at a table. The men would then sit with each of them in turn, moving tables every three minutes.

Ally wondered if there was gay and lesbian speed dating or how this set-up would cope with a mixed group but decided it'd be cruel to ask Fran difficult questions. She made a mental note to Google it later on.

She sat at the nearest table and heard Gran's voice telling her to sit up straight and push her chest out. She sat up straight but let her chest project naturally, and tried to feel enthusiastic. It shouldn't have taken an effort to be excited: she was about to meet ten single men, and it'd been far too long since she'd dated. But somehow, even with all her recent practice at faking happiness, it was hard to muster up enthusiasm.

'OK, gentlemen, take your seats,' said Fran. 'You've got fifteen seconds to settle in.'

Fran held up a stopwatch. Perhaps she'd be good as an army officer?

A man with black hair and blue eyes sat opposite Ally. She'd noticed him glancing at her during the forced silence, in between examining a picture of a sixteenth-century feast. Or was it the horse and cart with the hay? Ally flickered her eyes at the wall to check. Horse and cart. She should've remembered that.

As she looked back to her new companion, her gaze drifted down the row of tables and her mouth dropped open.

Marc sat there, four tables away, staring hard at her. When their eyes met, he didn't move and his expression didn't change. He'd already seen her. Maybe as soon as he arrived – obviously one of the latecomers who'd stood behind her. He'd have recognised her back, just like she would've recognised his. He probably hadn't been sure until he'd seen her face.

A shrill alarm jerked her out of her shock and into a new one.

'Go!' Fran shouted, waving her phone in the air as it blared a jarring note.

Ally's head moved of its own accord between Marc, still staring at her and apparently not registering the siren, and the man sitting opposite her.

'I'm Alan,' Black-Haired Guy said. 'Pleasure to meet you.'

'Pleasure,' Ally repeated slowly. It was a nice word and it meant nice things. What the hell was Marc doing here? He was dating now? Why did that make her so annoyed and . . . lonely? Either he'd moved on from her or he was trying to move on from her. That should make her happy. It shouldn't make her want to cry and demand to know if he still loved her and was it really his idea of love to forget about someone in a couple of months and join cringey speed-dating groups wearing an olive green shirt that really bloody suited him, the git.

'Yes,' she blurted out, with no idea what she was agreeing to. What had he said? Something about meat? 'Ah, I'm Ally. What's your name?'

'Uh, Alan.' A frown flickered across his features. 'It's my name. Not, like, a greeting.'

'Oh. Yes. Ally's my name. Ally and Alan. Funny. Funny's good.' Ally snuck a glance at Marc. He'd stopped staring, his face turned to his companion. Her expression was thunderous, arms folded, and when she caught Ally's eye she shook her head and jerked her thumb at Marc. Ally understood. 'This guy,' the gesture said. 'What a creep. Watch out when he gets to your table.'

Protective instincts demanded she defend him, but she kept her mouth shut. He wasn't a creep, but he could at least pretend to talk to the woman instead of staring at Ally as if his companion was invisible.

A hand waved in her face.

Shit, yes. Alan.

'Sorry,' she blurted out. 'I've been doing this brain thing. Damn it, what's it called?' She couldn't remember what the memory games were called, but she thought that was called irony. 'Uh . . . you know, like brain exercises?'

'Oh.' Alan nodded and sat back as if he'd had a big realisation. 'I see. Are you under a neurologist? Or a psychiatrist?'

He thought she was mentally impaired. Well, she was doing a pretty good impression of someone with brain injuries. Mum swore she'd never been dropped on the head as a baby but it would explain a lot . . .

'No,' she said, forgetting the question. She needed him to talk so she could pretend to listen while her brain processed things. 'Uh, what did you think of the painting?'

'Ugly and uninteresting,' he replied, without looking at it. 'Unlike you. I have a feeling it'd be hard to be bored around you.'

Flirting. This was flirting. Ally was good at that, so she could handle this. Only three minutes. Two and a half minutes? How long was three minutes?

Flirting. She could do that.

'Do you believe in Jesus?' she said.

Alan looked horrified. 'Um. Sure?'

''Cause he's the answer to all your prayers.'

No, that wasn't how it went. Who'd said it to her? Simon. Simon at the train station. There'd been another one too, about eyes . . .

'Do you have any eye problems?' Ally said. 'No, wait, that's not right. Do you have any problems with just your right eye?'

Alan shifted in his seat and turned his wrist so his watch was face-up. 'Not as far as I know. Why, is it red?'

'No, you look right.'

Silence from Alan but a snort of laughter from the next table.

The couple there bit their lips and grinned at each other when Ally looked at them. Well, at least her flirting was helping somebody.

'Do you – are you OK?' Alan asked, taking her wrist gently. 'Are you sure you should be here? Some men would take advantage, you know. Of your . . . problems, I mean. Is there someone you can call to take you home? Does anyone know you're here?'

Ally spent the remaining time convincing him that she wasn't a health and safety risk.

When the alarm made everyone's ears bleed a second time, each man moved one table to his left. Ally tried to smile at the man who'd snorted at her flirting.

'Don't worry,' he said, holding his hand out for a shake. 'My brother's autistic – pretty low functioning – and my best mate's bipolar. Bloody NHS don't know what to do with mental problems, do they? I'm Dave, by the way.'

In between watching Marc sitting stonily at his table and giving single word answers to his companion, Ally learned about several exciting developments in autism and a potential link to stomach bacteria. When the alarm sounded she was assuring Dave she'd try eschewing gluten for a few weeks to see if it helped.

Next on the conveyor belt was another black-haired man with beautiful black eyes and a gentle smile.

'Swap with me,' a voice said, just as Beautiful Eyes man went to sit down. Marc hovered over him, ignoring the snorter's companion next to Ally, who he was supposed to be sitting with.

'Excuse me,' said Beautiful Eyes, in a polite tone. 'One table to the left. I had a delightful conversation with Diane but now it's time to move on to . . .' He looked at Ally with questioning eyebrows.

'Alan,' said Ally. 'No, wait, not Alan. Oh god, what's my name?'

Beautiful Eyes looked at her name badge. 'Ally,' he supplied.

'Yes! Thank you. Close to Alan, right?'

'Right.' He slid into the chair.

Marc sat down with a thump next to him.

'Oh, I'm so honoured you deigned to sit down,' Diane said. 'Considering I'm so unappealing next to my neighbour.' She frowned and turned to Ally. 'I have nothing against you. It's this creep I'm insulting.'

Marc wasn't very good at this speed dating thing.

'Do you always carry a name badge?' Beautiful Eyes asked. There was no badge on his chest, and none on Marc's or Diane's either. Fran had evidently forgotten to give them out once people started arriving thick and fast.

'Uh, yes,' Ally said. 'It helps with my brain problems.'

The beautiful eyes blinked. 'Oh. I see. Er, what do you do?'

'I'm a businesswoman. I'm a bit overconfident at the moment but it's better than feeling like an imposter, isn't it?'

Beautiful Eyes didn't have a watch, but he looked longingly at the next row of tables. There was a long silence, not just from Ally's table but from Marc's as well. Diane had her arms folded and Marc, jaw set, drummed his fingers on the table.

'What about you?' Ally asked Beautiful Eyes. Her glass of Prosecco was dry, so she took his and poured it into her glass.

'I'm a doctor.'

'Oh yeah? Do you know about the link between autism and stomach bacteria?'

He didn't, so she explained it. It came out a little differently from the way Dave had said it, but she was fairly sure he wouldn't be putting any patients on a gluten-free diet until he'd looked up the studies. In any case, it used up the three minutes.

The alarm fought with Ally's heartbeat, both of them thumping in her ears, as Marc sat across from her. Finally he was still, not shuffling in his seat or tapping the table or running a hand through his hair.

'Hi,' she said softly.

'Hello.' His voice was so smooth, so melty. She could almost feel a square of chocolate melting on her tongue; Lindt with sea salt, dissolving right before he kissed her.

Her eyes stung. She swallowed, determined not to cry, and gripped the narrow stalk of her champagne flute.

'What are you doing here?' she asked.

'Pissing off all the single women in Camden.'

Ally laughed then sniffed. 'You know what I mean. Did you know I'd be here?'

'I was going to ask you the same thing. I thought Paul might have told you. He's been on at me for weeks to call you.'

'Paul . . .' Ally closed her eyes and tried to picture the email inviting her to the event. 'No. Someone called Iris emailed me.'

Marc let out a huff of laughter and nodded. 'Paul's wife. I knew it. They must have planned it together.'

'I always liked Paul.'

Marc reached a hand out as if he were going to touch her wrist, then let it drop on to the table between them. That fist had slammed into her jaw and left it sore and aching for days. Still, she wasn't scared of it, and never had been.

'I'm sorry,' he said. He'd followed her gaze to his hand, and now he slipped it under the table. 'I would never hurt you on purpose. I'd never hit you.'

'I know. I know you didn't do any of it,' she said, meeting his eyes. 'I was taken in for a few minutes, until you came into the room and I looked into your eyes. But I panicked. I wanted a reason to end it. I wanted Sam to forgive me.'

Marc didn't answer for a long moment. Maybe he couldn't forgive her for the betrayal, for not trusting him. Ally watched bubbles in the Prosecco until they burst.

'Has he?' Marc asked eventually.

'No.' Ally bit her lip to stop it trembling, and felt for her crystal.

'Me neither.' There was pain in his voice, too. 'Do you regret it? If you could go back, would you change it so we never met?'

It didn't require conscious thought to remember how happy she'd been in bed with him, in his arms, clothed or naked. She thought about it so much it was always there in her mind, springing to the surface at the slightest provocation. Instead, she paused to think about everything else she'd experienced since meeting him. Without him, she might still have started up her business eventually, but would she have stuck at it? Would she have believed she could stay interested in something long enough to be good at it? Would she be here, looking for love instead of sex?

'No.' She met his eyes and the urge to cry disappeared. 'I wouldn't.'

'Me neither.'

He reached across the table and pushed her hand away from her crystal. When he went to lean back, she gripped his hand and stroked his rough, gardener's palm. He stroked her fingers and closed his eyes briefly, like it hurt.

'I'm too old for you, Ally.'

All the time they'd been together he'd worried about that just as much as she'd worried about Sam and her fickleness and her fear of commitment. Couldn't he see himself how she saw him? Gorgeous, sexy, mature. Her equal, not her senior.

'You're perfect for me,' she said quietly. 'We were made for each other, even if I came into the world twenty years after you. I'm late for everything.'

He smiled, but he still looked sad. Unconvinced.

It was time to stop trying to convince herself this wasn't the real deal, and time to convince him *she* was the real deal.

'I love you,' she said.

Marc's intense expression hadn't changed since he sat down, but now his face split into the widest grin she'd ever seen on it. He stood, pulled her to her feet, and his arms slid around her waist as naturally as hers around his neck. The kiss wasn't hard but deep, rocketing right to her feet to make her toes curl. How had she lived without this for so long?

She thought of nothing at all until the alarm rang. She unglued herself from Marc's face and met a sea of shocked faces, the whole room frozen and gaping at them.

'See!' Fran shouted, rushing over and waving her list in the air. 'It works! Speed dating works! You'll all come back next week, won't you?'

'Not me,' Marc whispered into her ear.

'Probably for the best,' Ally replied, breathing in his cologne. 'I don't think you would've got any numbers.'

* * *

Despite only drinking a glass of Prosecco, Ally felt drunk walking through the streets of London hand in hand with Marc. She was giddy and unbalanced, but he tucked her arm in his and she leaned on him, letting him lead them silently to a taxi.

They didn't speak the whole journey, but it was the most comfortable silence she'd ever sat in. She curled up on the seat, rested her head on his shoulder, and tried to decide if it was blackcurrant or blackberry buried in all the other notes of his scent.

The driver stopped in the middle of the street – no parking on Ally's road, as usual – and she didn't register the car in front of her house until she nearly crashed into the figure on her doorstop.

Ally unstuck her tongue. 'Rachel? What are you doing here?'

'I'm having dinner with Mrs Cooper.'

'Oh.'

Rachel rolled her eyes. 'I'm here to see you, you doughnut. Are you drunk? Who's this . . . oh.' She took in Marc.

'We just met again tonight,' Ally said quickly, gripping his hand for support. 'We haven't been seeing each other. I haven't lied to you. I promised to never ever lie to my friends again. Ever. Or my boyfriends,' she added, looking up at Marc. 'Boyfriend. Singular.'

Marc smiled. Oh man, she loved those crinkles as much as she loved that expression that said, *Don't worry. I understand you.*

'Then great, you have to tell me the truth. Why aren't you talking to me? What have I done? If I've not been supportive enough, you can just tell me. I—'

'No! It's not that. You're great. You've been so great. I just . . . you can't juggle both of us, can you? Me and Sam. I don't want you to be stuck in the middle, or for Sam to be annoyed with you for still seeing me. Neither of you did anything wrong, and you shouldn't have to suffer. He deserves you more than me.'

'Well, he's not getting custody,' said Rachel, her head cocked to one side like it always was when she was impatient. 'You know the score. When parents break up the most important thing is to make sure the kids know it wasn't their fault and that Mummy and Daddy love them just the same. So you stop neglecting me, OK? I'm half yours for phone calls, social events and period days. Well . . .' She frowned. 'Maybe you get all the period days and Sam can have, I don't know, peeing on the toilet seat days. The point remains. I'm still your best friend and if you try to lose me I will cling on tooth and nail.'

Ally lurched forward and hugged her but didn't let go of Marc's hand. Helpfully, he stepped forward to relieve the strain on her arm.

Rachel patted her back. 'As much as I love you, this is like a scene out of *The Human Centipede* and I still have nightmares about that.' She drew back and raised her eyebrows at Ally and Marc's clasped hands. 'You've been apart for months, haven't you? Go inside. I'll post some energy drinks and snacks through the letter box.'

Ally hugged Rachel again as she leaned in for a cheek kiss.

Before she left, Rachel paused and appraised Marc again. 'Bye, Marc. I think she arrived at the right conclusion, but if you ever hurt her I will have you killed. I might look small but I know people. See you both soon.'

They watched her retreating back.

'I like her,' Marc said.

'Me too.'

'You?' Marc stepped into the house after her. 'I love you.'

A warm glow spread through her stomach. The butterflies were quiet for the first time in ages.

'I love you too.' It still tasted new and sweet.

'Prove it,' he said.

EPILOGUE

Ally revolved slowly on the spot, taking in the whole room, then dropped her paintbrush. 'Are we done? Are we really done?'

Marc peeled the last piece of masking tape from the skirting board and stepped back. 'I think we really are.'

'Oh, thank god.' Ally collapsed on to the sheet-covered floor and spread out like a snow angel.

'No time for naps,' he said, planting his feet either side of her waist. 'We're done painting but we still have to finish the bathroom tiling.'

Ally groaned. 'Do we really need a bathroom? We have the toilet downstairs, and Gran used to wash me in the kitchen sink. I'm sure that's more environmentally friendly than baths and showers.'

'Washing up liquid is bad for your skin.'

'Is it? OK, we need a bathroom.'

Marc hauled her to her feet. She sat in the bathtub cross-legged and filled in the last two rows of tiles while Marc finished grouting the sink.

Then they were really done.

'Our own house,' Ally murmured, curled up on the garden

swing with her head on his shoulder. Harry snoozed, his paws on Ally's feet and his head on his paws. She'd trained him to drool on himself rather than her. Blondie, the golden retriever, sat beside Marcus and watched a squirrel stealing seeds from the bird feeder.

At first, it'd seemed like they'd never save up a deposit for a house. He signed the marital home over to Julie, and left her most of the savings, too, for a clean break. They wanted a fresh start, their own place bought with their own money and no input from anyone else. Even though Julie had never contributed to the mortgage, it still felt like *her* house more than his, and neither of them wanted to buy a place with that cash.

But cash wasn't in plentiful supply at the beginning. Marc took a big wage cut to study graphic design, and Ally's bookings just about paid the bills. But then he was promoted, and she had so many bookings she had to quit her part-time jobs one by one. Summer had been a whirlwind of weddings and spring had been busy with makeovers, pet portraits and Ally's latest brainwave – colour consultations with personal shopping included.

She had other ideas. So many she had to record them on her phone and work through them when she had time. Her days now were far more varied than they'd ever been when she had three jobs instead of one business. Had she really put it off so long because she thought she'd get bored?

In the end, it took eighteen months and now here they were, in their own house, paid for through hard work doing things they both loved.

'You know how I'm an old man?' Marc asked.

Ally sighed. 'I'm not going over that again. Fifty is the new thirty and since I'm thirty, we're the same age.'

'Whatever you like. But I'm an old man, and you know if I keel over suddenly there'll be a tree-full of paperwork for you to fill out to keep the house. A whole tree, Ally. If you'd just marry me it'd be much simpler.'

'I'm not going over that again, either. I'm not getting married without my best man.'

'Ally.' He nuzzled her hair and tightened his arm around her shoulders. 'It's been two years. He's not going to come round.'

'Then I'm not getting married,' she said stubbornly. 'We made a pact. A *blood* pact. We stabbed our thumbs with compasses and everything and if we break the pact we get leprosy.'

'That's fine. It's curable these days. I promise you'll still have hands and feet for the ceremony. Look, we don't even need a ceremony. We'll pop down the registry office at lunchtime and we can be back at work for the afternoon. You can pick the rings, or you can go bare-fingered if you prefer. I'll call you Miss Rivers for ever if you like. I just want you to be my wife.'

'I want to be your wife. But not without my best man.' She clamped a hand over his mouth and stood up. 'Don't argue with me. I let you veto my cow mural on the bedroom feature wall but you're not going to win this one. I'll take my shoes off to cook dinner and it'll be just like we're married. You can even pretend I'm pregnant.'

'I don't want babies,' he called after her. 'Or barefoot housewives. I just want you.'

And she wanted him, of course. But marriage felt like the final nail in the coffin Sam had built for her, and a childishly optimistic part of her clung to the possibility of forgiveness, the possibility that he'd still be her best man. She couldn't plan a wedding, declare her happiness to all her family and friends, because one of them would be missing.

The sound of scraping metal accompanied her as she took coconut cupcakes out of the oven and made lime icing. Marc was doing what he always did when he was troubled – gardening. At least he wasn't precious about the garden, letting her help whenever she wanted. When she'd accidentally killed his favourite rose plant he hadn't been angry. He'd been amused at her insistence that the butterfly which'd startled her was at least the size of a housecat, with fangs to match. How could she have believed, even for a minute, that he could be violent?

His rap sounded at the door. Ha. She wasn't the only one who locked herself out occasionally.

'Did you—' She opened the door and lost the power of speech.

Sam shuffled his feet and focused on the door frame with a pained expression. 'Can I come in?'

Ally nodded like a puppet being jerked on a string. Sam didn't move, and she panicked that he'd changed his mind.

'Please come in,' she said, unsticking her tongue. 'Please, Sam. I miss you.'

'Er—'

'No, please, don't go. Please. I have lime cupcakes in the kitchen. They're probably still warm.'

'But—'

'Sam! Lime cupcakes! And, and I'll—'

Sam put his hands on her shoulders, turned her round, and pushed her gently down the narrow hallway so he could follow.

'Oh,' she said. 'Right.'

The kitchen door was open at the end of the hall, the scent of coconut and citrus strong in the evening air. Sam steered her to a chair at the scrubbed table and sat awkwardly across from her, examining the persimmons in the fruit bowl.

Before she could speak, scratching noises and whining from the door distracted her. The moment she opened it Harry bounded in and shoved his nose up Sam's T-shirt to sniff his back.

Sam was as delighted to see the dog as the dog was to see him. They couldn't have seen each other since Sam took Harry on that walk, and came back to find his world imploding.

'I'm sorry, Sam,' she blurted out. 'I was an idiot. I shouldn't have . . . without telling you. I'm sorry.'

Sam's grin faded but he continued looking down at Harry. 'Would you still do it, if you could go back and change things?'

Hadn't Marc asked her that once? These two were so alike. He was still more self-assured and more mischievous than reserved Sam, but their mannerisms and turns of phrase were uncanny.

She still wanted both of them in her life. One wasn't a substitute for the other, and either one of them left a hole in her when they were apart.

But she had to be honest. She would never lie to a friend again.

'Yes,' she said, her heart sinking. Now he would leave. 'I'd do it again. Maybe differently. Definitely differently. But I'd do it.'

'You really . . . love him?' Sam grimaced and hunched, like he was discussing sex with a grandparent.

Ally knew exactly what *that* was like.

'Yes,' she said straight away. 'I love him.' She resisted the urge to remind Sam that he was the only man she'd loved since she was young and even more naive.

The back door opened again and Marc reversed in, shaking off his gardening gloves so the dirt fell on to the patio instead of the tiles.

'Can we eat worms?' he said, removing the gloves with his back to them. 'Because if so we never have to go food shopping again. I—' He turned and saw Sam.

'Hi, Dad,' Sam said, clasping his hands together so hard his knuckles paled.

'Sam.' Marc looked much like Ally had felt when she'd been on the doorstep. She wanted to go to him, put an arm around him, take his blood pressure with that home kit he'd bought and obsessed over for days before it was abandoned in the medicine cabinet.

'I wanted to talk to you both,' Sam said to the persimmons. 'If that's OK.'

Ally resisted another urge – to pick up the fruits and mimic them saying, 'That's OK!' Now wasn't the time for jokes five-year-olds giggled at.

Marc started towards the chair next to Ally. Just as she thought *that's not a good idea* he veered off and sat at the head of the table instead, midway between Ally and Sam. That was better. Not her and Marc against him, but all of them equal.

God, she loved his powers of telepathy.

'I, uh, I hope you don't mind me dropping by,' Sam said. 'Rachel gave me the address. I didn't want to do it over the phone.'

Oh god. Do what?

'Of course we don't,' Marc said.

'Right,' Ally agreed. 'We're always talking about you. Well, not always, that'd be weird. But we miss you.' Should they be saying 'we'? She could hardly say *I missed you, but I dunno about your dad. Maybe he doesn't care.* Man, this was a minefield.

'I missed you too,' Sam told the fruit, his cheeks colouring. 'Anyway. I found out some stuff.'

Stuff? What stuff? What had they done that he didn't know about? Was he pissed off that they'd bought a house together?

The sight of Marc's tensed body made her take a deep breath and shake her legs and hands under the table to loosen her muscles. Keep calm.

'What stuff?' she asked.

'Mum—' Sam grimaced again and shifted like there was a splinter in his butt. 'She said she was ill. Cancer—'

Sam stopped abruptly, because Marc had made a convulsive movement and gripped the edge of the table.

'It wasn't true,' Sam said quickly. 'She's fine.'

'I know.'

Ally blinked at the hard edge in Marc's voice, and the grim set of his jaw.

'Oh,' she said. 'She's done it before.'

Marc gave her a meaningful look and flicked his eyes at Sam. He stared at his dad, ashen.

'Crap, Sam, sorry.' Ally winced. 'My big mouth. I just . . .'

'Did she?' Sam interrupted, still looking at Marc.

'It was a long time ago,' Marc said gently. 'When I first said I wanted to leave. It took me a long time to understand, but I think she's really afraid of being alone. Of people leaving. And so she makes it so they can't leave . . .'

'It backfired again, then, didn't it,' Sam said. Ally had never heard him sound so bitter, and she resisted an urge to hug him. 'I found out she was lying, and then other stuff came out. She said you'd taken all the money, so we all clubbed together to make sure she was OK, then Kaitlyn saw a bank statement. Gavin went through all her papers and found the agreements and the deeds and a bunch of other stuff. Even some printouts of bad reviews for your business, Ally. She must've kept them to . . . look at and enjoy.'

'That was her?' Ally felt strangely relieved. She'd racked her brains for weeks trying to work out which of her clients could've been so disgruntled when none of them had complained to her face. Marc had been convinced from the start it was just trolling, but it felt personal to Ally.

'Yeah. She denied it all, and Gavin said we should make allowances because she was lonely and scared and all that. Then when Brendan moved in, I—'

'Brendan moved in?' Ally bounced on her seat.

Sam nodded shyly, but his smile quickly faded. 'I didn't want to keep him a secret any more. And Mum said . . . she said a lot of things. I don't want to repeat them. I got angry and asked how she could call anyone perverted when she'd faked cancer. When I got home I had a call from Kaitlyn, saying Mum had accused me of stealing money from her under threats of violence. I think she's gone mad. Maybe she was always a bit mad.'

Ally couldn't bear his pain. She dashed over to Sam and hugged him tightly, relishing the once-familiar feel of his hot face and squishy stomach.

Sam patted her arm and leaned his head forward to look at his dad. 'I know she lied about you as well. I shouldn't have believed her. I've never even seen you shout, except when we were kids and did something dangerous. You were the best dad.'

Marc blinked, visibly taken aback. 'Me? I was a terrible father. I was never around.'

Sam frowned. 'Yes, you were. Every Saturday we'd go out. You must remember?'

Marc nodded slowly. 'Right. The bowling alley.'

'Or the ice rink.'

'Films, sometimes.'

'Yeah. And football.'

'I always hated football,' Marc admitted. 'I just pretended to like it because you and Gavin did.'

'Actually, just Gavin. I prefer cricket.'

'Really?' Marc's face brightened. 'Me too. I have tickets for Lords, the international semi-finals. I've invited Paul but screw him, you should come. I mean . . . if you want to.' He looked suddenly nervous.

'I want to,' Sam said, equally uncomfortably.

There was a short silence then Marc said, hesitantly, 'Sam, I know how you feel about your mum right now. Believe me, I've been there. But remember what I said, about how afraid she is of being alone. It's like how you feel about spiders.'

A shudder went up Sam's back, and he looked reflexively over his shoulder.

'No spiders,' Ally said, muffled, into his shirt. 'I'll protect your back.'

'Imagine,' Marc continued, 'that everyone you love shut you in a room with spiders. Just you and spiders, in the dark. That's how she feels right now and that's why she's lashing out. I'm not saying you have to forgive her, or that what she's done is excusable. But I also know she loves you and Gavin more than anything, more than life. She'd die for you without a moment's hesitation. She's not evil, and she needs help, and we can't leave her with the spiders.'

'No,' Sam said, after a pause. 'OK. Just . . . give me a bit of time. I'll call her.'

'Take all the time you need. I'll make sure she's OK until then.' He met Ally's eyes, and she nodded. They had enough happiness to spare a bit for Julie, if she would take it.

'I missed you,' Sam mumbled.

'I missed you, too,' Marc said. He patted Sam's shoulder, and Sam patted his back, and Ally didn't let go so the three of them looked like a human pretzel.

It was going to take a bit of time for Sam and Marc to develop the kind of best-friend relationship Ally had with her mum – who'd forgiven everything when Marc spent two weeks installing her a new kitchen and bathroom at no cost – but she was sure they'd get there.

'You forgive us?' Ally asked, smiling and rocking him from side to side like he was a rattle. 'You'll be my friend again?'

'Yes.' Sam patted her again.

'Best friend?'

'Yes.'

She glanced at Marc. 'Am I pushing my luck to say best man?'

Sam froze, and Ally wished she could snatch the words back.

'Sure,' he said, before she could try to cover her blunder. 'But I'm not calling you stepmum.'

Ally squeezed him so tightly he batted her hands away, moaning about not being able to breathe.

Mrs Ally Rivers had a nice ring to it.

HEADLINE
ETERNAL

FIND YOUR HEART'S DESIRE...

VISIT OUR WEBSITE: www.headlineeternal.com
FIND US ON FACEBOOK: facebook.com/eternalromance
CONNECT WITH US ON TWITTER: @eternal_books
FOLLOW US ON INSTAGRAM: @headlineeternal
EMAIL US: eternalromance@headline.co.uk